I0672894

Kultur's Keep

Louise Furley

Kultur's Keep

Copyright (©) 2021 Louise Furley

All rights reserved. No part of this publication may be reproduced, distributed, or transmitted in any form or by any means, including photocopying, recording, or other electronic of mechanical methods without the prior written permission of the publisher.

ISBN- 978-1-7369376-4-8 (Paperback)
ISBN- 978-1-7369376-3-1 (eBook)

Cover design by Pixel Mischief Design

The characters and events portrayed in this book are fictitious. Any similarity to real persons, living or dead, is coincidental and not intended by the author.

ALSO BY LOUISE FURLEY

A Mafia Romance series

Distilled Duplicity
His Winnings
Adara
Jozadak

Satan's Brood series

Devil's Prince
Devil's Seed

Dutch Military Special Forces series

Jungle Treasure
Jancarlo

Medieval series

Cini and the Beast
Kultur's Keep

Stand alone titles

Jezábel and the Assassin

Solitar

Halo Valley

Isle of Orainn

Anastasia

The Kissing Number

The Poser

Wrath of Wolf

Auction Block

Kultur's Keep

Chapter One

The enormous iron and wood door slammed open startling the group gathered in the great chamber of Castle Aenlic. A captain's guard, one of the League's Kirmen, a barrel-chested man with short shaggy hair charged inside dragging a woman with him.

His thick dirty fingers brutally gripping the back of her neck, he yanked her forward then shoved her to stand in front of a man wearing a long-sleeved coarse shirt, leather breeches and heavy boots, all in black.

Everyone in the room jolted in shock, there were gasps of surprise, but the man in black did not alter his rigid warrior stance, he did not flinch, and the callous expression in his dark eyes did not waver.

The woman tilted her head to look up at the imposing male she was shoved in front of. He towered many inches over six feet with a powerful chest like a rock wall. It was the eyes though, like bottomless black pits that made her visibly shudder. She struggled to get away from the guard's cruel grasp, his fingers dug into her neck with no concern for her pain.

The hefty Kirman squeezed his fingers tighter around her slim neck pushing her closer to the man in black. The cadence of questioning whispers and shocked murmurs from clusters of men and woman observing the intrusion bounced around the great room.

In a cool, deep yet quiet voice, the formidable man in black asked, "What is the meaning of this, Kirman Trogga?" He set huge strong hands on his hips and glared from the Kirman to the woman. He glanced with dispassion down the length of her small stature.

She was attired in a floor-length dress that was worn and tattered. A dingy kerchief covered the top of her head hiding her hair, and her skin was layered with dirt.

"Ahh," Trogga's triumphant grunt forged deep from his good-sized belly. Still gripping the woman, he reached inside his tan vest to scratch his chest over the rough linen shirt. His guttural voice stoked with imperious pride, he declared, "Atraam Kultiran, I found this villainous vagabond hiding in the near meadows. She was holding her head and stumbling out of the woods. Obviously up to no good, Atraam, she has no marking so she's not from the island."

At the fierce Atraam's silence, Trogga burst on, "Timmins claims he saw her a week or so ago near the shore with another man that also looked foreign. I brought her here for you to interrogate and torture before you behead her." Thick lips, his face was a mush of ample stupid. Dull brown eyes gleamed with uncouth pomposity at his fine capture.

The young female blanched at his words, her eyes dropped to the floor. Her struggles to get out of the hefty man's grasp were futile, she stopped fighting him. His stink of sweat, ale and stale urine assailed everyone's nose within ten feet of him.

His unemotional deep voice rumbling with slight sarcasm, the man in black, the Atraam, Kultur Kultiran asked, "Was she hiding, Kirman Trogga, or was she stumbling out of the woods?"

Trogga's slack eyes bugged nervously at the Atraam. "Uh, she, uh…" drool gathered in the corners of his thick lips.

In a quiet command, Atraam Kultiran ordered, "Clear the room." He waited while the people hesitated at first then seeing the harsh set of his mouth and the muscle tensing at his jaw, silently exited the hall.

Ignoring the people dispersing as he had bid, Kultur regarded the female in front of him. His dark scrutiny traveled from the top of her dirty kerchief to the worn ballet shoes peeping out from under the tattered dress, so worn the original color was undeterminable.

"What is your name, *koritsi*?" At her confused look, Kultur stated, "You are an obvious outsider, *koritsi* means foreigner. To be exact, it means 'little foreigner.'" He repeated calmly but the steel-edged undertone made even Trogga's skin crawl, "What is your name?"

When the young woman remained silent, one of Kultur's unruffled brows arched like a black boomerang. His deeply masculine voice low, he quietly asked her, "Where are you from?"

Her eyes on the floor, her shoulders rigid, she remained mute.

Trogga barked, "Heathen!" and backhanded her so hard she fell to the ground with a stunned cry.

Kultur crouched down in front of her to peer at her face. A hand to her injured face, her eyes wavered unfocused. Her head bobbing dizzily she cringed from his scrutiny as if expecting him to strike her too. He grasped her jaw and raised her head forcing her to look at him, but he asked Trogga, "Why did you strike her?"

Trogga tucked his stout fingers under the front of his belt. The image of a tall, stocky troll, his stance stretched wide in the leather pants, unpolished boots planted solidly on the marble floor. Scratching under the leather vest again, coarse lines creased his already mushed porridge-like face.

His beady eyes mulish, looking down at her, he said with disdain, "She did not answer your question. She shows disrespect to our great Atraam Kultiran."

Trogga sniffed, "Maybe the heathen would understand the word *King* Kultiran better." Looking down at her with a lewd glint in his eye, his vulgar intent plain on his homely face, his voice grandiose as if it was his right, he announced, "I request to- have the woman, Atraam, before you behead her."

Still clutching her face, Kultur leaned in closer to her. Shaking her dizziness off, she set her palms on the floor to brace herself and looked directly back at Kultur, her sheer terror of him blatant in her wide eyes.

Kultur let go of her chin and stood up. Bending over, he reached down, clinched his long fingers around her thin arm and pulled her up to her unsteady feet. He held her until she gained her balance.

His eyes still on her, Kultur said to Trogga, "There is another bruise on the side of her face besides the red mark from your hand. The bruise is recent judging by the bright purple color." His gaze drifted down the front of her.

He said quietly, "There are older bruises on her arms. There appears to be a fresh tear on her dress." The side of the skirt was torn and the bodice was ripped exposing the top swell of her breast. Kultur glanced at Trogga whose greedy eyes were glued to the woman's partially exposed bosom.

Kultur asked, "How did she get that bruise?" The Atraam was a big, powerfully built man but he spoke quite low and without inflection of any kind making his thoughts and feelings indiscernible. It left people uneasy, not knowing if they were digging themselves in deeper or if he liked what he was hearing.

One of Trogga's round shoulders rose slightly in a guilty shrug, his attention still plastered to the pale curve of the woman's breast. A bulbous tongue slurped out of the slack mouth and licked the thick lips.

"Uh, I was questioning her, she refused to answer me. I felt it was my duty to search her body for our marking. The fact that she does not have one proves she is a danger. She is probably one of those shore prostitutes that float in from the other distant islands." His attention to Kultur was fleeting, it went right back to the woman's exposed skin.

His voice hardening, the vein twitched, Kultur repeated, "You've not yet explained the bruise. Also explain how her dress got ripped." His brow arched with displeasure at the sluggard Trogga standing with his big mouth hanging open. Kultur snapped, "*Now.*"

Clasping his hands behind his back, Trogga appeared vaguely sheepish then turned indignant. "Uh, yeah, I hit her, so what? I had to look at her hip for the marking. While I had her dress pushed up, I tried to get a little, you know, feel. I mean," his cheeks reddened. "My hand was already up her dress and she fought me, her dress got ripped and then uh, I kind of had her on the ground and her bodice got torn, she bit me." Arrogantly outraged, Trogga sputtered, "The bitch bit me, so I hit her."

Trogga took a lumbering threatening step towards the young female. She cowered from him, bringing her hands up in front of her as if the small, slender woman could ward off the husky troll.

"She's just a filthy pagan whore, Atraam," he spat, "she was already dirty and scratched up when I found her, what's a little more fucking bruising?"

He didn't volunteer that if other Kirmen hadn't come along he would have just punched her harder to daze her then climbed on top of her and forced himself inside her, and that would have been that. But the other men insisted he bring her to the castle to the Atraam.

He gurgled on, spittle gathering in the corner of his mouth, "I will be quick with her, sir," he offered, "you can behead her right after I finish." Trogga's leering grin deepened at the putrid aghast look the woman shot him.

Reaching for her, he chuckled to himself, he couldn't wait to throw up her skirts and see that terrified look in her eyes go insane as she screamed while he forced those lilywhite thighs apart and pounded into her.

Kultur moved between Trogga and the frightened woman. He gave a short, sharp whistle, then cold as ice, he said to the Kirman, "You are too weak to control a woman you have to hit her? You are not man enough to be one of the League's Kirmen."

Several boots pounded into the room responding to the Atraam's whistled signal. Kultur did not look at them. He only saw the instant fear in Trogga's face, the sudden abject knowledge that he was a dead man.

Kultur's eyes narrowed with lethal intent, he said harshly, "You dishonor our League," and lashed his fist out striking Trogga in the bridge of his nose, his neck fractured with a loud crack. The Kirman was dead before he crashed to the ground.

Wiping the back of his hand on his pants, Kultur said with no emotion to the other Kirmen, "Get rid of him." He turned to the girl as the Kirmen picked up Trogga's body and headed for the door.

As soon as his black gaze struck her, the woman let out a tight scream, clapped her hand over her mouth and fainted.

Before she collapsed to the floor, the king caught her and swung her up in his arms.

Chapter Two

The Atraam easily carried the young woman up the stairs as if she were an infant. He took her to his chambers. As soon as he kicked the door closed behind them, she stirred.

Coming to, her lashes fluttered, she blinked then opened her eyes and saw she was in the clutches of the brutal killer, only inches from the monster's glittering obsidian orbs.

"Oh my stars!" The horror of the episode of only a few moments ago struck the color right out of her cheeks. "Put me down!" she cried pushing at his massive chest.

He obligingly set her on her feet. She immediately backed away from him. "You- you killed that- that man, in cold blood!"

His big hands twined behind his back, his legs akimbo, he nodded. "Aye. We have rules every Kirman, every man in the land is fully aware of. Timmins will also lose his head for allowing Trogga to do what he did."

Her eyes big and round she whispered, "Wha- what did he do?"

Kultur's brow rose surprised she even asked the question. "He brought a dangerous stranger into my home." He took a step to the door, opened it. There was a Kirman standing at attention outside the room.

"Guard," Kultur ordered, "have Timmins taken to the dungeon, prepare him for his beheading. I will be there momentarily." The guard bowed his head in obeisance and marched away. Kultur closed the door again.

Before he could say another word, the woman dropped to her knees, a green hue to her skin, she clasped her hands together as if in prayer and cried, "Oh, please, sir, please don't take another life because of me. It's not their fault they found me. They were trying to do the right thing. Please, please sir, I beg you- take me instead, punish me, it's my fault."

His astonishment at her behavior clear on his face, the rough angles sharpened, dark eyes unreadable, as earlier, he bent to grasp her arm and pulled her to her feet. As she gained her balance, he suddenly whipped his hand out, snatched her kerchief off her head and tossed it on the floor.

With a little cry she threw her hands up to stop her hair from tumbling down.

Reaching to her, Kultur lifted a lock of hair and studied it. It wound around his finger. "I fear," he said with a rueful half smile, "we will have to wait until you are clean to see the true color. It looks quite…unusual."

He let the hair uncoil around his finger then it fell to curl under her breast. His eyes on the curl then the torn bodice, he sighed and said, "Because it is strange circumstances, and you are but a slip of a female, and Timmins' young wife, Sadie, just had a new baby, I will, just this once allow a flogging instead of the beheading."

Her hands went back in prayer, her tentative smile grateful, "Thank you, kind Lord, that is so forgiving of you."

He grabbed her chin holding her head taut. Towering over her, the rugged planes in his warrior's face down to the strong jaw tightened to harsh stone, he said grimly, "You may not be so grateful when you view his flogging."

Enigmatic eyes so dark they appeared as night condemned her. "You will see what it means to disobey our laws. We live in a treacherous land, we must all act as one and follow the laws."

Her jaw trembled in his hand. "Please, I can't- please don't make me watch!"

"Woman, you will see that strangers who do not answer my questions are tortured as well until they spill all." Impassively, he observed the rosy pink that had just infused her cheeks dissolve leaving them stark white.

His gaze stayed on her cheeks. Contemplating them, he said, "The childlike roundness of your cheeks, clarity of your eyes, the smoothness and pureness of your skin indicate you have only shortly evolved from childhood to adult." His absorbed contemplation swept her body, "Hmmm, you may have the face of a child but you have the figure and the grace of a woman."

He suddenly grasped her arm and pulled her through the primary room down the short hall to his bedchamber. Releasing her, he started unbuttoning the cuffs on his sleeves, nodded to the huge bed. Matter-of-factly he ordered, "Get on the bed. Prepare yourself."

Her eyes popped, she took a step away from him then stood frozen.

Frowning his impatience, he repeated, "I said get on the bed. Spread your legs, make ready for me. I find I need to take you quickly then you can bathe before we go again."

Another step back, her voice shaking, she whispered in horror, "*No.*"

Both brows rose, he crossed his arms. "Oh? You want to strip first then?" He nodded. "That's fine. I cannot tell what your body looks like under that garment." His gaze lit on her bust. "You do look shapely. We will see. Go on now, remove your clothes. Quickly." He palmed his already swollen erection.

Wordless, she shook her head.

With no anger in his tone, just a bit of interest, he asked, "What do you want then? Do you want me to take you standing up against the wall- thrust into you without preamble? Don't you want to take off your clothes so I don't ruin them further?"

When she just stared at him with her mouth open, he moved towards her. "You want foreplay then? Or do you want it rough, bent over the desk, are you that kind of-"

She stumbled backwards but he shot his arm out and grabbed the front of her dress, shoved his hand inside the torn bodice and then with both hands he grasped the bindings covering her breasts and tried to tear them.

He hesitated, said in surprise, "Your binding is much tighter and thicker than most women wear it. Why? What are you trying to hide? Do you have weapons hidden?"

When she didn't answer and struggled to push his hands away, he grew angry. Clutching the binding material he tugged hard on it to rip it.

Frantically pulling at his hands, her voice shaking with fear, she cried out desperately, "Please don't, please stop!" Her small fingers fought with his huge calloused hands, yanking at his wrists in panic.

Letting go of her, he slammed his hands on his hips and snapped furiously, "What the hell are you playing at? I'm done with your games. Do what I said. Get on the bed. Now."

Her head swiveling back and forth, her eyes darted around the room looking for the quickest escape, or a weapon, she backed away as she searched the room.

All patience gone, he grabbed her arm, dragged her over and shoved her down on the bed. She landed on her bottom with a huffed cry, her hands fell behind her to stop her fall.

Without another word, he knelt on the mattress. Easily lifting her under her arms he pulled her to the center then splayed his big hand on her breastbone, pushed her flat on her back and climbed on top of her.

Ignoring her puny punches at his thickly muscled chest, and frantic kicks with her soft ballet slippers, he clamped ahold of her face, roughly lowered his mouth onto hers and took her lips with such a violent kiss he stole her breath, then he shoved her skirt up.

Her chest heaving with sobs, she beat at his chest, squirming under him trying for all her might to scramble away from him, screaming, "Stop! Stop!"

Pulling at his belt, he opened the buttons on his pants, then stuck his hand in a side pocket and drew out a protective lambskin shield and moved between her legs. Pushing her thighs apart, at the same time, bending over her, he forced her lips open then thrust his tongue in her mouth. He held her down with the weight of his big body while tearing at the strings on her undergarment.

Feeling her sobs hitching against his chest, Kultur tasted the salt of her tears in the brutal kiss. He became completely still.

Pushing up on his elbows to look at her, his forehead wrinkled in consternation. Seeing the tears pouring down her cheeks, bewildered, he asked, "Why the hell are you crying?"

Gulping back her sobs, the woman cried, "You're forcing me, raping me. I- I don't want this!"

He quickly rolled off her and sat up. "What the hell are you talking about? I am not raping you." His frown even more confused than ever. "*Koritsi*, I've never had a woman cry before, they never say no, they come to me, beg me for it. I thought you were playing."

Moving back slightly, he ordered, "Sit up." Black locks of hair hung over his brow, his breaths came quick from his exertions, and the thick erection throbbed at his undone breeches.

Unsure of his intentions, she hesitated; he caught her slim shoulders and helped her to sit up. Brushing her long curly hair off her shoulders, he gently cupped her trembling chin with a big, calloused hand and studied her tears. "You're not playing. You don't wish for me to fuck you?"

Her frightened eyes blinked at him rapidly, then lowered in embarrassment. Her voice small, she murmured, "No." The tears continued to stream, she tried to pull her face away but he held her still.

Kultur pulled a handkerchief out of his pocket and handed it to her. Releasing her, he said quietly, "Dry your eyes." He watched her in silence try to staunch the flood of tears.

When they subsided somewhat, he asked, "Are you not a shore prostitute as Trogga had said? Once in a great full moon one of them manages to land ashore here."

Pressing the hanky to her face she shook her head. Her hoarse voice hushed, she replied, "No. I don't know what that is."

11

He crossed his legs, twined his fingers and rested his arms on his thighs. "So, tell me who you are and where you are from. You are not from this land." His gaze lowered to her bosom.

Dabbing at her eyes, she crossed her legs too and primly covered them with her skirt. She pulled together the torn bodice and asked weakly, "How do you know that?"

His black gaze went to her head. "Your hair. Even under all that dirt I can still see that no one on this land has hair the color of pure chroma, like a varnished winter jasmine- the softest yet brightest yellow I've ever seen. Or skin that," he licked his finger then ran it down her face making a clean streak through the dirt, "is so, luminescent pearl."

He cupped her chin again, tilting her head to study her face. "High, round delicate cheekbones, almost childlike, your lips are tiny, but," he leaned in lightly brushed them with his full yet chiseled, bold mouth and said, "but very full, like pink pillows, they are exceedingly soft to kiss. And those eyes," he loomed over her, holding her tightly when she tried to shrink away.

She kept her lashes low over her eyes but he held her face up forcing her to look at him. His was a gaze of study, not lust.

"Your eyes are a mix of diamond and something like the blue of a mountain bluebird. When you look away they glitter like a many faceted clear diamond, when you look head on, they are a crystalline blue I've never seen the likes of before, can't really describe."

He said everything unemotionally, as a statement of fact like he was recording a statistic, not giving a compliment.

"No," he shook his head, "there is nothing about you that resembles anyone else on this land." Releasing her chin he suddenly clutched her wrist forcing her to roll onto her side. He pushed her skirt back up then twisted her to expose her hip.

Ignoring her short yelp of protest, he said, "And, you have no mark of your kinsmen on your right hip like everyone on this land does to identify them, when they're born, to which faction they belong. Some have the mark on other places of their body, but I've a feeling you do not have one anywhere."

He rolled off the bed to stand and yanked her up with him. His face dark with anger, he said in a low coarse voice, "Now, enough games, tell me who you are and where you are from." He buttoned his pants and buckled the belt, wincing as the material tightened on the hard lump beneath it.

She wrapped her arms around her body, stared at the floor and didn't answer him.

"Woman," Kultur clutched her arms and impatiently shook her. The dirty golden hair fluttered around her, spiraling down her back to her waist. "You answer me or I will have you whipped until you do." He shook her again, "Do you understand me? Now, tell me your name."

The sheen of tears distorted the blue of her eyes as she raised them fearfully to him. "I- I don't know."

Incredulous, Kultur shook her again until her teeth rattled. "What kind of bullshit is that? Stop with the nonsense, woman, and tell me who the fuck you are." His dark eyes pierced her with threat, his mouth full yet masculine, tightened into a hard line.

"I speak the truth, I don't know my name, I don't know who I am." So frightened of the fearsome huge man glowering in impatient anger at her, the woman's eyes rolled back in her head as if she was going to faint again.

"Oh no you don't." Kultur twined his fingers around her neck to hold her head up and helped her sit on the edge of the bed then stood back from her so she'd feel less threatened.

His voice calmer, he asked quietly, "How can you say you don't know?" His shoulders were solid and broad but his hips were narrow. He stood with his feet apart, bracing his heavy boots on the carpet. Crossing his arms, his biceps flexed obviously enormous even under his long-sleeved shirt.

She folded her hands together, set them gracefully in her lap, sighed deeply and stared anxiously at the floor.

"Look at me when I am speaking to you!" He bellowed so loud she jerked back. When her skin paled again he sighed grievously and said more quietly, "Look at me and explain what you said."

In a calming manner, she brushed her shaking palms over the sides of her head smoothing her hair back. She slowly rolled her eyes up at him trying not to flinch from the big fierce man, his face flushed red with ire. She cleared her throat, "Um, I…well, before your- uh, guard found me…I uh…"

"Quit stammering, *koritsi*, spit it out."

"I fear you won't believe what I have to say." She looked up with wary nervousness straining her soft face. He stood forbidding yet mute waiting for her to speak.

"Okay," she said, swallowing hard. "A few days ago, when I woke up I was lying on the sand in a cove by the sea."

When she stopped, he quirked a brow, said, "Go on, then what?"

"That's just it, I remember nothing at all before that."

He waited, his expression baffled disbelief. When she wasn't more forthcoming he prodded, "What do you mean? You mean you don't remember how you got to the cove?"

Her pained smile was without mirth. "What I'm saying is, I don't remember anything, at all, not my name, not who I am, not where I'm from, not how I got there, *nothing*."

Seeing his disbelief she continued, "I was very groggy when I woke. I have a lump on my head. I think I must have hit it and it caused, um," she sighed, "I don't know."

While she spoke, Kultur studied her. She held her back rigid, like a princess, but she wore a peasant's frock. The dress was worn and dirty. The ballet slippers on her feet looked like they were silk, but they too were damaged and dirty.

Her fair skin was scratched and bruised and also layered in grime. The long curly hair hung in crooked filthy ringlets down her back. It was as if she had tumbled down a jagged hill banging and bashing her body, her clothes and skin taking the dirt with her.

She'd need a good scrubbing and the bruises healed before he could determine what she really looked like. The only thing not covered in filth or hidden were those big, clear as crystal bright blue eyes.

Odd, he thought he saw purity and intelligence radiating out of them. He peered closely looking for fakery, but they just appeared wholesomely guileless. He grunted, she was probably a gifted criminal with good acting skills.

"So," he drawled, "if I'm to believe this unlikely tale of amnesia, what have you been doing the past few days or so?"

Her graceful shrug drew his attention to her elegant shoulders. "I have been walking and walking. Trying to find my way to- I don't know, I just kept going. I ate berries when I could find some, drank water from the streams and slept in the grass. That's why I look like this," she glanced down at herself in chagrin.

Speaking what he had been thinking, she said, "I think I must have fallen down a hill or something at some point. I have scratches and bruises," she blushed, "absolutely everywhere."

Kultur wrapped an arm around his waist, set his elbow on his arm and tapped at his chin with his fingertips. "Uh huh." His disbelieving frown swept from her toes to her face. "I tell you what. Let's go on down to the dungeon and view Timmins' flogging, then we'll see if your story changes."

Her mouth dropped, eyes widened. "What? No! Please, I'm being honest with you, I don't know who I am!"

He grabbed her arm and roughly hauled her to her feet. "Not another word from you until you decide to tell me the truth. Come with me." So strong, he practically lifted her on her toes as he marched her to the door.

Chapter Three

It was a long walk down the endless stone floored hall, then down the stairs to the first level. Braided rugs scattered across the hallways. They passed many people as they traveled through the palest of pink mixed with beige stone and marble building. The colors of the sky-high rounded walls were not feminine, but rather regal and softly ornate.

People looked at the couple with curiosity, especially at the foreign woman, but the grim hard look to Kultur's roughly hewn face precluded any questions.

He gripped her arm tightly and held it close against his side so she could keep up with his long-legged strides. She tried to glance around at her surroundings as he dragged her steadily along. The castle was bright and airy, acres huge with a vaulted arced ceiling over five stories.

It appeared numerous wings branched off from the main great room that Trogga had dumped her in. Skylights let in bright sunlight and torches flickered in glass lanterns strung along the marble walls.

Down on the first level thick rugs were spread throughout the structure partially covering the white and gold marble floors, a warm contrast to the stone floors above. There was at least one enormous stone fireplace in each room they passed.

He ushered her outside. They passed villagers herding sheep through the main, dirt road of the keep who stopped and gawked at the pair. Further on, fowl hung from ropes in front of a shop with hogs hanging on hooks behind them, and children raced around with dogs yapping at their feet.

In the distance long puffs of steam from a mill rose amongst the tall trees. Several fisherman traipsing by with their catches eyed the king and his captive with open curiosity.

The central area of the keep was a mass of one level, wooden, brick, stone and stucco residential huts and shops with the rest of the homes and farmlands rippling over small hills spreading in all directions. Mills and heavy forests ranged in the vast perimeter.

Chickens cackled out of the way as the couple quickly approached a structure made of solid stone.

Kultur's boots clomped on the stairs as they headed down to the belly of the building. As they descended, the building grew dim and damp, the inside walls dark grey cement.

Voices crying for help, others gruff and bullying bounded down the narrow passageway. He didn't slow until he reached a cavernous room. Narrow windows high up the cement walls let in faint light. It only showed the gruesomeness of the dungeon more clearly and grisly.

All kinds of whips and other torturous looking instruments and apparatus were hooked up around the room along with a variety of manacles attached to the walls.

In the center of the room were several posts, and stocks in square n shapes. They were to restrain the offender who was to be flogged. One of the stocks already had a terrified occupant chained on it.

A man was on his knees, his hands were cuffed to the horizontal board that was nailed to the vertical two boards holding it up, like a sawhorse. His wrists were already cut and bloody from his frantic struggles.

Although he worked hard biting his tongue to stifle them, the man's terrified whimpers crept out of his mouth. He was shirtless, sweat drenched his displayed, vulnerable back.

As soon as Kultur and the woman entered the room, she let out a wretched gasp at the sight of the kneeling man and the other man standing behind him with a bullwhip in his fist. She dug her heels in trying to keep from being hauled into the room. But Kultur pulled her further inside.

"No, mister, uh, Atri- uh, King, please," she tried to pry his fingers of iron off her arm.

"Atraam." The man with the whip bowed to Kultur. His eyes darted once to the woman then back to Kultur. His pants were as black as Kultur's but unlike the Atraam's neat breeches that fit snug on his muscled thighs and low on his tapered hips, the flogger's blood-stained trousers hung loose below his thick stomach. A leather apron more red than black tied around his waist, and his boots were stained dark scarlet.

His chest was bare, presumably so he wouldn't have to keep washing blood soaked shirts. He had a square head, long heavy nose, whiskers covered most of his blocky features, and his chest and biceps were bulging huge.

Kultur nodded imperially, and greeted, "Horace." He drew the woman forward, still holding her arm. Her shoulders were rigid up around her ears, her blue eyes frantic.

"We've come to observe." Kultur swept his hand out saying, "No beheading, just the flogging. Proceed."

Horace glanced at the woman, a shade of uncertainty shadowed his bulky ugly face. Darting a look at Kultur's cold expressionless face, he shrugged and lifted the whip over his shoulder.

The woman's legs buckled. Kultur moved her to stand in front of him and pulled her against his chest then wrapped his arms around the front of her to hold her up. He'd have to lower his head if he wanted to touch the top her curly hair with his chin.

Marks on her arm caught his attention. He looked closely at them, saw they were faint new bruises spreading. A frown drew the corners of his mouth down when he realized that the bruises were fingerprints. His fingerprints. Under his breath he expelled a curse, *damned frail female*.

Horace drew the whip back then flung it forward hard with a vicious snap, it slashed into Timmins' back. Timmins let out a howl.

The woman cried out and turned away from the sight. She fought to get out of Kultur's arms but he held her fast.

"You will watch, *koritsi*, so you can see what happens to people who don't tell the truth. Who don't answer questions from the Atraam."

Keeping an arm like an iron band around her, Kultur gripped her jaw with nail-hard fingers but light enough not to bruise any more of her skin, and held her head up straight so she was forced to watch Timmins being flogged.

Annoyed at the way her pert little bottom pushed against his groin eliciting a response he didn't need right now, shifting her roughly, he growled, "Keep your eyes open, or I will have you experience this first hand. You did offer your life for his after all." He pinched her chin with the calloused pads of his fingertips until she opened her eyes.

Horace swung the whip again and again lashing into Timmins' back, slicing the skin open.

Timmins' body wrenched, his spine jerked, with every strike he screamed in agony. Blood and sweat flew like visceral bullets with each of the twenty lashes. After the twentieth blow, Horace set down the whip covered with Timmins' blood and bits of skin.

The woman was gulping and heaving wretchedly like she couldn't catch her breath, her legs were so rubbery Kultur was the only thing holding her up. When Horace stopped the flogging, Kultur loosened his hold on her and the woman turned around and buried her face in his chest.

She sobbed against him, her tears thoroughly wetting his shirt. Ignoring the reproving look Horace gave him, Kultur rolled his arm around the weeping woman, her stomach still heaving, her throat so constricted she gasped tear-congested ragged breaths, and he drew her out of the room.

She tried but couldn't lift her trembling legs to go up the stairs. Kultur scooped her up in his arms, holding her high and tight against his chest he trod easily up the two flights of stone stairs and back to the castle where he strode through the great room and up another flight of stairs.

She didn't see people watching them in stunned interest because she kept her face buried in his shoulder as she sobbed.

He carried her down a long hall then stopped at a room. A guard followed him then when the Atraam stopped, he stood beside the door. Kultur nodded at the door.

The guard turned the handle, stood aside and opened it. Kultur strode through still carrying her; the guard closed the door behind them.

Kultur gently let the woman down to her shaking feet but held her arm gingerly to steady her. "Now," black eyes blazing, he ground harshly, "will you tell me the truth now?"

She turned horrified eyes on him; her skin had turned darker green. She clapped a hand over her mouth, jerked from his grasp and ran to a door. Fortunately it was the bathing chamber. Kultur stood stoically listening to her as she threw up. It was only dry heaves as she apparently was telling the truth about not having eaten for days.

The tips of his ears turned red, the vein beat at his temple, Kultur sat on the edge of the bed and waited. A few moments and he heard the water running in the bathing room.

More minutes passed before he heard her feet padding on the tiled floor then she appeared in the doorway. His expression a total blank he watched her clutch the side of the doorway to hold herself up. The hair around her face and her hands were damp.

The green tint was gone from her washed face, now it was so dreadfully without color her skin looked translucent. Her hand quivered over her mouth, shadows circled the huge blue eyes that stared over her hand at him in horror.

Taking one step into the room she sank to her knees. She pushed her long hair back with both hands, working to keep her mouth from trembling.

Kultur didn't stand up although his body had twitched when she dropped to her knees.

Her hand lowered from her mouth, she sat back on her heels. "Mister, uh, A- Atarri- uh."

It looked like he smothered a brief half smile. He murmured, "It is pronounced 'Atraam.' It is as Trogga had said, something like king. I am Atraam Kultur Kultiran, King if you will, of the Chamaine-Gris." His head bowed slightly. "It is a mouthful, you will call me Kultur."

She picked up a curl that fell over her shoulder and absently fidgeted with it. "Mister uh…"

His eyes narrowed, "Kultur."

Nodding, she swallowed and started again, "Mr. um, King Kultur, you can beat me, whip me, kill me," she took a shaky breath, licked her dry lips. "But I can't tell you what I don't know. I told you the truth, I can't remember who I am. Not even my name. If I could think of a good realistic lie to tell you to save my neck," she shrugged one shoulder, looked unwavering at him, "I would probably do so."

Her head dropped, the long hair covered her like a curly shawl. Her voice muffled by the veil of hair she said, "Please, all I ask, beg, is that there is at least a tiny marker so if I do have anyone who," a sob coughed out, "cares about me, they- they can know where I am buried." Keeping her head down she drew her shoulders in together as if preparing to lose her head.

She waited, her entire body quaking in fear. When she didn't hear him approach, the wretched fear getting the better of her again, she slapped her hand over her mouth with a short, terrified dry heave.

From his seat on the bed Kultur said, "Look at me, *koritsi*."

Slowly, fearfully, she raised her head and peered at him through her veil of hair. Her voice a tiny confused quiver, she asked, "What are you calling me, kora- kori?"

The corner of Kultur's mouth quirked. "I told you before. It means 'little foreigner.' You are not a girl, yet barely a woman." He stood up, catching her cringe.

Raking his long fingers through thick, black wavy hair, he said, "For now, young one, I will not force the issue of who you are or why you are here." He turned and walked towards the door.

Opening it, he said, "A maid will bring you some tea and crackers. When your stomach has settled she will provide something more substantial." Indicating her very slender form, he said, "You are quite thin, it appears it has been a while since you've eaten much."

Moving into the threshold, he noticed she held herself rigid as if waiting for a deathblow while bewilderment furrowed her forehead.

He said quietly, "No one will harm you, for now. You may take a bath. I will have the maid bring you some of my sister's clothes; you can't wear that shit you have on. You will stay here, in this room, until I decide what to do with you."

Gesturing to the window, he told her, "We are too high up for you to jump without breaking your legs, and the door will remain locked." Without another word he left the room and closed the door, the lock clicked audibly.

She didn't move for a long time. Unsure if he was just screwing with her and would suddenly pop back in and assault her, or behead her, she just stayed on her knees. Curiously, she carefully scanned the room.

It was almost round with cream painted walls, cream runners, pale rose and white ruffled curtains framed the window. The bed looked comfy with a fluffy cream quilt dappled in soft roses and matching pillows.

The nightstand beside the bed was painted white and gold and matched the dresser against the wall and the vanity with an attached mirror. A matching armoire took up part of the other wall. Atop the vanity was a comb and brush set with a hand mirror.

When she was in the bathing room she had barely noticed it was warm and pretty with the same cream and roses in the tiles with cushy rugs. She shivered. The soft pretty room was such a contrast to the flint hard, brutal man with the dark, ice-cold eyes that put her in it.

She didn't know how much time had passed when she heard a key in the lock and the door opened slowly. Her eyes shut tight figuring this was it, he'd returned to kill her.

"Miss," a soft voice filtered across the room to her.

Peeking out from under her lashes she saw a woman in a black blouse and black wide-legged trousers, a frilly black apron was tied around her plump waist. Her brown hair was in a knot on top of her head.

She appeared to be maybe in her thirties with wide chocolate eyes, the smile on her long plain face was friendly. Over her arm were some articles of clothing, and she carried a tray with a teacup, small teapot with steam gently spiraling out of the spout, cream, sugar, a plate of crackers with a bowl containing pats of butter, and a spoon and small butter knife.

The woman set the tray on the wide nightstand and laid the clothes out on the bed. She stood back and folded her hands benignly in front of her. Her thin-lipped smile big and warm, she bowed slightly and said, "Miss, my name is Onani and I am here to take care of your needs."

She motioned to the tray of tea and said cheerfully, "The master has ordered this for you. He said when you are able to keep this down I am to bring you dinner. Shall I pour for you?"

Still kneeling on the floor, the young woman's eyes flashed nervously around the room as if expecting a trick that the horrible man would suddenly appear like a demon and slice off her head.

"The Atraam said you are a bit, uh, skittish and to be slow and gentle with you." Onani smiled at the lift of the woman's disbelieving brows. "Yes, tis a bit surprising. He seldom shows kindness to any other than his close family, or sometimes to someone about to be taken by the sword for a misdeed- uh," her mouth shut at the girl's stricken face and quaking body.

She took a small step towards the young woman. Frowning unhappily when the girl cringed from her, she said kindly, "Please, Miss, I am not here to harm you. I will pour you some tea and

butter a few crackers then I will leave you alone to eat and bathe."
She nodded at the clothes on the bed. "Master Kultur retrieved
some clothing from his sister for you to wear."

Her head cocked in interest at the woman with a wary look
in her eyes slowly climbing to her feet. Onani asked amicably,
"What is your name?" She looked taken aback at the frightened
shadow that marred the woman's face before her eyes dropped to
the floor.

"Tis all right, Miss, I forgot the master said you couldn't
remember. That is so peculiar, huh? Anyway, the master said this
room was for you as the creams and roses matched your
complexion under all that dust. I swear, I've never heard him
speak so-" She brushed her pudgy hands down her apron.

"I'm so sorry to be babbling on like this. Please," she scurried
to the tray and poured some tea then buttered several crackers. Her
smile gentle, she said kindly, "You won't relax until I'm gone."
As she trod to the door, the wary girl stepped back so Onani
wouldn't pass near her.

"I will be back, in say," the maid pondered a moment,
"around maybe an hour and a half? That should give you plenty
of time to bathe, change, eat and relax a bit."

She hesitated as she opened the door, "Go on now, it will be
all right. No one is going to harm you." She slipped out of the
room closing the door quietly behind her.

Standing awkwardly unsure of what to think, what to do, the
woman's eyes were drawn to the tray. "Oh well," she sighed out
loud heading to it. "I might as well die with a full stomach."

She had eaten, bathed and was dressed in a floor length gown
made of a soft, light texture in white. It had capped sleeves and a
feminine, round neckline with a satin collar. It was long and a little
loose on her. The king's sister was obviously taller and heavier
than her. She brushed her hair until it dried then using pins she
found in the bathroom, pinned her curly hair up on the top of her
head. She had stuck the last pin in when she heard a strange noise.

Slipping quietly to the door, she leaned her ear against it.
Someone was crying. It sounded like a child. "Oh dear," she

murmured. Although he said it would be locked, she turned the doorknob anyway and was surprised when it opened. Onani must have forgotten to secure it when she left.

She carefully opened the tall door and peered out.

The crying was louder.

Looking down the hall she spotted a young child. His head was down, he was rubbing his eyes and wailing, "Mommy...mommy..."

Chapter Four

Leaving the door slightly ajar, the young woman stepped out and moved slowly to the boy. His cries grew louder and more desperate.

Reaching him, she slid down to her knees, the dress a white pool around her, and touched his little shoulder. "Darling, it's all right. Tell me what's wrong, why are you crying?"

Rubbing his eyes, the boy peered up at her through a thick fringe of yellow lashes. Huge, golden, wet eyes regarded her. He said, "I lost mommy," and broke into woeful wails again.

"Oh sweetheart, come here," the woman wound her arms around him and pulled him in close. Petting his silky hair that was cut like a yellow bowl around his head, she murmured, "Now, now, don't cry, little guy, we'll find your mommy. Now dry your tears," she leaned back and brushed at his tears with her fingertips. "What's your name, sweetheart?"

Sniffing and gulping loudly, the boy blinked his big gold eyes, pointed at her and announced, "Mommy."

She laughed and shook her head. "No, I'm not your mommy. What is your name, little guy?"

His mouth broadened into a gaping grin showing baby teeth. "I Bardon. Daddy calls me Bard. I be 4 in…" his face screwed up as he tried to remember. He gave up and asked, "Who you? What you name?"

A line slit between her brows, looking uncomfortable she said, "Um, I don't know my name, Bardon. I don't even know who I am."

He looked at her with concern. "You don know you name?" His dark yellow hair flopped as he shook his head sadly at her. "I sorry. What you mommy call you?"

Her eyes clouded, she said softly, "Bardon, everything is a blank except," her face twisted as some of the stark perplexity shifted, she fell silent. Her eyes closed, the corners pinching as she thought hard.

" 'Cept what?" The boy asked.

"I…I remember a kiss," she said gently stroking the side of her head, her eyes still closed, her head tilted. "And, I can hear a soft voice saying, "sleep now, Sislla." She opened her eyes and frowned.

Bardon's face brightened, he said happily, "So you is Sislla?" But he said it lispy like Sisa.

Her smile turned weak and confused, sad, she pressed her fingertips wearily under her eyes. "I…I…don't know…maybe? It could have been me saying it to someone, I can't tell. It might not even be a name, could be the name of a pet or the title of someone…"

"You scared you not know who you is?" He didn't look at her as if she were weird, he just regarded her with friendly childish eyes.

Her lips pulled in, and her own eyes now blurred with tears. She said, "Yes, Bardon, it's horridly frightening, it's-'' she broke off not wanting to frighten the boy. "Uh, anyway," she changed the subject, "you know you are a very handsome young man." She patted his soft round head.

He grinned showing where a tooth was missing. "You pretty like my mommy."

Smiling at him, she replied, "Thank you sweetheart. Come, let's go find your mommy." She stood up and took his hand and started to lead him down a hall, when suddenly Kultur materialized in front of her.

She gasped, her hand went to her mouth as she stepped back and pulled the boy behind her to protect him.

Kultur said smoothly with a hint of a sarcastic smile, "Let him go, you couldn't protect yourself much less the child. You are too weak. Come here, Bardon."

The little boy tugged his hand from the woman's and ran to Kultur with a big grin.

With a sly smirk that pulled in a dimple in one cheek on his harshly handsome face, Kultur bent over and handed the boy a sweet on a stick. "Good job, Bardon. Thank you. Now go find your mama."

"Thank you Unca K." The boy grinned cheerfully and said to the young woman, "Bye Sisa," and ran down the hall.

She stared wide-eyed at Kultur. "I- don't understand."

Crossing his arms over his chest, his legs braced, one side of his shrewd mouth curved up, Kultur said derisively, "I needed to find out your name and you weren't going to tell me." His gaze scrolled down her body taking in how the dress smoothed over her feminine curves.

Then he took in the clean shiny hair pinned atop her head before moving to the big blue eyes, his pupils flared when they settled on her plush lips.

Incredulous, she spouted with furious reproach, "You put that child in danger to get a stupid name? You don't know me, I could have killed him! You are arrogant and self-centered-"

He whistled, up and down the hall men stepped out from hidden doorways and alcoves just as he had. Her mouth dropped open, she swung around to see man after man, at the ready to get to her before she could have harmed the child.

The smile gone, his expression returned to its normal aloof stoicism. He inclined his head to her. Regarding her with puzzlement, he didn't hide the surprise in his voice, "Why didn't you run?"

Her eyes were still on the guards as they disappeared one by one as eerily as they had appeared. She rubbed her arms trying to scrub away the goose bumps that had popped when first Kultur and then the men had suddenly appeared.

An undercurrent of displeasure lining his words, he commanded, "Look at me." More severely he ground out, "And answer my question."

She turned to face him, anxiety trembled in her lips but she kept her eyes direct and steady at his. "I didn't want Onani to get in trouble for not securing the door, and I couldn't leave the boy lost and crying."

He couldn't hide his dismay at her answer. "Ah," his mouth pursed, "I see." A corner of his lip pulled in. "It's a good thing for Onani that it was a ruse to get information from you."

She didn't reply or move a muscle.

"All right." He pushed the half opened door wider and indicated for her to go inside.

When she stepped back into the room, her spine stiff waiting for some kind of retribution, he said, "I think you are stable enough for dinner. Someone will retrieve you, Sislla, shortly and bring you to the dining room."

"Oh! But wait, I don't know if that is really my name or not, it could be-"

Kultur said quietly, "It doesn't really much matter, *koritsi*, for the time being it is better than calling you Foreigner."

She shrank from him when he moved to stand in front of her then flinched when he reached up to her head.

He plucked out every single pin she'd put in her hair and watched it spill down flowing over her shoulders then spiraling down her back.

She exclaimed, "Oh!" Her mouth dropped open and her hands went to her head. "What are you doing?"

Kultur reached for her hand, held it palm side up and dropped the pins in it, then lifted a long coiled lock. Examining it closely, he rubbed it between his fingers then actually brought it under his nose and sniffed it before letting it go. He watched it settle back down into a ringlet down the front of her like it had earlier. His lip curled, with zero inflection he mumbled, "Just as I thought."

Without explaining his meaning, he stepped back and said evenly, "Leave it as it is. Upswept hair can hide weapons." He clipped his heels together and left the room. After the door closed the lock clicked.

Chapter Five

Shaking her head, she strolled over to the dresser and placed the pins on it. She set the pads of her fingertips on the white dresser and looked at her reflection. The woman looking back at her had very big bright blues eyes. She turned her head slightly and saw the crystalline diamonds the king guy had referred to.

She frowned at the small but shapely lips. Full but tiny, the king had described them. He said he would call her Sislla, her eyes narrowed at the reflection. The name meant nothing to her other than that hazy flash of the voice and the kiss on her forehead. She pursed her lips and studied the rest of her reflection.

Her skin was fair, she didn't see the luminescent pearl stuff he had talked about, she only saw a face that was quite pale except for a trace of pale pink in the very apple of her cheeks. Again, as the king had said, her cheeks were round and childlike. Because her eyes were big, cheeks round, nose small and straight, tiny mouth, it all made her heart-shaped face all that more pronounced.

She lifted her arm and looked at it then her slim neck, yes; he had mentioned that she was very thin. "He must find me so ugly and unshapely." If it weren't for her full cheeks she would look a prisoner of war.

"Huh," she snorted, "I apparently am a prisoner." Lastly, she drew her fingers through her long ringlets.

She didn't know about the chroma, the varnished winter jasmine weirdness he had called the color, what had he said? The softest yet brightest yellow he'd ever seen? The ringlets waved and curled almost to her waist. It seemed a hassle to leave it loose, but he'd told her to leave it that way.

She pushed the locks that curled down the front of her back off her shoulders. "Maybe he thinks it'll be easier to jerk me around by my hair like that animal Trogga had."

She shivered at the remembrance of the king killing the guard with one punch. Shivers ran up her spine again. If he could kill a thickly strong man like Trogga with one punch, goodness knows what horror he could do to her. The blue eyes gazed back at her in free-floating fright. She did not recognize the girl in the mirror.

Out loud she pondered, "I wonder how old I am. The king had said shortly out of childhood. Hmmm, how shortly I wonder?" She set her elbow on the dresser and stared at herself to see if she could remember or figure out her age.

A knock at the door startled her. By the time she turned around, a young woman was striding in. She had a wide mouth that was drawn up in a huge grin showing a mouthful of big bright, white teeth.

"Ahh, so you are the mysterious foreigner, Sislla." She walked towards her with a friendly gait and her hand out. "I'm Kultur's sister, Lexi." She wore tight blue denims and a flowery frilly blouse.

Eying the girl warily, the young woman said, "Uh, I'm not sure my name is Sislla."

Lexi grabbed up her hand and pumped it cheerfully. "I know. But that's what my brother is calling you so," she shrugged, "we'll go with that. Is that okay with you?" The smile faltered, she held her breath afraid she had insulted the foreign woman.

"I, uh," she brushed her hair back nervously staring at the king's sister. The pretty girl with a straight nose, oval face and the wide friendly mouth that had barged into her room now regarded her with an unsure smile. "I guess Sislla is all right. I mean, it could be my name..."

Lexi let out her held breath in a loud whoosh. "Good. Now that that's settled, let's visit." She grasped the chair at the vanity, turned it around and sat on it while gesturing for Sislla to sit on the bed in front of her.

Sislla moved warily, this could be another trap, a trick to make her feel at ease and then- then what? She sat down and smiled with uncertainty at Lexi. Her brows drew down in a leery frown, "Aren't you concerned I could harm you?"

"Ha!" Lexi's laugh a barking clap. Mischief glimmering in her eyes, she smiled. "As if. First of all, you appear younger and are obviously smaller than me. Besides, there are guards outside the door. So," changing the subject, Lexi said amiably, "Kultur says you have like amnesia, that you can't remember anything before you woke up in a cove. Is that right? You have no recollections at all of family or..." one eye almost closed in a wink, "men friends?"

Sislla's shoulders flicked, her eyes narrowed in confusion. "Men friends? What do you mean?"

Blushing slightly, Lexi giggled. "I mean do you have a boyfriend?"

Folding her hands together, Sislla set them in her lap. Bunching her shoulders up, she said, "I don't know. Do you?"

Giggling again, Lexi reached up and gathered her dark brown hair on top of her head then let it fall. It fell in thick waves just past her shoulders. "I'm trying to get a guy's attention. His name is Van." She hugged herself grinning.

"He is so good looking. He's pretty tall, he has nice shoulders but he's a little lean. His hair is a very light brown and he has the most gorgeous light golden eyes." Sighing, she looked at Sislla sitting so primly in front of her. "You have the most brilliant blue eyes, Sislla, and glorious buttercup colored hair just like Kultur said."

Lexi played with her own hair some more. "Everyone on this land has some form of brownish to black hair and brown, golden or dark grey eyes. A handful of children, like my nephew Bardon have yellow hair but it will darken before he's a teenager. My eyes are dark, but not as dark as Kultur's, his look black. Plus I have these God-awful freckles. You are gonna stand out like a sore thumb."

At the sudden look of embarrassment on Sislla's face, Lexi said quickly, "A gorgeous sore thumb, believe me, the men will all ogle you and the women will, well, let me say, I can't wait to see Araina's face when she gets a load of you!"

At a loss to know how to respond, Sislla stammered, "I...uh...who is Araina?"

Lexi's loud burst of laughter shook the room. "Oh yeah, it's gonna be fun." Wiping an eye she said, "Araina has been after my brother for years but he has not yet given in."

"Oh. Um, why not? Is she, um, unattractive?" Sislla felt so odd having this intimate conversation with the beast's sister like they visited as friends every day. She fidgeted with her fingers. But it was hard to be suspicious of this fey-like cheerful young woman.

Rolling her eyes, Lexi twittered. "If only. No, she is quite beautiful. Tall and willowy with long, sleek black hair and gold eyes that are shaped like a cat's. She's kind of panther-like if you know what I mean. She is *very* vain, especially about her eyes."

"Oh," Sislla murmured. "So, does the king- uh your brother not like women?"

Lexi let out another loud burst of laughter. "Oh yeah, Kultur likes women just fine. But he doesn't date anyone steady, ever, and he only uses women for, you know, release." She grinned awkwardly.

"And he never sees anyone here, he goes into the deep part of the village and seeks out, uh," her eyes flicked around the room then she giggled. "The loose kind of women, like prostitutes. He doesn't want any chance of a woman latching onto him seeking a serious relationship."

Sislla digested all the crazy information Lexi had just divulged. Her brows drew down, she asked, "Why doesn't he want a serious relationship?"

Lexi's eyes widened when she looked at the clock on the nightstand. "Oh my gosh, we have to go, we're gonna be late.

Kultur will just kill us!" She jumped up, grabbed Sislla's wrist and dragged her hurriedly out of the room.

Speechless, Sislla allowed herself to be hauled out of the room and down the hall. She wondered if Lexi meant the king would *literally* kill them for being late.

Surely he wouldn't murder his sister, but Sislla? Undoubtedly. In the short day she'd been in his presence the king had threatened her repeatedly, forced her to watch a man get whipped because of her, and killed a huge guard with his fist.

One of the guards outside the bedroom door followed the girls silently. Sislla glanced over her shoulder at him.

"Don't worry about him, Sislla, Kultur put him there to make sure you don't leave. He won't hurt you. So," Lexi leaned in conspiratorially and whispered, "tomorrow, after breakfast we'll go for a walk and I will tell you all the juicy details about my brother and his women. But for now, we hafta hurry!" She dragged Sislla faster.

They went down the stairs and across the great room and down another hall. As they reached a wide arch to a room, Lexi stopped so abruptly Sislla almost crashed into her.

"What?" Sislla whispered.

Whispering, "Shh," Lexi smoothed her frilly blouse over her pants and took a deep breath. She looked at Sislla and quickly combed her fingers through Sislla's hair and straightened the satin collar on the ivory dress.

Then she took a step back and gave a faint wolf whistle. "Girl, you sure fill out my dress! You're shorter and thinner but you have curves in all the right places. Okay, let's go in."

Her entire body taut with trepidation, Sislla allowed Lexi to pull her into the vast room.

The pale peach wallpaper had a hint of silver sparkle in it. White trim bordered the ceiling and around the doors and the bottom of the walls. A huge crystal chandelier with several interspersed peach gems twinkled over a very long, crowded table.

Several servants were lined up near a door on the opposite side of the room. The table was set with cut crystal glassware, and light beige porcelain plates with tiny blue flowers dotted along the gold trim. Just inside the door Sislla froze like a statue.

Lexi tugged on her hand and whispered feverishly, "My other brothers aren't here. Come on, we have to sit down."

But Sislla's feet were cemented to the door. All she could see was a blurry haze of faces, at least 20 or 30 people all staring at her.

An older woman near the far head of the table pushed back her chair and went to stand up but a voice stopped her.

Chapter Six

"Sit, Mother." At the head of the table, Kultur rose, dashing a hand through his hair he walked around the long table to the girls. One of his dark fathomless eyes narrowed at his sister. "You are late. Take your place."

Lexi sent him a mischievous grin, released Sislla's wrist and sauntered off to sit at the table.

Still frozen, Sislla stared unblinking at Lexi's back as she deserted her.

"Sislla."

His deep manly voice stirred shivers in her. The name Sislla was already becoming familiar to her ear. Acutely aware of the crowd of strangers staring at her, she didn't move her gaze from where Lexi had been standing and swallowed hard. She felt something on her arm.

Her eyes lowered but her head didn't. Kultur had gently clasped her arm. When she looked up at him, his eyes were sweeping her from head to toe and back. She thought she saw a dark flame flicker in his eyes. But then mentally shook her head, she must have imagined it.

He leaned over towards her ear, "Come, Sislla," some of the hardness lessened in his whisper. His hand moved from her arm to her lower back. He gently nudged her forward.

If she didn't move her feet she would fall on her face. Kultur ushered her past all the gawking people to the far end of the table where he had been sitting.

When he reached the end, he looked at a man that had been sitting to Kultur's left. Without a word, the man stood up and moved to a different seat.

The room was expectantly silent.

His hand on the curve of Sislla's waist, Kultur glanced around the table. "I want to introduce, Miss Sislla. She is my…guest. There are too many of you now and it would take too long to announce each and every one of you, so introduce yourselves to her if you meet her in passing." He pulled the vacated chair out a little further and indicated to Sislla to sit.

She slid gracefully on the seat and he pushed it in for her then reclaimed his seat at the head of the long oval table.

No one moved. All eyes were fastened on Sislla. Her head was lowered.

Kultur sent a slight glare around the table, and said curtly, "Everyone, attend to your business." There was a brief stillness before a ripple of awkward conversation started up jostling around the table.

Kultur turned and nodded to the servants. They immediately came to attention and a quiet bustle of movement stirred around the room as the servants moved quickly yet with professional grace.

"So, this is our little intruder." The woman on Kultur's right sneered. Her eyes flit up and down Sislla, the curl of her lip indicated she didn't care for what her small, sparrow dark eyes saw.

She continued, "Darling, I do not understand why she is sitting with us and not safely ensconced in the dungeon. After all," she looked contemptuously down her regal nose at Sislla then sniffed. "That is what the dungeon is for isn't it? Criminals and the like?" She sniffed again and fluffed her greying hair that was curled and pinned around her head.

"Mother, your soup is getting cold." Kultur nodded at the bowl of creamy soup in front of her.

A woman sitting next to Kultur's mother squinted disdainfully at Sislla. "Harrumph. Kultur, whatever are you thinking? You can dress a felon up, but you can't make a silk purse out of her."

A man several chairs down didn't hide his blatant leer at Sislla's chest. "Yeah you can. There's proof right there."

Across the table, a woman glared her derision at Sislla. "Really, Kultur, I agree with Suzzane, you've dressed her up as if she were an angel in that white satin, what are you thinking having that- that trash at our table?"

Watching Sislla's fair skin staining red with shame and embarrassment, Kultur slammed his hand down on the table and shouted, "Enough!" Everyone jumped.

"I do not have to explain my actions to anyone." He looked straight at his mother who sniffed again and looked away. "Carry on as you were before our guest entered the room."

"You go, K!" Lexi yelped from down the table. "You tell these stuffed-shirts-"

Warning, "Lexi," Kultur swung his dark gaze at his sister. She grinned at him but didn't say another word. His glare next went to the man that was ogling Sislla's chest. The man quickly ducked his head and grabbed his wine glass.

Kultur picked up his soupspoon and dipped it in his bowl. Taking a few sips, he cut a glance at Sislla sitting stiff and motionless in her chair, her eyes were focused on the bowl in front of her but she hadn't even picked up her spoon.

He murmured so only she could hear, "Eat, *koritsi.*"

Still she didn't move, the red had drained from her face leaving it starkly pale. She didn't dare look at the half-barbarian, half-gentleman king next to her.

Moving the spotlight off Sislla, Kultur said to the man beside her, "Georges, I heard Tenthekens were spotted near the mountains. Prepare a troop to check it out."

The man nodded but his eyes were all over Sislla. Then he saw Kultur's frown and quickly averted his eyes. "Of course, Atraam. We will leave before daybreak. What are we to do with any we capture? Run the swords through them or-"

"Ahem," Kultur cleared his throat and frowned more deeply. His eyes flit to Sislla who if possible, had turned even whiter. He could see the tremor in her chin as she clenched her teeth against tossing her cookies again. Or, crackers. To Georges he said, "Just have the men ready before dawn. I will take lead."

The servants cleared the soup bowls. One woman hesitated at Sislla's untouched soup. She ferried a quick look at Kultur who nodded and she scooped up the bowl and scurried from the room.

The rest of the dinner of succulent roast, gravy covered potatoes, vegetables and warm buttered bread was served. Most of the people at the table were drinking wine; they continued to sneak quick glimpses at Sislla over their wineglass and whisper behind their hands.

Kultur had quietly instructed to Sislla several more times to eat, but although she picked up a fork, the only thing she consumed were a few sips of cold water. Her relief when the dessert plates were cleared was palpable.

Kultur pushed back his chair. As others started to move, he said to them, "Please, stay if you wish." He turned to his mother and inclined his head, "Mother," then he turned to Sislla.

Much to his mother's dismay, Kultur pulled back Sislla's chair and held his hand out to her. She hesitated then set her small icy hand in his large warm one allowing him to bring her to her feet. Moving his hand to her lower back, Kultur led her out of the room.

"See ya in the morning!" Lexi's cheerful shout followed them. Conversation burst as soon as they left, Sislla the salacious topic.

Kultur looked up to the heavens, muttering, "Ah, my recalcitrant sister." He moved his hand to the small of Sislla's back where her curls tickled the top of his hand, and led her down the hall and to the stairs. In a quiet voice he said, "You must be careful and not let Lexi lead you astray."

He almost chuckled at her puzzled look. "Ah, never mind." He brought her back to the cream and rose room. A guard stood stoically beside the door.

Without acknowledging the guard, and the guard did not blink, Kultur opened the door and his hand still at her back, ushered Sislla inside.

He closed the door and clasped his hands behind his back. He frowned, displeased at the frightened look on her face as Sislla backed away from him.

He gestured to the chair Lexi had sat in earlier. "Please sit before you faint on me again." He waited until her shaking legs brought her to the chair and she sat down quite elegantly for a woman whose entire body was shaking like a leaf.

Not wanting to watch her get sick again with fear, Kultur leaned against the door keeping his distance from her. She was staring blankly towards the window. He said quietly, "Sislla."

She didn't respond.

Clearing his throat, Kultur said patiently, "Look at me," he waited until the blue eyes turned up to him.

"You are my prisoner and will do as I direct. As I said earlier, for now, you will stay in this room unless I or a guard under my command is with you. The door will remain locked from the outside, only I, the house guards and Onani have the key."

Seeing her forehead crinkle he sighed, "Yes, my sister finagled the key from Onani. Speaking of Lexi, she appears to have made plans for tomorrow to take you on a tour of the castle and grounds."

Still making no response, unsure if she was supposed to say something or not, Sislla just looked at Kultur keeping her gaze on his chin. Those black inscrutable eyes were just too scary to look at head on.

Deciding such a dainty female that upchucks at a mere flogging, poses little threat, he continued, "I don't see a problem with that as long as there is a guard with you. Lexi is aware of this.

You are not to leave the castle's premises, or there will be severe punishment, or death.

"And, let me make myself clear," he stopped talking. Gesturing with irritation to his eyes with two fingers, he said sharply, "Stop looking at my chin goddammit. Look me in the fucking eyes." He could see the sheen of tears even from several feet away as she raised her frightened eyes to his.

He didn't move from the door but his tone hardened and his pupils glittered ominously. "I'm warning you, if you try to run, or hurt anyone, especially my sister, then what you saw today with Trogga and later with Timmins in the dungeon will seem like child's play to- *ah shit-*"

Clamping her hand over her mouth Sislla jumped up, ran into the bathroom and threw up her tea and crackers.

His back against the door, Kultur crossed his ankles and his arms listening to her pitiful retching sounds. He had not wanted to scare her into heaving again, he only wanted to make sure she understood that he would not brook his sister being harmed or Sislla running away.

At least until he discovered who she was and why she was in a land few people in the world knew about and was almost inaccessible unless by accident.

For her to have survived for days without any of the factions coming across her was either a cunning trick of hers, or she was just plain lucky. His head turned as he heard the bathroom door open.

She stood weak and ashen in the bathroom doorway.

"Sit down," Kultur ordered.

As if her legs were made of wood, she crossed the room and perched on the first thing she got to, the edge of the bed.

His deep inhale was audible across the room as was his heavy sigh. "All right, Sislla. You understand the rules. One other thing," he ran his hand over his thick hair and folded his arms over his chest. "I would prefer you don't starve to death in my castle. Fleeing is one thing, a woman dying from malnutrition is quite another. I don't need any more demerits on my name. If I allow you to leave this room, you are going to have to agree to eat."

Her arms were wrapped tightly around herself, she looked everywhere in the room except at him.

His mouth turned down, his voice lowered and his eyes tapered at her. "I have had enough of this. You will look at me when I speak to you, and you will answer me when I ask you a question." He glared at her trying to disregard how her lovely face and delicate figure affected his body.

She looked at him but said nothing.

He shouted, "Answer me!"

Her mouth parted slightly like she was going to say something, then she closed it. Then she said, "I- I- uh, did you ask me a question?"

His eyes thinned to slits. "Are you fucking with me?"

Sislla's brows flew up to her hairline. "No! No sir- uh, King, I'm not sure what you, um," she petered out not wanting to anger him further.

A rush of irritation growled out of him. Painstakingly he said, "I said, if I allow you to leave this room then you have to agree to eat." He waited, she said nothing. He barked. "If you don't answer me-"

Squirming her bottom on the bed, Sislla murmured, "You didn't, uh, you haven't asked me, a…question…"

Staring in disbelief at the frightened, bewildered young woman practically cowering from him on the bed, Kultur snapped his mouth shut. He thought for a second, uncrossed his arms and tucked his hands in his pockets, lowered his shoulders and sighed deeply.

"You are correct. My apologies. I incorrectly assumed you would understand that I was offering you an agreement and that you would either accept it or decline. Let me rephrase. "If I allow you to go out of this room, do you agree that you will eat every meal?" He watched her mouth firm as she took in what he was saying.

She murmured, "I- I suppose so."

"Good sons above!" Kultur bellowed. "What is 'I suppose so' supposed to mean exactly? You either eat or you don't. You either say yes or no. What is so fucking hard about this?"

Her fingers clasped more tightly in her lap, her chin raised haughtily. "Mister King-"

"It's fucking just Kultur, just fucking call me Kultur, no king, no mister, just *goddamned Kultur*." His furious voice banged off the walls, he pounded his fists against the door at his side.

She flinched but her chin stiffened and moved higher in the air. "You don't have to yell. I didn't understand what I was to call you, you have made it clear." She frowned down her small nose at him, "And you don't need to curse at me. Intelligent men do not need to use profanity to make their point."

"Oh yeah, who told you that?"

Her lids blinked up and down as she thought about it. "I, uh don't know. It just came to me."

Trying to rein in his temper, Kultur forked his fingers through his thick dark hair turning it unruly. "Sons above, woman, you can push my buttons." A sharp rap on the door interrupted him.

He opened it and stuck his head out. "Everything is fine," he snapped shortly to the guard. Closing the door he set his hand on the knob and let out a long pained exhale. "You still have not answered my question. If I allow-"

"Well," she interrupted primly, pressing her palms over the white dress. "If all I have to do to have some freedom is eat, I will do my best to oblige."

"For the love of-" he jammed his hands through his hair again. "A simple yes, all I ask is a simple fuck- uh miserly yes." All the air scraped out of his lungs. He looked like he had just fought a battle. "Can you just say yes?" He couldn't believe, all the vicious, bloodletting battles he's fought and he's standing here arguing with a slip of a girl over foolishness. But he felt compelled to do it. He didn't understand why, but he was reluctant to leave her.

A polite patronizing smile softened the fear in her face. "Of course I can."

He waited. She cocked a brow at him. He hissed, "Sislla, say the word *yes*."

"Oh, okay. Yes. Is that all right?"

The guileless tone just about killed him. Without another word, he yanked the door open, stepped through and for the first time in his life lost control and slammed it behind him so hard the windows in the castle shook.

Chapter Seven

Sunlight fingered through the ruffled curtains pushing at Sislla's closed lids. It didn't wake her but the knocking on the door did.

Rubbing one eye, she sat up in bed with a yawn as the door opened. She had just enough time to take in her surroundings and remember where she was.

"Hey sleepyhead, time to blossom and glow girl." Lexi skipped gaily into the room. She had a bag in her hand that she set on the vanity while admiring her reflection.

Another yawn and Sislla swung her legs off the side of the bed. "You look really pretty today, Lexi," she said watching the young woman preen in the mirror. "Your hair is all wavy and shiny."

Lexi swung around, her eyes twinkled merrily. "Thank you, Sis. Hey, that's kinda cute. Your name shortened is Sis, like sister. Maybe we can be like sisters. I have three obnoxious brothers and no sisters. I can use some more estrogen in the castle! My uptight old mother doesn't count." She giggled meanly and snickered, "There's probably not a drop of estrogen in her old eggs anyway."

Sliding to her feet, Sislla smoothed down the long white nightgown Lexi had loaned her and asked, "Why do you say your brothers are obnoxious?"

"Ugh, they're men," Lexi grunted as if that answered the question. She arched her neck and let her head drop back. Then

46

flopping her head forward, she bent over and shook her brunette hair then tossed it back. Taking the brush off the dresser she drew it through her wavy tresses. "Get dressed, I want to get out of the castle. It's gorgeous outside."

"Okay." Sislla went into the bathroom and ten minutes later came out in denims like Lexi was wearing only in black, and she wore a pale pink blouse with lacey collar. "Thank you so much for lending me your clothes, I don't know what I'd do without them."

"It's okay, that's what sisters are for. Except you make me look like a rail compared to the way you fill out my clothes. You should roll the cuffs on the pants up a little or you'll trip."

Sislla bent over and did that. "You were telling me why your brothers are obnoxious," she prompted Lexi to talk. She wanted to learn more about the place she was in and the people, especially the dark brooding king of said castle.

Lexi opened the bag she'd brought. She pulled out a pastry and handed it to Sislla. When Sislla started to shake her head, Lexi said, "You have to eat it. Kultur said he would not allow you out of this room at all if I don't make sure you eat. So," she held the pastry out.

Her lips pulled in, Sislla took the pastry but didn't eat it.

"Seriously, Sis, take a bite. When Kultur says something, believe me by the sons above, he means it. Here," she took a juice bottle out of the bag, stuck a straw in it and gave it to Sislla.

Pinching off a tiny piece of pastry, Sislla tucked it in her mouth and spoke through the wad, asking again, "Tell me about your brothers."

Gobbling her own sweet, Lexi gulped some juice before answering. "I'm the baby of the family. The oldest is Lucas. He's married and has a son, Bardon who is three."

"Almost four," Sislla interjected.

"Huh? How'd you know that?"

"I met him. He's adorable but sneaky. Your brother used him to play a trick on me." She took another miniscule bite of the pastry.

Lexi half closed one eye at her. "You need to tell me about that later. Anyway, the next oldest is Gabriel. He is wickedly handsome and a player."

At Sislla's expression, she explained, "He loves the ladies and goes through them like a shark through a school of minnows. Girls are flocking here night and day trying to get his or Kultur's attention. Actually," she gave a little snicker, "they come first for Kultur. Women are attracted for some strange reason to the aura of violence and mystery and danger that hangs around him.

"If I wasn't his sister I'd be scared to death of him. Even as his sister I must admit I fear him some. He has this cold frightening temper, his eyes shut down and you can tell he's on the edge and he is capable of doing anything. Even to me."

Sislla took another tiny bite and set the pastry down behind the clock on the nightstand and drank her juice. She was just too nervous to eat, her stomach was tied up in knots over her strange situation.

She concurred with Lexi, "I can see how that is. After he killed that poor guard and then the flogging," she wrapped her arms around herself and shuddered, and prayed the bit of pastry she'd had would stay down. The violence just turned her stomach over. "But I don't think he would harm you, Lexi, no matter what you did."

Lexi's pretty mouth turned up in a grin. "You're right. But he can be scary nonetheless even to me. And he has threatened to spank me on occasion."

"Why is he so- so-"

"Cold and volatile?" Lexi shoved in the last of her pastry and looked around Sislla suspiciously for her breakfast.

"Uh, yes. I guess," Sislla muttered, innocently wiping her mouth with a napkin.

Lexi gathered up the napkins put them in the bag, tossed in the empty juice bottles and dumped them in a small trashcan near the vanity.

"Well, our father was a...a difficult man. Kultur is notorious as the most ruthless, vicious, brutal warlord in the land; he needs to be that way to protect the people. But Father was even more… violent, more brutal; he was horridly sadistic and bloodthirsty. And he was a tyrant. He was tough on all the boys. Me, he hardly ever bothered with because I was just a useless girl." She shrugged at Sislla's look.

"Anyway, he was the hardest on Kultur. I guess although he was the youngest male, he felt Kultur had what it took to be a warrior king. Trust me, Lucas and Gabriel are as fierce as it gets, but Kultur is…" she turned up a palm. "I guess he is harder and smarter, faster and tougher and more merciless than my other brothers."

"That's, um, interesting." Sislla combed her hair while Lexi wandered around the room.

"Yeah. So Father was actually pretty horrible to Kultur trying to toughen him up. He brutalized him as a young child, beating him, locking him in the dungeon for weeks. He even made him fight with wolves to make him fear nothing and be able to fight, and defeat, anyone or anything."

"That is…heartbreaking." Sislla grew quiet picturing a young Kultur left alone in the woods to fight off a pack of wild wolves. Shaking her head to dispel the picture, she said, "Last night you said he only went with, uh, women that…"

Lexi let out an unladylike snort. "True that. Basically whores that he can screw quickly and move on without any attachments." She shook her head morosely; her long brown hair flopped back and forth.

Still combing her hair, Sislla asked, "Why is he that way? It seems, you know, sad. Lonely."

Lexi nodded in agreement. "It is. Sometimes I feel bad for my brother. What happened was," she glanced around the room as if to see if anyone was lurking about and listening then said in a low voice, "Kultur was pledged to be married to this girl, Cassandra. She was from one of the other factions on our island. Supposedly, Father and the girl's father were using them to form a union between the two warring factions.

"Well, to make a long story short, she betrayed Kultur. She was sleeping with the Atraam, the king of the Tenthekens and they used a meeting between Kultur and Cassandra to set up an ambush for my father so they could take our clan over, and…" her wide mouth drooped, the twinkle left her eyes.

"And?"

"Father was killed. Kultur never forgave himself for not seeing the scheme. I don't think he was in love with Cassandra, but she was very beautiful in a- a cold kind of way. Her long straight hair had a hint of red in it, matched that bitchy fiery temper of hers. Her dark eyes were like ice, totally bereft of any warmth." Lexi snarked, then sighed.

"I guess Kultur never got over the betrayal or the guilt, he thinks it was his fault Father was killed." Her mouth twitched. "But he is obviously loaded with alpha testosterone so he needs to, you know, see women," she trailed off wiggling her eyebrows.

Running the comb through her ringlets, Sislla's voice holding sadness, she commented, "That is a terrible story, and I'm sorry for your loss, Lexi. It doesn't sound like there was anything King- uh Kultur could have done to change the outcome."

Lexi snatched the comb out of Sislla's hand and tossed it on the dresser. "Come on, let's go, enough about my dopey brothers." She yanked open the door and took Sislla's hand and almost ran down the stairs and out of the castle.

Right at their heels was the guard.

Chapter Eight

Lexi took Sislla on a tour of the castle. There were so many wings and hallways and rooms Sislla was lost right off the bat.

All the rooms were all painted in airy pastel colors with gold or white trim had luxurious, plush cushioned furniture. Paintings hung on all the walls, the carpets were thick and squishy. The staircase and floor of the great room were cool, smooth, white marble veined with gold.

"This place is stunning, Lexi, beautiful," the awe in Sislla's voice rang clear and honest. "Somehow I don't think Kultur had a hand in the decorating."

A giggle erupted from Lexi as she shook her head. "No way. It would be dreadfully dark and brooding and very plain, no frills, no color. No, Mother is the decorator. Except I think the boys had a say in their rooms because Kultur's and Gabe's are tastefully masculine. Lucas had to go with his wife, Cindra's desires. Here, let's go out this door." The girls rushed out the door to the outside.

"Ahh," Lexi breathed in deeply. Raising her arms, she twirled, her hair flowing. "See, blue sky, lovely and warm, and smell that fresh air, girl."

Sislla agreed it was nice out. She walked beside Lexi as she strolled around the lawns pointing things out like the men's training center, stables, fragrant pastures. A few horses lolled in the meadow.

The girls leaned their arms over a wooden fence and watched the horses wander lazily and chomp grass.

"Lexi, how old are you?" Sislla asked. Picking a yellow flower, she sniffed it then brushed it over her cheek.

"I'm twenty-two. Lucas is thirty two, Gabriel is, um, twenty uh eight, and Kultur believe it or not is only twenty-seven." She laughed at Sislla's disbelief. "Yeah, it's all that harsh hardness in him, makes him seem older. Plus all that fighting, it adds years at least in experience, bruises shadows into his eyes, you know?"

"Yes, I can certainly see that." Sislla turned her serious face to her new friend. "How old do you think I am?"

"Hmmm," Lexi studied the girl next to her. "I'm not really sure, but I think you're younger than me by a few years maybe."

"Oh." Sislla twirled the flower. "Can you explain to me this- this- land, I've heard it called an island."

"Sure." Lexi bent and yanked a long blade of grass out of the ground and stuck the end in her mouth. "It is an island. It's huge, with mountains and lakes and fields but still an island. It's basically inaccessible, but," she eyed her friend, "people sometimes come in by accident. No one leaves, and no one, on the outside knows about us except one other distant island."

Nodding thoughtfully, Sislla asked, "There was something said about a- um, marking to- I don't know, an identification or something?"

"Yes. It's called an Epita. Everyone on the island in all three factions is born with the mark. Ours is like a tiny star shape, mostly on a person's hip but lots of people have them elsewhere, arms, legs, necks, a few have them on their faces. We're born with it."

Lexi studied her new friend with a smile. "That's how Kultur, along with your unique coloring, believes you are not one of us. Because you don't have our marking. Or do you? I didn't hear that, I mean, Kultur didn't say," she blushed and stammered, "I mean did he see you naked-"

"Oh heavens no!" Sislla's cheeks turned bright red. "He did not. And no, I do not have the marking. I don't know where I'm from." She dropped the flower and put her hands over her flaming cheeks. Changing the subject she asked, "Tell me about the, what do you call them, factions?"

Chuckling at Sislla's embarrassed red face, Lexi could barely picture her tough brother with hardened, faceless prostitutes, there was no way he would be with someone as young, dainty, and sweet as Sislla. As far as coldly stripping her naked to see if she was marked, she shrugged, that she wouldn't put past him. She smiled, and he would do it with the same impersonal attitude as he does everything else.

"Lexi?"

"Oh, yeah, sorry, I was thinking, uh, never mind." She explained about the occupants of the island. "There are three factions or you could say, I don't know, clans maybe, on the island. There's us, the Chamaine-Gris, and then there's the Ulmas, and the Tenthekens. We three are continuously at war except when the Iminims come on raid from across the sea, then we all fight the Iminims together because they are wild and vicious enough to end us all if they got the upper hand."

Sislla crossed her arms on the fence and set her chin on her wrist. "Why are you always at war?"

Lexi bumped one shoulder up and tickled the side of her neck with the blade of grass before sticking it back in her mouth.

She replied, "Well, I guess it's because our land is the only area that the turesenes that make heat can be found, and the Ulmas have the special papyrus that makes boats so we can catch fish for food. The Tenthekens have the metals, and the pines for the tar to line the boats. We all have mills to make clothing, oil wells, and sand to create glass."

"But, so why do you fight?"

Lexi's arms flopped over the top rail of the fence; she set a foot on the bottom rail. Her shoulders hunched. "We all need what each other has so we steal what we need from each other and so there are constant skirmishes to stop the stealing. We lose men all the time when caught stealing or when warring. I worry for my brothers, and now for Van, he is in training to be a warrior." She grew quiet and contemplative.

"What about the women? Don't they fight too?"

Pulled out of her revelry, Lexi shook her head. "No. Women are not allowed to be soldiers. Kultur refuses to have our womenfolk raped, tortured, mutilated, killed-"

"Okay, got it." Sislla cut her off as her stomach roiled. "Um, you said something about when you group together to fight the-somethings?"

"The Iminims," Lexi provided. A dark grimace marred her face, "They are the only people outside of the island that know about us. Once or twice a year they come ashore and like I said, they go warring on all of us. If we didn't all fight them they would kill us all and take the island over. It's really quite scary."

"I can imagine," Sislla agreed. "So…why do you clans fight and steal amongst each other instead of buying from each other what you need?"

It was Lexi's turn to look puzzled. "What does that mean?"

Not sure how she knows this without knowing her own name, Sislla said, "You give money, or like you trade your stones for their wood and the metal and then you know, visa-versa."

Lexi stared at her friend trying to grasp what she was saying, then she shook her head. "That makes no sense when you can fight for it. Besides, I think it was tried many years ago and someone didn't abide by the rules."

"But Lexi, listen, let me explain it better-"

Suddenly an ear-splitting siren rent the air. Lexi grabbed Sislla's hand and yelled, "We have to go into the castle- now!"

The two young women raced across the grass along with others to the castle. There was immediate pandemonium and noise.

Sislla yelled over the noise, "What is happening?" Considering all the loud chaos she was surprised to see Lexi relatively calm and unafraid.

Lexi leaned close so Sislla could hear her. "It's the Bowlem Siren. When it goes off it means there's some trouble with the other factions and all the women, children, the elderly and non-warriors are to immediately go inside their homes and bolt their doors."

She glanced around nodding here and there. "I see my cousins, my mother, my aunts, a few of the warrior's wives who live with their men here are present."

"But you seem not distressed at the-"

There was a thunder in the ground and yelling in the air. The thunder was pounding hooves that grew louder and louder as they came closer and closer.

Seeing her friend's new terror, Lexi laid a hand on her arm. "It's all right, it's our men, the siren is just a precaution. They will arrive in a minute, we need to get inside."

It seemed the horses would roar right through the solid wood and steel front door, but they passed down a tunnel that ran alongside the castle walls. It took a while, but the pounding hooves finally lessened, but then the door to the castle flew open and several horses charged inside.

Lexi slapped her hand over Sislla's mouth as she opened it to scream. "Tis okay, Sis, it's Kultur, but something is wrong."

Kultur, in black leather and iron mesh jumped off his horse, grabbed a man that was slung over the front of his steed with both hands and as he slung him down, another warrior who resembled Kultur strode over to him and helped him bring the man down.

They carried him to a table. With one hand, Kultur swept everything on the table off- vases and glasses and picture frames crashed to the floor.

"Kultur! Lucas! What on earth-" Kultur's mother, the Altra, Queen Darathia gathered up her long skirts and marched over with a furious expression and scarlet dots on her cheeks.

Ignoring her, the brothers laid the man on the table. In the commotion, Lexi grabbed Sislla's hand again and dragged her over so they could see what was going on.

They pushed through the crowd until they were in front of the table. A man was stretched out, he looked near death.

"Tis Cortland McGovern," Lexi whispered. Obviously not knowing who he was, Sislla remained silent.

"Get towels, bandages and ice!" Kultur bellowed, pulling off the man's boots. He tossed them on the floor. A sickening murmur passed around the crowd. Cortland's trousers were shredded and drenched with blood.

Sislla yanked her hand from Lexi's and moved right up to the table. Seeing her, Kultur held out an arm blocking her. His grave fear for the man on the table made his voice heavy and gruff, he said tersely, "Get back."

But Sislla proceeded to the table. Glancing briefly at Kultur then down at the injured man, she ordered Kultur, "Give me your shirt."

His shocked look turned furious. "Sislla, you have no business here, especially with your weak stomach, get away."

She turned fierce eyes to him and repeated calmly with authority, "Give me your shirt. Quickly."

Chapter Nine

"Woman, what the hell-" something in Sislla's eyes and voice made Kultur hesitate. He yanked at the ties on his leather vest, ripped it off and let it fall to the floor. Then he reached over his shoulder and grabbed the back of his shirt pulling it off and handed it to her.

But her eyes were like wide goggles gaping at his chest. Even though he seemed to be covered in tons of blood, it was clear to see that his chest was powerful with hard carved muscles and partially covered with dark hair, scars crisscrossed all over his torso. Sislla acted like she'd never seen a man's bare chest before, she just froze, riveted.

"*Sislla*," Kultur's bark broke the spell.

She snatched the shirt out of his hands and bent over the man. "King Kultur, I need you to remove the lower leg of his pants-quickly."

He didn't ask why, he just grasped the bottom of the man's pant leg and tore the hem up past his knee. A surge of retching and horrified gasps rent the air in the room, people backed away.

The man's leg was a mess, so bloody and destroyed; it was a grisly wreck that no longer resembled a leg.

Kultur's brother Lucas said despondently, "There's nothing to do. We will have to amputate to save his life. Someone give me your sword and bring a flame." Grievous crying and wailing filled the chamber.

Ignoring the men, Sislla moved right to the man and wrapped Kultur's shirt tightly around his thigh above the injury. She said to Kultur, "Every four minutes, loosen the shirt for no more than thirty seconds then tie it back up tight again. Do this until I return." She pivoted and started for the door.

Kultur snagged her arm and held her back. "Where the hell do you think you're going?"

Tugging at her arm, Sislla said impatiently, "I must get to the field. I saw earlier there are medicinal herbs out there, I must collect some strand-bines to stop the bleeding, it will cause it to clot, and I need some broad clavertail, and blue thistle and- other things, and if someone could gather needle and thread, alcohol- any kind."

Kultur held her arm. "*Koritsi*, you are not going anywhere. Women are not allowed to leave the safety of the castle. The Tenthekens are on a rampaging raid, no way-"

"If I don't go he will die. Even with the amputation, he will bleed to death before you kill him with the cauterizing. Release me!"

The black eyes glowered at her; he still held her arm, denying, "No. You are not leaving." He called out, "Zane!"

A young man in warrior gear like Kultur was wearing popped up beside them. "Atraam?"

"Kirman Zane, you are to go out to the field, bring at least two others with you. You will retrieve," Kultur turned to Sislla, "tell him what you need, describe the herbs, where they are located and how much."

Cortland's agonized screams twisted even the sturdiest man's heart. He thrashed and writhed so violently several burly men struggled to hold him down.

Her sigh laborious, Sislla described the herbs she needed, how much and where they were to be found, while Zane wrote notes. She declared with a heavy breath, "You must hurry, Kirman Zane, time is of the essence."

"You get everything she told you?" Kultur asked the young man.

The tall, lithe young man nodded with eager competence, his thin light hair bounced over his forehead. "Yes sir!"

"Go then, take men with you, hurry, and," Kultur let go of Sislla and caught Zane's arm, his voice steady, low, he urged, "be careful. Keep your eyes open, if it tis too dangerous, return. I'd rather lose one man than three. Understand?"

"Yes, sir." Zane nodded sharply.

Kultur patted him on the back and the boy was gone.

A guard brought Kultur another shirt, he quickly shrugged it on, buttoned it up.

While they waited, Sislla instructed Kultur on how and when to work the tourniquet. Someone brought the needle, thread, towels, alcohol. Kultur ordered the room cleared except for a few select men. His brother was one of them.

His hair lighter than Kultur's but with shoulders as wide, they had the same powerful physiques, but Lucas had a hint of warmth in his eyes that were a lot lighter than Kultur's ruthless obsidian orbs. But at the moment he was scowling darkly at Sislla. "Brother," he started, "what is this woman doing here?"

"We will discuss it later, Lucas. It can't help anyone now for us to hash it."

Shaking his head with a scowl, Lucas questioned, "But, why are you listening to her? What the fuck does she-"

Kultur ground out with quiet intensity, "I said later."

"Huh." Lucas closed his mouth but he glared at Sislla, that is when he wasn't checking out her curves. Her borrowed black denims and blouse were already covered in blood.

Ignoring Lucas' resistance, Sislla quickly catered to the injured man. Kultur did everything Sislla directed. Reluctantly Lucas joined in.

They worked in silence with the sounds of Cortland McGovern's pregnant wife's sobs in the back of the room. Keeping her away from the sight of her husband's gruesome injuries, and the possibility of his dying on the table, her family circled her in support.

Kultur and Lucas kept pouring the alcohol down the groaning man's throat to help dull the profound pain, and fear, that he was in. He was writhing and crying like a pitiful deer being torn apart by a voracious lion.

The door finally burst open and a grinning Zane followed by two other young men strode swiftly to Sislla. He handed her a cloth bag. "It's all there, Miss, everything you asked for." He bowed then stepped back.

Sislla opened the bag and poured out the herbs on the table beside Cortland. She handed several small yellow leaves to Kultur. "Put these in his mouth, force him if you have to. He must chew them, they will stop the pain."

Kultur took them from her. Without a word, the men held Cortland down, while another man and Lucas held his head and pried his mouth open. Cortland was out of his mind with agony. Kultur shoved the leaves in and he and Lucas forced his mouth to grind back and forth, making him chew the leaves.

Kultur said to Sislla, "We can't make him swallow them, what-"

"It's all right, they will work anyway. Please have someone pour the alcohol all over his leg." Sislla was knotting a needle.

Kultur tipped the bottle over the injured man's leg.

Lucas said through his teeth, "Hold onto him boys, when that alcohol hits that open wound he's going to go insane with pain."

The men stood stupefied with their mouths open while Kultur poured the alcohol, and Cortland not only didn't scream and thrash, he actually appeared quite calm, even seemed to have a faint smile on his face.

"What – the- fuck-" Lucas gawked from Cortland to Sislla and back to Cortland. "Well I'll be damned…" He and the other men warily let go of the injured man and slowly stood back. They watched in silent awe as Sislla quickly laid broad leaves all over Cortland's leg. As if by magic, the blood slowed, then trickled, then stopped completely.

When the bleeding stopped, Sislla said quietly, "Can someone wash his leg clean?" As soon as she spoke two men dipped towels in a pail of water mixed with alcohol per Sislla's earlier instruction and washed the blood off Cortland's leg. Half the men turned queasy when the chopped meat of his leg was visible without the cover of the blood.

Kultur and Lucas were the only ones to stand solid and not look away, even when Sislla stuck the needle into the ravaged skin.

All eyes followed her swift movements as she knit his flesh, veins, and muscles together. When she made the last knot and cut the thread, she set the needle down and picked up some leaves with a purple hue and laid them over the wound.

After wrapping a cloth around the wound, Sislla stood up straight, one hand at her lower back, the other pressed on her forehead, she stepped back.

Everyone in the room let out a collectively held breath. Curious people were wandering back into the great room.

"Put him in his bed and cover him with a warm blanket. Give him water every half hour. Someone should stay watch over him through the night. By morning he should be better. If he starts a fever I must be called." Before anyone could say anything, Sislla turned from the table and strode across the room to Lori, Cortland's wife.

Tears streaked down the young, pregnant woman's face. She watched Sislla approach with trepidation. Her family members closed in around her, protecting her from the stranger. Kultur was right behind her.

Sislla held her hand out towards Lori and opened it. Tiny whitish leaves were nestled in her palm. Her voice gentle, she said, "Make a tea out of these. Sip through the night. They will ease your nerves and take away that blinding headache you have."

The young woman's eyes widened. "How did you know-" she looked from Sislla to Kultur to Sislla, then down at the leaves.

Lori's mother took the leaves from Sislla. "I vaguely remember these from when I was a little girl. I recall my granny saying the same thing you just more or less said." She smiled at

Sislla and then turned to her daughter's frightened face. "I will heat these up right away. You will be fine, my dear daughter."

She patted her cheek then said to Sislla, "Thank you, for…everything." She leaned in and kissed Sislla on the cheek, bowed to Kultur then scurried off to heat the leaves.

Another woman in the group said urgently to Sislla, "I've had terrible stomach pains for months do you think you could-"

Kultur dropped his heavy hand on the inner curve of Sislla's lower back and turned her away. "Enough for now. You are dead on your feet. I will take you to your room."

Sislla resisted him slightly to say to the woman, "Come back tomorrow and I will help you."

The woman complained, "But, I need-"

Kultur cut her off. He addressed all the people left in the room, "Everyone, please go to your chambers, let's clear this room." He stepped between Sislla and the rest of the people, turning his back to them.

With grumbling and muttering, and whispering, the rest of the occupants trod off to their respective rooms leaving Sislla and Kultur alone.

When the room was empty, Kultur said, "Now that you have healed both Cortland and his *avithé*," seeing Sislla's question in her expression he said, "Lori is his *avithé*, his wife. Come, I will take you upstairs."

"Oh, no, your arm," distressed, Sislla reached out and touched Kultur's upper arm. "There is blood. You are injured. Here," she took his hand and brought him to the table Cortland had been laying on. "Sit here."

Then she took off to get her needles and leftover herbs that had been moved to another table, light spiraling hair fluttering behind her.

"No, wait Sislla," he called out, "I don't need anything, I'm fine, stop."

She hurried back. Frowning at the big man, she gave him a little push. "Sit." She laid out the herbs along the table.

Shocked at this dainty frail woman pushing him around and he was twice her size, but he sat down on the table with the herbs lined up beside him. Still protesting, "I am fine, woman, you don't need to-"

"Hush," she remonstrated. "Can you uncover your arm, please?"

His brows drew down in an annoyed frown, but he unbuttoned his fresh shirt, which was already wet with blood, and shrugged his left arm out of the sleeve. "Really, *koritsi*, this is all quite unnecessary." When she kept working ignoring his words, he sighed and closed his mouth and watched her prepare.

She poured the alcohol over the wound. When he didn't flinch, she peered up at him. He was staring at her. "Ah," she murmured, "you not only look like you are made of iron, you apparently are." She put her attention back to her work.

When he saw her laying the pain leaves on his injury instead of having him refuse to chew them, he said in irritation, "I do not need that. I am-"

"Yes, I know. You're fine." She patted the leaves in place. Seeing his arm become slightly less tense, she hid a tiny smile, he was feeling the pain, but the pain leaves were causing it to rapidly diminish. Cortland's injuries were so severe it was necessary for him to chew the leaves to hit his pain interceptors in his brain and at the wound as fast as possible.

Her nimble fingers set a layer of broad leaves over his wound and in seconds it stopped bleeding. He was still astonished at the magic of it. As usual, no emotion showed in Kultur's hard face, but lines around his mouth deepened when he saw her pick up the needle and start to thread it.

Now she did have a hint of a smile. "Don't worry, you won't feel much, the pain leaves will help dull the pain of the needle."

"Humph," he sniffed. "I am not worried or scared of a little pain. Do not concern yourself."

Her face split with a wide grin. "Oh, don't worry, I am not concerned. I know you can take it."

His eyes were on her mouth. He looked at her bright white teeth, the way her cheeks rounded more with her smile, her plush lips curving- "Ouch! Hey-" he growled at the sudden jab of her needle.

"Oh, I'm sorry, the leaves will lessen-"

"Yeah," he grumbled, "I know, they'll lessen the- ow!" He glared at her. "Are you doing that on purpose?"

Her hair rolled back and forth reflecting the light in her bright curls as she shook her head trying to hide her mirth. "No. I guess because you are so big with all those muscles it's taking the leaves longer to bleed through to ease the pain. I'm sorry."

She kept sewing, ignoring his not amused grunts. On her tiptoes then she set back on her heels. "I need to get closer, I can't see far enough."

"Oh. Here." He opened his legs and she moved between them to get closer to the wound.

Leaning over him, her hair brushed over the side of his face. Instead of pushing it away, he nudged his nose in the curls and breathed deeply.

She set her hand in the middle of his chest to balance. His eyes dropped to stare at it. But he didn't move her away or comment on it. Instead, his hands came up and cinched her waist to help her hold steady.

"So, uh, Sislla," feeling the warmth of her skin through her light blouse, his voice shook slightly, "it's been so chaotic I haven't had a chance to really speak with you."

Mumbling, "Uh huh," she kept sewing.

"This…healing skill you have. Did your memory come back? Do you remember who you are now?"

Her hair moved across his face as she shook her head. He pushed his nose further into the curls. "No. It's strange. I don't know how, or…anything." She hesitated for a second before resuming sewing. "It's kind of like you warriors. You train and train and then when something happens you just act by rote, muscle memory, without thinking about it."

She shrugged. "My hands and mouth seemed to have minds of their own. I told everyone what to do before the thought was even in my head. My hands just," she shrugged again, "do what they do. I still have zero recollections of anything. Even how I learned this...healing I guess as you called it."

"Hmmm," he didn't say anything else, just continued smelling her fragrant hair, he seemed unaware that his fingers tightened on her waist and his thumbs were stroking her belly. When she suddenly stepped back announcing she was done, he blinked rapidly as if he was hazy in a trance.

"Um, you can let go of me now," Sislla said softly with a trace of a smile in her voice.

He didn't move, just mumbled, "Huh?"

"Your hands, you can let go of me, I won't topple into you, I promise."

Kultur looked down at his hands as if surprised to see them holding onto her. He instantly released her and coughed. "Uh, I was concerned you would, uh, lose your balance." He cleared his throat and dragged his shirt back on and started to button it.

Now she did grin at him. "You don't need to concern yourself about me." She started packing up her herbs.

His dark eyes flashed up at her. At first he frowned, then seeing she was teasing him, repeating the words he'd said to her, his mouth relaxed into some semblance of a smile. "Fine." He stood up. "If you are done healing for the day, I will take you to your-"

"Oh dear."

He cringed. "What now?"

"Your leg. I can see the blood oozing through your pants. Take them off and sit down." She turned and set the herbs back down on the table.

Impatience stretched across his face. "Listen, there is no need to-"

Setting her hands on her hips she looked up at him, her brows crescents over blue eyes that weren't backing down.

His eyes rolled heavenward, a big sigh let out like the weight of the world was on his shoulders. "Bless the sons above," he plopped down on the table, cursed, "goddammit."

"Um, you have to remove your trousers, I can't see your wound or be able to sew it through the material." The blue eyes now regarded him as if he was a dense child.

His mouth dropped, he looked like he was about to argue, but he sighed again and stood up. When he reached to unbuckle his belt Sislla's cheeks turned crimson and she spun around so fast she almost fell backwards.

Chapter Ten

Tugging at the buttons on his trousers Kultur smirked at her back. "You all right there little doctor?"

She nodded. Her shoulders twitched at his snicker. She heard him kicking off his boots, then the pants fall to the floor. The table creaked when he sat back down on it.

"I'm ready, Doc." The smirk was evident in his voice.

Before she turned around she asked timidly, "Uh, can you be sure you, uh, you know, cover yourself?" His deep chuckle surprised her.

"You're mighty shy and modest for a doctor, *koritsi*."

There was some shuffling then he said, "Okay, Doc, I'm decent. Sort of. You can turn around."

She gingerly turned around with a few leaves clenched in her hand. Her body eased when she saw he was sitting on the table with one of the unused towels draped over his lap.

"Will that do?" he chuckled at her embarrassed consternation, watched the red cheeks turn scarlet.

Stepping to him she mumbled, "Sure." She gathered up the pain leaves and was relieved when he didn't protest. Keeping her eyes on his leg and not his face, she said, "You need to move the towel, uncover the injury."

As soon as he moved the towel and she saw how severe the gouge was she became instantly cool and confident. Layering the leaves over the wound, she said, "It is quite a wicked injury. An inch deeper and you would have likely bled to death before making it back to the keep."

As she trickled the leaves up and down his thigh and then patted them down, it was his turn to become uncomfortable. His body reacted to her light touch. He cleared his throat several times but couldn't speak through the constriction lodged there.

She stepped back a bit and looked around the room. "I need you to put your foot up on something so your thigh is away from the table and I can stitch you." Spotting a small footstool she hurried over to retrieve it.

While she did that, Kultur readjusted himself and the towel to hide his growing erection. By the time she came back and set the stool down in front of him, he had an undisturbed calm expression, but the vein at his temple was beating madly.

When she lowered to her knees in front of him only inches away from his groin, his tan turned pale. "What the hell are you doing?" he slid back on the table.

Setting a hand above the wound, high up on his thigh, almost to his hip, she leaned over with the needle in her hand. The leaves stopped the pain but they didn't kill the feeling in his lower extremities. She scolded him, "Stop moving, hold still."

When he saw her glancing around the room he asked, "What are you looking for?"

"Hmmm. I need to tie my hair up, maybe there is a piece of cloth I can use."

"No problem. I will hold it for you." To her astonishment he gathered the curls up, combing them with his fingers then held her hair back in a ponytail.

"Well, uh, okay," she set her hand back on his thigh and picked up the needle.

A low growl rumbled in his chest as he fought to not squirm under her touch. He prayed she couldn't see the center of the towel rising. Kneeling in front of him, between his legs, her face was scant inches from his private parts. Her hand slid down to press against his inner thigh to hold his skin while she plunged the needle through his flesh.

So tense trying to control his body's reaction to her he didn't feel the prick of the needle at all. Just her warm fingers and breath on his legs, making him harder, *Oh shit-*

"Kultur! What is the meaning of this?" An austere, shocked voice made them both jump.

"*Ow*," he grunted when the needle pressed harder than before.

Sislla apologized, "I'm sorry, she-"

"Kultur!" His mother was stalking across the room straight towards them. "You disgusting tramp, you get your filthy mouth off my son's-"

"Mother!" Kultur stopped her with a fierce snarl, still holding Sislla's hair with one hand. "She is stitching up my leg. And you shouting like that is only making her *ow*- poke me harder." At least her sudden entrance had helped his erection fade, a little. He held onto the towel and scowled darkly at his mother.

Her heels making jarring clacks on the marble, in her anger, Darathia stomped right up to them and looked over Sislla's shoulder. "My sons above, Kultur, you are in your underwear and she has her face in your- privates!"

Her describing the situation did nothing but re-arouse his erection. Kultur's irritated exhale was loud. "I have an injury, she is stitching it up so I don't bleed to death. Now," he tensed at the plunging needle, apparently his mother was making Sislla nervous, "leave us so she can finish."

Beet red steaks ran up both of Darathia's gaunt cheeks. Her lips, shaped like her son's but a bit leaner and not chiseled like his, were pressed in a mutinous line. Her rectangle jaw was clenched and her eyes narrowed to accusing pins.

"My word, Kultur, why are you holding the wretched girl's hair? Really, my son, I will not leave you alone, naked and in this criminal's treacherous clutches. She is obviously about to service you with her mouth, I refuse to leave you!"

His voice frigid and quietly low, Kultur said through grit teeth, "Mother. Leave the room. Now." He was hunched over with one hand grasping the towel and the other Sislla's hair. His head lowered, black hair hanging over his brow ridge, he rolled his acerbic black eyes up, glaring through unarguable slits at her.

Darathia's lips pursed in a tight pucker, then she turned on her heel and stomped out of the room. Her steps could be heard clacking across the marble floor until she reached a carpeted hallway.

Sislla had not moved except to keep sewing. Her hand was shaking; she was having a hard time keeping a straight line.

Kultur laid his big hand over hers. "'Tis all right, *koritsi*, don't take offense. Unfortunately she has a very narrow mind. Once she gets to know you she will learn to like-" he broke off. There was no way of knowing how long Sislla would be with them. A day, a week, a year? He moved his hand back off hers to grab the towel that was sliding.

He couldn't explain his own instant trust of her. Seeing her so tender and protective towards Bardon started it. In her fury she thought Kultur had endangered the child. She could have escaped, but instead, she stayed to protect a maid from punishment and to comfort a small boy. Adding now, saving Cortland, and sewing Kultur himself up.

Snorting, "Wow," almost finished sewing, Sislla said with small awe, "even your mother obeys you without question." She tied a knot and clipped it with scissors. "You may let go of my hair now."

Opening his hand, Kultur watched the bright spirals fall, bouncing around her shoulders and down her back.

She said glumly, "Why was she so mad that I was close to your thigh, I mean, what on earth did she think I was doing? It was obvious I was attending to your injury." Huffing her annoyance she put her implements back in the bag Zane had brought them in.

Kultur's gaze lit on the top of her head as she closed up the bag. "Sislla," his voice was pondering slow, he waited until she looked at him with those big innocent blue eyes. "How much...experience have you had with...men?"

Her forehead wrinkled. "I suppose I know some, I mean, what do you mean?"

Feeling the heat rise up the back of his neck, Kultur palmed it. Rubbing it, sounding slightly uncomfortable he persevered, "I mean, how many men have you been with?" Somehow the question bothered him; he almost didn't want to hear her answer.

Her chin jutted forward and her brow wrinkled more, "What do you mean, go with them where?"

The heat was rolling around to the front of his neck. "Uh, I mean like in the Biblical sense." She looked even more confused, he exhaled in discomfort. "I mean how many men have you had sex with?"

He assumed she had been with men, even as young as she might be. She was too beautiful to get by without men sniffing after her. He put his hand on his stomach feeling it twinge at the thought.

As the blush took over her face, her eyes were like mortified saucers and her mouth fell open. "I- I," her mouth shut and she turned her face from his scrutiny. "I don't know."

Then she turned back and said furiously, "I don't know my own name, how in all the heavens would I know if I've had...lovers?" Her hands snapped on her hips, her embarrassment turned to anger, she scowled at him. "Why are you asking, anyway? It is certainly none of your business."

She was right. It was none of his business. "I just wondered because you didn't seem to understand my mother's," he dragged his fingers down over his face, "never mind. You are exhausted. Let's go." He went to slide off the table when she held a hand up to stop him.

"Wait," she spun around quickly turning her back to him.

Pulling his pants up he chuckled, he still had a hard-on and it was a chore to button his pants but she amused him. "I forgot what a shy little doctor you are, *koritsi*." By the time he had his belt buckled and his boots on, she was sitting in a chair with her head in her arms on a table. He trod over to her. "You ready?"

Sluggish with weariness, Sislla pushed from the table and stood up. Tucking her hair back behind her ears, she rubbed her eyes and started walking to the stairs. He matched his stride with her shorter steps, but each step she took was slower and slower.

"It seems this…healing thing takes a lot out of you, Sislla." Feeling uncommon sympathy, he slid his palm under her elbow to help her walk more easily.

She put a weary hand to her head not realizing she leaned heavily on the support of his strong hand. "I guess. It's strange, really, it kind of feels like there's a piece of me, my energy or something leaves and enters the- the- injury. I can't believe I can hardly walk," she stumbled but he caught her up holding her steady.

When they reached the stairs she stopped. Like when she was in the dungeon, she gazed at the steps, tried to lift a tired leg, her lids drooped almost covering her eyes, she was so spent she could hardly move. Kultur slid his hands under her and swept her up in his arms.

The protest flew out of her mouth, "Oh, no, King, uh, Kultur, I can…" her voice weak, she was barely audible, "…walk…you don't have to…carry…me…" he ignored her as he strode up the stairs. Concern chased away some of her lethargy. "Please, you are badly injured, you're going to hurt yourself. Put me down."

"Believe me, *koritsi*, I have endured way worse than this. These injuries are nothing but mosquito bites. Now, rest your head on my shoulder and hold still."

Doing as he instructed, Sislla commented, "You know, you never say please. You just order. Even with your mother and sister." She yawned and snuggled against him.

He looked down at her cuddled against his chest, smiled until he felt an odd pang. "If I said, 'Oh would you please' or 'would you mind terribly if you please' or 'if you would be so kind to,'" her giggle interrupted him. He smiled, "Or if I said, 'thank you ever so much.'" She giggled more.

He said with a chuckle, "Half my troops would be massacred before I got past the please. I hate to think what would happen if I 'begged their pardon whilst I stab them?' "

"Okay, okay," she giggled harder, "I get it. You don't have the time to be polite and it's become a habit even when you are not battling." The giggles kept erupting. "I can't imagine you with your pinky out and simpering, 'If you don't mind, please pass the cream,' " she pressed her face against his shoulder to stop laughing at the picture she'd made.

He smiled down at her. Her one arm wrapped around his shoulder to cling to his neck, the other clutched a handful of his shirt while she giggled into his shoulder.

They reached her room. Her guard was suddenly behind them. He had made his presence scarce downstairs but he had never let her out of his sight per the Atraam's orders. He opened the door for them to pass through and closed it after Kultur brought her in.

Kultur carried her to the bed and set her down so she was sitting leaned back against the pillows and headboard. The mattress sank as he sat down beside her.

Less than a foot from her face, he leaned to set his palm on the other side of her hip so he was facing her, fencing her in with his arm. He reached his hand out and tucked a wayward curl back off her shoulder. She smiled, her eyes closed in weariness.

Hoping to make her laugh again, Kultur said, "Your face, *koritsi*, gets all pink and shiny when you giggle." Her smile broadened but her eyes stayed closed.

"Ah, *koritsi*, you need to sleep. But you must bathe that blood off of you and get out of those clothes. Shall I undress and bathe you?" he said it teasing but his pants tightened with hopefulness.

Rubbing an eye, her lips curved up lazily. "Hmm, that would be nice. I wouldn't have to move then," her head drifted to the side as she spoke.

Kultur's shaft jumped, he resisted the urge to put his hand on it and press it down. He shouldn't be playing like this with her. Still, he drew a finger down the side of her cheek and brushed her hair off her face.

"*Koritsi*," he sighed reluctantly as she snuggled against his hand already half asleep. It was not a good idea for him to undress her. He knew he would not stop once he had her naked. Sighing again, he muttered, "I will find Onani to assist you."

Standing up, he watched her for a moment.

Long lashes splayed on cheeks that were still pink from her giggling. Soft lips tranquil, her chest rose and sank with shallow breaths as she fell into sleep.

His eyes slid down to her bosom. It strained against the blouse with every inhale, his shaft grew harder and damned uncomfortable.

Damn, he turned quickly and left her room to get Onani.

Chapter Eleven

Before dawn the next day Kultur was leading his League in a sparring practice. Most of the men wore only breeches and boots. A few hundred shiny backs of all shapes and sizes glinted in the twilight while grunts and curses strew across the meadow.

All of a sudden, one-by-one the men stopped fighting. His back to the castle, letting out a blue cloud of curses, Kultur asked his men what the fuck was their problem?

"What the hell? Get back to work, men!" He commanded.

They were all staring at something. He turned around to see what it was. His mouth dropped.

Sislla and Lexi were sauntering across the field carrying baskets.

Repeating in a gruff bark, "*What the hell-*" as he started for the field Kultur caught sight of his brother, Gabriel grinning like a loon at Sislla.

"Hot damn, K, the stories are right. Babe is a looker." His hair a lot lighter and longer than Kultur's, his eyes light brown contained a hint of lurking mischief, he set his hands on his hips.

Pushing his hair back off his forehead, Gabriel's eyes followed Sislla like an eagle stalking a field mouse. "Shit, K, check out those fine tits they are bounce-"

Kultur punched him in the arm and snapped, "Shut the fuck up, Gabriel, and get these men back to work."

Gabriel didn't move or take his eyes off Sislla. "Come on, brother, I didn't know she was so hot, I need to make some time with that-"

Kultur punched him again, hard.

"Hey," Gabriel scowled rubbing his arm, "that hurt."

"It will hurt worse if you don't get these men moving." Kultur barked, "*Now*."

"Geez, K, all right, don't get your breeches in a twist." Gabriel moved to take over the practice, like the others he was dressed in leather breeches and boots, sweat dripped down his bare back.

He marched through the group shouting, cursing, and threatening all the men that if they didn't stop gawking and get back to sparring he would remove their balls with a garden trowel.

Kultur strode through the tall grass, his heavy boots mashing down a trail. The madder he got the faster he moved, the closer he got to the women the madder he got. Several yards from them he called, "Lexi!"

The girls stopped and spun around. Lexi grinned, "Kultur! Aren't you busy with the men?"

As he got closer, Lexi's grin withered at the fury darkening her brother's face. He was glaring at Sislla, his gaze traveled up and down her tight pants and cropped shirt that hugged her perfectly round breasts so-

"Kultur," Lexi started but he cut her off.

"What the fuck is going on here, Lexi? What trouble are you getting Sislla into?"

Astounded that Kultur would speak so roughly to his little sister, Sislla moved between the siblings. Keeping her eyes averted from his powerful bare chest, she said quickly, "It wasn't her, King, um, sir, it was me. We came out to-"

He cut her off too, his eyes narrowed in insult at Sislla, he demanded, "And what the fuck are you wearing?"

Sislla's skin flushed at his nasty tone, she tipped her chin up and sniffed. "We are out to collect herbs."

His mouth dropped. "Huh? For what?" His eyes flicked to Lexi who was smirking at him. She stopped when his pupils hardened and glittered with unquestionable threat, her own eyes lowered. His glare swung back to Sislla.

Sislla answered him calmly, "For the ill."

Towering over her, when she didn't cower from his obvious wrath. His brows slashed down like black arrows, his huge hands clenched into fists, he moved a step closer to her. Danger was in the set of his mouth, a deadly stillness in his bearing, through a throaty growl, he said, "What?"

Lexi tugged on Sislla's shirt to pull her back out of Kultur's reach and interjected, "There are sick people lined up outside the castle asking for Sis to heal them."

His formidable stance didn't change but his eyes drew down to Sislla's chest. She was starting to breathe a little harder in growing pique, her chest drew in and out rising higher making her breasts press against the thin material of the shirt.

Jerking his gaze from her, he switched his angry, confused eyes to his sister. "Who the fuck is Sis?"

"Honestly, King Kultur," Sislla said quietly, "you shouldn't swear at your sister, it's not-"

His glare was so frigid with fury Sislla's mouth snapped shut.

The growl deepened, "For the last time, it is just Kultur. No Atraam, no Mister, no *fucking King*."

"Sis is Sislla for short, get it?" Lexi cooed still tugging Sislla away from her brother's inexplicable wrath. "Gee, Kultur, what is the matter with you? What is wrong with us collecting a few stinking flowers for crying out loud? She's kinda right about the cursing, you know really you shouldn't-"

"*Lexi*," the ferocious warning came from deep inside him. He shook his head then scrubbed his fingers through his dark hair trying to calm himself. He stopped until he felt he could talk more peacefully.

His sister was right. It was not like him to lose his control like this, and he could see the shock on his Lexi's face at his lack of keeping a cool head.

He cleared his throat. His voice hoarse from the effort it took to keep it low, he rasped, "I do not want *her*," he jerked his head at Sislla, "outside the castle walls."

"Why not?" Both Lexi and Sislla asked at the same time.

Kultur put his hands on his hips and gripped them to keep from lashing out. "I don't need to tell either of you my reasons for anything I do or say. But," he spoke over his sister's protesting words, "there was a raid just last night and neither of you females should be out here. Lexi, you damned well know better."

"Oh come on, Kultur," Lexi complained, "it's obvious the raiders are gone since your troops are out here practicing, you..." She looked past him to search the group of men looking for a tall, lean, light brown haired young man, her voice trailed off when she spied him.

"Lexi," Kultur hissed seeing her fascinated gaze land on Van.

Sighing her irritation, his sister turned her attention back to Kultur. "You don't need to worry that Sislla will kill me or run off," she gave her brother a crafty wink.

"That's not fuck- uh, not funny, Lex." He faced Sislla and pointed a finger like an iron peg at her, his eyes so slatted only a gleam of black showed. "You were clearly told you were not to leave the castle without my permission or the guard with you." He made a mocking pretense of looking at the castle and then around for the guard who obviously was not with them.

Her face blushing in guilt, Lexi mumbled quietly, "We ditched him."

Crossing his arms over his chest, rocky biceps bulging, Kultur kept his head raised up but lowered his eyes to look down at Sislla. "I see that yet another guard must forfeit his life on your behalf." He shook his head sadly, "It's too bad he has to lose his head, he has three small cousins to feed and-"

Sislla grabbed his arm with both hands and cried, "Oh, God, no, please, King- Kultur, please don't hurt him!"

Beside her, Lexi's face was stricken to ash. She knew he would do it in a heartbeat. "Kultur, it wasn't his fault, we tricked him."

His eyes were on Sislla's small hands gripping his arm so fiercely they were white. He shook his head, "Nonetheless, he is a seasoned Kirman, he should not have been tricked by two," his gaze swept the young women with a sneer, "tiny weak females." He bit back a bare smile at the suddenly angry look that crossed Sislla's face at his insult. But her fear for the man's life was stronger.

She begged in a small quivering but sure voice, "Please, please, take me, not him. I will take his place."

"Sislla!" Lexi cried aghast at her friend's selfless offer. "He will do it, my brother will have you at the very least flogged, or- or you could lose your head!" She slid her terrified gaze carefully to her brother.

He didn't look as angry as he had; his skin had lightened from the enraged darkness that had flared when he'd first approached them. He hadn't pushed Sislla away or struck her as he normally would when someone had the audacity to touch the Atraam like that. He was just calmly observing her through his lowered lids.

When Sislla went to drop to her knees in front of him, a perturbed expression briefly crossed his face. He grasped her arm before she reached her knees and kept her standing.

The straight black brows ticked up, the hard mouth tightened, his eyes fell to look at his big fingers wrapped in irritation around her thin arm. He released her immediately knowing her fair delicate skin would bruise quickly under his hard grip.

Both women held their breaths watching him with fearful unease. Smoothing his face of all emotion, Kultur said without nuance, "I will think about it." Zero emotion now in his cold gaze he ordered, "For now, you will both return to the castle and go straight to your rooms and stay there until I decide what I will do."

Sislla's feet shifted, she clasped her hands in front of her. "Uh…"

Trying to contain his aggravation, Kultur said shortly, "What now?"

Seeing her brother's wrath had cooled and he wasn't going to hurt Sislla, drawing his attention away from Sislla, Lexi shook her head and said smoothly, "You forget there are a lot of sick people lined up outside the castle waiting for Sis to heal them. We have to get the herbs or you," she jabbed a finger in her brother's chest, "can go tell each and every one of them, including those holding sick babies, that they need to go away." She crossed her arms and tapped her foot in the grass.

Gritting his teeth to keep his mouth from dropping open, realizing he was trapped, Kultur snarled, "Goddammit Lexi," if he sent the villagers away he would look callous and uncaring. Which he was, wasn't he? It's not like it ever bothered him before.

He shook his head and dragged his fingers through his hair like he was digging furrows in a field. Scrubbing his fingers down his face he said, "Very Well. I see your poor guard scurrying in a panic towards us. You collect the items you need, with your guard quickly, then get back to the castle and to your chambers. If you need more you will send a man to gather them."

"Oh, Kultur." Lexi grinned.

His eyes rolled. "What the fuck now, Lexi?"

"Sislla will need to see to the people, she can't do that in her room."

"For the love of-" he swiped a hand across his face exhaling his aggravation that he had to keep making concessions. This was not how he ran his realm. He ordered, they obeyed, simple. The foreign woman had only been there a couple of days and she was already complicating things.

His hands planted on his hips he said crossly, "Do what you have to do. Just do not leave the castle." Sarcastically he arched a sarcastic brow at Lexi and asked, "Anything else baby sister?"

She gave him a glowing grin, stepped to him on tiptoe and kissed his cheek. Grinning at his embarrassed expression, she wiped the painted lip smear off his cheek. "No, dear brother. Thank you."

Scowling, he grumbled, "Yeah." Then turning to Sislla gesturing to her with a dirty look he ordered, "You will change your clothes as soon as you get back to the castle and you will never wear shit like that again," he pivoted and strode back to his men.

"Wow," Lexi snickered, "you can practically see the steam coming out of his ears. He never said that to me when I wore those clothes." She eyed her friend with a smile. "Of course, I didn't fill them out like you do. And since I wore them when I was much younger they are pretty tight on you." She mused, "Since when did he ever care what anyone wore?"

Watching Kultur stride angrily through the field, Sislla asked, "Why is he so mad? What's wrong with helping sick people get better? He was fine with it last night."

"Hmmm." The edges of Lexi's wide mouth turned up in a cagey smile. "'Tis not the sick people, Sis, it's you."

"Me?" Sislla sputtered in horror. "I- I don't think I've done anything wrong....have I?"

Lexi grinned at her and motioned to her body. "You have no idea what you look like, girl, you are scorching hot with that body in my tight clothes. I think he didn't like it that you paraded past his men dressed like that and took their attention away from their practice.

Sislla's brow wrinkled as she tried to make sense of her friend's words. "But all he had to do was tell them to pay attention to their work. Why would he get so upset for a few seconds of curiosity?"

"Hmmm. I think my brother was feeling territorial...ah...possessive."

"I don't understand. Is it because I intruded into his castle? When that man brought me inside he was so deadly enraged."

An inelegant snort burst from Lexi. "You have no idea what you look like, honey. You are in his castle. Even as apparently a prisoner, he considers you his possession. I'd say looking the way you do and with your sweet disposition, I'm thinking he is feeling proprietorial jealousy."

Flummoxed with the conversation, Sislla started walking, the faster they got the herbs the faster she could get back to the castle and get busy. "People are not possessions. You make no sense at all. Come on, let's go."

Chapter Twelve

After hours of working, his mind not into the practice, Kultur released his men. As much as he fought it, his curiosity got the better of him.

Shrugging his shirt on but not bothering to button it, he strode through the front door to go to his chambers to shower, and stopped like he'd hit a brick wall. The room was teeming with people. *"What in the sons' name-"*

His head and shoulders above most of them, like the parting of the Red Sea, the crowd moved instantly for him to pass. He made his way through the throng to where it appeared the majority was waiting.

When he pushed past the last few, he stopped in his tracks. Sislla was leaning over a table. A child was sitting on the edge nervously swinging his little legs. Beside the boy, Kultur saw piles of leaves, a bucket of what looked like soil, alcohol, towels and infirmary implements.

He made his way around the table to the side, standing almost in the shadows to quietly observe. The people closest to the table facing away from him didn't notice him so they continued talking and circulating.

Smiling gently, Sislla was softly running her palms over the child's body. Asking him questions, she spoke tenderly to him as if to inspire his confidence. After her examination, she picked up a few leaves and told the boy to open his mouth. After a quick glance at probably his mother, after her nod, he did and Sislla slipped the leaves inside.

"Okay, Rand, honey, now don't chew them. The leaves will melt away on your tongue, and by tomorrow morning your tummy ache will be gone. Okay?"

His hand on his belly, the boy nodded warily. His mother stepped forward to help him jump off the table. She said to Sislla, "Thank you, Miss Sislla. I saw that Jon and Glenna and the others all left here looking and feeling so much better I knew you could help my son. Bless you. Here," she pulled some pieces of jewelry out of the pocket in her skirt and handed them to Sislla.

Shaking her head with a smile, Sislla closed the woman's hands over her jewels and said, "There is no cost to healing. Just watch him closely. If the yellow spots return, bring him back immediately."

The woman thanked her gratefully, took her child's hand and made a path through the crowd to leave the castle.

Kultur watched as a man stepped in front of Sislla. He was a big man and he glared down at her in an overbearing manner announcing in a rude loud voice, "I'm next."

Sislla wiped at dark shadows under her eyes and pushing aside her obvious exhaustion, she smiled at the man. "Of course, sir. What is your name?"

"Give us a minute," Kultur's deep voice broke through the chatter in the room. He moved around the table to Sislla.

Her surprise at seeing him there resounded with the rest of the people that just noticed him. They all instantly hushed; most of the men bowed their heads. Their respect and fear of Kultur set a chilling silent atmosphere like a sudden snowfall.

After mumbling a few words to the guard, Kultur commanded Sislla, "Come with me," he turned but stopped when Sislla didn't move. He frowned at her. "I will speak with you, come with me."

"Sir," her breathy voice softly firm, "no, I need to help these people."

He wound his fingers around her wrist. "Now." Ignoring the gasps in the crowd, he pulled her through them out of the room and to a chamber he used as his office. Unlocking the door, he brought her inside and shut the door.

When he released her, she stepped away from him and twined her fingers tightly together, her lips pressed, she looked guardedly up through long lashes at him.

Seeing her anxious fear of him, Kultur relaxed the perturbed lines around his mouth. Pointing to a dark brown leather couch he ordered quietly, "Sit down."

She hesitated. He stood immobile, black eyes inscrutable.

Unease in the tautness of her shoulders, she went to the couch and gracefully sat down. Her hands folded together in her lap, clearly holding her breath, she waited. Keeping her watchful eyes on him she only saw the room peripherally.

It was large, masculine in its dark wood furniture, bookcase, beige braided rugs scattered on the stone floor. No pretty marble in here.

There were several dark wood-framed windows that he could see out from sitting at the big desk. Ledgers, papers, books, even a few tools and intricate metal pieces were on the desk. A mug still half full of coffee was set precariously on the edge like he'd absently set it down without looking.

Sislla recalled seeing the red coffee berries bright against the green of the plants in the crop fields as Trogga had dragged her to the castle.

A few feet from her, Kultur leaned a hip against his desk, crossed his arms and said lightly, "I am not mad at you, Sislla. Relax. Please." His lip quirked at the unfamiliar word, please, on his tongue.

"Then why-"

"My grand chamber is filled with villagers, most who should be working in their fields, in the mills, caring for their animals, fishing, or collecting the heat stones or repairing their homes. There is a myriad of chores to be done daily to keep the people fed and comfortable."

"Yes," she said nervously, "but you said it was all right that I heal the people." Her brow arched confused. "Did I misunderstand? I meant no wrong, sir."

"You will call me Kultur. Not sir." Only a tightening around his eyes betrayed his annoyance at her continued lack of obeying him regarding his name. He demanded the respect of the villagers and his soldiers, but, somehow, it irritated him when she called him King or sir or the like.

Her mouth dropped then she shut it.

"You did nothing wrong, Sislla, I gave you permission to heal. But I did not give you permission to be unsafely surrounded by hordes of people who are strangers to you while you work yourself to the bone."

"Oh, I was quite safe, um, Kultur. The guard, Ryan," she smiled, "he never took his eyes off of me. I don't think anyone here means me any harm anyway. So," she went to stand up, "may I return to-"

"Sit down."

She sat.

Cocking his dark head to the side, he regarded her through his narrowed lids. "A single guard is not sufficient protection in such a crowd. Although foreigners who infrequently find their way to us bring us new vocabulary words to add to our language as well as new clothing and home building ideas, some of our people fear and resent them. There have been...situations."

"But-"

He held a hand up. "There are rooms here that can accommodate people waiting, but not so near you, and there are shelves and drawers and cupboards you can set up for more ease. That is if you insist on continuing this...healing thing."

She nodded vigorously and agreed quickly, "Yes, the poor people have not had any medical care except for midwives. So, as long as I'm here...however long that is..."

Scratching a black sideburn, Kultur appeared vexed. "We have been so busy warring we have not had the time to study, to learn better healing practices." He looked her over, she'd put on a long looser shirt. Fortunately for her.

Kultur was still livid thinking about her strutting through the field in full view of his men, including his lusty brother the way she was dressed. She could have easily started a damned riot with men fighting over her.

He needed to have a talk with his brother about chasing after her skirts. It was unseemly. After all, she was a prisoner. His prisoner.

The shirt she put on thankfully covered the top of the tight, low-rise pants. It was very warm in the office with the sun shining hotly through the windowpanes. Before he knew it, she was unbuttoning the shirt revealing she still had the crop top on under it.

She moved to stand up. "That is all right, I can teach anyone willing to learn. It will take a while, some things I seem to feel, that can't be taught, but I will do my best. Now-"

"Sit down."

"But uh, Kultur, they are waiting for me," she stood.

Staring with impassive patience, his eyes flicked to the couch behind her and back to her. She sat back down.

"The room and the people do not concern me, *koritsi*," he moved so quickly and with such stealth, he was sitting beside Sislla and she never even saw him move.

He drew a fingertip under her eye. "You are fatigued. I'm betting, although you promised, that you have not eaten anything today except maybe some foolish sweet my sister gave you for breakfast. And I'll bet again that you didn't eat all of it."

He smiled crookedly when her eyes widened in surprise that he knew that she hadn't eaten, and guilt that he surmised the truth of the 2nd half-eaten pastry hidden behind the clock on her nightstand.

Her gaze lowered to her hands folded in her lap. "I promised I would eat so I could leave the castle. I have not left the castle since this morning, so," she limply raised a palm. She just hadn't had an appetite since she'd been brought to the castle.

And now, she was so busy, so many ill people needed her that she rushed to get dressed, get the herbs and hurry to help them.

Kultur leaned back against the cushion, sitting like men do with his legs open, his knee touched hers. An odd tingling started where he felt their knees touching, it strolled up his thigh. He turned to face her. "Ah, so you build loopholes into our contracts."

"No," she shook her head, opened her mouth to deny it. Her hair was pinned up to keep it out of her way while she worked, but loose tendrils spiraled alongside her tired face and down over her chest, curving over her breasts that pushed against the tight shirt.

He set two fingers over her mouth. "Hush, do not lie to me, even unknowing. You may not be deliberately making loopholes, but that doesn't make you any less guilty of violating my orders." His fingers pressed against the softness of her lips tingled like his leg that was touching her knee. He dropped his hand.

Keeping his eyes on her face, he said, "We will now have a new contract. You want to heal the people; you will eat and have proper rest. No-" he shook his head, a lock of black hair fell over one brow, he impatiently pushed it back. "You need food to give you strength. There will be no discussion about it. You eat, you heal. You don't eat, you don't heal. That's it."

He watched the emotions flicker over her face. Anger, hunger, weariness, resignation. His fingers itched to touch her lips again. He kept his palms flat on his thighs.

She went to stand up. "All right. Fine. Starting tomorrow I will-" he grabbed her wrist and pulled her, she sat back down with a thump. He didn't release her wrist. Her eyes turned cautiously to him.

"First, *koritsi*, you never leave my presence until I give you consent to do so. Second, you are done healing for the day." He looked down at his hand holding her. Her bones were so small his fingers almost wrapped around her wrist twice. Bemused, he thought, if she was to hold his wrist she'd need two hands.

Feeling her tense, building up to argue, he rubbed her skin with his thumb.

She blinked, as if she forgot what she was going to say, and looked down at his hand around her wrist. The warmth of her skin grew hotter under his fingers. Her gaze rolled slowly up to his.

In her big clear orbs he could see the reflection of his eyes blazing black heat at her. She tugged her wrist, he let her go.

Remembering what she was going to say, growing irate, she stammered, "I am not done healing, there are dozens of people waiting, so," she put her palms on the couch.

"You're done. I told Kirman Ryan Shaws to clear them out, send them home."

"What?" She went to move to the edge of the seat to stand up, he touched her arm, she sat still. Her voice rising in her objection, she declared, "But I still have so much to do!"

The angles of his face turned hard. "I said you are done for the day. You argue with me and you will be done for tomorrow too, and the next day." He leaned forward resting his arms on his legs.

"Now, I will see you to your room. Onani will bring you food, which," his voice firmed, "you will eat. I understand your nerves from being here upset your stomach, nonetheless, you will eat dinner this evening. I will be there to ensure you do. If you want to see to the people tomorrow, then you will be enjoying a hearty breakfast in the morning." He sounded almost cheerful.

He bit back a smile at the tortured look on her face. But she said nothing. What could she say? She was under his will.

Rising to his feet, he held a hand down to her. "Ready?"

Her furious eyes glared from his hand to his face. They narrowed at the perceived stifled smile at her expense. He was standing directly in front of her. She knew she wasn't leaving the room unless he let her, and did it his way. Huffing her displeasure, she put her hand in his.

A corner of his mouth tugged up as he pulled her gracefully to her feet. Slipping his hand under her elbow, he led her to the door and walked her out. After locking his office, he slid his hand under the unbuttoned long shirt and around to her lower back as they headed down the hall.

Below her cropped shirt, his fingers were flush against her bare skin. He felt her shudder under his touch, and his pants tightened. Kultur was dismayed. He'd never had such immediate arousal to a woman before. It has happened so many times now he knew it wasn't just a fluke.

Yes, he has many dalliances when he chooses, but he is very particular with his choices. Still, the second his eyes light on her he feels an instant spiking frisson rush up his body heating it with prickles and white hot tingles.

True to his word, the grand chamber was totally empty. Including the table where she'd left her supplies. Before she could question, he whisked her to the stairs, propelling her up them.

At her room, the guard, Ryan Shaws, his eyes straight ahead unblinking, opened her door. His neck flushed. Kultur didn't have to look at him for him to know he was in deep trouble for letting the girls give him the slip earlier.

Kultur drew Sislla inside and shut the door. His hand still on her back, feeling her heat against his splayed fingers, he didn't remove his hand, only slid it around to her side as she faced him. She tried to move back but he increased the pressure of his hand.

Her lashes lowered, she said, "So…you said you would spare Ryan…"

Not knowing why he did it, Kultur set his other hand on her bare waist. Seeing her trying to hide a yawn behind her concern for the guard, a deep breath pulsed before he spoke, "As I said, Onani will bring you food. You will eat, then rest," he lifted his hand to brush under her eyes, then he stepped away from her.

"But, Ryan-"

"I will see you at dinner." He clipped his heels and left the room leaving Sislla staring at the closed door.

Chapter Thirteen

Two days later, Sislla rose early. She picked up the list of herbs and their description she'd made and added another one that popped into her mind.

Showered and dressed, she hurried downstairs with Ryan the guard, who thankfully still had his head and apparently was not suffering from a whipping, at her heels. When she veered down a hall towards her workshop instead of the dining area, Ryan coughed loudly behind her.

"Miss," he croaked, "you know the master says you are not to go to the workshop before eating breakfast."

Her feet churned a little faster with her chagrin, "Oh, Ryan, you know the people will be lined up, I can't make them wait." She kept heading for the workshop.

"Please, Miss," Ryan said, right behind her, "you know it will be my head if I let you go and he finds out."

Her stride slowed, her head tilted back in frustration, she glared at the ceiling. "Ugh. It's hard to eat this early in the morning. Fine, but you are not to make any comment about what or how much I eat. If he asks you, just, tell him I ate." Hearing his distinct sigh of relief, she rolled her eyes and changed direction.

Speaking of eating reminded her of last night at dinner she sat in total silence trying to choke down enough food to satisfy old Eagle Eye Kultur.

How was she to eat when all the horrible people gawked at her and gossiped about her behind their hands? Not one of them was civil to her, even when Kultur threatened them, which only made it worse.

Her pushing around food on her plate did not fool him. At one point he had laid his big hand over hers covering it entirely and said quietly in her ear, "You promised to eat." He had claimed that having her wander around his castle emaciated made him look bad as a torturer of women.

She whispered, "It's okay, I'm not leaving the castle."

His fingers squeezed hers; he whispered back, "The new agreement was that if you eat, you heal. No eating, no healing."

She had peered up at him through her lashes. She could have sworn there was a smile in there lurking with his stern admonition. The black eyes actually seemed to not pierce her as coldly as usual.

His mother glowered so fiercely at their hands that Sislla feared she would lunge over the table at her. She tugged her hand free, picked up a fork and forced some mashed potatoes down.

After that, Darathia glared cold hostility at her all the rest of the dinner, and Kultur stayed engaged in deep discussion with his brother Lucas over the recent raids.

No one else spoke to her, just shot some curious, some fearful, some hostile, some lustful, glances at her. She missed Lexi who had corralled her Van and was having a private evening with him.

Last night thankfully, Kultur and half the men had gone out on reconnaissance and Sislla was allowed to eat in her room.

But that was last night, today was a new day.

"I'm curious," Sislla said to her guard, he tilted his head indicating he was listening. "There is a mix of, oh, I don't know, tones, accents, ancient words, and modern words, curses, and my brain tells me slang, although I don't recall how I would even know about those things. Anyway, there's this mixture in the people. How is that?"

His hands behind his back, Ryan bumped his shoulders. Nodding his head, he had dark hair with a deep overtone of red in it, he replied, "Over hundreds of years people do wash up once in a while on our shores. One time an entire ship wrecked on the island. The Atraam allowed the men to stay, but they had these...weapons.

"Metal tubes that discharged solid iron pellets that could go a good distance and were almost always lethal. The Atraam made our people take them out to deep sea and dump them. They brought all sorts of new words such as okay, and yea, I mean yeah, things like that. And new kinds of clothing too."

"Oh. It's just strange, jarring sometimes hearing the olde world with the new as I seem to know them."

They reached the smaller kitchen. Sislla grabbed an apple and gobbled it, with Ryan on her heels, shaking his head in disapproval at her breakfast choice as she hurried to her workshop.

There was a long line of people waiting. She rushed inside the room Kultur had assigned to her.

It was big and roomy with varnished cupboards, drawers, marble flooring, an examination bed on wheels and plenty of counters and jars to keep her supplies.

The first patient was already inside sitting on the bed.

Sislla gave her a big warm smile. "Hi, I'm Sislla, who are you?"

The woman's tiny, marbled virulent eyes bobbed up and down Sislla's length with seething disapproval. She turned her long skinny nose up and said, "I just wanted to see the peasant witch everyone is talking about. I wouldn't let you touch me with ten-inch thick gloves, you hussy. The Altra, Darathia is beside herself with mortification that you are in her home, at her dinner table."

The woman dressed in finery such as Darathia would wear. Her brunette hair slivered with grey was swept up in a fashionable chignon, her longish nose was even in length with her pointed chin that shook with hostility, beady eyes sneered at Sislla.

She suddenly leaped off the bed to stand in front of Sislla and with harsh rancor pushed Sislla's shoulder, As Sislla stumbled backwards the woman shoved her again harder. Sislla's elbow and head banged against the wall.

Moving towards Sislla, the noxious woman raising a hand to her as if to strike her said with scathing gall, "You, Miss, you are abominable, you need to clear out of here. You are a danger to Darathia's entire family. The Iminims will be here in a few months and they will detect you and come for you and kill family members in nearness to you!" She swung her fist at Sislla.

"Madam!" Ryan threw his arm around the woman's neck and dragged her away from Sislla. When he got her clear, he twisted her arm behind her back and used it as a lever to usher her to the door. He jerked the door open and stepped outside with her to take her out of the castle.

Rubbing the back of her head, Sislla stood stunned at the viciousness attack and vile hate the woman had directed at her. A knock at the back door took her attention from the horrible assault.

She opened the door. A woman in a cloak with her face covered beckoned Sislla to come outside. Without thinking, Sislla stepped right out.

"Are you ill? Do you need help?"

The woman waved her closer. Sislla could see the woman was young and in terrible fright. "My-" she tried to talk, her voice broke.

Sislla set her hand on her shoulder and said gently, "It's all right, take a breath, tell me what you need."

The woman heaved in a deep shuddering breath. The cloak half covered her eyes that darted all around nonstop.

"Can I trust you?" the woman asked with a quiver in her voice and in her hands.

Sislla moved closer assuring her, "Of course you can." She waited while the woman made sure no one saw them talking.

"My- my child is ill. I'm so afraid."

"Where is he? Bring him inside right away I will do what I can." Sislla looked all around but didn't see anyone else in the area. "What is your name Miss?"

"I'm Noni, please, you don't understand," the woman whispered, "Dond is not Chamaine-Gris, we are Tenthekens." She moved back from Sislla preparing to flee.

"I don't care if he's from the moon, bring him. I will help him. I have to go back inside now or the guard will sound an alarm. Just knock on this door when you return with the child and I will come right-"

"No." The woman shook her head adamantly, her eyes filled with tears, "I've hidden him down by the east river. It is an hour's walk from here. I can't bring him. If we're caught," her eyes traveled urgently all around the keep, "we could be killed by the king or imprisoned. Please, you must come to us. Please."

Sislla considered what the woman was saying. She seemed to be truly worried for her child and scared of Kultur and his men.

"Give me directions, the League will be out again tonight doing reconnaissance. I will tell them I am eating in my room and will slip out and meet you."

The woman told her how to get there and quickly hurried away.

When Sislla went back inside Ryan was standing there with a horrified look on his face.

"Miss! Where have you been? I've looked for you everywhere! I was about to sound the alarm! The Atraam would have my head if I let anything happen to you." He shook his head fretfully, first the old bag attacking her and now Sislla disappearing. He was about to have a heart attack.

"Everything is all right, Ryan, relax. I am here, bring in the next patient."

When he didn't move and stood there looking sick she asked, "What?"

"I have to tell him about the woman, her hurting you. If he finds out and I didn't tell him," he made a slashing motion across his neck.

"Really," Sislla was getting annoyed at this whole 'off with their head' thing. Kultur needs to find another way to deal with offenses. "We don't need to tell him, only you and I know."

His head swung hard back and forth. Serious eyes that had seemed so intensely stoic were now jumping all over the room. "No. The old lady knows and she could brag to friends," he shivered, "it could get back. I have to tell him."

Ryan was a tall beanpole, all arms and legs with narrow shoulders. One shoulder would twitch up then the other would then the other like he was so tied up in knots inside he couldn't be still. Ruddy freckles covered his long rectangular face.

Sislla set a hand on his arm and looked up at him with a comforting smile. "All right, calm down. I will tell him, he will see that it was nothing and you did your job."

"No." Ryan's shoulders slumped. He was probably in his mid-twenties but at the moment he looked 100. He had run his hands through his hair so many times in his frantic search for her the reddish-brown locks spiked up all around his head. The house guards wore white pants and a red jacket so they could be spotted easily. "I have to tell him."

Sislla's chest rose with her deep inhale. "I will be with you when you do. I will let him see it was not a big thing. Now, let's get back to work."

It was hours before Kultur returned. He entered the castle from a back entrance and went to the kitchen to get something to eat before heading to his chamber for a long, hot shower. They'd been in the field all day tracking the raiders to see if they could find their last hiding place. He was covered in dirt from head to toe. He felt grubby and sticky and tired.

The cook made him a sandwich on a plate, Kultur took it and grabbed a cold barley ale and headed for the stairs.

"Kultur."

His shoulders flinched at his mother's voice. He turned slowly. It took an effort to keep the annoyed impatience out of his voice. "Yes mother."

She caught up her long black skirt in both hands, her heels clacked across the marble floor. "I need to speak with you."

"Mother, it's been a long day, I need a shower and a change of clothes. I want to check on...the woman." Swigging the ale he didn't see the look on his mother's gaunt face.

She was quite tall too. Unlike most women, in heels she could almost look him in the eye. Her crisp white blouse made him feel grubbier.

"That is what I want to talk to you about. That witch."

"Desist Mother. I already know how you feel; I don't need to hear it again. I will make the decisions here and no one is to question them." He tilted his head forward slightly towards her, "No one."

"Huh." Darathia crossed her arms over her thin bosom and looked down her nose at him. "Have you given any thought to the Epita? The marking? They will be here soon and she will draw them to us. Any of us, little Bardon, could be injured or killed when they trace the unshielded woman."

Kultur had been about to take a bite of his sandwich, that stopped him in his tracks. "Actually, Mother, I have given it some thought."

"And?" her grey eyebrows arched superciliously, her arms still crossed, she cocked her head and waited. Wisps of grey hair mixed with brown strayed in escaped curlicues from her bun. On any other woman they would soften her stony face, but not on Darathia's snobbish bony features.

He took a big bite out of the sandwich and half was gone. Chewing, he pushed the bread to prod out his cheek and said, "I will let you know what I decide. Now, I need to bathe."

She moved to stand in front of him so he couldn't go up the stairs. "I think you need to give her to one of the village men quickly to mark her. It takes weeks to complete."

His brows drew down like black daggers; he shoved the rest of the sandwich in his mouth. Talking while chewing, he told her, "I said I would think about it." He started around her but she stopped him again. He looked heavenward with a sigh.

97

"Kultur," she spoke as if in a conspiracy, "I think she already has a young man."

That brought him up hard. "What? What the hell are you talking about?"

She smiled with smug glee. Now she had his attention. She leaned in close to him and said, "This morning she was seen outside of the workshop, outside of the castle, Kultur, speaking with someone in a black cloak. My source says it was a young man. They were very close to each other before the man suddenly ran off."

The contentious smile curled up her gullet seeing the dark color that rode up his neck then slowly flooded his face. "So, perhaps it should be as soon as tonight you turn her out to find her way to the village and get with her young man."

Kultur took one of her hands, pulled it forward and set his empty plate in it then pulled out her other hand, downed his ale then put the empty bottle in it, turned and made for the workshop.

Darathia stared her satisfied sneer at his retreating back. She had hoped siccing Marolie on that little witch this morning might incite the girl to do something foolish she could catch her on. Ryan had run Marolie off before anything could happen.

But even better, Darathia rubbed her arms with anticipation, Marolie saw Sislla meet out back with a cloaked figure. Sure, she'd said it was a female, but who said anything was fair in love and war? She scurried off to tell Onani to prepare to clean the room as the occupant of the rose room would be gone as soon as tonight!

Chapter Fourteen

Striving to stifle his burgeoning rage, Kultur's boots clomped in staccato across the floor then down the carpeted hall to the workshop. It was late, around eight; he was stunned to see people still lined up to see Sislla. He barged through the door and saw the blood drain from Ryan's face. Guilt. The guard knew something.

Sislla was just about to walk her patient out when Kultur burst in. Recovering from the door being suddenly thrown open and an obviously furious Kultur stalking into the room, Sislla hurried the patient out, closed the door and smoothed her shirt and then her mussed hair. "Kultur?"

Ignoring her, Kultur said sharply to Ryan, "Clear the people out. Send them home."

"Uh," Ryan's shoulders stiffened.

The Atraam's shadowy eyes closed to murderous slits, he said with haughty menace to the guard, "You dare to question me?" His huge shoulders seemed to grow broader, taking up even more space in the room.

Ryan's lanky body curved back like a parenthesis but he held his ground. His reddish hair seemed to stand on end. "No- no- sir, Atraam, but I need to tell you-"

Sislla moved to stand between them. "Kultur," she started.

Kultur stared over her head at Ryan, ignoring her. "Kirman?"

"Atraam, there was a situation today," the words fell weakly out of Ryan's mouth. Trying to stare unwavering, bravely at Kultur, his maple eyeballs shook with the effort.

"Kultur, please, let me explain." Sislla put her hand on his chest.

Ryan about died on the spot. No one touches the Atraam except family, and even then not many of them dared...

Kultur's attention went from Ryan to the dainty hand pressed against his chest. All thought fled. The warmth of her small hand spread, radiating out over his entire chest and down his stomach to his loins, the blood rushed to his head and buzzed in his ears.

The trio stood in silence for several minutes. It was hard to tell who was breathing harder, Ryan in his terror or Kultur in his anger.

But Kultur forgot what he was angry about. He couldn't think until she took her hand off his chest. "I am filthy and covered with burrs, you shouldn't touch me."

Seeing him somewhat calmed, Sislla stepped back near Ryan, still in front of the guard as if she could protect him from Kultur. Kudos to the young guard, he discreetly maneuvered Sislla to stand behind him.

The buzzing in his ears dissipated, his face a blank sheet, Kultur looked from Sislla to Ryan. His brow low and granite, Kultur lowered his head to look up at the guard through it. "You deign to protect my...prisoner, from me?"

Ryan wisely said nothing but kept his place, trying to keep between Sislla and Kultur.

Secretly, although fiercely pissed the guard would stand between him and his prisoner, or anyone under his rule for that matter, Kultur commended the young man's protective balls. "Tell me, Kirman, *please*," his mouth hooked in at the corner, "do tell me what happened today." He clasped his hands behind his back and braced his legs apart.

Ryan's forehead jumped at the Atraam saying the unfamiliar *please*, to him, albeit with sarcasm. "Uh, well sir, this woman came into the shop."

Kultur's brow twitched not hearing what he was expecting, but he remained mute, just nodded for Ryan to continue.

"So, uh," Ryan's eyes flashed to Sislla who was smiling unworried, with encouragement at him. "This woman, Mrs. Wintaspel, Marolie Wintaspel came in under the pretense of seeking healing."

"Pretense?" Kultur's brow cocked.

Ryan nodded, gulped, swallowed hard. His bony Adam's apple bobbed in his thin neck. "Yes sir. She told the maid at the front door that she was ill and needed help. But, when she came in and the Miss," he glanced at Sislla, "asked her how she could help her the woman attacked-"

His face darkened, Kultur barked, "*Attacked?*"

Sislla moved in front of Ryan again. "No, she didn't actually attack me."

Kultur put both his hands on Sislla's shoulders and moved her to the side, out of the way. "I will have the Kirman tell the story. Continue," he told the guard.

Ryan's fists clenched in fear at his side, he gulped again, "Uh, she told Miss Sislla that she was a witch, that she was going to bring the Iminims, and without her having the Epita-"

"What does that mean?" Sislla asked.

Kultur ignored her but his skin started darkening again and the lines around his eyes sharpened. "Continue, Kirman."

Clearing his throat, Ryan swallowed again, "She said the family, your family will be in danger because she," he nodded to Sislla, "does not have the shield, the marking."

"What is the marking?" Sislla asked, growing frustrated that the men spoke about her but not to her.

"Is there more?" Kultur asked coolly.

Nodding, Ryan tried to keep his face from cringing, revealing the stark terror he was feeling. The cooler Kultur was sometimes he was even more dangerous than when enraged. "She uh, well, she pushed Miss Sislla," he struggled to keep his feet cemented to the floor at the ire that flooded Kultur's face.

"She touched her? Pushed her?" Kultur's voice was eerily strident.

"Uh, yes sir. Twice. Miss Sislla fell back, um, was shoved into the wall. I think she hurt her head and elbow, and the lady raised her fist to strike Miss Sislla-"

"And you stood there doing *nothing*?" his thundering voice rocked the room; he took a step at Ryan. Although near the same age, Kultur, taller, broader, twice as muscular as Ryan, could pulverize the guard to dust in seconds.

Sislla leaped between the two men. "No, she did it so fast, but he grabbed her - like in a flash- around the neck and marched her out of the castle be- before her hand could reach me. He did what he was supposed to do, he protected me, Kultur. He doesn't deserve to be...punished."

Kultur reached out and twined his fingers around Sislla's lower arms to move her out of the way again but halted when he saw her wince. He let her go immediately. "Let me see, push up your sleeve."

Thanking the stars she declined to wear the tiny outfit Lexi pressed on her this morning, after his wrath the other day at the cropped shirt she didn't want to be the brunt of that anger again. So, instead she had on a long baggy shirt and trousers. "It's nothing, Kultur, really, it's nothing."

"Woman, if I have to ask you again..."

"All right, all right. Here," she pushed up the long sleeve. Even she was surprised how black and blue her elbow was, and it was swollen. It had been hurting but she was so busy she ignored it.

Kultur's eyes flattened to flinty creases at the sight of her swollen elbow, then he said, "Come here. Show me your head."

"Kultur," she hesitated.

"Sislla, every time I have to ask you to do something twice Ryan will receive another lash," he said it so steely cold, Sislla blanched and Ryan all but fainted.

She moved within his reach and turned her head then pointed.

"I can't tell where, *koritsi*, show me exactly."

Knowing it was going to hurt, her head had throbbed all day, she tried to touch the lump as lightly as possible, yet she still winced.

Kultur shifted a cluster of long curly locks that had escaped her bun to the side, then curled his thick, strong fingers gently over her slender shoulder to hold her steady. Putting his other hand to her head, and as softly as if he were touching a cloud, he felt the lump with the pads of his fingertips.

The room was dead silent again, except for Ryan's rapid shallow breaths.

Kultur gathered up the hair he'd moved and brought it back to where it had been, then combed his fingers through the few ringlets back over the front of her.

Ryan turned blue holding his breath. He'd never seen the Atraam touch another person, a woman, except family. Kultur smoothed Sislla's hair like he was ardently petting her.

"All right," Kultur finally said. "Now, tell me about the man at the back door." He studiously watched both their expressions.

Ryan looked confused, Sislla looked guilty. Neither said a word.

"Sislla," Kultur nodded his threat towards Ryan. The young man's narrow shoulders twitched uncontrollably, nonstop.

Pink suffused Sislla's cheeks. "It was nothing. There was a knock, I opened it, a distraught young woman in a cloak asked me to step out to talk with her."

Kultur waited, when she was not more forthcoming his eyes narrowed as they flicked from her to Ryan. Ryan's gulp could be heard it was so loud.

Quickly Sislla said, "That was it, we talked for a moment and I came back in."

She wasn't looking him in the eye; he knew she was not telling him the truth, or at least not all of it. She'd said a woman came, his mother had said it was a man. It would not be beyond Darathia to say it was a man to stir Kultur's blood.

"What did she want? Let me make myself clear, Sislla before you speak. Spit out the truth, the entire truth, don't make me drag it out of you or Ryan here will suffer. You are a terrible liar. Now, speak."

Sislla's mouth opened and closed like a fish, her face was now bright red. "She- I mean she only said her child was ill. I said bring him inside and I will help him. She was very frightened. She said he was here then, um, suddenly ran off."

It sounded much as his mother had told it. He stared at her for a silent moment. She was struggling not to squirm under his glare. He was pretty sure there was more, but other than throttling Ryan in front of her, and as he was a second cousin he was loathe to harm him. Now anyway.

Forking his fingers through his hair he sighed. "All right. Kirman, you are dismissed to get dinner after you clear the people out. I will take Sislla to her room."

Ryan only blinked once before quickly sidling out of the room.

Kultur frowned when he stepped towards Sislla and she shrank from him. It did nothing to help his ill humor. He put his hand on her upper back and moved her out of the room.

Neither said a word all the way to her chamber. He ushered her inside and without preamble said, "Sit."

Kultur could see she took offense at being spoken to like that but tough shit. She sat on the vanity chair without a word.

He said, "Tomorrow, I will assign some helpers to assist you. You are working too hard. In a week you will waste away to nothing and not have the strength to stand. You make me look like a heartless scoundrel."

He held a hand up as she started to object. "Yes, I know, you're tougher than you look. I don't want to hear a word from you right now. I mean it. As I was saying, you will have aids and you will not work more than three hours a day."

"But-"

"Not a word. You fight me on this and you will not work any hours, any days. I will stop the whole healing thing and you will stay imprisoned in this room. Don't push me. I am tired of threatening you to eat. I will not revisit that issue again. You eat or you don't heal, that's final. You will not leave this castle without my permission. At all, for anything, with anyone."

"Kultur," her voice was soft, she asked, "why do you keep me here? Why don't you send me away? Let me go off...to...wherever..."

His lips formed a hard line. "I don't have explain myself to you. Besides, I've already told you you're not leaving until I know who you are and why you are here on this island. Now," he put his thumb on one side of his forehead and his fingers on the other and rubbed his temples.

"It's late, it's been a long day, for both of us. I am in desperate need of a shower. Onani will bring you food and ice for your head and elbow."

He walked slowly to the door, turned and said, "I mean it, Sislla. You work no more than three hours a day and you do not leave the castle without my permission." He grasped the doorknob.

"Kultur," when he hesitated she asked, "if you fear who I am why do you not keep me in the dungeon?"

Not answering her, he turned the knob.

"Kultur?"

He turned back to her.

She asked, "What is the- marking thing?" Her big blue eyes, so guileless, even when she wasn't telling him the whole truth. It was more as if she feared for someone else if she told all that had occurred, not fear for herself.

His eyes rose to her hair pinned on top of her head to keep it out of the way while she worked. He looked at the few ringlets that had slipped from the pins that he had fondled a few moments ago; they floated in swirls around her shoulders.

His mouth worked as he thought about what to tell her, how much to tell her. He let go of the doorknob and moved very slowly to her so she would not cringe from him and piss him off. She didn't move but stiffened as he reached up, and plucked the pins out of her hair.

When done, he handed them to her like he had before then slid his fingers into her hair and rubbed her head avoiding her lump. Her eyelids drifted down, he could feel her relax under his touch. He combed the spirals, drawing out some of the ringlets.

Her eyes closed, she was almost purring like a kitten. It was interesting seeing her relax so thoroughly that she wavered uneasily on her feet. His fingers slipped down to cup her chin; he raised it so she would look at him.

The big eyes always so striking peered like a tired blue mist, looked trusting at him for once. Her pretty mouth, if not for her kind spirit and sweet smile, would look pouty. He felt drawn to kiss her- he let her go and stood back. Her eyes fluttered.

"Yes, the, ah, marking." Hearing the rasp in his own voice gave him pause. His hand moved to touch her again but he forced it to stay at his side. "You've been told that everyone on the island is born with a mark indicating their clan?"

She nodded. "The woman said I will draw the- Imm- somethings because I don't have one."

"Iminims."

"She said it would be, could be harmful to the people, your people. I don't understand. Kultur," she set her palm on the center of his chest. "I don't want to be a danger, the cause of anyone to get hurt. If it's true, you must send me away."

He didn't look down at her hand; he could feel it more without seeing it. Gathering his thoughts, he said, "Ah, a couple times a year the Iminims come across the water to our island. They seek to war with all of us here, with all three factions. They want to destroy, dispose of us and take over the island for its resources.

"When they come, everyone who is not a warrior hides in hidden tunnels in the mountains until we run the Iminims off. The Epita, that is what the marking is called, is a kind of...shield. It shields the person from the Iminims detecting them."

"How do they detect?" Her hand still on his chest, she was relaxed. She looked up at him with interest.

Kultur lowered his head so their eyes could meet more easily. His hands moved to set loosely on her waist. This caused her to rest her forearms on his chest. She plucked at one of his buttons acting as comfortable as if she had always been encircled in his arms.

Watching her fingers fidget with his button, Kultur struggled to center himself, to not react to her touching him. He wasn't used to this kind of contact with women, gentle, almost affectionate. His way was to use them and move away as quickly as possible.

The law of the Chamaine-Gris was that no one, except close family, was allowed to touch the Atraam without prior consent. He should strike her for her audacity. However, he was touching her as well, he could feel her heat on the calloused skin of his palms burning right through her shirt.

Clearing his throat with a tiny cough, he replied, "I don't know how they detect those without the marking. There's some kind of a vibe, or energy, vibration, we don't know. If a person does not have the marking, the Iminims can find them.

"Then if that happens it leads them to all of the people, women, children, the weak, sick, elderly hiding in the mountain. They could be, would be, killed. Even with all three factions fighting them, we don't have the manpower to fight and protect everyone at the same time."

He paused, gazing at her to see if he held her interest. Her wide eyes were trained up at him, her head tilted slightly indicating she was concentrating on his words.

Thus, he continued, "Once marked, a person can never leave the island again. Opposite to being able to only detect the unmarked on land, out on the open sea the Iminims *can* detect the *marked*. A person would be vulnerable, completely open to them as if a neon target was on their back."

She was quiet while taking this in. Then, "So," she said thoughtfully, "since I am not marked, I could lead the Iminims to the vulnerable people." Her eyes flit back and forth as she pondered this.

"Sislla," he started.

She shook her head. "Of course, I must not be with anyone who is hiding. I would have to hide alone or just, sit there and wait out in the open for them. I guess."

"They would detect you the second they stepped out of their boats onto our land. They would find you within minutes and then kill you, and not quickly, or with mercy. They are brutal, bloodthirsty sadists. They would enjoy passing you around for days before slowly taking your life."

He tried to sound matter-of-fact but he couldn't still the faint stress in his voice. He was picturing what would happen to her if they caught her.

Then realizing she would read it on his face, although her innocent mind would not be able to conjure up the full horrifying extent of the atrocious rapes and pitiless torture he was well aware of, had unfortunately seen in the past, she would read enough in his face and understand enough to grasp the dire situation.

Her cheeks were no longer pink. There was not a shred of color in her ashen face. She moved a hand off his chest to cover her mouth, her eyes watered. Kultur took her other hand and held it.

Through strained vocal cords she said, "I...you must let me go out to sea. I can't put anyone here in danger, I have to go. If I leave then the villagers in hiding will stay protected and as I am unmarked they won't be able to detect me if I'm on the water." Looking away from him, her brow furrowed, she shook her head. "Yes, that's the only way. I must leave immediately."

"No." He linked their fingers, her hand was so cold.

"But," wide with fear but pinched with distress, her petrified eyes turned up to him, "what can I do?"

"You will be marked. Once that is done, they cannot detect you and all will be well."

"But, how? I obviously wasn't born here."

He cleared the disconcerting knowledge of how to do it out of his throat. "You, ah, have to mate with a man. One of the islanders, any male can mark you. Mating will cause the Epita to rise on your skin."

"Oh?" her quailing fear went down a notch. "How can he do that? Is it easy? Painful? It doesn't matter, I will endure it to keep everyone safe."

Kultur never thought that he would ever, in his life, feel embarrassment. Especially as experienced as he was with women. But he could feel the heat roil up his neck.

He put his palm to the back of his neck and rubbed it. "Ah, mating means, sex. You would have to have sex three times over three golden moons, then the mark comes. You cannot leave the island again after that. Ever."

Her brows shot up like missiles. "What?"

His lips pulled in but he said nothing, just watched the understanding dawn over her as she comprehended what he said.

"I- I don't, what, uh…I can't stay here, Kultur, this is not my home…I don't want to mate with a man, a stranger…" she sputtered off.

"You don't need to worry about it now. We have time. For right now," he dragged a weary hand over his face, "Onani will see to your food and ice for your injuries. I need to get out of these filthy stinking clothes." He hesitated as if he was going to say more, then shook his head and strode to the door.

As he opened it she asked, "That woman, the one today, who, you know, what will happen to her? Please don't hurt her."

A heavy sigh rolled out of him, his head dropped. "I don't have the strength to argue with you about her, *koritsi*, she will be punished."

At her swift intake of breath he sighed again. "She must be. She touched, hurt, insulted a woman under my protection, she knows that comes with consequences."

He jerked the door open and stepped out closing it, but was not fast enough to shut out her plea, "*Mercy, Kultur.*"

Chapter Fifteen

While Onani was preoccupied with setting up Sislla's food and ice for her injuries, Sislla slipped to the door, opened it quietly and stuffed a wad of paper into the lock where it went into the door jam.

Then, she waited patiently while Onani fussed around. A storm had kicked up in the last thirty minutes and now the wind and rain pounded the window. The glass rattled and crackled under the assault.

When the maid was done she trod over to Sislla with a big smile on her long plain face, warmth in her plain round brown eyes. "All right then, Miss, do you need anything else? Would you like me to fetch you a nice glass of wine to go with the food or some sweet tea?"

Sislla nudged her to the door. "No, no, Onani, I'm fine, you did everything just perfectly. Now you go to bed, I don't want you coming back for the tray. No," she said at the maid's shaking head, "I won't hear of it. It's late, the tray will keep until the morning."

"Well, uh, if you're sure, Miss. Oh!" She hopped at the harsh sound of the storm bashing harder at the glass. "I don't know how any of us will be able to get a wink tonight with all that noise! Well, then, if you're sure…"

"Yes, yes, I'm sure." Sislla shooed her towards the door.

"All right then, you have a good-"

Sislla closed the door in her face. She heard the lock click but it was more muffled than usual. She hurried to grab a coat and a tiny bag of emergency supplies for the child, and waited until she was sure Onani was not coming back.

She gingerly turned the knob, it turned, it worked! Slowly opening the door, she stuck her head out looking up and down the hall. It was empty and only a few lanterns were lit so it was fairly dark.

Slipping out, Sislla carefully closed the door and tiptoed as quickly as she could down the hall then down the stairs. She hesitated every few yards to listen if anyone was coming.

Satisfied everyone was in bed, she hurried to her workroom where she knew she could slip out the back door with less of a chance of being seen.

As soon as she opened the door she was slammed by the whipping wind and driving rain. The wind snatched the door right out of her hands. It took all her strength to wrestle the door closed.

When she stepped away from the shelter of the castle the storm really beat at her. She knew it was foolhardy to go out in such a gale, but Noni said she would be waiting with her child no matter what. Sislla had to go.

Noni had told her an hour's walk, but trudging through rain and mud while being knocked around, sometimes even slammed to her knees by the storm it took longer.

She kept going and going, her clothes were soaked through the minute she'd left the castle and she hadn't eaten, again, she was in too much of a hurry to leave so her strength was waning. She prayed she would get to the woman soon.

After what seemed a brutal eternity, she saw a flash of color near some bushes.

As she reached the bushes, Noni, clutching her cloak around her head stepped out and beckoned to her.

****

After a hot shower, another sandwich and another barley ale, dressed in clean warm clothes, Kultur thought he would be drowsy and ready to go right to bed. But, something was itching inside him. He had a funny, not a pleasant funny, feeling.

Maybe it was the talk with Sislla about the mating, and the Iminims. He knew his own stomach turned at the thought of it, he could imagine how bad she felt. Maybe he should go discuss it further with her, ease her mind, tell her his plan. No, remembering the feel of her hand on his chest, her silken hair sliding through his fingers, it was best that right now he keep his distance from her.

He paced, drank another ale, but the uneasy feeling persisted. Tossing the ale bottle in the trash, he left his room and strode down the hall to Sislla's. Although he had a key, he knocked.

When he knocked, the door opened. His body went rigid, on alert. He slowly pushed the door open further and moved inside.

The room was empty. She was gone. Now his stomach really roiled. He checked the bathroom then went to the door and saw the paper stuffed in it the lock slot.

He ran to Onani's room and woke her uncaring that she was sound asleep and screamed when she saw him looming over her in the dark like a fearsome snorting bull.

"Onani, where is Sislla?"

Her face screwed up in confusion, "What? She's in bed of course. Where else would she be?" The maid dragged the sheets up to her chin cowering from her greatly disturbed master.

"When did you see her last? Tell me quickly," Kultur had to shout over the deafening storm that raged outside.

"I- I brought her food and ice as you instructed, I left ten or so minutes after. She practically pushed me out the door, she-"

Without waiting for her to finish, Kultur bolted out of her room. He contacted some of his Kirmen and sent them to search the castle.

The windows rattled all around the building, the wind whistled, the rain struck like shattering hail. Everyone returned with the same answer. Sislla was not in the castle.

"She's gone, I saw her leave," Darathia's cool, aged voice informed him.

Kultur stomped over to her. "What the hell are you talking about? When? Where-"

"Calm down, son. It's for the best. I'm sure she snuck out to meet that young man of hers from this morning. I told you she was a whore. Good riddance to bad rubbish I say- Kultur! Where are you going?"

Not responding to his mother, Kultur went to his men. "Get the horses ready, now. Meet me in the tunnel beside the castle." The men left immediately, he went to gather weapons.

Darathia yelled, "Kultur! You can't be meaning to go out into that storm? It's a death trap, come back here! She's not worth it!" her shrieks rang off empty walls.

In the tunnel, Kultur mounted his horse and gave the signal to head out. They left the shelter of the tunnel walls and were instantly, violently pummeled by the storm. There was only one easy way that a woman on foot could go, so he took to that path.

For an hour the men fought through the sleeting rain and cold vicious wind. Kultur thought, there is no way that petite young woman could withstand this storm.

After going as far as he thought she could have gotten on foot in the storm, he started thinking it would be her dead body he would be bringing back.

Then he saw movement down the path near the river. Blinded by the biting wind and rain, Kultur held his hand up for his men to wait. He continued on heading down the path towards the movement. Then he saw her through a curtain of rain.

Sislla was bending over something; the wind whipped her bright hair and coat like a whirlpool.

Kultur slid off his horse and stalked in a blinding rage over to her through the havoc of the wild storm. He bent and grabbed her coat jerking her up and around.

Over the howling storm he yelled, "You little fool, you brave this deadly storm just to be with your lover?" He shook her so hard her head snapped back and forth. Cursing furiously he swore, "I will remove his head for this!"

"No, Kultur-" Sislla pulled from him and pointed to the ground.

Kultur saw a woman in a black cloak, then he looked at something wiggling next to her. Peering through the sheets of rain, Kultur saw an infant lying under the bushes.

"What the hell are you-" Kultur crouched down to look at the child. Wrapped in a sodden blanket, the baby was not crying, his eyes were puffed and closed, his skin was a hue of blue. He was obviously very sick.

Insisting, "I have to help him," Sislla knelt back down beside Kultur. The whipping wind tossing her hair over both of them, she struggled to push it out of her face. The rain struck them as a solid wall of cascading water. She reached for the child but Kultur slid his hands under the baby and stood up with him.

Over the crescendo of the squall, he shouted to one of his men, "Get her on the horse with you, and see to the mother as well." Without another word, he strode to his stallion and mounted it still holding the child. He tucked the baby under his coat to protect him as best he could from the violent elements.

Kultur waited only until his guard lifted Sislla to sit behind him on the guard's horse, then he kicked his steed and tore through the storm.

When they reached the castle, he instructed his men to take Sislla and the mother to her workshop. He handed the child to Sislla, ordering, "Change into dry clothes first, then you may deal with the child."

As soon as they went inside, he called for Onani who was already coming.

He instructed, "Get dry clothes for both women and hot tea and blankets, warm the blankets up with the stones." He sent his men to their beds then went to his own chambers to change his wet clothes before returning to the workshop.

When he reached the workshop he observed Sislla standing in her still soaked clothes, working on the child who was dry and wrapped in a heated blanket. Beside her, the mother in dry clothes with a warmed blanket wrapped around her stood watching.

His fists clenched, Kultur wanted to march over and rip those wet clothes off Sislla before she got ill, and wrap her in one of the heated blankets. But he knew she'd fight him and it would only waste time. He had to stuff his anger and impatience until she was finally done.

He nodded to Onani and two other maids. They came forward. "Take the woman and child and put them in a bedchamber, bring them food." Kultur grabbed Sislla's arm roughly and hauled her from the room.

"Kultur wait," she protested.

Gripping her arm while he dragged her along he snarled, "Shut up. Not a word." He hauled her up the stairs, tripping on the steps she would have tumbled back down several times if he hadn't held her so tightly.

When they reached her room he shoved her inside.

She stumbled but caught her balance. She couldn't meet his eyes, she had known what would happen if she didn't get back before anyone realized she'd gone.

He threw the wad of paper she'd stuffed in the lock at her feet.

His face was so hard and sharp, dark with fury, so angry his shoulders shook.

She wrapped her arms around herself and stood shivering, her wet hair plastered to her face, not daring to say a word.

His voice harsh and unyielding he commanded, "Get out of those wet clothes, now. Right now."

Her eyes widened at him. She glanced at the bathing room.

"No." He shook his head, his damp hair shifting. "In front of me. You had your chance for privacy downstairs when I told you to change. So, you will change right now, right here yourself or I will do it for you."

Still she didn't move, he took a step towards her, she grabbed up the dry clothes, a pair of soft pants and matching soft shirt and a blanket.

He clasped his hands behind his back, legs akimbo; he gave her the decency of bowing his head and staring at the floor while she changed.

When she was dressed, he raised his eyes to her. He could only imagine how frightening he looked to her, aware of the rage he was radiating; he would be scared of him too.

The emotion cleared out of his voice leaving it frigid and so empty it made her body that was still shivering quake harder. He barked at her roughly, "Get in the fucking bed."

Knowing she'd worked his last nerve, without a word she hurried to the bed and climbed in. He turned and stalked out the door, slamming it. For the second time in his life.

Outside the room, Onani waited nervously holding a tray with a cup and a plate. When he came out, seeing the look on his face, she wondered if the Miss was still alive.

"Dry her hair, then give her the tea and sandwich. And by the sons above, Onani, you sit there and watch her eat every single bite. You tell her if she does not, that *you* will be flogged within an inch of your life. You hear me?"

She nodded, her head bouncing up and down like a ball. "Yes, Atraam."

Kultur turned as Ryan joined them. "Onani, you will stay in her room all night with her." He said to Ryan, "Kirman, you stay outside, on the door. I mean on the fucking door. She leaves this building again and you both will pay with your lives. Do I make myself clear?"

The pair nodded too frightened to answer him.

He stalked off down the hall to his own chambers. On the way he considered bringing Sislla to his room. He'd make damned sure she didn't sneak out of the fucking castle again, if he had to tie her to his bed. Great. *There's a thought to try to sleep on, Sislla tied to his bed.*

Sighing, he shucked his clothes, pulled the sheets back and slid in, dragging the sheet and comforter over him. The sheets were cool on his skin. If he shared his bed he'd feel warmer. But he's never before had a woman in his chambers. He pictured Sislla lying on his bed with her hands tied over her head, *Yeah, don't go there*. No doubt they'd both be warm.

He reached over to the lantern beside his bed and turned the knob killing the light.

Chapter Sixteen

Before the sun broke through the morning clouds, Kultur rose, dressed and went to his office. He had statistics to record in his ledgers.

There was a quiet knock at the door, then it opened. A guard came in with a mug of hot fresh coffee and a plate of eggs, a hunk of ham, bread, and skillet potatoes. He set them on the corner of the desk.

Kultur muttered, "Thanks, Edgar." Without looking up, he picked up the coffee and although it was steaming, drank a good quarter of it. His attention on the ledgers, he didn't notice the guard leave as quietly as he came.

After an hour, he tossed his pen on top of the open book of numbers and rubbed his eyes. Damn he hated the paperwork part of maintaining a village. He pushed the book away and the empty plate of eggs. Edgar had come in three more times with a fresh cup of coffee.

Having enough of numbers, he shoved his chair back. It was time to get ready to join his men. Some will be doing reconnaissance, some sparring practice, some policing the village, still others had different tasks. He had one of the older League Kirmen working up the schedules, but he wanted to be present as it was reviewed.

A double-rap sounded then the door opened. It was his older brother Lucas.

Lucas greeted, "Brother." Seeing Kultur still at his desk he wandered in and plopped himself down on one of the chairs near the desk. "You on your way out to the field?"

Kultur gave a rare and brief smile at the close mirror image of himself and his younger brother, Gabriel. Like Gabriel, Lucas' hair and eyes were on the light side, they were both an inch shorter than Kultur, as powerfully built, but Kultur was bulkier by 25 pounds of sheer muscle.

Most of Kultur's bulk was in his upper torso, there wasn't an ounce of fat on him. His hips were so lean his trousers tended to hang low on them, whereas Lucas' bulk was distributed around his body, his back and legs were beefier than his brother's.

Lucas' head was a shade squarer and his face was thicker than Kultur's, and a touch softer than the unrelenting rock harshness of Kultur's icy mien.

Kultur replied, "Yes. Jon is probably already heading out there to organize the schedules and tasks. What about you?"

Lucas tapped his fingertips on the chair arms. "After I go back upstairs and get Bardon his breakfast I'll head out. Mama is feeling a tad under the weather." He settled his back against the chair cushion and crossed an ankle over a knee.

Lucas glanced out the window, the first ray of morning sun streamed through the window lighting the side of his face. "I hope the sun dries up all that mud from last night's storm. Speaking of storm," he angled his head and smirked at his brother. "I hear that hot little foreigner of yours is giving you a rough time of it."

"Hmmm." Kultur sat back in his roomy leather chair, the cushions made of stuffed cloths and covered with slick cowhide. He picked up the quill pen that contained mineral oil and twirled it between his fingers.

His non-response only deepened Lucas' smirk. "I hear tell from Gabe you're having a hard time controlling her. That all your threats fall on deaf ears." A lop-sided smirk on his handsome face, not hiding his mirth, he said, "She's just a slip of a girl, K, you can't strong-arm her?"

When Kultur still said nothing, Lucas kept on, "For *kriités* sake, K, you are known as the most ruthless, vicious, brutal warlord of this side of the world. I've seen you take down a man as big and ferocious as a charging tiger with one punch, strangle with one hand, crush a skull-"

"All right, Lucas, all right, I get it." Kultur threw the pen down. "The thing is, threats don't scare her. I've threatened the worst of the worst, she saw me kill Trogga with one strike and beat another senseless. I forced her to watch a flogging. For the sons above, she puked after the flogging she was so disturbed, but when I tell her I'm going to have her whipped, she stands like a terrified shaking branch but says, go ahead and do it."

"Uh huh. So why haven't you?"

One of Kultur's brows rounded over a scornful eye, he snorted, "Really, Luke? You would bind Cindra and whip the hell out of her?"

"Come on, K, she's my wife. We're talking about a foreigner, she could be a spy, a thief, an assassin."

Kultur's speculative gaze sneered at his brother. "She's a woman, Lucas. You telling me you would beat, flog, kill, even slap a woman no matter what she was?" He knitted his fingers, set them on the desk and hunched over facing his brother.

Lucas shook his head with a grin. "Nah, not me, but we're talking about you. It's been said you have no soul, little brother. That anyone who doesn't abide by the rules, our laws, they are vigorously punished or killed." He watched Kultur's face darken, his mouth stiffened, the black eyes glinted inscrutable as usual.

Kultur sat back again, shrugged his big shoulders. A faint smug smile brought out the dimple in his left cheek. "Doesn't matter. I figured out how to control her without laying a finger on her."

Lucas' light brows arched with interest. "Oh yeah? Do tell."

A half smile tugged at the corner of Kultur's mouth. "I can threaten to whip her all day long, but if she thinks someone else is going to be punished because of her she goes all monkey-shit. Practically throws herself at my feet begging me to take the penalty out on her hide instead of theirs." He almost chuckled as he recalled the other day. "Kirman Shaws, you know, lanky Ryan Shaws with the reddish hair?"

Lucas nodded. "Of course, one of our distant cousins. He works hard, trains hard, he'll be a great warrior I think some day."

"Hah. The girl thought I was going to do Shaws in and she stepped between us telling me to punish her instead, the boy about died of mortification."

Leaning forward at the waist, Lucas gave a whoop of laughter. "No kidding? Way to emasculate a guy, cut his balls right off."

"Yeah. I had to bite my tongue to not call Shaws a sissy. He redeemed himself by maneuvering her behind him. Anyway, you've heard she heals?"

Lucas nodded wiping a mirthful tear from his eye. "I've seen her first hand, remember? Cortland?"

"Oh, right. Anyway, when she argues with me or disobeys my orders, I tell her she can't heal anyone that day, and maybe even the next, she gets freaked that she can't help the ill and gives in."

A discerning eye narrowed at his brother, Lucas said, "K, you have ensconced this woman in a comfortable room in your home instead of the dungeon where most foreigners go. You have allowed her to run roughshod over your commands, you allow her to hang out with Lexi," he hesitated with a grin.

"Well, I guess it's the young woman who should watch out for Lexi. Our sister has been mischievous, like Gabriel, all her life. Whatever poor slob that marries her will have his hands full that's for sure."

The corner of his mouth tugging up, the dimple deepened, Kultur nodded his agreement.

"Anyway, my point is, why are you treating this woman so...softly?"

Kultur's lips pulled in. He stood up. "We need to get out to the field."

Smirking, Lucas suggested, "If she were old and fat and ugly, or male, I'm betting she'd be in the dungeon."

When Kultur didn't jump at the bait, chuckling, Lucas rose lazily to his feet. Stretching his long arms over his head, he yawned then shook his head. Combing his hair back with his fingers he grinned at Kultur. "Okay, you don't want to talk about her. I'll let it go, for now." He strode to the door, "Meet you in a few," and started down the hall to the stairs to care for his son.

Watching his brother leave, Kultur stood for a moment thinking about Lucas' words. He couldn't answer why he was so damned soft on Sislla. It was just…that *she* was so damned soft, and kind, and sweet and compassionate. Too compassionate for her own good. Her selfless actions could get her sick or hurt, or worse.

He almost felt like he had to protect her from herself, from being too guileless and naïve. Too gullible. For crying out loud, the girl left the castle in the black of night in a killer storm to go meet a strange woman she wanted to help who could have had ulterior, devious plans. It was only by luck it had turned out all right.

His mother had told him Sislla had gone out to meet a man. He recalled his blind rage at the thought that she had risked her life to go out in that tempest to meet a lover. Even now the thought pinched a prick in his stomach. He shook his head, enough pondering for the day. He had work to do.

Dressed in a long-sleeved white shirt, brown trousers and boots, he swiped a hand across his jaw. He should have shaved. His men didn't care what he looked like; he'd tend to it later. If he was going to be around the inside of the castle or to the village he would be better groomed, but outside working and sweating with his men it didn't much matter.

On his way to go outside, he decided to check on the sick child they'd brought in last night. He thought maybe Sislla would be there caring for the infant.

Last night he'd given the order that people seeking healing would be turned away today. They'd had a late night last night, and he wanted his little healer not to have to heal herself if she gets sick from exhaustion and malnutrition.

The door to the room he had assigned them stood open.

Kultur walked inside expecting to see mother and child and Sislla. The room was starkly empty. The bed was stripped; all evidence of the guests was gone.

"What in the hell," instantly on edge, Kultur strode out of the room and headed to Sislla's chamber. Almost there, Kirman Ryan, breathing heavy from jogging, flagged him down.

"Sir, Atraam, here I am." The guard stopped in front of Kultur.

Kultur stood staring at him. Ryan stared back.

Impatiently, Kultur snapped, "What is it, Kirman?"

Confusion wrinkled Ryan's fair skin. "Uh, you sent for me, sir."

"Kirman, I don't have time for this shit." Kultur made to move past the guard but stopped and turned to him. Ryan was a picture of bafflement. "Who told you I wanted to see you?"

Almost clicking his heels together, Ryan announced, "Madam Kultiran, Atraam. Your mother."

A frown tugged uneasily at Kultur's brows. "What exactly did she say?"

"She just told me that you said for me to go to you. She said you were probably still in your chamber. I was going to your office next but then I found you here."

Kultur pinned his guard with a hard look. "Do you know where the woman and ill child went?"

His lips didn't move, but red started staining Ryan's already ruddy cheeks.

"You've been hanging around Sislla too much, Kirman. Do not make me ask you questions twice. I'm at my last thread with that shit. Answer me."

"Y- yes sir, Atraam. Uh, well, Miss Sislla was concerned because, ah, the woman and child were, are, uh, Tenthekens." He braced himself to be struck by the brunt of the Atraam's lethal fury. It was all he could do to keep his eyes open and not flinch.

Shock held Kultur immobile. It was so beyond belief, beyond acceptable, beyond- The incredulous, the terrifying idea that the murderous enemy had been within his walls, his mouth opened, closed.

He said, "She brought Tenthekens into the castle? The keep? Into my family's home?"

"Um, actually, sir, you brought them in." Ryan's eyes dropped to the floor, he stared at his boots waiting for the blow that would end his life. But then, he thought he heard a short laugh. He raised his eyes a hair to peer at his leader.

Kultur was rubbing the dark stubble on his jaw, then he wiped his hand over his wry smile. He rolled his eyes to the ceiling. That woman. No one but she could have finagled him into bringing the enemy into his home. And without a word.

In truth, she never asked. She was prepared to treat the child in the dead of night, knee-deep in mud, with a total stranger, on treacherous land, in the middle of a damned cyclone.

He's the one that had stalked over, picked up the child and took him and his mother to the castle so Sislla could help the baby. That woman has him so in circles he doesn't know what he's doing half the time. He smiled again in disbelief shaking his head.

"Stand up straight, Kirman," he snapped at Ryan. The guard slapped his heels together, stiffened his spine like a poker and looked straight ahead with his head high.

"Why did Sislla make them leave the castle?"

Ryan's Adam's apple bobbed nervously. "She was concerned that if anyone discovered they were Tenthekens that they may be in danger here. She had, uh, one of the villagers," he blinked hard, said swiftly, "I don't know who, sir, she said she wouldn't tell me who it was, that what I don't know I can't tell. Sir."

One side of Kultur's lips curved up in another wry smile. "Of course she did." Then he remembered his mother had lied and had deliberately separated Ryan from Sislla. "Kirman, you left Miss Sislla's side, again against my orders. Why?"

Keeping his eyes straight ahead, Ryan said, "Your mother said, sir, she told me you asked for me."

Kultur stared at the guard for so long Ryan thought he'd turned to cement. "Where was my mother headed when she told you I wanted to see you?"

"The dungeon, Atraam."

His heart started quickening. "Was Sislla with her?"

"Yes...sir..." What Kultur was thinking was now dawning on Ryan. "Oh sons above, sir, she wouldn't-"

Kultur turned and ran. Taking the stairs two and three at a time he sailed down them, raced through the main great room out the door and to the dungeon.

Chapter Seventeen

The heavy wooden door crashed open.

Darathia Kultiran's imperious head jerked to the door. A sneer of tyrannical annoyance, and a snarled promise of severe punishment for whoever had dared to intrude on her plans curled on her wrinkled lip.

Seeing her enraged son on the threshold, what little color there was in her gaunt face hemorrhaged in an instant, leaving her surprised and bone-shattering petrified.

But Kultur's eyes were not on her, they went first to the bare-chested behemoth standing with powerful legs spread to brace his bulky, muscle-bound body. He held a whip held high overhead in his massive fist about to swing down and flail a deep strip of Sislla's fair skin off her back.

Not the regular flogger, Horace, this man had a huge head, bumpy and mutilated from too many fights. His scarred body gleamed with perspiration. Trousers stained with filth and blood clung to thick thighs, his eyes stupid with no brains but showed glee as he stared down at the slender, white bare back of the young female he was about to destroy.

He was standing behind and over Sislla.

She was on her knees, bent over a wooden stock. Her arms were stretched out to either side, and her wrists that were cuffed to the horizontal board were bloody from her struggles to get free.

Her face was on its side resting on the stock between her trapped hands. The long curly tresses had been pulled over to flow between her neck and shoulder to keep her back clear for the whip. Her dress had been torn completely down her back, a scant few threads kept only a part of her breasts covered.

"Stop!" Kultur commanded, shoving past his mother.

Darathia quickly melted into the shadows out of her son's direct wrath.

The flogger so intent on stripping off Sislla's skin didn't pay any attention to Kultur. He started to pull the whip back to fling it against her.

With a thunderous roar, Kultur ran and charged, leaping and battering into the behemoth as he slashed the whip.

Kultur hit him so hard both men were airborne before slamming onto the straw layered stone floor. Before the flogger could get his hands up to fight him, Kultur bashed his fist into the man's face. He hit him so hard the behemoth's head bounced off the stones spraying straw and blood.

Kultur didn't stop with one punch, he hammered at the man so hard and fast the flogger never got a hit in. It took only seconds and the behemoth was out. But Kultur kept pounding him.

Through the black rage and red haze blinding and deafening him, a small voice cried, *"Mercy, Kultur, please,"* he shook it off and kept battering the man's face until it was almost obliterated.

Then the faint, *"Mercy,"* broke through again, stalling Kultur's rampage.

He sat back on his heels and wiped his bloody sleeve across the sweat that poured down his brow. His thick chest rose hard and fast with heavy panting. He tugged his shirt out of his belt and wiped his face and hands with it then turned to Sislla.

Her eyes were half closed from swelling, someone had struck her. Her lips were also swollen and bleeding. Tears fell on the board her head was lying on. Her arms stretched from either side of her head manacled to the stock dripped blood. Still, the words, *"Mercy on him, Kultur, please,"* kept falling softly from her bruised mouth.

127

Gasping, "Oh my sons' breath, Sislla," Kultur stood up, stumbled away from the behemoth and fell to his knees beside her. He dropped his arm over her shoulder, laid his head next to hers and wept tearless for a few breaths.

Climbing back to his feet, he lumbered to the wall where the keys hung, snatched the ring off and stumbled back to Sislla. He unlocked the chains, and as her body fell loose he sat cross-legged, pulled her onto his lap, gathered her up in his arms and held her against his chest.

He cradled her head, smoothed her hair back as he felt her tears soaking into his shirt. Murmuring against her head, he stroked her hair to soothe her, when his hand brushed down her bare back he gently held her forward until he saw her dress and under-bindings had been ripped almost entirely off.

Sislla weakly drew her arms across the front of her to cover her half-exposed breasts.

When Kultur didn't move his wide-eyed stare from her bosom, she whispered, "Kultur, please," her breasts were plumped up over her covering arm.

Muttering, "Ah, yes, here, *koritsi*," blood and sweat soaked though it was, Kultur quickly unbuttoned his shirt, pulled it off and helped her put it on. While he did that he turned his head to his mother who still lurked in the shadows.

"Mother," his tone indicated for her to come forward. She did, cautiously, her face mutinous.

Her long skirts swished over the floor, the straw cracked under her heels. She stood in front of the couple, her lip curled in a sneer at the girl her son held in his arms.

"Why, mother, why would you do this? You know I forbid beating or flogging of females."

Darathia crossed her long arms over her flat chest, her bony chin raised in the air. Red spots jarred on her sallow cheeks, her mouth pinched in snobbish contempt. Patting her greying hair back, she pushed some loose strays back up in her bun and sniffed defiantly.

"The filthy tramp continues to disobey you, the Atraam, the Lord of Chamaine-Gris, King of Aenlic Castle, mighty warlord of the Isle of Aniniva Kinthara. She should have lost her head the day that beast Trogga brought her here. He should have used her as he wanted to in the woods then just buried her body."

"That is enough, Mother," Kultur snapped, turned his attention to Sislla on his lap and did up the buttons on his filthy shirt to cover her. Her hands hung useless in her lap, her wrists were bruised, bloody and torn.

Her voice bold and strident, Darathia said vehemently, "No, it is not enough, son. She will bring the Iminims straight to our door. We will be murdered in our beds. Children slashed and tortured, she will have-"

"I said enough!" Kultur bellowed. He stood up with Sislla, half dazed in his arms.

Darathia stood in front of him, her claw-like fingers curled on boney hips. "You should throw her to the sea, but if you insist on keeping her, Kultur, she must be marked. I will bring some suitable men in," her eyes fell to Sislla's bruised and cut face, "in a week when she will be more presentable. One of them will do the deed. That will take care of the problem."

Kultur pushed past her, tromping to the door with Sislla tucked tight against his chest.

Passing in and out of consciousness, her head lolled against his shoulder. He went out the door.

Darathia shouted after him, "It is the only way, Kultur, either throw her out to take her chances alone with the Iminims, or get her marked! Any of the single men will be eager to take her."

He went around the back of the manor so people wouldn't gawk at them. Taking the stairs two at a time to her room, he stopped when he reached the door. Ryan had waited just outside the dungeon and had followed him.

"Shall I open it, Atraam?"

Kultur hesitated, then turned. "No." He pivoted and started down the hall until he reached his own chambers. "Open the door, Kirman," he ordered.

A dismayed look on his ruddy face, Ryan opened the door to Kultur's chambers.

As Kultur stepped in, he said, "Get Onani. Tell her ice, bandages, alcohol, and food for Miss Sislla."

Not waiting for Ryan's affirmation, he marched inside and gently laid her on his bed. He pulled her shoes off and dropped them on the floor then sat down beside her. The mattress was thick but it dipped slightly under his weight.

When Onani timidly entered the room, Kultur was sitting on the bed stroking Sislla's arm.

"Sir?" Onani asked, her voice quivered slightly with nerves. The big man scared her half to death all the time. She'd seen his anger and cold ruthlessness too often to be comfortable in his presence.

"Ah, Onani," Kultur acknowledge her then said to Ryan standing behind the servant, "Kirman, get another maid to assist Miss Onani." Ryan left the room.

When Onani moved closer, Kultur's mouth curved ruefully at her stunned gasp.

"Oh, my poor Miss," she cried, seeing Sislla lying bloodied and bruised wrapped in Kultur's shirt. She kept her eyes averted from his bare chest, but her accusing glare sliced at him.

His voice gruff with irritation, Kultur said with a scowl, "It was not me. Now, I need you and the other maid to strip her, bathe her, clean her cuts with alcohol and bandage them. When Kirman Shaws returns, have him retrieve Miss Sislla's bag with her healing stuff in it. Maybe she can do something more for her wounds"

Onani nodded wordlessly, her face taut with distraught grief at Sislla's brutal beating.

Kultur continued, "Then tell Shaws he is to stay with her and the other maid while you retrieve bedclothes for her to wear. Be leery of her wrists." He nodded to Sislla's hands.

Glaring harshly at Onani he said roughly, "Shaws is to stand guard outside while you tend to her. No one but you two maids and Shaws are to enter this room. That includes my mother."

Another sharp intake of shocked breath at the sight of Sislla's damaged skin, Onani could only nod. Then she quivered, "Uh, we are to attend to her in your, uh bath?"

His eyes on Sislla, he said, "Yes. She will stay here for now." He ignored Onani's shocked inhale. He was tired of seeing Sislla, a young woman under his charge, be in constant danger and harm. If she was here under his nose he could see that she was safe, and, another rueful smile, fed.

He wouldn't let her get away with tricks and wheedling. She works too hard and doesn't eat enough because she's too tired. He will have no woman die on his watch from exhaustion or starvation, foreigner or not.

He stood up. "I will be back. I left someone alive that needs to be dead." He'd not killed the behemoth because Sislla pled for his life. She would not be there now to see him complete the job. He stepped from the bed when a faint voice stopped him.

"Kultur, please, mercy."

His hands, knuckles cut and bloody, clasped behind his back, he frowned down at her.

The bright blue of Sislla's eyes peered dimly at him through her swollen lids. The cut on her lip gave her a painful lisp as she begged for the behemoth's life.

"No."

"Kultur," it came out in a sluggish wisp.

"No, *koritsi*, not this time." He turned on his heel.

She whispered, "Please, Kultur, you must show mercy."

A tightening in the backs of his eyes threatened to loosen, god- forbid, tears, at the sight of her pretty face so badly battered. The light dimmed in her bruised eyes yet she still pled for another person's life.

One that would have, after he'd already beaten and half-stripped her, would probably have flogged her to death. Judging by the way the man had leered at Sislla's naked skin, he likely would have, without showing *her* any mercy, brutally raped her before she died.

"No, *koritsi*," he spat through clenched teeth, "who showed you mercy?"

He started to walk away, but still heard her murmur barely audible, "You did."

His throat constricted, heart pinched, Onani's sob in his ear, he hesitated, then left the room.

Chapter Eighteen

Sislla slept like the dead for a week. Slowly wakening, she felt the slight ache in her head and pain in her wrists. Her eyes fluttered open. Staring up at the ceiling, she became suddenly aware she was not in her room.

She sat up abruptly, wincing at the pain in her stomach and again in her wrists as she used her hands to brace herself on the mattress.

"Miss!" Onani hurried to the bed. "Please, move carefully, you don't want to re-injure yourself. Let me help you." She put her arm around Sislla's shoulders and helped her lean back against the pillows.

Sislla touched her head, slightly dizzy from her quick movement. Nestling back into the pillows, wincing, she gazed around the room. She was in a huge, very comfortable bed. The heavy, dark wooden dresser, armoire, chairs with dark blue cushions and curtains to match indicated she was in a man's room. It was vaguely familiar.

Her eyes shot to the divan against the wall. It had rumpled blankets and a couple of pillows on it. She rolled her bewildered eyes to Onani. "Where am I?"

Her hands folded in front of her, a warm smile on her plain face, Onani answered, "You are in the master's suite, the Atraam's."

133

Sislla's eyes few open. "What? How?" She went to throw off the sheets and blanket and get out of the bed, Onani put out a hand to stall her.

"It's all right, Miss. The Atraam brought you here. You don't remember?"

Her heavy lids pressed down, Sislla shook her head, it hurt. "No."

"Oh. Well," Onani explained cheerfully, "you were about to be flogged by Gregor the Giant, when the Atraam burst in and rescued you. He beat Gregor to a pulp and brought you here. Sonnett and I undressed and bathed you, we bandaged your wounds."

Onani's face darkened, "Gregor tore off most of your dress and beat you before he was going to whip you." She grew cheerful again, said with a smile, "But like I said, the Atraam annihilated him and carried you from the dungeon up here. It was so romantic." She frowned. "Um, except for your injuries of course."

Sislla was mortified. "Oh my stars, Onani, that sounds dreadful and humiliating. Why- why was I to be flogged? Because I secreted the woman and child out of here? But then it would have been Kultur who would have ordered the whipping. I don't understand, why would he order me whipped and then stop it?"

Vigorously shaking her head, her face crunched in an angry scowl, Onani said, "No Miss, it was," she swallowed, spreading gossip could cause one to lose her head. Ryan had told her what had transpired. She continued, figuring it would come back to the Miss eventually anyway, although, she already had trouble with recalling her past life, Onani shrugged.

"It was the Atraam's mother, Altra Darathia Kultiran who brought you to the dungeon."

At Sislla's baffled expression she explained, "The Madam was angry that you keep disobeying the Atraam without consequences. She felt you needed to be brought into line." Her face fell. "I am so sorry, Miss that she did that to you. She doesn't know what a sweet, kind, gentle person you are."

Being dragged down to the dungeon by Kultur's mother was vaguely returning to her memory. Sislla looked around. "But why am I here? In Kultur's room?"

Onani smiled broadly. "The Atraam said he was tired of you being in harm's way and the only way to prevent that was to have you under his supervision. He has slept every night on that couch," she nodded to the one with sheets on it. "I slept in the sitting room," she indicated a doorway to the back of the room. She blushed and said, "For proprieties sake, you know."

Her eyes scrunched in a wince of pain, Sislla asked, "Where is Kultur now?"

Her mouth pursed, the maid shrugged again. "I'm not sure. He is probably seeing to the sparring practice. So, for breakfast would you like-"

Sislla swung her legs to the side of the bed. "I want to get dressed. Do I have clothes here?"

Shaking her head a bit distressed, Onani said with some anxiety, "No, you have no clothes. You've been in bed for a week. I helped you with your, uh, bathroom issues, and the Master helped you eat."

"What?" Flabbergasted, Sislla repeated, "He helped me eat?" her voice rose high at the end of her question.

Onani nodded. "Yes, Miss. Mostly soup. He said his feeding you would ensure you could not use any trickery to not eat properly...um..."

"Huh," Sislla snorted and slid to her feet. A little wobbly she clung to the bedpost. "I will go to my chamber and change. Onani, are there people here today seeking healing?"

"Yes, Miss." She eyed Sislla with trepidation, she didn't think the Atraam would be pleased to return and find the Miss gone, and, again, without eating.

She told Sislla, "They are here every day even though the Atraam tells them you yourself are too ill to tend to them. So, perhaps you should get back into his bed...I mean, the bed," she urged Sislla but the girl kept moving to the door. Onani trailed after her.

Outside the door, Ryan came to attention. His gaze met Onani's. At the maid's shrug and worried face he said quickly, "Miss, where, uh, are you going?"

"Good morning, Ryan," Sislla greeted, sweeping past him and down the hall.

Onani whispered as they followed her, "She's going to get dressed." She added with dread, "I fear she's going to go downstairs to heal."

"Oh shit," Ryan sputtered. Onani nodded in agreement.

Finding she had no clothes that weren't torn or bloody, Sislla hurried to Lexi's room.

The girl welcomed her with a big happy hug. "Sons above, girl, I heard what happened to you." Lexi scowled. "Kultur would not let me see you. He hogged you all to himself. What-"

"Never mind that now, Lex, I need something to wear to go down and heal. Do you have something I can borrow?"

Her brow knit with uncertainty, twirling a length of dark hair around a finger, Lexi said, "Well, um, Sis, I don't think my brother wants you to-"

"Please, Lexi. It's been over a week since I've helped the people. I've let them down, I feel terrible. I just need something to wear."

"Well," seeing the concerned crease in Sislla's forehead, and her adamancy to go downstairs, Lexi reluctantly gave in. She went to her closet and peered in. "Tomorrow is wash day, I don't have a lot of clean stuff, I mean that would fit tiny little you."

She pushed some clothes aside. "Here, this should be okay." She pulled out an off-white dress and handed it to Sislla.

"Thank you, Lex." Sislla promptly shucked off the nightgown and yanked the dress over her head. Smoothing it down, she stuck her feet into the shoes she'd grabbed from her room.

"Wait," Lexi ran to her dresser, opened a drawer. "Here, you need underwear girl." She thrust a pair of silk underdrawers into Sislla's hands. Sislla stepped into them and pulled them up, tied each side then smoothed the dress down. She headed for the door.

"Omigod, Sis, wait, you need bindings for your bosom-"

"I'm fine, no one can tell, I need to hurry." Sislla raced out the door.

"Oh crap." Lexi seeing the red of Ryan's jacket as he fled after Sislla muttered, "Kultur is going to kill one or both of them." Then she grinned. "At least Ryan finally smartened up. He's staying glued to her ass this time, no matter what. Too bad he's not going to be smart enough to have someone send word to Kultur about Sislla's intentions." She shrugged one shoulder. "Oh well, I'm not going to be the bearer of bad news."

Sislla worked all day healing, constantly admonishing Ryan to hush and quit telling her that she needed to return to Kultur's room.

Seeing to the last of the villagers for the day, she wearily trudged back into the main part of the castle. She came to an abrupt stop as she entered the great room. It was filled with women. Young, beautiful women.

At the door, she asked one of the maids what was going on.

The maid replied, "Madam Kultiran is throwing a party for every single girl in the village to come so the Atraam can choose a bride."

"What?" Sislla's big blue eyes scanned the room in astonishment. "Why would she, I mean can't he do his own searching?" Her stomach suddenly twisted painfully, it must be hunger pains.

"I guess his mother has lost her patience with him. A few more years and he will be thirty years old and she thinks he should get married already and produce an heir. But," the maid leaned in whispering with a snicker, "everyone knows he won't marry. Why should he? He has the pick of the town. He's been known to sleep around without bothering to stay the night with women or even learning their names.

"The word is he goes into the city and does whores, prostitutes, 'cause there's no strings then. But, he could sleep with a different girl every night for years and not do them all. As they say, 'why buy the milk when you can milk the cow?' "

The girl rambled on but Sislla had stopped listening. She'd spotted Kultur. It was easy, so tall, big, confident; his steely cold eyes could pierce a dark cave. He was standing across the room surrounded by a group of women. One was cuddled up to him, his ear was lowered to her mouth, his hand was on her back.

Feeling her stomach twist even more, as she headed towards the stairs, Sislla remember Lexi telling her no one was allowed to touch the Atraam without his permission. Well, I guess he gave the woman, a statuesque willowy woman with long straight dark hair that was rubbing her breasts against the front of his shirt, permission to touch him.

A few feet from the staircase she didn't see the willowy brunette detach herself from Kultur and follow her.

"*You*," Sislla heard a voice say right behind her. "You're that foreign bitch come to have us all slaughtered in our beds."

Sislla froze with her hand on the bannister. She turned slowly towards the brunette until she was eye to eye, almost, as the woman was a foot taller than her.

The woman appeared older than Lexi, her almond shaped golden eyes were like sharp accusing rapiers. She slithered until she was between Sislla and the stairs.

Without a word, Sislla started to move around the woman to go up the stairs. The woman moved to block her.

Her eyes lowered, "Please let me pass," Sislla murmured politely.

A harsh laugh came out of the woman's mouth like a shrill clot. "No, you little whore, we need to talk." She put her arm out to link with the railing. Sislla would have to physically push her aside to get by.

Slowly, her head high, Sislla turned to face the woman. She waited for her to speak first.

The woman's insulting gaze trailed up and down Sislla's body. "You shouldn't even be in this castle. You weren't invited to the party, you're foreign trash, no one wants you here. Kultur has probably already fucked you and moved on from your weird appearance." Lip curled in contempt, the woman glared scornfully at Sislla as if she could bury her with a sneer of disdain.

When Sislla remained mute, her nose in the air, the woman said, "I am Araina Delgata, you don't measure up to me," she swept her arm in an arc across the room, "or any of the young women here. Just look at the way you are dressed, like a disgusting slutty washerwoman. You are not near good enough for our Atraam."

When Sislla didn't respond to her nasty words, Araina's nose wrinkled with repugnance as she looked pointedly at her head. She said with disgusted disdain, "With that ugly unusual yellow hair, and obviously weak eyes they are so…blue, light, spooky, it's a wonder Kultur has let you stay around for even a second. Maybe he gets off on fucking weird ugly women."

Araina shook her head; her sleek hair shimmered against her back. "But he won't keep you, he won't marry you. You need to move on and stop putting the rest of us in danger."

Neither woman was aware Kultur was standing behind them.

Sislla said calmly, "I am not vacuous as some to want what is not mine to have."

Her dark brows arched like pointed wings, Araina looked confused by Sislla's words. "Are you insulting me you ugly whore? How dare you!" She hurled her hand at Sislla to slap her, like lightening Kultur caught her hand.

Both women looked at him in surprise.

Sislla took the opportunity to try to push past Araina and run up the stairs.

Kultur threw Araina's hand down, his mouth hard with anger.

Rubbing her wrist, Araina scowled at him, her snide voice deep for a woman, she said, "Kultur," then faltered at the darkness that crossed Kultur's face and into his eyes. "Uh, Atraam, she is nothing but fucking worthless trash. You need to get rid of her before she brings calamity down on all of us. The Iminims-"

Kultur reached around her and grasped Sislla's wrist as she tried to escape up the stairs. He held onto her until he got to the step she was on then took her upper arm guiding her up the steps.

Araina glowered at the pair. She said loud enough for anyone in earshot to hear, "Watch your back, Atraam, she is dangerous, alien trash, nothing more. She is not one of us. You will tire of her oddness soon."

She turned preening to her audience because the couple was gone, "And then he will come to me for comfort and relish being with a clean, normal, beautiful woman again. One of his own clan. He will come to me."

Upstairs, Kultur let go of her arm and she went straight to her room. "Wait, Sislla, I want you to stay-"

She opened the door and went in. Right behind her, he said, "Where do you think you're going?"

Taking a deep breath, she turned to him. He was taken aback at the shadows under her eyes. The bruises and cuts had diminished, but she looked bone tired. "I need a bath." As she headed towards the bathing room he stuck his hand out and grabbed her arm.

"Kultur, please."

He pulled her over and sat her down at the vanity. Then he stomped over to the nightstand and picked up a plate, clomped in his heavy boots back over to her and practically threw it down in front of her. She jerked back when the plate clattered on the table.

Kultur stomped back across the room, grabbed a chair and dropped it down beside her, tugging his leather breeches up at the knees to loosen them, and sat down.

He was acting so chilly and rough, Sislla didn't move, just watched him. Kultur crossed his arms over his strong chest, leaned back and snapped, "Eat. All of it. Right now."

Sislla looked down at what must have been her breakfast Onani had brought her. Her stomach grumbled realizing she hadn't eaten all day. She'd been so busy.

"Eat!" he barked.

She jumped, glanced at him. His black eyes glowered ominous and cold. She lowered her gaze to the egg sandwich then picked it up. But her stomach churned, she just stared at it.

"Uh, Atraam, sir," having followed them, Onani's timid voice jittered. She almost shook to death when Kultur slanted his forbidding dark gaze at her through tapered lids. He looked like a fiercely angry panther ready to sink his fangs into a cornered quarry.

Bravely, Onani edged to the door with her eyes nervously prodding him to follow her.

He set his big hands on the chair arms and pushed himself up with an irritated grunt. He trod over to where Onani stood by the door then verbally struck out, "What?"

Keeping her head averted from his glare, Onani stared at her fingers picking at them. "I beg your pardon, Atraam. But she is still recovering from…last week, and she's worked hard all day on an empty stomach. She was just verbally assaulted in public downstairs, I- I fear if you force her to eat it will only make her sick." She didn't dare look up at him. The angry heat radiating off his large body was enough to keep her on edge.

Not acknowledging the maid's words, Kultur went back over to Sislla. He said quietly, "*Koritsi.*"

She kept her head down staring at the sandwich in her hand.

"Look- at- me-" the words ground out with frustration.

The blue eyes rolled up at him. She was so bushed her lids were half down over her eyes, so translucent, blue veins were visible through her thin skin.

He took the sandwich out of her hand and set it on the plate. His voice softened, "Come with me." He held out his hand and waited until she put hers in it and he helped her up. He walked her to the window.

She looked out the window then at him perplexed.

His hands clasped behind his back, he nodded to the window. "Tomorrow, there will be people lined up to see you, seeking your help."

Wordless, she looked out the window, nodding, her lips pulled in trying to follow him.

"They will be sent away."

Her eyes flashed to him, she opened her mouth to protest.

"Sislla, I told you that you were not to work more than three hours a day, and you were to have your two assistants with you, and you were to eat. You did not follow even one of my orders. There will be no healing tomorrow or the next day. After that we will see."

Aghast, she protested, "No, Kultur, I need to help them."

Unmoved, he said calmly, "I was going to leave it at two days, but since you argue with me I will add a third."

"But you can't, that's not fair-"

"You wish me to add more days, Sislla?"

She shut her mouth with chagrin, tears of frustration gathered in her eyes.

"I don't have to be fair to you, Sislla. Or to anyone. I only need to keep this realm running. Do not mistake my not physically harming you, *yet*, that I am soft or kind. I am not. I am only waiting until I know who you are. If you are some great king's daughter, I don't want to insult him and bring down his ire for injuring, mistreating...or killing you."

The hurt and shame was apparent in the stiffening of her shoulders, so thin her shoulder blades were sharp against the back of the dress. The hurt pulled in her soft lips, and the darkening of her blue irises as the pupils enlarged to hold in her pain at his cold impersonal words.

She looked so sad and drawn he considered rephrasing his statement. But no, he would not negate what he'd said. "You are still recovering from a bad...beating. You are not giving your body time to heal and recover, and if you won't, goddammit I will." Kultur's sigh coursed out, "You may bathe now then you have an hour to eat that sandwich when I will return to make sure you have."

"Kultur, the people need-"

He pounded his fists banging them on the windowsill and roared, "I don't give a fuck about the people!" Both Sislla, and Onani still standing by the door jumped.

Sislla's shoulders bunched in fright. Her eyes like blue wavering torches peered up at him as if she expected him to strike her.

He spread his fingers then set his palms on the sill, hunched his back and glared out the window. Getting control of his temper, Kultur wiped his mouth then shoved his jet black hair back off his head. He put a hand up against the side of the window frame, the other on his hip; clearing his throat he shifted slightly to face Sislla.

She looked so damned tired, and scared. Of him. He said gruffly, "Just, uh, get some rest. I won't disturb you the rest of the night. Onani will stay with you." Without looking away from Sislla, he could see Onani nodding.

Noticing what Sislla was wearing for the first time, Kultur glared at her dress. It was a thin, tight material; the bodice was cut a little low exposing a bit of her cleavage.

Seeing his attention on her chest, she moved slightly to turn from his view. Her breasts jiggled with her movements.

His eyes pinpointed at her nipples budding through the slight material. "You have no fucking bindings on under that? You wore that all day while working in the shop- showing everyone your damned breasts?"

"Um," feeling awkward, Sislla crossed her arms over her front. "No one paid any attention to what I was-"

"Are you at least wearing," he bent and snatched up the bottom of her dress exposing the borrowed tiny wisp of pink silk underwear Lexi had given her. The tips of his ears burned red, he dropped her skirt like it had scalded him. He heard Onani's sucked in breath shock from the doorway.

He'd forgotten himself; he was acting like a barbarian. Yet he couldn't help picturing her sashaying through the castle and her workshop in front of men in that practically sheer dress with her tits half exposed and bouncing everywhere. His ears grew redder and his cheekbones thinned knife-edged with his gall.

"I can't believe you wore that slutty shit in public. Men were probably drooling all over you all day. Did anyone make a pass at you?"

She just stared at him in disbelief.

He grasped her thin wrist and pulled her close to him, so close her chest was pressed up against his. His eyes dipped down to her breasts that were forced up mounding out of the top of the dress from being pressed against him.

"No one touched me, Kul- Kultur. I didn't have anything to wear-"

"*Shut up!*" he barked. Still looking at her breasts, his eyes narrowed. "I take it that's my sister's. You give it back to her. If I see you in it again I'll burn it." Releasing her abruptly he started for the door, he turned back at her voice.

"Kultur?"

"Yes, Sislla?" He fetched the rage out of his voice making it steady and cool.

"Are you going to marry that woman, that, uh, Araina is her name?"

Sighing and rubbing his eyes, he told her, "Eat and go to bed, *koritsi*." He started for the door again, when she said, "Kultur?"

He tilted his head, observed her through lowered lids, one brow arched under a flop of black hair.

"If I can't heal, can I at least get my herbs and leaves?"

"Of course. Good night now."

Onani opened the door before he got to it. He nodded to her on his way out.

The maid's eyes were lowered, she couldn't face him after the way he'd manhandled the poor Miss. She closed the door behind him and went over to Sislla still standing by the window.

"He was so mad, Miss. I've seldom seen him like that. He usually carries no expression at all, and keeps his cool under even extreme circumstances. I don't understand why he gets so mad at you."

Sislla wandered over to the vanity and took a bite of the sandwich then set it down. "Me neither. For some reason I push his buttons, but I don't mean to upset him. He has actually been very kind to me."

"Yes, that's true," Onani agreed. "I've never seen him bring a woman, who was not family or married to family, or a relative of one of his warriors into his home. That Araina has continuously tried to scheme her way in here. As have countless other hussies. His mother snuck the surprise party on him today. Trust me, he was not pleased."

"Hmm," was all Sislla murmured recalling that woman rubbing herself all over him.

"Anyway, Miss, he's put you in the prettiest room. He had the men transform that room downstairs in the back so you could have that for your workshop. Other than his direct family, you are the only one he allows to call him by his given name. When he's here he brings you to the dining room for dinner, which," Onani's shoulders went up with her snicker, "really pisses off the old bat." Referring to Kultur's mother.

"Onani!" Sislla blurted with a grin, the pair giggled together.

"Come on, Miss," Onani said, nudging Sislla to the bathroom door. "Let's get you bathed and in bed. One thing the Atraam was right about, you do need rest."

Chapter Nineteen

Mid-afternoon the next day, Kultur was in the field sparring with his League. He and two of his men were charging at and grappling each other. Grunts and curses, spitting and more curses abounded the field as others were doing the same thing.

Tackling one of his men taking him to the ground, Kultur rolled him on his stomach and held him down with his knee while grabbing the second man's foot as he tried to kick Kultur in the head. Kultur jerked his foot causing the man to go off balance and crash to the ground.

Kultur jumped to his feet and held a hand down to one then the other of his defeated men and helped them up. He clapped one of the men on the back and said, "Marco, you are much improved."

The young man grinned ear-to-ear then quickly hid his thrill at the compliment from the Atraam. Nodding serious and solemn, he bowed to Kultur.

At that moment Kultur caught a glimpse of red scurrying from the direction of the castle past the archers practicing near the forest, towards the sparring men. His brows drew down and his eyes narrowed when he recognized Ryan running to him. His stomach clenched.

Ryan was huffing and puffing when he reached him, he bent over with his hands on his knees to catch his breath.

"What is it, Kirman?"

So winded, Ryan couldn't speak.

"Is it her? Sislla?" Hating the anxious note in his voice, Kultur lowered it and spoke more roughly, "Tell me, now Kirman!"

Through exhalations Ryan gasped, "Yes, it's the Miss."

"Goddammit, Kirman, you tell me what the hell is going on." Kultur gripped Ryan's arm with steel fingers digging them into the young man's skin and squeezed until the guard cried out.

"Oh sons above, sir, Kirman Jonhassen was with her, with Miss Sislla in the far meadows. They went too far, the- the she was taken by Ulmas, she-"

"What?" Kultur grabbed both of Ryan's arms and shook the piss out of him. "What are you talking about? Where? Goddammit you fool, tell me what happened!"

"It wasn't my shift to be with her, Atraam, it was Jonhassen's. He took her to gather her herbs and weeds and whatever-"

"She left the castle? But she knows I said-"

Ryan shook his head. "Jonhassen said that she said you told her she couldn't heal today but you gave her permission to go collect her plants. So he took her...to the...meadows. I guess there were Ulmas casing the far side of the woods on our land, and one of them spotted her." Sucking in several ragged breaths Ryan struggled to shove down his hysterical panic.

"Ah, Atraam, the man charged up on his horse, reached down and grabbed her up- right up on his horse in front of him and dashed off with her before Jonhassen could even shout out!"

Winded from running and his long speech, Ryan doubled over again with his hands on his knees heaving for air.

"Why didn't Jonhassen go to you and not me?" Kultur was already yanking his shirt off a fence post and shrugging it on.

"He was scared...sir." Before Ryan had the sir out, Kultur was racing to the stables. He called over his shoulder to Ryan, "Get my brothers, tell them to meet me at the stables, then gather the League to follow us."

Ryan paused, scanning the field until he spotted Gabriel and Lucas, he rushed to get them.

By the time Kultur was pounding down the road on his horse, his brothers were beside him. He knew where he was going. Both the Ulmas and Tenthekens' strongholds were well known.

If the Tenthekens had taken Sislla, she would already be dead or their Atraam's new concubine. Then there would be catastrophic bloodshed because Kultur would either be massacring half their warriors to rescue her, or killing them all in revenge for her death.

During the times when the Iminims attacked, there was an uneasy truce between the three factions. When it wasn't during those times, it was each faction for itself. If a person of a different clan was captured, they were either outright killed or taken for torture and imprisonment. The women were normally but not always, kept alive.

If captured by the Ulmas, if the female was plain, she would be given to whichever warrior wanted her, if beautiful, the Atraam kept her for himself.

If the Tenthekens take a woman from a clan other than their own, if homely, they might use her body or kill her right out, after tremendous torture. If beautiful, the Atraam keeps her for as long as he wants, then he passes her to his men, when they're done with her, they cut her up in tiny pieces and scatter her.

When his men capture a female, Kultur does not believe in keeping the other clans' women. He returned them.

Since it was the Ulmas that took her, he still had a chance to retrieve her. The Ulmas weren't as bloodthirsty and sadistic as the Tenthekens and normally chose to have as little friction between them and the Kultur's people, the Chamaine-Gris.

Kultur was too well known as a relentless, ruthless warlord and they know he could wipe them out of he chose to.

The only time Kultur slowed his stallion was when he passed through the meadow and spotted Sislla's baskets in the grass near the muddy trail where she'd dropped them when she was snatched.

When they reached the start of the Ulmas' stronghold, the three brothers slowed their pace. Kirman Ryan came up the rear with a league of backup.

One of the warriors trotted up to Kultur and handed him a pole with a blue flag on it.

Kultur knew the Ulmas would already be coming to meet them as he had deliberately not been quiet and did not use any sleuth to avoid detection. He wanted their approach to be heard and the fact that they entered the stronghold clearly wanting to be seen. The flag meant they were not there for war, but to talk.

Flanked by an assembly of warriors, with many more around and behind them on horseback as well as on foot, a big man, the Ulmas' Atraam, Rosh Boshor, came forward on his steed.

When Kultur and his brothers dismounted, Rosh Boshor followed suit and signaled his lead men to do the same.

The two Atraams cautiously approached each other to meet in the middle ground.

Atraam Boshor bowed to Kultur. He said with a wary smile of greeting, "What do I owe the honor of the Great Atraam Kultur Kultiran's unexpected visit?"

Like Kultur, Boshor was immense with huge cordons of muscles, bulging biceps, and although with frighteningly lethal appearances depicting they were clearly capable of cold, brutal murder, they both were good-looking men. With harsh hard features and taut angles, scars, and inscrutable eyes, they were dangerous looking, but handsome.

"Atraam Boshor, you dare take what is mine?" Kultur said calmly without a trace of anger or threat.

The smile slipped slightly from Boshor's masculine lips. He looked disappointed. "Oh, the woman is yours?"

Dashing Boshor's anticipation of keeping his new captive, Kultur nodded grimly, but said cordially, "Yes. She is mine. She belongs to the Chamaine-Gris."

His hands twined behind his back, Boshor rocked back and forth on his heels. "I don't suppose you would be willing to discuss a trade? I could offer you another girl, or girls, maybe ten, twenty for her?"

"Afraid not."

Boshor bowed reluctantly. "Ah, I can understand your desire to keep her. She is quite beautiful and unique. Forgive me, Great Kultur, I did not know she belonged to you. Please take her and accept my deepest apologies." He nodded to the man standing rigidly beside him.

The man disappeared into the crowd of warriors behind him. He returned clutching Sislla's arm. He brought her to Kultur.

The terror screaming in her blue eyes did not lessen when she stood in front of Kultur with his impenetrable mask of ice. His gaze barely flicked over her with zero expression.

Boshor twisted his torso and stabbed his knife into the stomach of the man who had brought Sislla out. Apparently expecting it, the man sunk to his knees, then fell to the ground, his eyes wide open.

A mild glance down at the dead man, Boshor remarked, "Kirman Nosren will not be plucking females out of your meadow again."

Kultur's face remained impassive, his eyes flicked to Sislla's green complexion. At least she was smart enough not to scream or faint at the callous murder.

Boshor said, "Atraam Kultiran," drawing Kultur's unfathomable midnight eyes back to him.

Kultur regarded him in silence.

With curious interest, Boshor commented, "She is not marked."

Without a response to him, Kultur stuck his hand in Sislla's hair, grabbed a fistful and dragged her to his horse ignoring her soft cries. As he turned to offer his salutations to Atraam Boshor, he crossed his arm over Sislla's chest and cupped his big hard hand possessively over her breast squeezing it.

"Kultur! Please!" Sislla's breathy mortified cry, she struggled to get free of his tight, humiliating, painful grasp.

Kultur growled coarsely in her ear, "*Be quiet.*" Releasing her, he waited until Lucas mounted then he lifted her, swinging her up to sit behind Lucas.

Lucas said to her kindly, "Put your arms around my waist, honey, hold on." Feeling Sislla's body quaking against him, and her sniffing back tears prodded at Lucas' soft heart, after all, he had a wife and child. They had softened some of his brutal warrior rough edges.

He whispered to her, "He had to show that you are his possession but that you don't have his heart. If they think you are important to him they could return to steal you later and use you as a bargaining chip or a threat to him. Today, Kultur took Boshor by surprise, but as I said, if they thought you were important to him, they would plan next time."

As she dashed at her tears with the backs of her hands she saw Kultur's dark gaze cutting through the burgeoning night at her. All in black leather, he stood hard and regal like the warlord he was.

His eyes on Sislla, one hand holding his horse's reins, Kultur turned to squint with intense seething fury at Rosh Boshor who was waving cheerfully at him.

Gabriel leaned over and said quietly, "You butcher them, even as terrified as she is right now, she would never forgive you for killing hordes of men in her name."

Hiding his deadly thoughts under lowered lids, Kultur inclined his head to Boshor and mounted his horse. Pulling the reins, he swung his steed around and led the League out of the stronghold. A hundred horses galloped like thunder over the land back to the castle.

When they neared the entrance to Aenlic Castle, Kultur dismounted and handed his reins to the man beside him indicating for the Kirman to take care of his horse. He strode over to where Lucas waited for him, holding his steed still, only the horse's tail swished.

Without a word, Kultur reached up, cinched his hands around Sislla's waist and lifted her off the horse, her long skirt swishing over the saddle, and set her on her feet.

He said nothing to his brothers, just wrapped his hand around Sislla's arm and walked her inside. He heard her quiet sigh of relief. As much as she didn't want to be there, as much as she feared Kultur's wrath, she was clearly relieved to be back in the castle.

They walked in silence through the dark building. Night had fallen and only the lanterns lit the grand chamber. Thankfully it was empty as they trod through it. That was until they reached the stairs. Darathia was waiting in the shadows.

She stepped out at the same time Kirman Ryan closed the castle door and roamed up discreetly behind them.

"Mother. We are on our way up," his voice stiff, cold, Kultur kept moving forward bringing Sislla with him.

"Kultur, it is time. You should have left her with the Ulmas, let them deal with her. Now, you must either cut her loose, send her to the seas, or give her to one of the village men, maybe a warrior."

Without responding, if possible his face grew darker, hardened even more grimly and rigid. He kept moving up the stairs.

"Kultur!" Darathia called up the stairs. "I will make plans for her!"

His long legs strode so fast he was almost dragging Sislla down the hall. He slowed at the door to his chamber as if considering something, then shook his head and continued to her room.

Unlocking the door, he handed her inside then about closed the door in her face and locked it.

He turned to Ryan who had hurried up behind them. "You stay in front of this door. I don't want anyone to go in, or come out of this room except Onani. Kirman Jaspar will relieve you in the morning, then I want you two to take shifts until I tell you otherwise." He leaned in towards Ryan, the young Kirman tried not to bend back from his livid eyes like fierce ravens glittering at him.

The timber low and strained, like he was doing everything he could to keep his temper tamped, Kultur said, "I repeat. You do not leave this door for any reason. Kirman Jaspar will be receiving the same instructions from me. If something odd occurs, you tell Onani or someone else to go and get Lucas. I will be out of the area for a few days. The ill are to be sent away until further notice. That is all."

He swiveled on his heel and stalked away down the hall, even the walls seemed to shudder from the big man's anger.

Chapter Twenty

Kultur's best friend, Danel had sent word. His coded few words indicated they caught another stranger. An unmarked stranger.

Kultur and Gabriel rode without a sound through the woods, a day's march to where Danel was holed up. Danel had been on the far side of the forest tracking rogue Tenthekens when he captured the stranger.

The brothers slipped through the dense forest until they came to a crooked tree. Kultur whistled as they approached. The horses stood almost completely still, even their tails didn't swish.

A man was only as good a warrior as his horse was trained. Too many had been ambushed, killed because their horse's tail brushed a bush or a hoof stomped or a snort echoed.

In moments, a man emerged from the woods, invisible and soundlessly as if he was a tree come to life.

Kultur and Gabriel dismounted and left their horses knowing the mounts would not leave, and followed the man back into the woods.

A few yards in and they came upon a large shed that was built of timber and so covered with leaves and dirt it was not discernible in the forest. At the door, Kultur asked, "How did you find him?"

Danel, as big, broad and powerfully built as the two brothers grinned. Being outside most of the time his skin was tanned dark and weathered. He looked older than Kultur but they had grown up playing as toddlers together.

His brown hair was shorn close to this head. Keen eyes, a rare golden color like Araina's, shone light like dark yellow finches against his darkened skin smiled warmly at his friend.

Scratching a few days' growth of bristled stubble, Danel set his hand on the doorknob and said, "He was stupid and clumsy. Obviously not used to being in the timberland, or outside at all. Has to be a city fella from across the sea. I heard him crashing and lumbering through the woods cursing a blue streak.

"I stood next to a tree and as he stepped past loud as an ox in a glass house, I slugged him once. He dropped like a sack of turnips. I hauled him inside and sent word to you."

"You said he's unmarked?" Gabriel asked, sharing a look with his brother.

"Yes. Otherwise I would have just questioned him then killed him." He opened the door and the three men went inside.

A few small windows let in a thrift of light in the dim room. Smelling of old musty wood, the room, more like a cabin, was large, only one room with a counter in the corner for a kitchen and supplies.

A few plain wooden chairs as well as a couple of cushioned chairs, worn with stuffing poking out, and a couch that was also a bed, and a small square table were the only furniture. A bow and sheath of arrows, swords and other weapons leaned against a wall by the front door.

In the center of the room was a man tied to a chair. He wasn't a small man, maybe around mid-forties, he looked fairly strong but he didn't look hardened and crafty like a warrior. His skin was dirty, sunburnt and covered with scratches.

He looked like he'd been wandering around in the forest for a few weeks. Even under the filth, the shock of light hair, almost as fair as Sislla's, was noticeable, and his eyes were a light grey, they were pinpointed with terror at the three men.

Kultur halted to stand about two feet directly in front of him with Gabriel and Danel flanking him on either side.

"What is your name?" Kultur asked, his calm voice jarred with the dead ice in his dark eyes.

The bruise Danel had given him colored purple under one eye. Trying to look brave and irritated, the man said with an affronted air, "I don't have to tell you anything."

Gabriel took a step forward and punched the man and was back standing still before the man even felt the slug.

His mouth bleeding, the man now cowered behind his hair that hung long over his gaunt face, his frantic eyes peered through the dirty blond locks in a panic at the men. He struggled in vain to quell his trembling lips.

As mischievous and playful as Gabriel normally was, he was just as lethally cold now. His hazelnut eyes were absent of any kindness or mercy. Without a trace of emotion, he said, "You can die quickly, or not. It's up to you."

The small room was cramped with massive amounts of testosterone exuding from the three big warriors waiting for the stranger's response.

His gulp palpable, the man's voice wobbled as he said, "My name is Apris Tinnian," the words gushed out before his throat closed in fright. The light eyes swung back and forth between Kultur and Gabriel then to Danel.

Even when he clocked him and brought him to the cabin and tied him up, and searched every inch of his skin, Apris shivered anew at the remembrance, Danel had never said one word to him.

The way Danel had studied his flesh, Apris thought he was considering, cooking- and eating him. When he hadn't, Apris sighed in relief when Danel had left the shed, until now.

Apris glanced at Gabriel who stood with his hands loose at his side revealing none of the tight energy coiled in his body. He was a warrior, designed to spring into combat in less than a blink of an eye.

Kultur was the same, but he had a deadly calm, cool detachment that differed from the aura of eagerness to get to fighting in Gabriel.

Penetrating Tinnian's skull from the abyss of his ebony eyes, Kultur questioned, "Where are you from?"

When Tinnian hesitated, Gabriel slammed him again, then stood back as if he hadn't moved at all.

Tinnian's head snapped to the right with Gabriel's punch, blood spurted from his nose, then his head bobbed back center. He looked up at Kultur with unfocused eyes. "I...I am from Ghesecular Providence."

"Where is that in location to this island?" Kultur asked.

Sniffing back blood, Tinnian licked his bleeding lip. "It is two months of travel across the sea towards the west." His head hung, he was afraid to look into Kultur's soulless orbs.

With calm ease, Kultur asked, "You came with Sislla?"

The pop of uncertain light in Tinnian's eyes told Kultur the answer.

Tinnian's wavering gaze flit around the room as he considered his answer. Gabriel raised a fist, Apris quickly croaked out, "Yes, yes, we arrived here together."

Kultur moved to crouch in front of Tinnian. Bound to the chair, the stranger backed as far away from him as he could, the sheer unemotional ice in the depth of the endless blackness made him mind-numbing terrified.

"Listen to me, Apris Tinnian, I will only say this once. You will tell me, from the start, how you got here, why you are here, and precisely who Sislla is and what happened to her once she arrived on this land."

His expression like uncompassionate granite, Kultur continued. "If you stop talking, if you don't answer properly, if you lie," he stood up. "By the way, in this land, many have the gift of hearing the inside of a person's mind. My friend Danel here," he nodded to his friend who stared with empty ghostlike eyes at Apris, "is one of those people. He will be keenly aware if you lie."

Kultur clasped his hands behind his back in a casual, faux benign stance. He waited until Apris raised his shaking gaze up to him. "Now, start at the beginning."

Apris blinked at the sweat that dripped in his eyes, coughed out some blood and said in a slow rasp, "We were sent here."

Gabriel interrupted, "But this island is unknown to all, and almost impossible to get to. How did you know about it?"

Licking his lips, bone dry except for the bleeding cut, Apris said, "A man came upon the island many years ago by accident. He was able to scout the land without being seen, got back in his boat and travelled home. He was wealthy and powerful, but his dynasty began crumbling under growing debt when he remembered this place."

Apris sucked in a shaky heaving breath and swallowed the blood that flowed in his mouth and nose. The three warriors remained silent, but their expressions clearly read pain and death to the stranger.

Another shuddering breath and Apris went on, "Uh, he, the explorer, recalled the island's lush meadows filled with ripe fruit, unique papyrus to build unsinkable ships, stones that heated homes without fire or smoke, and a font of metals and gems. It came to him that he could take over this…land and reap its assets. So he made a plan." Apris broke into paroxysms of coughing.

The three men waited until Apris caught his breath and was able to speak again. The coughing ceased and now he heaved in shallow rasping breaths.

"The plan was?" Gabriel prompted him to continue.

Apris' head bobbed slightly in a weak nod. "The wealthy man had learned in his time here that a mighty, unbeatable warlord," he glanced at Kultur, "was ruthless in his quest to keep the island remaining pure and simple, archaic even and safe from intruders. Judging by your looks and demeanor," Apris eyed Kultur's hard expression, his cadaverous black orbs revealing nothing of his thoughts. He started coughing again.

Lucas helpfully slapped him very hard on the back.

Apris' eyes watered at the smack. Blinking hard, he said, "It was probably your father. King, uh," he looked up, squinted, trying to remember. "Yes, it was Atraam Khonan Kultiran. Black hair and eyes, cutthroat and feral, huge and powerfully built, like you. Even down to the same dimple in your left cheek."

Kultur nodded. Gabriel crossed his arms over his chest, braced his legs, feet planted on the wood floor. Danel stayed motionless and silent.

Gabriel said, "He was our father, continue. What was the plan?"

After another brief coughing fit, Apris swallowed more blood in his mouth and said, "We've had a few other citizens make it here and back. They advised that Khonan Kultiran had passed, and his son, Kultur Kultiran, was now Atraam. His plan was to send an extremely innocuous person to the island and have that person insinuate themselves into the stronghold of the Chamaine-Gris. Get inside the Castle Aenlic, and..." he gulped, gasped for air that was trapped in his terrified throat.

Gabriel punched him. Apris' head snapped again, when it bounced back a cut over his eye bled profusely. Gabriel commanded, "My brother said spit it out without hesitation."

Tilting his head back, Apris shook it to get the sweat out of his eyes then dropped forward staring at the floor. "The person was to get close to Atraam Kultur Kultiran, and, kill him."

The blood rushed into Kultur's head, he could feel Gabriel tighten beside him. Getting a grip, Kultur said, "And who was this person?"

His voice hushed out with a bit of thin air, "Sislla. The woman you mentioned."

There was stark silence in the room. Kultur could feel his brother's eyes on him. He ignored him. He had a gut feeling about Sislla and his gut feelings were never wrong.

Keeping his hands clasped behind his back, Kultur said, "This Sislla, tell us what happened to her when you came ashore."

Feeling this was a safer topic, Apris' voice firmed. He snorted, then sniffed back blood, swallowed with a twisted mouth.

Stretching his neck, he coughed and told them, "The bitch argued and fought with me the entire way here." He didn't catch Kultur's and Gabriel's arched brows and quick, almost knowing smirks at each other. "Her orders were to get here, as I said, insinuate herself into the Chamaine-Gris stronghold, get into the keep, and hopefully gain entrance to the Castle so she could get close to-" he gulped, swallowed hard, "ah, you, and kill you, Kultiran."

Kultur and Gabriel's expressions were stoic, unmoving and unreadable.

He continued, "Once you were eliminated, as the biggest landowner and the most powerful faction, the Chamaine-Gris would become weakened, enough that the other two factions would wipe you all out then fight each other, furthering weakening any stronghold on the island. I would return home with the good news, then our own troops could come and easily take over the entire island."

"Hmmm," Kultur pondered. "How was this woman to get away? It would seem she would most likely be caught either in the castle or quickly outside as she tried to escape."

For once Apris' countenanced hardened. He shrugged. "It didn't matter. She had a mission to complete, it didn't matter how it ended for her." He didn't see the narrowing of Kultur's obsidian eyes shielding his thoughts.

"So," Kultur said, "she argued about what on the way here?"

Apris snorted a laugh. "She said she would not kill anyone. Not the Atraam, or anyone. I told her she had no choice. She had been specifically, physically, put into the boat for the soul mission to come here and kill...you."

Rolling his eyes, he groused, "It had been so damned annoying. They threw her aboard kicking and screaming, until the master came aboard and had a...serious...discussion with her. When he left, there were actual fingerprints around her neck. She was quiet after that. Until we were days out at sea, then she started again with her protests."

"Hell," Apris' snorting laugh turned ugly. "I thought we could at least fool around to while away the time, but she was seasick most of the time and threatened to throw up on me if I came near her, the little sow."

Biting back his grin, Gabriel asked, "What happened when you came ashore?"

Apris rolled his eyes. "That's when the shit hit the fan. I told her she could probably get work as a maid, or as comely as she is, a concubine, whatever, anything to get inside your castle. Then I tried to give her a knife she could hide on her person, secret it into the castle and kill you with it. But," he sighed aggravated at the memory, "she refused. Said she wasn't killing anyone, that she would take herself out before she did, then she started back towards the water.

"I chased after her, asked her what the hell she thought she was doing. '*Killing myself*' she said, the dumb bitch." He shook his head in disbelief. "She was knee deep in the sea about to drown herself when I caught up with her."

"So? She's not dead, what happened?" Gabriel prodded, his gaze flipped to his brother and back to Apris.

Apris' mouth curled in a vicious snarl. "Boy did she piss me the fuck off. I dragged her out of the ocean by that beautiful hair of hers and up the side of the mountain of the cove where we'd come ashore. I thought I could still talk some sense into her. But no," he sneered, shaking his head, face red with anger.

"The fucking bitch just flat out refused. Then I thought we could at least have a little fun now that we were out of that endless sea. But no. I mean, fuck, so what if she was a virgin? She would have to give it up sometime anyway. I put a couple of moves on her and she knees me in the nuts."

He shrugged, twitching his head to toss his sweaty hair out of his eyes and said matter-of-factly, "So I beat her fucking senseless." He dug in a deep wheezing breath.

Gabriel held a hand out to still his brother. He could feel Kultur burn, about to attack the man and tear him to shreds. He said to Apris, "Then what happened?"

He let out a long laborious sigh. "When she came to, I gave her one more chance to agree to the assassination. Still, she refused. So, I threw her off the cliff. I assumed she landed on the rocky shore and then the tide would wash her back out to the raging sea. The body would never be-" he suddenly looked with wary incredulity at Kultur, "did you say she was still alive?"

Gabriel murmured to Kultur, "She must have hit her head hard on a rock or the ground, that would have caused the amnesia."

"Who sent Sislla here?" Kultur asked Tinnian.

Apris again gave an unconcerned shrug, and replied, "Haarold Andersson, her grandfather."

The two brothers couldn't hide their shock. Gabriel said with dismay, "Sislla's own grandfather sent her here, to certain death?"

A corner of his bloody lip pulled in, Apris sniffed in blood then spat it on the floor. "Yeah, so what? Nothing as simple as kin would get in the way of Haarold Andersson claiming the riches of this land. He planned on slaughtering all of you, what's the difference in one small girl?"

A hint of hope in his voice, he said, "So, I've told you everything, will you let me go? Maybe give me a boat so I can get back home? My boat was dashed against the shore, crushed and splintered into pieces."

He looked a bit peaked when he said, "Uh, I was going to have to take over her task, you know, assassinate you, King Kultiran, but," he grinned sheepishly, wincing at his split lip. "Now of course I will abort that mission. You can feel assured I will simply board whatever boat you allow me and off I'll go. No harm no foul? Right?"

Kultur turned on his heel and strode out the door. Gabriel and Danel followed him. Kultur went straight to his horse and mounted.

Gabriel did the same then grimly saluted his goodbye to Danel.

Danel asked Kultur calmly, "What shall I do with him?"

Grabbing up the reins in one hand, as he jerked them for the horse to move, Kultur said, "I don't care how you do it. As long as he can't return home and tell what happened, or harm Sislla." He shook off the sound of Sislla's gentle voice in his head saying,

'*Mercy, Kultur.*' Fuck that, Apris Tinnian was yet another who had shown Sislla no mercy.

He snapped the reins on the horse's back and the brothers galloped off through the forest.

Danel casually strolled back into the cabin.

The brothers passed through the village. Clusters of stone and thatch houses knotted the valley and the foothills. Evening had fallen, a few villagers were out and about tending to animals or last minute chores, or just visiting. They waved to them as they trotted by.

The Keep was quiet. Kirmen guarded the village and clustered throughout the Keep on watch.

When they dismounted at the stables, Gabriel asked, "You going to tell her?"

Kultur shook his head. "No."

Gabriel gaped at him in surprise. "Why not? She has a right to know who she is, K."

"If I tell her she will leave," Kultur replied impassively.

The light eyes shot a sideways glance of surprised query. "So what? Besides, why would she?" He watched his brother's nonchalance. "Or more importantly, how would she leave?"

Kultur stopped walking. Holding his horse's reins, he ran his hand down the side of the stallion's belly and then down his long nose. "She will feel obligated to return to her homeland where she probably has family, mother, father, siblings..."

"A boyfriend, husband," Gabriel inserted, smirking at Kultur's frown. "Anyway, like I said, how would she get home? Her land is months of travel away by sea."

One shoulder bumped up in a half-shrug. "She is smart and resourceful. The people are always trying to pay her with food, jewels, etc. for her healing, she could accept a boat as payment."

"You think she would go on the high seas alone? A lone woman?" Gabriel sounded like he didn't think it was possible.

"She would have to. If anyone went with her, they are marked. The Iminims would detect them and be on them like a

fucking magnet. She wouldn't put someone else in that jeopardy."
Kultur started walking into the stable.

Following him, Gabriel asked, "K, you really think she would
hop in a boat and go it alone, especially not even knowing where
she was going?"

"Oh, I know she would. She'll think somehow she'll just
automatically float there or something. She's smart but not too
worldly, quite naive. She would hate that she was sent here to kill
me, she would hate that Apris Tinnian, was...disposed of...
because of her. She would feel bad that her family would be
worried for her. She is one stubborn, selfless, hard-headed little
female."

He reached for a bucket to get food for his horse before he
rubbed him down. "Oh aye, she would go. And she would die out
there, alone. Either by the treacherous sea itself or starvation, or
by the Iminims. Stubborn wench." His horse stepped sideways
from him at his irritated growl. "She doesn't know it yet, but she
will get marked and will then be forced to stay here."

"Stubborn, huh. Sounds like someone else I know." Gabriel
grinned at his brother, a twinkle in his light brown eyes. "You two
would make a helluva hard-headed pair. The rest of the world
wouldn't stand a chance if you two hooked up and ran this
kingdom."

Kultur ignored him, filling the bucket with food.

"But, K, she's is going to be one mighty pissed off woman
when she finds out you knew the truth about her and didn't tell
her."

"I know." Kultur's mouth tightened grimly, he brought the
bucket of feed to his horse. "Only you and Danel know, you two
will keep your mouths shut. She shouldn't ever find out."

Chapter Twenty-One

The next day Kultur allowed Sislla to return to her workshop.

The people lined up every morning. But after three hours, Ryan, or whoever was guarding her that day closed the shop up and she was escorted back to her room to eat lunch.

She usually ate with Lexi. The girls gossiped and giggled about the other residents of the castle. Lexi confided about her burgeoning romance with Van.

Several days passed uneventfully. Kultur spent from dawn to past dusk in the field training his men. Today he felt like cutting the day short, he thought maybe he and Sislla could visit over an early dinner. He hadn't seen much of her; apparently she was managing to stay out of trouble. The corner of his lip pulled up, yeah sure, and the sky is green.

When he went in through the front door of the castle into the great room, he stood stunned with his mouth hanging open.

The room was filled wall to wall with young men. A few women wandered around, but it was 95% men. He saw his mother near the bar they set up when they had parties, and waded through the crowd to her.

"Mother," he said when he reached her.

She smiled broadly at her son. "Darling," she kissed him on the cheek. She was wearing a fancy, long printed skirt with frilly white blouse, a sparkling red necklace with matching earrings; her

165

hair was in an intricate swirl around her head. With a glass of wine in her hand, she was chatting quite animatedly with a clutch of young men.

"Mother, what is going on?" His gaze traveled the room. He recognized many of the young men, many of his warriors were present.

"Why don't you get yourself something to drink, honey, or," her eyes took in his rough clothes, grass stained and dirty, his hair was damp with sweat and he had a heavy five o'clock shadow. "I suppose you should go and get cleaned up first."

He growled crossly in her ear, "I asked you what is this all about? Answer me, I am quickly losing my patience."

Darathia held the stem of her wine glass with both hands down in front of her. "Well, I told you that, that creature you insist on keeping as some kind of a pet needed marking, and you refused to do anything about it, so I took matters into my own hands. I invited the eligible Chamaine-Gris young men to come and meet her."

Araina popped up out of nowhere and wrapped her hands around Kultur's arm. Trying to grasp what his mother was saying he ignored her. "For *kriités* sake, what are you talking about, Mother?"

Her eyes rolled, "Darling, exactly what I said. She should easily be able to quickly choose one of these fine men to mark her. He can begin the deed this weekend, when the first golden moon rises. I'm sure this meet will work out better than the one I did for you." She had been scathing to anyone within earshot the evening she'd brought all those single women to him and he'd up'd and left before anything had even gotten started and fled up the stairs with that- *foreigner*.

"What the hell are you saying?"

"Darling, don't sound so grumpy because you didn't think of it yourself. It's only a matter of time before these young wolves come after her anyway. The only thing that has held them off is that she is here under such tight guard. But now, I've brought the candy store to her!"

She went to slip her hand through Kultur's other arm. "Isn't that a grand plan, son?" Darathia smiled broadly and proudly surveying her handy-work. The room teemed with young men.

Looking out under his ridge of hard brow, Kultur searched the room crowded with horny young men, and not seeing the bright ringlets anywhere, ground out through clenched teeth, "Where is she?"

Araina pawed him while Darathia glanced around. "Oh, I think she said something about just wanting a glass of water. The cretin doesn't care for alcohol, she might have gone to the kitchen. I had to have her dragged out of that workshop of hers and practically tied down to get an appropriate dress on her. For heaven's sake, she fought me tooth and nail. So darling, what do you think of-"

Shaking both women loose, Kultur muscled his way through the crowd, then stormed down a short hall to the kitchen.

There was a big kitchen for the parties and a smaller more intimate one for the occupants of the castle to use. He pushed the café doors open and instantly saw Sislla across the room. She wasn't alone. She was with a man.

Sislla was pushed up smack hard against the wall, the young man had one hand curled over her neck trying to hold her head still, and the other was making its way up her skirt, the side of his hip pressed against hers pinning her to the wall.

Whipping her head back and forth to keep the man's mouth off hers and pushing at his hands, Sislla cried, "Let go of me, Sergei! Stop this!"

Sergei's predatory smile did nothing to mar his handsome face. With classical good looks and a full head of wavy brown hair, he was used to women falling at his feet. His hand still on her neck he grasped her jaw hard to hold it still.

"Come on honey, you want it. Atra Darathia served you up on a silver platter. But, I don't mind a little playing hard to get, it just ups the anticipation. Now spread those pretty legs for me," he forced his mouth over hers stifling her scream and shoved his hand up her skirt.

Sergei was jerked so hard off Sislla she almost fell over with him. Kultur grabbed Sergei with two hands and hurled him across the kitchen into the wall.

Before he landed, Kultur was tramping over to him. He bent, clutched the front of the young man's shirt and pulled him to his feet then slammed his fist into his face. Sergei was a big strong fellow but Kultur lifted him off his feet and pulled his fist back to strike him again.

"Kultur!" Sislla flew over and threw herself between the two men before Kultur could hit him again.

His voice tight with drenching fury, Kultur ordered, "Get out of the way, Sislla." He tried to move her aside with his arm, but she clung to it with both hands.

"No, let him go, please." She said it so quietly it permeated Kultur's brain harder than a shout would have.

Kultur lowered his fist and released Sergei's shirt. The young man ran before Kultur could change his mind. His eyes on Sislla, Kultur didn't watch Sergei flee. His gaze swept the red dress his mother had forced her into.

It skimmed her body tightly from the bodice to her hips then it flared out to the floor. The neckline was scandalously low exposing a lot of her soft, round breasts which rose and fell with her distraught breaths.

It took an effort to pull his eyes away. Without a word, he took her hand and led her through a back staircase up to the floor their chambers were on.

He brought her to her room and took her inside. Pulling out the vanity chair, he pointed and instructed, "Have a seat, Sislla, we're going to have a talk." Squelching his ire with difficulty, he raked his fingers through his hair several times.

Unnerved at what happened downstairs and now the way Kultur's artic obsidian eyes glittered dangerously at her, he was so tensely wound she could feel it. Sislla sat down. She tried not to shrink back from him when he came to stand nearer to her, yet she did.

His eyes narrowed, vexed at her fear of him. He stepped back a bit, spread his legs a foot apart and crossed his arms. His long-sleeved white shirt was clotted with grass stains and dirt, his breeches had mud on them and his boots were dusty.

He wished he'd had time to clean up before having this talk, but it had to be done now. His mother had pushed the matter and now he didn't have the time to do this more...pleasantly.

"Sislla, you are aware of why my mother brought those men here today?" He watched the scarlet color her face, she looked away and nodded.

A deep breath flowed out; he took another one in and said, "You must be marked. I had hoped to do this in a...slower, smoother...way, but, it is unfortunate that my mother has rushed the issue."

Sislla opened her mouth to reply but he said evenly, "I will mark you." His lips pulled in as he waited for her reaction. As he feared, the color now drained from her face as her mouth dropped open.

She stood up, whispered, *"No,"* and started to walk away. He grabbed her wrist holding her back.

"It has to be done, Sislla. You understand enough about why by now, and you must have already accepted it." But she hadn't. He could tell by the distress rapidly clouding her blue eyes.

Tugging at her wrist, she adamantly shook her head. "No. If I am marked I will be forced to stay here. I can't do that."

Refusing to release her, he said crossly, "Why not? What is wrong with this island? This castle? The land is beautiful and fruitful, the castle is big and strong and warm, it's modern and attractive, you have every comfort. You love to heal the people. Why can't you be content to stay here?" He drew her close to him so she had to look into his eyes.

He could see his reflection in her big, crystal blue orbs. His face was hard angled and grim, covered in dark stubble he looked downright menacing.

Fierceness smoldered in the dark depths of his eyes, and he towered over her, she was so dainty in his hand. Along with notorious ruthless violence, he was also known for possessing an ice cold soul; he could easily understand her fear of him. But that was too bad. She would learn to be at ease with him.

"I can't stay here, Kultur, this is not my home. I have a family...out there," she arced her arm, "somewhere."

Gabriel's comment about a boyfriend or husband rankled in Kultur's ears. He didn't care who she had at home waiting for her, her home was here now. She could not go back. Some day she would understand it and accept it. For now, she had to be made ready.

Without warning, he slid his large hand along the side of her jaw. His fingers cupping the back of her head, he lowered his mouth on hers. Her lips parted in surprise, and he used it to his advantage and thrust his tongue inside.

Letting go of her wrist, he rolled his arm around her back holding her close and ravaged her mouth, tasting, licking with heady desire, he sucked her lips taking control of her. When she brought her hands up to push against his chest and tried to move her mouth from his, he released her, she stumbled backwards, the back of her hand pressed over her mouth.

Feeling the innocence in her response to his kiss, he asked, "Sislla, are you a virgin?" Then he remembered Apris had said she was.

The back of her hand over her stunned mouth, her face turned blank. He could see her struggle to remember.

Tears formed in her eyes. She said in a hushed voice, "I don't know." Embarrassed at his question, and shocked at his behavior, she dashed in confusion at the spilling tears with her palms. "Go away, leave me alone."

He stared at her for a frozen second, his burning eyes on her trembling mouth behind her hand, craving to taste her again.

Instead, he strode to the door and flung it open. "It will be done. I will come for you on Saturday, the first golden moon. Be ready."

As soon as the door closed, Sislla let out her held breath. Weak at the knees, she staggered to the vanity and flopped down. She looked in the mirror like she was looking at a stranger, which, basically because of the amnesia, she was.

There was a soft knock at the door. Too soft to be Kultur returning. She rose unsteadily and opened the door. It was Lexi.

Lexi slipped in with a half sad, half happy, guilty look on her face. Her dark wavy hair was tied up in a bouncy ponytail, a smattering of light freckles trickled over her nose and cheeks. "Sis," she whispered.

Sislla closed the door and sat down with a heavy groan onto the chair. Tears streamed down her face, she crossed her arms on the vanity and dropped her head onto them. "Lexi, you won't believe-"

"Uh, yeah I would." Lexi's face tinged with pink and a lop-sided grin. "Ryan and I were listening at the door." She trod lightly over to her friend. "Why are you so upset? You will stay here and become family, I am so excited!"

Sislla raised her head, her eyes red with tears. "I can't stay here, I have to return to my home. Your brother, he wants to- to, uh, be with me, he's going to mark me, how can he just," the red eyes looked at Lexi with extreme embarrassment, and fear.

"Are you scared of him?" Lexi pulled a chair over to her and sat down. "He's big and extraordinarily strong, rugged and tough, damned overbearing, and yeah, prone to extreme violence, and that cold hard temper of his, yeah he can be-"

"You're not helping, Lex." Sislla wiped at her tears.

"Yeah, well, I've never heard that he damaged any of the uh, women he's been with, actually, to think about it, they could have been easily disposed of and no one would know-"

"Lexi!" Sislla shrieked. "Stop it!"

With an abashed slight grin, Lexi muttered, "Sorry."

"Oh, Lex, what am I going to do?"

Lexi thought about the situation and shrugged. "Sislla, there's really nothing you can do. You have to be marked or you will die, a terrible death, and, Kultur says he will do it. Take my word for it, when my brother says he's going to do something, nothing will stop him. He's like a charging bull."

Sislla smiled sarcastically through her tears. "Gee, Lex, thanks for making me feel so much better."

Lexi scooted her chair closer, leaned over and hugged Sislla, "Sis, that's what friends are for!"

Chapter Twenty-Two

She should have figured it. It was Saturday, and Sislla had gone and hidden somewhere. He had specifically told her to be in his chambers at six o'clock.

It was now seven. Damn the woman. He wanted her to come to him so she would feel she had some control of the situation, that she was acquiescing to what they were about to do.

Cursing, Kultur went in search of her. His mother was having a party in one of the downstairs salons. He didn't think she'd be in there, but he'd looked pretty much everywhere else.

As he stepped over the threshold, he didn't have to search long. She was on the far side of the soft peach room standing amidst a group of people. He knew she saw him, her face suddenly paled. *Great*, she was still terrified of him. That's not going to help the evening.

Nonetheless, he started to move through the crowded sea of people when someone unexpectedly threw themselves at his back and wrapped their arms around his waist.

His instinct was to throw his head back and head butt them then twist and snap their neck before they could hit him or use a weapon.

However, he was in the castle, in the bright, cheery salon with its white furniture and peach and white cushions, and his mother was holding court in the middle of the room. Therefore, he hesitated.

173

"Kultur, darling," Araina purred seductively in his ear while stroking her hands over his chest. "Sons above, you have such a ripped chest, and oh," her hands stroked lower over his abdomen, "you are so hard and shredded. Your chambers are on the second floor, why don't we just go up-"

"Sorry, Araina," Kultur clinched her wrists, pulled her hands off him and swiveled her around to face him. "I have plans."

Leaving her standing with her mouth open, he elbowed his way through the room straight to Sislla. He didn't see the venomous look Araina lashed at Sislla.

"Don't pretend you don't know I'm here, Sislla," his deep voice rumbled next to her ear. Even without seeing him come in, he knew she had felt the undercurrent of the room change when he arrived.

He didn't touch her but he knew she could feel his heat burning her from inches away. His cool breath stirred her hair into the side of her face.

Still, she refused to acknowledge him. Instead, she observed both Araina's and Darathia's furious glares at her.

"If you don't come with me peacefully, *koritsi*, I will throw you over my shoulder and carry you out in front of everyone, and they will know why." He slid his hand around her settling it on the curve of her waist.

That was when her body started trembling. She fought to control it, but she knew he had to be well aware of it with his big manly paw on her. When he started to nudge her forward, she didn't struggle. The fight wasn't over, but she wasn't going to go at it in this room full of people.

The closer they get to his room the slower Sislla trudged. Kultur was almost dragging her. He wrapped an arm around her shoulder to keep her up with him.

His voice short and brusque he said, "Stop acting like you're on your way to the gallows, Sislla." He opened the door and drew her inside, releasing her to shut the door.

Her voice small and tight, she said, "You tell me you have to rape me to save my life, to prevent me from ever returning to my home, it is the gallows, Kultur."

He moved to stand in front of her and grasped her upper arms. "I don't want to force you, Sislla. I don't assault women. This is a necessity and you damn well know it. I've explained it, Lexi has explained it, it has to be done. Please don't make me force you."

He stroked a knuckle gently over her pale cheek. "Be a willing partner, *tiris koritsi,* my little foreigner, I will make it good for you, I promise you."

He moved his knuckle under her chin to raise it so she had to look at him. "We don't know if you are a virgin or not, I think you are. Nonetheless," he ignored the red flushing her face, "I will be gentle, we'll go slow, if you cooperate it shouldn't hurt."

Her yellow brows slashed down in anger. "Cooperate in my own rape? No, Kultur, I will not cooperate. You know I don't want to be marked. You know I need to return home," she jerked away from him.

She could hear his heavy, exasperated sigh from a few feet away. Maybe she could lock herself in the bathroom until the stupid golden moon passed. She suddenly lunged to run to the bathroom-

He caught her in two steps. Flinging his arms around her, he pulled her, pressing her back against his chest. Then, he wound his arms tightly around her, holding her arms down so she couldn't move them, and held her while she struggled and screamed. Good thing the castle was built so strongly it was soundproof.

After a few minutes of her violently trying to break free of him, he said quietly in her ear, "Stop this, *koritsi,* I fear you will hurt yourself."

Ignoring him, she kept twisting and squirming. Her hair was pinned up on her head, he sighed against her ear, blowing tendrils,

"Sislla, I am over twice as big, a hundred times stronger than you, and a fierce warrior. Do you think you can stop me with your womanly struggles? Please, don't fight me, be with me in this, enjoy our joining."

"No!" she exclaimed, twisting and jerking harder in his arms.

"Fine," he sighed again. "I will try not to hurt you. You will forgive me one day."

In a shot, he bent and grabbed one of her feet and yanked her shoe off and then did the other. Before she could stand again on both feet, he grasped her wrists and pulled them gently behind her lower back and held them there with one of his hands while still keeping her back against his chest.

Her body turned rigid when his loose hand went to the top button of her dress. He deftly unbuttoned it and then went to the next one.

"Kultur, please, I'm begging you, don't do this!" She tried to bend over to stop his hands but to no avail.

He whispered against the side of her face, "Don't fight me, *koritsi*," but when he went for the next button and the next she fought and squirmed with all her might. He could feel she had no bindings on under the dress. His mother no doubt wanted to entice the men with Sislla's physical delights.

"Why don't you just push me down and do the damned deed, Kultur," she sobbed, her chest heaving. "Just do it and get it over with and let me go. You don't need to undress me."

He murmured against her face, "Because I don't want to hurt you. I have to make you ready to receive me." A few more buttons parted, his lips pressed against her cheek. He murmured tenderly, "Because I don't want you to remember this day with pain and fear and horror."

"Too late," she mumbled.

Still holding her wrists behind her, he skimmed his hand up under her chin, held it and took possession of her mouth.

Her attempts to fight his kiss were as futile as her struggles to get out of his grip. He tasted her lips, her teeth, her tongue, tugged on the pout of her upper lip then moved his mouth to her neck.

"Sons above, you taste even better than I remembered. You have a lovely slender neck, *koritsi*," he sucked down the length of her neck, and at the same time releasing her, he used both hands and pushed down the front of her dress exposing her breasts.

He did it so smoothly and quickly it was a few beats before she reacted. "*Kultur!*" Her freed hands flew up to cover her breasts.

He wound his fingers gently around her wrists and pulled her hands away and behind her. "Look how beautiful you are, *koritsi,*" he nodded towards a full-length mirror on the wall in front of them. He carefully pushed her dress down until she was bare to her hips, like an hourglass with a skirt.

She kept her head down, refusing to look at her nudity.

He cupped her chin and raised it. "Open your eyes and look."

She did, slowly, fretfully. She saw him with his lips on her bare shoulder, his hair hanging over one eye.

He looked up at her through the lock of black hair and smiled at their reflection. "Your breasts are perfect, *koritsi,* soft and round, there is no other woman in this land as breathtaking as you."

Sislla had never looked at herself naked in the mirror before, it would be like looking at a stranger, too weird. But this was shocking, and mortifying, and...mesmerizing.

Her skin was pearly luminescent, her breasts plump and high, her waist curved in, her hips flared out. He released her hands; she immediately used them to cover herself.

Kultur watched her watching them in the mirror. He brought his big hands up and pushed his palms under hers to close over her breasts. His darker skin a contrast to her fairness. Her fingers wrapped around the backs of his hands, shyly tugging them off her.

He let her go and turned her around to face him; before she could catch her balance he cupped her breasts again and leaned over first kissing each one then sucking them. He tugged a nipple into his mouth and Sislla surprised them both with a moan.

Her neck seemingly of its own volition, arched back. His mouth moved to her throat, kissing her skin and biting it gently but with pressure while he kneaded her supple globes. Then he licked his way back up to her mouth and captured her lips.

He pushed at her mouth with his tongue and was surprised again, and pleased when she opened it. Nibbling at her lips, he swirled his tongue inside. Sislla's own tongue came to join his, drawn to taste him too.

Kultur's ardor heated up at breakneck speed, his strong hands tightened on her breasts, his mouth intensified its exploration of hers. Kissing her hard, too roughly, he urgently tugged at her tongue with his teeth. Suddenly she stiffened and tried to push away from him.

He abruptly swung her around so her back was against his chest again and pushed her dress down to the floor.

He lifted her slightly and shoved the dress aside with his foot.

She was now clad in only a wisp of sheer white undergarment. In a panic, she tried to jerk hard and run but he caught her wrists and again held them behind her back in one hand.

Even as his other hand skimmed down her belly, she pleaded, "Don't Kultur."

His hand slid lower until he reached the sheer underwear and he cupped his hand over her mound.

Shocked, Sislla cried out and twisted violently from him.

"Shh, *koritsi.*" Holding her immobile, Kultur moved one of his feet between hers, pressing against her leg, making it almost impossible for her to move her body.

His mouth slid over her jaw, then her neck, nipping and kissing, continuing despite her struggles. He slid his hand inside her silk undergarment and touched her woman's core. She bucked against his hand and whimpered. When he stroked her tender sex with two thick fingers she froze.

He nudged her feet further apart with his foot and continued stroking her soft flesh while murmuring in her ear, "Shh, baby, relax, I swear it will be okay, just feel my fingers, get out of your head and into your body and feel my fingers against your soft skin."

He drew his fingers up the outside folds of her vulva then down over her sensitive slit. She shivered against his hand, he felt her silk dampen his fingers.

"Your body betrays you, *koritsi*, you are wet for me. I knew you would be all right if you let yourself relax." She stiffened at his words.

Frowning that he caused her to move back into her head, Kultur slid his fingers up her slit until he reached her young bud. Her whole body jumped at his touch, then shivered more violently than before. He ripped the undergarment off and dropped it.

Her body burned from his touch but she cried out fearfully, "Kultur, please, I'm...scared...I...don't..."

He released her wrists and crossed an arm over the front of her securing her taut against him, and holding her up at the same time.

"It's okay, it's okay, look at us," he murmured, his voice deep and husky with his own arousal.

Eyes frightened, yet the lids over them heavy with the feelings he was stirring in her body, Sislla peered at the mirror.

Under hanging locks of black hair, the onyx of his eyes blazed at hers in the reflection. The muscles in his arm bulged holding her up, she watched him rub her bud with one finger, then two, pressing it, stroking it, tugging on it until her legs grew rubbery and she leaned back into his chest, her eyes gleaming under limpid lids watching their reflection.

She watched his big body behind her, bracing her like a delicate white swan against his dark shirt and pants. His burly arm holding her with ease while his hand was over her sex. She could see his fingers stroking, touching her, "*Uhh,*" her moan came unbidden with another shiver.

Sislla couldn't believe she was standing there, totally nude, while a fierce strapping warlord, fully clothed, held her from running, or falling, so gently he would leave no bruises, while his fingers skillfully strummed and caressed her.

She could see his fingers touching her, it was strange to watch it across the room like it was happening to someone else, but actually feel it.

The skin of his arm tanned and covered with dark silky hair, he put his large hand against her white thigh and pushed it, spreading her legs further apart. He suddenly cupped her sex rough, hard, then let go.

When another moan escaped her, Kultur pinched her bud lightly and surfed his fingers over her wet opening. At her stiffening again, he murmured, "Shh," in her ear, stroking her core again, then feeling her wet silk on his hand he slipped just a fingertip inside her.

"Kultur, no!" in a panic she started fighting him.

He kept his arm wrapped around her holding her arms pinned down, and didn't stop stroking her sex, pressing and brushing and circling her clit until tiny moans purred from deep in her throat. His lips on her neck, he kissed her satin skin, licking and biting down to her jaw.

Her eyes back on the mirror, she saw his masculine lips sucking her firm flesh, leaving a trail of red marks.

He raised his hands and covered her breasts. Cradling them in his big palms he turned her slightly, bent over her and kissed first one rounded globe and then the other. He licked a nipple, lathing it, then sucked it then bit it until Sislla was now writhing in his arms.

Kultur slid his arm under her ribs to support her using that hand to still cup her breast while his mouth sucked and licked her skin. He lowered his other hand back down to stroke her clit, his eyes tilted up to watch their reflection.

This time she didn't freeze, her hips writhed gently. She was so wet when he dipped his finger inside her she didn't jerk away, her soft moan scraped up her throat. Both their eyes on the mirror, they watched him push his finger up in her gently; he groaned feeling her womanhood close around it.

He pulled his thick finger out slowly then carefully pushed it back in, waiting for her tight body to adapt to it before pressing it in a little further. It was odd watching themselves in the mirror, but hot, sexy.

Sislla was mortified, but the feeling was drifting away being replaced by such unfamiliar sensations that made her body ache and tingle and thrum, with what, she didn't know.

Pushing his finger gently in and drawing it out, sweat started gathering at his temples, feeling how small and tight she was, Kultur felt a twinge of concern.

She was a petite woman; he was a very big man. Maybe he should have given her to another male after all, a smaller one, one a less tough- he closed his eyes, he could never do that.

He wondered why she didn't question him as to why he was the one doing the marking. Even Gabriel had said he would be more than willing to do it.

Kultur bit back a wry grimace, Sislla was probably so scared and angry she wasn't thinking about anything other than this moment. Besides, he never would have given her away to another male, even to his brother.

He just needed to move very slow and very gently. He hoped he could, his body was already entering damned meteor streaking status. He needed to keep a tight lid on his intense desire for her or he'd be like an out of control shooting star and ride roughshod over her.

His erection was pounding so hard against her curvy little bottom he was amazed it wasn't freaking her out. Of course, if she was a virgin she might not be aware his body was indicating how badly he wanted her.

And he had wanted her badly ever since she looked up at him in such fright when Trogga had thrown her to the floor. Even plied with dirt, she was the most beautiful thing he'd ever seen in his life. In the back of his subconscious he had started plotting right then and there how to keep her.

Bending his head, his mouth seized hers; he closed over it, ransacking her tender sweetness like a tiger devouring its catch. He moved the hand between her legs to knead her breast then stroked it back down. Inserting his finger back inside her soft flesh, he thumbed her nub, feeling her moving against his hand, bucking at his fingers.

He kissed her, demanding everything she had while thrusting his finger faster and faster, until she was crying at his mouth. Her breaths fast and shallow, her spine arched, Kultur pulled his head back to watch her.

Sislla's face widened as if she were in pain, then scrunched, her lips parted, as her body grew rigid, Kultur whispered, "Let it go *koritsi,* I have you."

His arm tightened around her, his hand still grasped her breast, his finger thrust in and out of her and around her clit until she took a deep guttural breath. Kultur covered her mouth with his and took her scream right down his throat.

Her sex clenched his fingers, she thrashed against his hand then her knees buckled and she fell forward over his supporting arm, her body jerking with spasms and hoarse sobs.

He supported her as tremors shook her body. As they diminished, her breathing slowed, deepened. While he held her he plucked the pins out of her hair letting each one fall to the floor. Then he slipped his hands under her, lifting her into his arms he carried her to the bed and laid her down.

Looking down at her bountiful nakedness, Kultur kicked off his boots and started unbuttoning his shirt. Seeing him undressing, his lusty gaze, fiery onyx burning at her, Sislla pushed her loose tresses out of her face and off her shoulders.

Dazed, she blinked to clear her vision, shake off the impact of the orgasm. Licking her lips, she shifted up and started to skitter away from him.

Kultur put his knee on the bed and clinched her waist, pulling her back, he moved his knee to between her legs in a loose straddle to keep her pinned.

He murmured soothing, "It's okay, honey, don't be afraid. I swear it will be all right for you," and he quickly finished unbuttoning his shirt, tugged it off and tossed it to the floor.

Chapter Twenty-Three

Sislla's eyes were like huge blue moons looking at his mammoth chest rippling with muscles, dark hair matting it. Her awed gaze moved to his huge bulging biceps.

Watching her studying him so intently, his erection hardened to the point Kultur feared his pants would split before he could get them off.

He unbuckled his belt. Her attention dropped to his hands, watching him undo his breeches. He moved his leg off the bed, shoved the trousers down and off, putting his knee back on the mattress as she made a move to back away.

Her eyes popped with startled fright when she saw his heavy manhood swaying like a tree trunk.

Sislla gasped, "Stars above, no Kultur, please," the size of his hard thick shaft about took her breath away. Her heart thundered out of her chest, she rolled to the other side of the bed getting up to get away.

He reached out a long arm snagging her waist and pulled her back to the middle of the bed then climbed on the bed on both knees, the thick mattress barely sinking under his weight.

He put his big hand half on her breastbone, half on her collarbone, pressed her down on her back and rolled beside her.

As she moved away again he dropped his leg down between hers to hold her. The warmth of their skin touching sizzled up his body.

"Kultur, please, you're too- too big," she pushed at his chest as if she could actually move him away from her.

"Hush, *koritsi,* since we don't know your virginal state I will go very slowly. It will be easier for you if you go with me, don't fight me."

He covered her protests with his mouth and cradled her breast, kneading gently at first then as his erection enlarged even more, hardening like steel against the firm skin of her thigh, he squeezed her plump flesh harder, his kisses turned fierce. His increasing intensity didn't seem to scare her as he feared. Quite the opposite, it seemed to spur her own already primed desire to heighten.

Kultur bent his head to suckle her breast. Kissing her tender flesh, he tugged at her nipple with his lips then sucked all of the plump suppleness.

At the moan that trembled from her lips, he stroked his hand back down to her core to build her desire to breaking point again. Brushing and swirling, tugging and stroking her nub until she was panting and thrashing against the mattress. He circled her clit with his thumb and slipped in a finger, then a second one to stretch her.

At the intrusion, she started struggling again, pushing at his chest. His arm under her neck, Kultur caught her hand and held it; the other was trapped under his heavy body. He gently probed inside her, seeking her sweet spots and thumbed her nub until she was squirming again with passion.

"You're soaking wet for me, *koritsi,* you are ready to take me. Don't be afraid." His own body jacked up, he roughly seized her mouth, kissing her deeply and moved over her, and between her legs. Lifting his mouth from hers he gazed for a moment into her clear blue eyes.

"Sislla, I don't want to hurt you, I will be as gentle as I can at first until I see how much of me, and how much of my strength you can take. I swear I'll be as careful of you as I can, for as long as I can. If you yield to me it will be less painful, less uncomfortable." He knew once he was inside her lush body he was likely to lose control, become a fireball and he hoped to the sons above that he wouldn't hurt her.

"Kultur," she responded in a tight small voice infused with anger hitched with passion, "you are hurting me by raping me no matter how gentle. By taking away my will and violating my body, and by forcing me to stay in Aniniva."

His head dropped, his hair brushed on her face but he didn't argue with her, she was right.

"There's still time," she whispered, "you can stop, let me go. I will leave, right away, tonight, and not draw danger to your people. Please."

In answer, he nudged her knees apart and wrapped his big fist around his thick erection and positioned it against her opening.

He started pushing the broad head into her, she cried, "Please don't, Kultur, please," her cries twisted his heart and pierced it like a knife, but he had to complete the deed or she'd die. Even so, he was beyond the point of stopping.

She tried to clench her rigid legs together. Wriggling his lean hips between her legs to spread them further apart, he pushed deeper into her and covered her cries with his mouth. She whimpered at his lips as he slowly pushed in further.

She was so tight he knew she had not had a child, or many men, if any. He shoved the thought of her lying with other men out of his mind and stopped moving to give her a chance to adapt to his intrusion into her soft tender sheath.

"Ah, sons above," he groaned at her mouth. He had to wait anyway, had to get a grip or he'd come unleashed. "You feel amazing, Sislla, I need to uh, get control of myself," or he'd be banging into her like a loose cannon and damage the hell out of her.

"Relax your legs, baby, try to feel me throbbing inside you." He pushed in a little more but she was so tight he had to go so painstakingly slow.

She squirmed under him, tears rained, she whimpered, "You're hurting me..."

He stopped. Braced on his forearms, Kultur lifted his hand and wiped at her tears with his thumb. The words, 'I'm sorry' pushed at his mouth, but he kept them in. She wouldn't believe him.

A few minutes passed and he could feel her ease around him. "*Koritsi,* stay relaxed like that, I have more to, uh, go."

He started gently, pushing deeper slowly so she could keep adapting to his size. He was still worried that he could hurt her with the size of his phallus, or if he loses control, his violence and strength could injure her.

He was used to tough, sturdy, experienced whores, not a dainty, fragile, frightened young woman like Sislla. Her vagina clenched suddenly, in reaction his shaft throbbed and jerked, he almost lost it.

Then, he hit a wall. It was confirmed, she was a virgin. Damn, now he had to hurt her. "Sislla, ah, I'm so sorry, but I have to," he groaned at her tight sheath squeezing his shaft so exquisitely. Nothing ever had felt this good in his life.

He could easily harm a man, but this beautiful creature? Yet it must be done to save her life. As he thrust through her maidenhood he nipped her ear hard- two conflicting pains- and her breath caught, then a horrible cry emitted from her gorgeous lips and Kultur about died inside. He stopped moving.

Sislla turned her head, gasping, tears rushed out. Stroking her hair, Kultur murmured gently, "Tis done my precious. Just…wait a moment."

She squirmed beneath him but he used his weight to still her. After a minute or so, he heard her breaths settle and, holding his own breath, he started pushing again, slowly, so damned agonizingly slowly.

Finally, blowing out the held breath, he murmured, "All right, *koritsi*, I am fully inside you." He waited a minute again for her to accept him, meanwhile her wet silk saturated them making it easier to slide.

His voice soft, he asked, "Are you all right, does it still hurt?"

Her fingers clenching his biceps, she didn't answer him. He pulled almost all the way out then pushed slowly back in. Her tears dwindled, he thumbed away the last ones, bent and kissed her gently while rocking in and out of her.

When his thrusts grew deeper, faster, he could feel her sheath clenching and releasing him. Pushing on his forearms he moved his body, tilting so his shaft would brush her clitoris with every plunge.

Her moan ruffled at his throat as her hands stroked up his chest, sifting through the hair to his shoulders. Instead of pushing at him, her small hands were clutching his shoulders, her hips started moving with his as he surged into a rhythm.

"*Ahh*," his groan reeled like his breath coursed over craggy ridges, he shifted slightly to the side. "Sislla," his growl deep in his chest, a rumbled command, "look at me."

He caressed her breasts, stroked down her belly to her core, pressing and circling her nub until she was clinging desperately to his shoulders, her fingers digging into his flesh, gasping whimpers hitching in her throat.

He brought his hand up to cup her face, kissed her then held her chin until she opened her eyes and looked at him. Her eyes misted with arousal, disoriented, her passion heavy lids started to close, he said, "Look at me Sislla."

Her unfocused eyes drifted back open. Kultur watched her glazed orbs connect with his, her pupils huge and black and gleaming.

From the depths of his soul, his voice low, serious, he chanted, "Tiris devoleb, Iegdelp oteb sruoj rererof, ewera won eno," then suddenly thrust fast and hard, his skin darkened, his face stiffened as his teeth clenched with the strain, she gasped, groaning his name as he pounded into her.

Although he was moving more vigorously, going deeper with rougher vehemence, she kept up with his rhythm, her fingers now knotted in his hair pulling on it.

Her inhalations grew ragged and rapid, breaths squeaked up her throat, the rushing severity of her gasps, her body thrashing beneath him signaled she was at the edge.

He could feel her vagina clutching him, milking him, and her hips twisting, bucking, her spine arched hard and her legs went rigid- then with a harsh cry, her eyes rolled back in her head and he watched her, feeling her body clutch and arch and shake against his in her climax.

Then he let go, thrusting forcefully, fast, penetrating so deep until he was engorged to bursting. With a growling roar he hammered into her until he exploded, releasing his seed deep inside her. Thrust after thrust, grunting and growling and shuddering until he finally slowed, his shaft still emptying his seeds, his body jerking, tremor after tremor, until he collapsed on her.

Lying atop Sislla, even through his own shredded heavy panting, Kultur could hear and feel her, she had climaxed again when he did, her breaths still gasping with keening gulps.

He reveled in her breasts still pressing, undulating against his chest until they both slowed, until they stilled. He lay motionless, enjoying the feel of her under him, her breasts now soft and slightly heaving against the hard surface of his chest.

Knowing he was too heavy for her, he moved most of his weight to beside her on the bed and reluctantly drew his length from her lushness. Still semi-hard, he pressed his manhood against her thigh, laid a leg carefully over hers, a hand settled possessively on her breast. She didn't push him away.

He was so relieved he had been able to take her with him in their mating. It killed him to force her, but she would die if he didn't, whether or not she believed him. He had seen firsthand what happened to the victims after the Iminims captured them, and left what was left of their carcasses to bake in the sun.

If he had time, he would have taught her to care for him, want him, love him, and want to stay with him. He would never have forced her, he would have tried to romance her, seduce her to desire him. He would have had to learn how, he'd never had to, or wanted to, seduce a woman before he met Sislla.

But his mother had pushed the issue by shoving other men at her. Plus, the time was nearing when she would need the marking for protection. He realized he had taken her choice away, but hadn't she said she wouldn't mate with anyone anyway, that she would leave? Regardless, he still wasn't about to hand her over to another man, or let her die.

They lay in a wordless, drowsy state. His contented revelry was disturbed when she shifted, trying to move out from under him.

His voice relaxed, low with satisfied release, half his face nestled in her hair, he asked quietly, "Sislla, are you all right?"

She didn't answer him, just kept trying to move from him. Her struggles were weak, as if she lost her energy.

Kultur slid both his arms around her, cuddling her to his chest, but she resisted.

One of her delicate hands pushed against his pecs, a useless waste of energy as his chest was as powerful as a brick wall, she couldn't leave unless he let her. Her other hand curled against her own bosom as if to keep him from being close to her. There was no way he was going to have sex with her, break her virginity and let her just get up and leave.

With a grunt, Kultur rolled grudgingly off the bed, and said, "Stay here, I will be right back. Please." The word please tasted funny in his mouth, when he saw her lashes flicker he knew she'd heard it.

When he returned, she had curled into a tight ball; her ringlets covered her naked body like a bright, messy, curly cloak. He bent and scooped her up in his arms.

"Come," his voice low, rasping husky from their lovemaking. She kept her eyes shut and stayed curled up tight, shutting herself off from him.

He was alternately concerned over her withdrawing from him, and pleased that she had responded so amazingly, it only made him want her more, and again, right now. He had thought perhaps once he had her, the craving desire that had been building since the day Trogga threw her at his feet would diminish. But since tasting her, he only wanted her even more intensely than ever.

He admitted to himself he had lusted after her, but if it wasn't necessary to mark her, he would never had touched her unless she had wanted him to.

If she weren't so closed off from him he would take her again right now. But, she was distant, withdrawn, she hadn't said a word or looked at him. Apparently she was mad. Understandably so. He smothered the sigh in his heart.

His footsteps muffled on the carpet started padding as his bare feet slapped on the marble tile while making his way into his salon.

The huge, round room was bright in all white marble veined with gold, thick gold and white towels hung from rails. Carrying her inside, he adjusted a dimmer which lowered the light of ceiling and wall lanterns.

The room was big and warm. Taking up the center was a massive marble tub, almost a pool. Turesenes, the stones that heated without fire or smoke were implanted along the bottom of the tub, the intensity of the heat could be controlled by touch, and Kultur had devised an invention, miniature water-weighted wheels, to keep the water in the tub continuously swirling and bubbly.

Besides the swirling froth, Kultur had added a powder that made sudsy bubbles and also fragrant bath salts. The room was balmy and smelled faintly of lilac. Candles interlaced around the room and the tub lit the atmosphere with soft, mellow light. He had prepared the room earlier while waiting for her to come to his chambers.

As he neared the tub, Kultur could feel Sislla tense even tighter in his arms. "It is warm and tranquil, it will be a pleasant environment while we talk."

"Huh," her snort almost graceful. Her anger obviously simmering under a cold demeanor, Sislla said with sarcasm, "As if after being raped we could have a lovely sweet chat about it while taking a romantic bubble bath."

Kultur knew there was nothing he could say that would appease or soothe her anger or resentment. Mentioning how wild she'd been in bed, how wonderfully receptive, would probably just piss her off more and make her more withdrawn.

Still carrying her, Kultur stepped carefully down on a couple of steps into the tub. There were several long, wide rounded steps; he sat down with her in his arms on a middle step so that only their hips and legs were submerged.

She moved to slip away from him, but he held her firmly on his lap, saw her frown deepen and a sheen of tears cover her pretty eyes.

An arm around her, he held her loosely against his shoulder and gently pushed bubbles over her, watching the suds slide down her silken skin. The splash of the swirling bubbles and the suds sliding, dripped a low echo against the marble walls.

Cloths, soap, salts and oils and other items covered part of the rim of the tub. Kultur reached for a bowl of pins and clumsily pinned her hair up. Then he retrieved a cloth and bar of soap.

Dipping the cloth in the water, he rubbed the bar of soap on the cloth until it was foamed with lather, then drew it lightly, languorously down her back. Her flesh quivered at his soft touch.

He lifted her arm, ignoring the rigidity of it, and peacefully drew the sudsy cloth over it. Down to her fingers, he washed each slender digit. Gently tugging on her fingers caused a reflexive tugging in his loins.

She stayed curved in the crook of his arm but kept her body stiff. Kultur lifted one leg, lazily washed it then did the other, tenderly soaping each tiny toe.

He dipped the cloth soaking it with warm water and bubbles and squeezed it at her neck so the warm sudsy water streamed down and over her breasts.

He smiled at her surprised pleasurable gasp, saw her nipples tighten to cherry buds. Soaking and soaping the cloth again until it was like velvet, he rubbed it over her breasts. Over the thick soft cloth, his big hands massaged and caressed her breasts.

Feeling the slight arch to her spine, and an almost unnoticeable backwards tilt to her head, her breasts imperceptibly pressing into the cloth, Kultur knew, even against her will, her body was turning on.

He kept lightly drawing the cloth over her breasts, her belly, her thighs.

****

Damn him, Sislla muttered a rare curse under her breath. He thinks he can assault her then pet her and she would fall lustfully into his arms? Big, overbearing arrogant brute.

She refused to look at him. Even as her body was firing up under his touch, everywhere he stroked with that sudsy cloth left a burning trail, goose bumps popped under it.

Heat struck between her legs, she shuddered remembering his hands there, his…shaft…inside her. He kept stroking her, lazily washing her, his barbaric arm around her keeping her locked in his embrace.

What could she do? He was as strong as a gorilla, she was totally helpless in his arms. And her traitorous body was reacting to his ministrations, growing pliant, melting under his hands, and he knew it, the miserable man, darn him.

"Kultur."

"Hmmm…" He dipped the cloth in the warm water and laid it over her chest, left it for a second, then wrapping his fingers around it so he was clutching the cloth with both hands over her, he slowly pulled the cloth off her skin, tugging and stretching her breasts with it. He smiled at her involuntary shiver.

"Will you be seeing Araina, later? Taking her into your bed? Will this not make her mad…or do you not intend to tell her? Am I to keep quiet, keep this- thing a secret?"

His hands froze. "What the hell are you talking about?"

Her skin goose bumped again but now it was because she was cold from the lack of his hands on her. "I saw you, uh, cuddling with her before. Lexi says as the Atraam, it is not appropriate for anyone to touch you without your permission. I assume you and she will marry?"

He squeezed the cloth irritably in his hands, twisted until it almost tore. "Sislla, why would you bring up another woman while you are naked in my arms?"

Her shoulders shrugged delicately. "She is a very beautiful woman."

Closing his eyes, he let out a gravelly sigh. "For *kratiis* sake, Sislla, we just got done making love-"

Her head snapped as she fired anger at him from her blue eyes. "No, you raped me."

Rolling his head back with an exasperated groan, he grumbled, "Sons above, Sislla, you could stop calling it rape and partner with me willingly, at least for the next two markings. You know the markings are for your own good."

He dropped his hands on her slim thighs with a little aggravated splash, then slid his palms down the firm meat of her thighs to her knees.

"Yes of course, a little rape is always good for a woman."

"You liked it."

"Oh!" With an explosive gasp she sat up straight, sputtering, "How dare you. You used your superior strength to hold me hostage while you- you- well you know what you did," her hands flailed at him in resentful fury.

Wrapping his big arms around her, he pulled her back into his embrace. He spoke quietly, patiently, "I had to prepare you to take me, whether or not you were a virgin. Without getting your body ready to receive me, because of my size, and you are so small, it would have been excruciatingly painful and you would have been injured if I hadn't."

Recalling the three orgasms she had, he added with a tiny smirk that pulled in his dimple, "And your body loved it." He knew that would infuriate her, he held her arms as she tried to strike him. When the fight drained from her, he relaxed his hold.

"You didn't answer me about Araina," her voice had cooled.

Now he was mad. "Goddammit Sislla, how could you ask me such a thing? You think I bed you then get up and go get her and make love to her?" He spat, "Don't be asinine. Where do you get this shit from, anyway?"

"You don't have to curse at me, Kultur, I told you, I saw you two all over each other the other."

"We were not all over each other, goddammit. Her mother and my mother have been best friends forever, and, after…" his voice grew heavy, "after my first…engagement broke off…" he dragged an arm across his eyes and let out a frustrated sigh.

"The three of them have been scheming for years to get us to marry. I have told them all again and again, I would never get married, to anyone." His lips pursed, he had something to tell her but the way she was right now it would be better to wait and tell her later.

Forking his fingers through his hair, in defense he said, "The truth is, Araina has thrown herself at me, on me, under me, so many times it was too exhausting to fight her off all the damned time. So yeah, sometimes I just let her,"

"Stroke your chest, and run her hands down your pants?"

Furious, Kultur grabbed her jaw turning her to look at him. "Yeah, maybe she rubbed up against me a few times, but her hands have never been down my pants."

"I don't understand, she's so beautiful, why wouldn't you want to have sex with her? You must care greatly for her, I can feel your desire for me lessen as you talk about her," she squirmed on his lap, "your, um, equipment has softened."

Glaring into her eyes, his face twisted with disgust. "My *equipment*, as you call it, is softening because we are sitting here with each other, naked, after just being as intimate as a couple could be, and you insist on talking about another goddamned woman.

"Araina is repulsive to me, Sislla, she is forward and pushy in her pursuit of me, and she's mean, and belittling. I wanted to slap her face and make her bite her vicious tongue when I heard what she was saying to you that day my mother brought all those women here. But it would have only made a scene, and made things worse."

"Yes," Sislla agreed with a nod. "Your mother already hates me enough. She would love for you to marry Araina. So will you eventually?"

His head fell back, he blinked at the ceiling, "For the sons' sake, Sislla, are you not listening to me? I do not have sex with one woman and marry another a day later."

She sniffed. "You did not have sex with me because you wanted to, you were only marking me."

"For the love of-" he grasped her chin again and took her in a hard, deep kiss, then pulled back and said slyly, "I have the most beautiful, sweet, hot little angel in my arms. Believe me, honey, I wanted you. Now, unless you're jealous of Araina and only want me to set your mind at rest-"

"Oh!" She jerked her face out of his hands and tried to stand up. "Do not be ridiculous. I am most certainly not jealous of you and that woman, or any woman for that matter."

"Good." He pulled her back down. "Then we're done with that topic. I don't want to hear her name again, especially when we are naked together."

"Then it's a good thing we will not ever be naked together again."

Splaying his hand over her belly, he settled her on the step between his legs with her back against him. "You need to give us a chance, Sislla, you will like us together if you let yourself."

When she struggled, he skimmed his hands up from her belly to cup her breasts. Netting his fingers around the firm flesh he strengthened his hold and murmured against her ear, "Is my *equipment* soft now, *koritsi*?"

Her struggles to get away from him only made him hold her breasts harder, squeezing them to keep her from slipping away, and her squirming between his legs only made his, *equipment*, harder. She could feel him swelling against her bottom. Maybe she should sit still and he would soften again and let her go.

When she stopped struggling, Kultur laid the side of his face against her head and, amazed that she didn't fight him, he caressed her breasts, kneading them, letting his fingers fill of her supple flesh.

Molding them in his hands, he licked down the side of her neck, stopped to suck on her skin, then kissed her shoulder while pinching her nipples lightly; he pulled on them and was rewarded by her bottom wriggling against his erection, and not in trying to get away.

Then, as if she turned a switch off in her mind, she stiffened and pushed against him.

With a groan, he tightened his grip on her, and watched a tear trail down her cheek. He wiped at it with his finger. "Why do you fight me, Sislla? Are my caresses so awful? Was it so terrible?" She pulled from him but he wouldn't let go.

Her gaze lowered to stare at the water. "You raped me, Kultur."

Shaking his head with a cold frown, he lowered his hands. Eyes deathly empty, his chilled voice dropped so savagely coarse she stiffened, shivered in fear.

His body seemed to grow even thicker and bigger and suddenly darkly menacing.

Chapter Twenty-Four

Through the ridge of his hard mouth, Kultur ground out, "Let me tell you, Sislla, I am an Atraam, a savage cutthroat warlord. In this slice of the world, if I chose to rape every woman in the land, no one would question it, or try to stop me. The other warlords, the other Atraams, do rape.

"They take any captured woman they want, when they want, and as brutal as they want. It is the way of our warring country, no one, not the women," his eyes dark slits deliberately cast down her body, "not their families, husbands, no one can, or does, complain. If I hadn't come for you, trust me, before the sun set, Atraam Rosh Boshon," his voice grated harshly, "and probably countless others, would have taken you, without gentleness, without *preparing* you, and without mercy."

Kultur had turned from softly cuddling and kissing and stroking her into a chilling, angry, frightening barbarian.

Sislla bit her tongue hard to keep her lips from trembling. She twisted her knotted fingers, and turned her head so he couldn't see her blink back the tears of terror he had just induced. Her body quaked so hard she clenched her teeth to keep them from chattering.

His indomitable shoulders a stony fortress, Kultur stared down at her impassively in silence, watching her quake in fear of what could have happened to her when the Ulmas snatched her, and now of him.

197

Having him behind her, so angry, so dangerous and volatile, the harder Sislla tried to still her body, the harder it shook. She yanked at her knotted fingers, chewed her lip to pieces.

"Sislla," he sighed in frustration. "If I was a depraved beast like the other Atraams, I would have forced you that first day Trogga brought you to the castle. I would have fucked you while you cried and not cared how I injured you. And, I would have fucked you every day and night since, because I want you that badly."

With another big sigh, he wrapped his arms around her and pulled her against the warm wall of his chest. Her shivers were so wracking she vibrated against his skin. A ragged breath flexed his taut muscles releasing the tension; he set his hands over hers to still her anxious mutilating of her fingers. She trembled against him.

A loose ringlet looped over his arm. He picked it up, rubbed it between his fingers then set it back where it was and gently stroked her shoulders.

Softening his harsh voice, he told her, "I have explained it again and again to you, Sislla. I did it to save your life. I can't help it if you do not believe me. I had hoped you would make love with me, willingly. Maybe if I'd had time to properly seduce, romance you, but…" his sigh drew out sad and jagged, "there was no time, it just had to be done."

Her throat so constricted her words came out tiny and broken, "You did not use protection. I could get…pregnant."

His hands slid down her ribs to cover her belly. "Aye, but the marking would not work with a shield. My seed had to go in you." He asked softly, "Would a child be so bad, Sislla? My child?"

In a small voice, she said, "I cannot stay here."

His hands moved back up stroking and caressing her breasts as if he couldn't get enough of their supple plumpness. "Why not stay here, Sislla, this is a wonderful place to live. You see how beautiful the countryside is, we have every comfort you could want. You are happy with your healing work. Why do you want to leave?"

His palms tightened, gripping her breasts as she again tried to move from him.

She said nothing.

His voice sounding a little tough, he said, "If I thought a child would keep you here, Sislla, we would make love every damned day all day until it happened. Would you stay willingly if we had a child?"

When she didn't answer him, his hands stroked down her body again, over her belly and to her thighs. Her legs stiffened. He pushed them apart and cupped her sex.

"Kultur…"

It wasn't a strong objection. Holding her thighs, he pulled them further apart and slid his thick fingers along her slit several times before delving his fingertips inside her.

"*Kultur*," this time it was a moan.

Letting go of her, he leaned to the side, folded up a towel and put it on the rim of the tub, then he clinched her waist with his strong hands and lifted her so she was standing facing the side of the tub. He took her arms and rested them on the towel on the rim of the tub.

Her voice muffled against her arms, she asked in a small panic, "Kultur, what are you doing?"

"Hush, *koritsi*, relax." He positioned himself behind her and nudged her legs apart. Her legs spread, he leaned over her, pushed her mostly fallen loose hair to the side and kissed the back of her neck down to her bare shoulder, and moved his hand around her to fondle her womanhood.

Squirming, Sislla tried to draw her thighs together, "Wait, Kultur…" her voice trailed off when he trickled his fingers up her slit then light as a feather touched her nub. She couldn't help it, a groan shivered out of her. Her hips pushed out against his hand to make him touch her harder.

His skillful fingers pressed her clit and tugged at her folds. He circled her nub with his fingers like a whisper, barely touching her. Her hips moved in a slight circle with them. He slipped a finger inside her.

She didn't fight him, instead, she pushed so it would go in deeper. He probed the tender inner walls of her lush sheath, when she groaned again he thrust his finger in and out, then added a second finger, her hips meeting each thrust.

Reaching around her, Kultur shoved another towel flat on the side of the tub in front of her. He pulled his fingers from inside her and put both hands around her waist lifting her so the front of her torso was flat on the side of the tub, her bottom in the air and her legs dangling down the inside of the tub.

"Kultur, what are you doing? I'm not sure, this is-"

"Uh huh, wait, *koritsi*," he stood up in the tub behind her, using his knees, he spread her legs apart and reached to caress her sex. Feeling her silk wetting his hand, he got closer and bent over her slightly.

Her breathing quickened short and shallow, her hips followed the circles he made on her clit. Sliding his fingers inside her, he leaned over further to put a hand beside her on the edge of the tub to brace his body.

It felt awkward to Sislla to be lying flat out face down on the side of a tub with her arms outstretched and her bum in the air and her legs spread, but she couldn't deny the surge of heat and desire that burned between her legs.

His thick fingers rubbed her swollen flesh, then he again inserted them inside her, gently thrusting them, curling the digits, putting pressure against her inside walls.

Her limbs felt weightless but her core and her brain simmered, she felt about to explode, her hips wiggled wantonly pushing at his hand.

Then he leaned back, pulled his fingers out, skimmed the fingertips of both hands down the center of her slender back then spread his hands on her bottom.

"Every womanly part of you, *koritsi*, is perfect and round." He squeezed and kneaded her cheeks, then drew his fingers down the crack between them and her hips bucked at his hand. His chuckle misted warm air on her back.

Groaning, "Uhhh," she twisted into his hand wanting more.

He squeezed some more then strolled his hand under her to touch her sex then he took his hand away. Before she could think, she felt the blunt head of his shaft at her opening. She sighed back into it, but he didn't move to go inside her. He stopped moving entirely.

"Kultur?"

He nudged her legs as far apart as he could get them and rubbed the head of his shaft against her swollen pulsing lips.

"Sislla," he said, pushing in her just at her opening, then whispered, "do you want me to stop?" Lifting his other hand he stroked it up her side to her breast mashed on the tile. He slid his fingers under it to cup it, squeezing it while holding his manhood in his fist and nudging it at her open core.

Her arms stretched out on the marble, she clutched the towel, crushing it in her fists. His huge phallus was hard as iron and he rubbed it over her sex then prodded into her but only just to her rim. She said not a word.

He pushed inside her a tiny bit and stopped. His hand clenched her breast and his phallus waited just barely inside her small channel. "Sislla?"

"Hmmm?" The heavy murmur oozed out of her.

"Do you want me to stop?"

Her bottom squirming against him, her breathing fast and loud, her hands crushing the towel in her fists, she still said nothing.

He pulled out and didn't move, neither did she. "All right, Sislla, this is up to you. You tell me to either stop or go ahead. You don't say anything and I will stop and we're done."

She didn't say anything.

He sighed deeply and started to step back from her.

"Don't stop, Kultur."

His held breath whooshed out. He asked anyway, he didn't want any recriminations later, at least about this time. "You're saying go ahead and take you, right, Sislla?"

Her head was turned, the side of her face flat on the towel, her hair covered half her face. He couldn't see her face, she nodded, a growly whimper culled deep inside. Her entire body pulsed and burned, her voice tight with a soft sob, she cried with need, "Yes, Kultur, do it."

His head dropped in relief, and he shoved hard in one stroke into her from behind. She cried out, her hips hit the marble.

Kultur wrapped his brawny arm around her waist and pulled her back then used his arm to cushion her against the wall of the tub, her hands slid to brace against the rim.

Kultur set one hand on the edge to hold himself balanced, kept the other wrapped tightly around her and he thrust with rough strength hard into her again.

She gasped but didn't cry for him to stop so he plunged in and out, hard and fast, each thrust deeper, again and again building the inside pressure. His mouth near her ear he said, "You ready, *koritsi baby*, come with me?"

Gulping heavily, her breaths quick and harsh, she nodded.

"Okay, honey," he pounded into her so hard she grunted with every thrust, his tight testicles slapped against her. Feeling her spine grow rigid, her chest heaving, Kultur clutched her tightly and they both came together, rapidly, violently. His seed erupted deep inside her, she cried out.

Hearing her call his name spurred him to thrust deep one more time, and he held it pulsating like crazy, then still holding her he collapsed on her back, his arm under her, protecting her from smashing onto the marble tile. Their panting breaths filled the warm, humid room.

After a moment, withdrawing from Sislla's soft body, Kultur turned to sit on the step. With his back against the wall, he pulled her with him and settled her on his lap. Her head fell on his shoulder, his arms strung around her.

Sislla could feel his racing heart beating against her back; his chest still rose and fell rapidly with heavy breaths.

She got to her feet so quickly he was caught unaware. Gracefully, she trod up the slippery steps out of the tub.

Still catching his breath, below lowered lids, Kultur watched her. His gaze burned a trail down her smooth back to her lush bottom and down the long slender legs.

The water whooshed as he stood up and moved up the steps following her. Snatching a clean towel off a table, he came behind her and dropped the towel over her shoulders, then rubbed it across her neck, her back, down her arms.

He could feel her body stiff and unyielding again. Drawing the towel across her back like a shawl, he pulled the ends around to her front and dried her breasts.

Only moments ago she was moaning and whimpering, and screaming in his arms, calling his name, now she was like a statue.

"What is it, *koritsi*?" He turned her around still holding the ends of the towel he pulled her in against his chest. His wet chest hair rubbing against her dry fair skin was turning it red.

Curling two fingers under her chin, he tilted her face up. "I did not force you, *koritsi*, you know that. What is wrong?"

Her mouth turned down, lips in a pursed pout, she accused, "You didn't force me, Kultur, but you knew what you were doing. You deliberately, uh, made me want you until I couldn't say no."

He let her towel drape over her and he grabbed another one. Dragging it across his big chest, he rubbed it hard in his pique.

"Yeah, so what? That's how I feel every time I look at you. I want you so badly it takes everything I have to not touch you."

"Huh, well," she croaked, "apparently you decided you were done with being a gentleman and decided it was okay to molest me."

The angles on his rugged face sharpened as his skin grew dark. "You wanted me to molest you just now, Sislla, I asked you if you wanted to stop. I repeat, I did not force you. I am not going to apologize for being a red-blooded male with a beautiful naked woman in his arms and wanting her, for *kratiis* sake. This is bullshit."

Her earlier fear of him was replaced with a rush of anger, she turned a furious face to him. "You are the experienced one, Kultur. Don't forget you removed my clothes against my will making me naked, you forcefully held me in that tub, and touched me deliberately to make me...hot."

Her cheeks warmed with blushing pink. "Besides, why did you force me in your bedroom but ask my permission here?"

His shrug lazy. "The first was the marking. I had to do it whether you were willing or not. The second marking will be in a week at the next golden moon. Since today was a mandatory marking and you wouldn't acquiesce I had to force you. The second time, in the tub, was not. You had the right to say no and I would have abided by it."

She thought about it and snorted. "But you made it impossible for me to say no."

He shrugged again with a small smug smile. "Like I said. I am obviously loaded with testosterone and you are beautiful, I would want you regardless of the need for the marking." His features hardened, "After today, I warn you, when I'm alone with you, I will try to seduce you. I will touch you.

"You can't," then, "wait, what do you mean, second marking?"

Letting out an annoyed sigh, Kultur said, "I've told you. Three markings are necessary before the Epita, the true mark is there. We had to mate on three golden moons, now only two."

Her mouth dropped aghast, "You mean we have to do this again?"

He scowled. "Dammit Sislla, don't make it sound so horrible. Don't you dare deny you enjoyed what we did, both times."

Her face colored. "It doesn't matter. We're not doing it again."

His brows drew down, then flattened into an annoyed line. "Don't start that shit again. There is no reason for this to be a big argument each time. We've done it once, well, twice; you see it's not so bad. The next time will be easier and even better without you fighting me."

She stepped back from him. "There will not be a next time. There will be no second marking, or a third for that matter."

His eyes narrowed to charred slivers, fiery black lasers cutting from them. "Yes there will, there has to be. Goddammit, Sislla, even if I have to hold you down and force you again."

She backed away further, shaking her head adamantly. "No. One assault in my lifetime is enough, thank you very much. Apparently one mating, marking, whatever, is not enough so I am still able to return home. I will be leaving, I have to."

Kultur traipsed over to a cupboard, opened it and took out a white robe. He brought it to her and held it out. When she didn't take it, he grabbed her towel and jerked it off her and threw it on the floor. He was about to put the robe on her when her nudity struck him still.

His heated gaze burned over her breasts so hot she wriggled like she could feel the scorching heat of it. His eyes seared down to her belly then to where her legs joined.

Dark color rose up his neck, his eyes ignited like burning embers inside the black coals. His manhood had not fully softened completely; it was now already turning to granite.

When he swallowed hard and licked his lips, Sislla scowled and snatched the robe out of his hands and shrugged it on, slapped it closed over her front and tied the belt.

His gaze rolled up her with a wolfish grin. "That won't help." He reached for her; she danced out of his way and moved several feet away from him.

His face fell cold. He didn't bother with a robe, just dried himself off and padded naked down the short hall back to his bedroom.

******

It had grown late; the huge golden moon was visible through a window. Kultur pulled on night sleeper bottoms and waited for her to come in the room. It was several minutes. He chuckled; she must have been seeking another way out. She would discover there was none.

Eventually, her chin in the air, she marched into the room and straight for the door. She grabbed the knob and turned it. But it didn't turn. It was locked.

Spinning around, "Kultur-" she stopped, he was standing behind her an inch away. She was eye-level with his thick chest hair that did little to hide the pulsing muscles in his powerful torso.

"The- the- door is locked."

"I know."

Frowning, she didn't want to look at his harrowing eyes so she stared at his chest. "Well, you need to unlock it so I can leave."

"Why would you leave?"

She stamped her foot. "Stop it, Kultur, I am going to my room. Open the door."

Instead, he caught her arm and drew her to his bed. "You will sleep with me every night from now on. Get in."

Her astonished eyes flashed before she scowled. "I most certainly am not. You got your stupid marking; you don't need to come near me for a week. I'm going to my room."

Ignoring her, he stomped over to his dresser, pulled out the top to his pajamas and tossed it to her. "Put that on. Unless you want to sleep naked, I won't mind," and he went and climbed into the bed, flopped on his back and laid his forearm over his eyes.

"Isn't Araina going to be mad when she sees there's no room in the bed for her?"

"Stop it, Sislla."

"Is she just going to stand aside the next two golden moons while you rape me?"

She was goading him and he knew it, but it frustrated him anyway. "You're starting to really piss me off. Sislla."

"Oh, what are you going to do to shut me up? *Rape* me?"

Groaning under his arm, he growled, "A thousand fucking women out there would throw themselves bare-assed naked in front of me with their legs spread like hot butter, and you kick and scream."

"Hmm. I've heard you've already had those thousand or so women. Go mark one of them."

"That's it." Kultur sat up and threw his legs over the side of the bed.

Knowing she'd gone too far, Sislla turned and ran into the smaller bathroom, quickly closed and locked the door. She yelped, jumped startled and afraid when he slammed his hand on the door. At his chuckle, her shoulders loosened.

"Believe me, Sislla, this door would not stop me if I wanted to get you. If you were on the other side of the wall and I wanted you, the wall would not stop me. Now, cut out the bullshit and come to bed."

He went and lay down. Although sated and relaxed from the sex, Kultur was still semi-hard. Just thinking about her stiffened him right back up. He forced his eyes to close and managed to doze for an hour or so.

He rolled on his side and reached a hand out to touch her. She wasn't there. He slit one eye open and peered out. The bed was empty, and he could see she wasn't in the room.

Muttering, "Damn, stubborn," he scooted to the edge of the bed and swung his legs over then got to his feet with a groan.

"Why can't she just fucking accept..." he grumbled his way to the bathroom. He turned the knob, she'd locked it. "For the love of," he leaned his head near the door.

"Sislla, open it or I'll knock it down. You've got one second." He rolled his back against the frame of the door, leaned against it, crossed his arms and waited. Nothing.

An exasperated sigh grated out of him. He pressed his forearm horizontally on the door and hung his head; he said wearily, "Stand away from the door."

When he moved to step back to throw his shoulder against the door he felt it move. He tried the knob again, it was locked but she hadn't closed the door all the way for the lock to fully bolt the door. When he slammed his hand on the door earlier it must have popped the lock up.

Shaking his head, he mumbled, "Silly chit." His heart stopped at the thought of her taking some boat out on the high seas, alone, when she couldn't even get a door closed properly.

His palm flat on the door, he lightly pushed it open and stuck his head in. His throat constricted. She wore his pajama top and was curled up in the corner. Sound asleep.

"Ah, *koritsi.*" He padded over and crouched beside her. Gently brushing the hair off her face, she looked so sad, and small, and young, and way too vulnerable.

She must have cried after her shower, there were tear tracks down and over her cheeks. Slipping his hands under her he stood up with her in his arms and carried her out of the room and back to the bedroom.

He laid her down on his bed then got in and stretched out beside her. Pulling the covers up, he tucked them under her chin then levered up on his elbow, propped his head on his hand and studied her in repose.

He lifted a ringlet, it was still damp and it curled around his hand. He set it down and splayed the rest of her curls across her pillow. Laying his head on his pillow, he slid his arms around her and pulled her over so her head rested on his chest, his hand cradling her bottom.

His eyes drifted closed then he felt something trickle down his chest. He raised a hand and gently touched her cheek. Tears were spilling.

Moaning, "*Tiris koritsi,*" he petted her face and stroked her hair, "everything will be all right, trust me. Please, trust me."

The tears only fell faster; she turned her head, pressed her face against his skin and sobbed softly into his chest.

He held her and stroked her until she fell asleep again.

Chapter Twenty-Five

It had been difficult for Kultur to sleep with Sislla in his arms. With an erection that could pound nails, he managed to doze off and on.

The sun had not yet risen but he slept all he was going to. Sislla was on her side with Kultur curved around her back, his knees tucked up behind hers. He kept his hips back so his shaft wasn't pressed against her bottom. Then he could not have resisted.

She was still asleep, he could feel her back move slightly with her relaxed breaths. He wondered how sore she might be. *Good move*, *think about her hot little body, fool*, *damn*, his shaft flexed towards her.

Gently, he brushed her hair to the side off her neck and pressed his lips on her warm skin. She looked so adorable in his pajamas. *Gah*, he'd never thought of a woman as adorable before.

His one arm was under her neck and the other was draped over her arm in front of her. Before the thought to do it reached his brain, Kultur's hand had moved to cup her breast over the pajama top. Damn, it was hot feeling her soft female curves that were under his masculine pajamas.

He fondled one breast then the other, surprised his touch or his lips and warm breath on the back of her neck didn't wake her. Pushing his hand up under the shirt, he caressed her bare skin, he'd never get used to how perfect her supple globes were. Unable to stop himself, he skimmed a palm down the front of her to curl over her tender mound.

Sislla stirred, groggily aware there were hands roaming all over her body. Big, warm, rough hands. Instinctively she pushed at them and tried to move away.

Feeling her growing panic, he whispered a raspy, "No, *koritsi,* baby, don't struggle." He rolled over on his back taking her with him. Settling her with her back still on his chest, he pushed her legs to drape over the outside of his thighs.

Sislla tried to put her palms on the mattress on either side of him to press down so she could sit up, but her shoulders were on his chest, her arms weren't long enough to reach around the width and depth of his chest to get any kind of leverage to lever up.

"Shh, *koritsi,* just let me pet you," a deep rumble purred into her ear. "I won't touch you sexually unless you want me to. All right?"

He drew his knees up so she couldn't pull her thighs together or use them to get off of him. It also forced her legs to spread further apart. She wasn't wearing an undergarment.

Objecting, "No, Kultur, I feel vulnerable like this, let me up," she raised her head. Her breathing now faster in panic mode, her body tensed.

"Please, Sislla, let me soothe you." He set his hand gently on her head and pulled her back down. "Give me five minutes and I will stop if you still want me to. All right?" His fingers combed through her hair a few times then skimmed softly down her arms.

Her body was rigid but she didn't say anything, so he stroked down the sides of her waist and over her belly. His palms slid so lightly he was barely even touching her skin, just like a warm breeze. He drew his fingertips up the front of her thighs, and then the sides. She shivered but didn't object.

His fingers drifted from her thighs, over her stomach, to her arms. When he stroked the sensitive insides of her arms she shivered again. He just trailed his fingertips all over the nonsexual areas of her bare skin. Caressing her neck, he brushed over her shoulders.

When he pushed her shirt up to the bottoms of her breasts so he could stroke under them, her ribs, abdomen, she didn't protest. In fact, to Kultur's ears, her breaths were coming faster; her bottom shifted over his hips.

His phallus was like throbbing steel. She had to feel it pressing hard into her bottom. Although he couldn't see lying flat on his back, he was acutely aware she was nude from her ribs down.

She felt relaxed but not fully. She was definitely being affected by his roaming touch. Lifting his head slightly, he could see her nipples now hard little buds poking through the pajama top.

Finally he could feel her stiff body loosen, her breathing changing from shallow and tense to rapid, deeper, she writhed slightly on his torso. He smiled, she was turned on and he hadn't touched her sexually. *Sons above, so receptive, she was made for love. For me.*

He took a chance and very slowly skimmed his hands up her thighs, over her stomach, up her ribs to palm her breasts. Her moan encouraged him to knead them and tug, twist her nipples.

She made a feeble effort to push his hands away but when he kept caressing them, her hands fell limply to the bed against either side of his waist.

Encouraged, he stroked his fingers down to cup her mound with both hands.

"Kultur…" Again, she made a small struggle to stop him, but when her faint pushes at his big hands didn't move them, she let her hands fall again. He widened his knees forcing her legs to spread further apart and still using both hands he lightly squeezed and pressed and tugged her sex.

Her head rolled over his chest in building desire, the soft curly hair streaming over his bare skin like silk would have been enough to get him off even without his hands all over her half naked body.

Keeping one hand cupping her mound, he drew his fingers up her body, over her stomach, ribs, up between her breasts to her neck and behind her ear.

She shivered deliciously all over his body. His erection jumped. He lifted her arms over her head and pulled the pajama top off her in one smooth move.

He trailed his fingers back down, circling them over her breasts, then palmed her swelling globes. At her purring whimpers, he drew his hands back down to drift up and down and around her sex. Using his other hand, he pulled her nether lips apart and sunk his finger into her.

The top part of her body folded forward, her hands clutched his wrists, she tried to sit up but her legs were held apart by his knees. He could feel her vagina clenching around him in small spasms like she was climaxing, but not yet.

"*Kultur*," she exhaled his name. His finger moved in and out of her, she whispered, "You said you wouldn't, *ahh…*"

Stroking a hand up to cuddle her breast he kept the other with his thick finger moving inside her, then he added a second long finger.

His voice a soft, low rumble, he said, "Do you want me to stop, Sislla?"

Her hips bucked with a whimper, her sheath undulated around his fingers. Her head rolled back against his shoulder, off his neck. He stroked her from her breast to her core, his fingers still gently thrusting.

She didn't answer him, but she moaned as her writhing body pushed her nub against his hand.

"Tell me, *tiris koritsi,* tell me you want me, this time is on you." His shaft was straining to push up her bottom, she wriggled against it making him groan out loud.

"Make up your mind fast, *koritsi*, we either go ahead or I have to stop right now." He pushed his pajamas down his hips, moved his hand to hold his phallus and rub it from under her up and against her core, slightly putting it in her opening then pulling back, teasing. Of course he was putting himself over the top too, the teaser was also being teased.

Her breaths short panting hics, she whimpered, "No."

"No what, Sislla?" One hand splayed over her belly, then slid back down to stroke her clit. "Tell me…"

"Uhh," she groaned, her hips undulating. "I- I want…" her lips parted, her eyes were closed but her lids fluttered.

"You want what, baby?" he whispered against her ear, her hair flurried from his breaths. "Tell me what you want."

She writhed harder, trying to move her core against his hands. "You…Kultur…" her words poured out in a breathy sigh. "I want you, Kultur."

Grinning against her neck, he put his hands back, stroking, swirling, dipping his fingers in and out of her until her body arched against his fingers.

Her legs tightened and her toes curled, knifing forward with a loud cry she pressed her sex at his fingers, hard. Her climax throttled her body until she fell back with wheezing short breaths, then she let out a deep throated wail and lay on Kultur with bone-breaking shudders.

He grasped her breasts, cupping them and pinching her nipples while her body wracked with tremors making her jerk and moan. Then he wrapped his hands around her waist and flipped her over to sit on top of him, straddling his hips.

Half dazed, she threw out her hands to his chest to brace herself from falling on him, but he was holding her steady. He wriggled his pants down further and off and pushed them off the bed.

Sislla wavered slightly, reeling and woozy. He chuckled at her shocked, disoriented expression, then his eyes darkened with burning lust.

Her eyes were bright and glazed, pupils hugely black, her lips separated, begging to be kissed, her cheeks shone rosy and dewy.

His gaze shifted down, her long curly hair swirled down and around and over her breasts, the pink nipples poked flirtatiously through the strands. Her thighs were astride his; her sex was pressed against him, actually right on top of his phallus.

Her back arched as she unconsciously pushed her hair back. Kultur's shaft lurched at the sight of her with her arms raised, lifting her hair up off her shoulders, her plump bare breasts exposed, so fair and round and made for his hands.

His gaze dropped to her thighs spread over him and her sex sitting on his shaft.

"All sons above, Sislla, you are so damned gorgeous you take my breath away." His throaty rasp urged her, "Put me in you, Sislla."

Confused, she seemed to just become aware of her position, that she was sitting fully nude atop Kultur. His palms were on her thighs stroking up and down their firm smooth length, his thumbs just lightly touching her core.

He planned on keeping her primed before her brain took over again and told him to stop. "It's okay, *tiris koritsi,* just hold onto me and sit on my shaft, slide down on me. I will help you."

His fingers gripped her waist to hold her hips to balance her. On her knees, she moved up off him and hesitated, then shyly put her fingertips on his thick hard erection, he almost jumped out of his skin.

"*Ahh*...sons above, baby," he moaned, his eyes scrunched closed. He instructed, "Hold me tighter," and wrapped his hand around hers to show her, squeezing her hand around his shaft. His groan growled out, his shaft swelled, hardened and pulsed in her dainty hand.

She leaned over to set a hand on his chest to balance. He put his palm on her back and pulled her down further so he could lift his head and nip at her taut nipples. With a gaspy mew, her head arched back and her body quivered.

Still holding his hand over hers, trying to talk around the tight growling grunt in his throat, he hissed, "Lean forward more, baby." A hand still on her back, he pulled her so her bum was raised and he tried to help her guide his shaft inside her, but she resisted.

Her face bunched up with worry, she said, "I- I can't, Kultur, please don't make me."

"Ahh, baby, don't fret. This is all new for you." Releasing her hand, he smiled up at her.

They were both taken aback when Sislla reached down and tenderly brushed locks of black hair off his brow.

His dark head was cushioned on the white pillowcase, his tanned skin a manly contrast on the white sheets. His shoulders were so broad he never would have fit in a double, or even a queen-sized bed comfortably.

Flinty orbs gleamed lustily up at her. He cupped her breasts, caressing them. "I'll never get enough of feeling your beautiful breasts in my palms, *tiris koritsi.*" His fingers clenched and molded them; he rubbed her nipples with his thumbs.

"What does that mean, what you called me?" Sislla asked with a tiny frown, "You said something before about foreigner but it sounds different than it did before."

She leaned over to press her bosom against his hard chest, to feel the silk of his chest hair on her bare skin, forcing him to release her breasts so they could chafe skin to skin.

Chuckling, he admitted, "I added a word. It means '*my* little foreigner.'" Then he held her and rolled over in one movement so she was on her back and he was over her.

Levering between her legs, he nudged her thighs apart. His fingers drifted down to stroke her clit, he said, "Is it still yes, Sislla?" Soaking from her orgasm, his finger dipped inside her with ease. He watched her eyelids flutter, her lips part and her back inverted slightly.

When she didn't answer him, he stroked her clitoris while gently plunging his finger inside her. "Sislla, answer me."

Her head tilted back, mouth opened further as she breathed harder and her eyes lolled.

"Sislla."

Gulping, she swallowed hard then licked her lips. Her voice small and hushed, she said, "Yes, Kultur."

His fingers still stroking and moving over and in her sex, his voice as soft as hers he asked, "You want me inside you? Say it."

Her head rolled on the pillow, her fingers dug into the sheets, she nodded with a lick of her lips. "Yes Kultur, uhh…" her moan racked her body with shivers. "Yes, I…want you…inside… me…"

A hint of mirth in his husky voice he said, "Say please," and watched her brows frown, she licked her lips. He kept his fingers pumping until he had her on the brink of orgasm then he pulled back, again and again.

Then he pulled his fingers out and braced one forearm on the bed and slid the other under her, raising her hips.

She cried, "Please, Kultur, I want you inside me…ahh…please…now," her chest rose hard she sucked in deep.

"*Ohh!*" Her breath wrung from her lungs as he slammed into her with one sudden, powerfully hard thrust.

Hesitating at her cry, his own guttural sounds of intense pleasure washed over him in waves from his impact of thrusting so savagely into her tender body.

Waiting to see if he'd hurt her, he watched her under lowered lids and saw her face tighten, eyes shut and crunched, he saw a streak of pain slash across her face, and he faltered.

Then her lids flickered and she took a deep breath and he felt her melt around him. With an inner sigh of relief, he slid more gently in and out of her soft as sweet cream sheath until her hips started moving in rhythm with his, then he drove with more power. The speed of his thrusts increasing with every deeper plunge.

"*Damn,*" he grit out, he didn't want it to be over so soon. The other times should have taken the edge off his lust for her, but the opposite was happening. It would be some time before they could have a long, languorous lovemaking.

But now, he couldn't hold back, he pounded her until he heard her hitching gasps speed up and her fingers dig into his shoulders. Her nails scraped his arms, *it felt great*, her womb clenched him sculpting his phallus in sharp pulses.

As she took a deep inhalation to cry out her climax, he let go and went with her.

Stabbing fiercely into her tiny channel, his teeth ground under the strain of holding part of him back. She was so small and delicate, he had to make sure. It would be a while before he could determine if he was too strong, too big to harm her if he lost total control. Women were designed to accept and adapt to men, but he needed to be sure before he really let go 100%.

With that thought, while her body shuddered around him in orgasm and she cried her pleasure against his neck, he rammed into her as much as he dared then he burst, erupting his seed into her womb with a breathless hoarse shout.

His own body wreathed with his fury of thrusts before he slowed, then heaving, he dropped beside her, pulling her with him to face him while he stayed inside her.

They rested, heartbeats throbbing out of their chests. Kultur wound his arms around her holding her close.

She lay half across him now, soft flesh over iron flesh with her arm curled around his neck and her face lying on his mat of chest hair. Her head rose with his lungs filling with air, then deeply exhaling as his body settled back down to normal.

Sislla moved away, out of his embrace, making him slide out of her. When he reached for her, she rolled to sit on the edge of the bed with her legs dangling off the side.

Huskily, Kultur demanded, "Sislla, come back here."

She scooted further away, her head down, she covered her face with her hands.

Chapter Twenty-Six

Qultur pushed to sit up, tucked his legs cross-legged and stared at her back. "Sislla, don't do this."

Out with an angry sob, "Do what?"

Leaning over, he clutched her arms, turned her around to face him, her legs pulled up to curve gracefully to the side.

She set a palm on the bed, her arm straight, and rested the other hand in her lap. Her crown of hair spiraled down almost completely covering her front except for her nipples. When she saw his eyes pinpointed on them, she slipped an arm under her hair to cross over and cover her nipples.

Dragging his fingers roughly through his thick mass of hair, he leaned his hulky body back slightly to be less intimidating to her. His mouth settled into a testy line, he set his arms on his thighs.

"You get pissy the second we get done making love. Like you regret it when in truth you reveled in it. Tis really aggravating me, Sislla."

Her eyes peered up irritably and shameful through her furl of lashes. "I do regret it. First you raped me, now you force yourself, your hands, on me while I'm asleep then, until I- I- can't say no. And then you take advantage of me and then say it's okay because I gave my permission."

"So what? I'm helping you let your body do the thinking, and your body said yes. We both get pleasure, it's not hurting

218

anything. When we are fully mated you will be happy to be in my bed."

"You're not being fair."

"Are you truly saying you regret these times we've made love?"

She opened her mouth, but shut it. Kultur could see the truth without her answering by her blushing cheeks. She ducked her head letting her hair fall over her face covering it.

Kultur pushed back both sides of her hair, tucking them behind her ears and lifting the bulk to flow down her back.

Keeping his eyes on her face and not her nude body, he put two fingers under her chin and tilted it up.

"Let me ask you this, Sislla. My mother brought all those other men around for you to choose one to mark you. Would you have chosen any of them if I had let you?" *Which never would have happened.*

Pulling some ringlets back forward to cover her chest, she leaned back from his fingers and shook her head. "It doesn't matter, I should have had a choice. You gave me no choice."

Annoyed she never answers him directly, his voice dropped lower, turned dusky like there was smoke in his lungs. "Answer my question."

When she turned her head from him, her lashes lowered over her eyes, she could feel his burning gaze on her breasts. Looking around for her robe and not seeing it, she pulled more hair forward to cover them.

Shaking her head, she said, "No. I would not have chosen to be with any of them. I still would have been forced to…have sex against my will, and forced to stay here."

He didn't know whether he was relieved or not. She hadn't answered if she had desired any of the men, only that she would have still had to stay on the island.

"What about me? I know I am a violent crude barbarian, and you are…the opposite, but, would you have chosen me if you'd had time to…get to feel comfortable with me?"

"I told you, Kultur, it doesn't matter. You will make me stay here. I can't. I have to go."

Trying to keep the irritation of her still not answering his specific question out of his tone, he asked impatiently, "Why? Why do you have to go?"

She was quiet because she didn't know why. She thought it was because she assumed she had family somewhere that cared about her, worried about her disappearance.

They both sat silently. Keeping her head averted from him, Sislla twisted the bottom of her hair between her fingers. He stared blankly at her.

Then, she asked, "Kultur, tell me, what would you do if James down the lane raped Mellie the maid?"

He frowned. "I would beat him within an inch of his life."

"Uh huh. What would you do if Van raped your sister?"

His confused frown furrowed deeper, he said quickly, "I would kill him."

"So, what would you do if Donni raped Gaya from the village?"

Shrugging, he said matter-of-factly, "I would beat him within an inch of his life."

"Okay, what would you do if Sams raped your mother?"

"I would kill him."

"What would you do if Graham the guard raped me?"

His hands balled into tight fists, he answered with anger, "I would beat him to death."

"What would you do if you raped me, Kultur?"

He was silent. Now she looked at him. His mouth parted, then his lips pulled in, he pushed them out and glared at her.

Huffy, he growled, "See, like I said, you get pissy every damned time after we make love. It won't make me want to touch you any less. I told you I would not stop touching you. If the marking had not been necessary I would never have forced you. But since it is and I did, we are not stopping now. The way you react to me, your body is made for making love. With me."

220

His chest rose and fell with his irritation. "I have told you again and again, Sislla, I've done what was necessary to save your life. But tis done now, and," the side of his lip lifted in a smirk, "there is no reason to stop now, as clearly you respond to my touch."

Her snort sarcastic mild, but uneasy, "I'm sure you know how to skillfully touch any woman and they would get as…disoriented…as me." The blue eyes shifted up to him then dropped quickly but not before he saw her embarrassment in them.

"No. You are different, Sislla. I don't do all this with any other woman." His hands itched to touch her, stroke her, he kept them still, and kept his eyes off her lips or he'd be kissing her senseless and she'd be on her back again. And this conversation would start all over again and she'd probably be even madder.

"What do you mean, all this?"

Losing his irritation, he said patiently, "We've made love three times in one night, basically counting today as last night as it's still early. I would have woken you up earlier for more but," he looked sheepish, "I knew you were exhausted and probably sore."

"But you did wake me up."

One broad shoulder rolled. "Uh, aye. I waited as long as I could. I found I couldn't help myself with you all adorable and luscious in my pajama top and curled in my arms. So kill me, I've told you I'm a man and that's what men do when there's a gorgeous woman in their bed."

"I don't understand, you just said you don't do what you did with me with other women, but now you say you would whenever there's a woman in your bed. What do you mean?" Her forehead wrinkled with confusion, this time she looked directly at him without lowering her eyes.

Understanding she was young and inexperienced he was still patient. "I said I don't normally have sex more than once with a woman. I take what I want and leave." His lips pursed, that was not the best way to say that.

"You're saying you don't make love- have sex- with a woman more than once?" Recalling the last lust-saturated hours, even now she could see he was aroused. He looked like he was struggling to keep from pouncing on her. She shook her head. "I don't believe that."

Shrugging without emotion, he said, "Believe what you want. For me to take the time to do it more than once they would have to be in my bed and I don't bring women here. When I fuck- uh, see them, it is elsewhere. It would be too uncomfortable if we were somewhere like outside or something to do it again, why bother, I already got what I wanted.

"Moreover, I do not stay overnight with them at their place. I have no desire to sleep with any of them. But, I do desire to have sex multiple times with you in a day. So yeah, you're different. You're the only woman I've had in my bed, and the only one that I've literally slept with."

One eyebrow quirked at him. "Oh really? When that creature, Troll, whatever his name was brought me here, you took me to your room and put me on your bed."

His gaze rolled coolly down her body and back up to her crystal blue orbs. He shrugged. "The second I laid eyes on you I wanted you. As I told you then, I thought you were a shore prostitute. We were already in the castle, it wouldn't have made sense to leave and go somewhere else."

He reached over and picked up a curl watching it twine around his finger, then let it go, "Plus, you were injured. When we were done, that is if we had had sex, I would have seen to your care."

Her hair separated around her full breasts, his eyes devoured her soft white globes. He was almost sitting on his hands to keep them off her. Then he couldn't help it, he reached for her, she leaned back from him.

Frowning, he said, "I warned you, when you're near me, I will be touching you. If we were fully mated, married, you would not put me off, you would expect it. It's hopeful that you would be touching me, too."

He had also hoped that if he taught her a few times that her body enjoyed the sex, with him, that she would become a willing participant, maybe even come to him of her own free will without him initiating it.

Seeing the flames glowing in his dark eyes staring at her flesh, Sislla grabbed the sheet and pulled it up to cover herself. The growing anger apparent in her tone, she said, "You don't have the right to touch me when you feel like it."

Unhappy, then comically, he watched her cover her nudity from him. Like she could stop him from touching her, having her, if he chose to, but he would keep his thoughts to himself.

His lip quirked up in resignation. "Sislla, there is no point in arguing about it. You are my mate. Tis done. Or almost done. Doesn't matter regardless, it is a done deal but for the two remaining markings."

Her lips compressed into a firm line, she wriggled to sit back against the headboard and held the sheet over her chest like he might snatch it away. "I am not your mate."

A short laugh, and he said, "Yeah you are, technically." He reached over and took a handful of her sheet and clenched it. "So, *tiris koritsi*, I should change my little foreigner to my little mate, you will be staying with me, every night, in my chambers, in my bed. Get used to it."

Her mouth dropped, eyes pinned wide then slid narrow. "So you can seduce me every time I'm asleep? I don't think so. Besides, even if we completed the three markings that doesn't mean we are a couple. You can go be with your other women and I will go on my way."

Red color flushed up his neck darkening his face up to his livid eyes. "What the fuck, Sislla, cut it out. We will not go our separate ways. We will live together in my chambers, in my home, in this castle. End of story." Fuming, he crossed his arms and glared at her hands clutching the sheet so tightly.

Holding the sheet closer to her chin, she sniffed, "Why? As you've said, you are marking me to save me, but that doesn't mean we have to live together."

His teeth clenched, eyes slit to furious gashes. "No fucking way. You will stay with me, permanently. I'm done with this fighting, we are done with this, there will be no more talk like this. Done."

She blinked rapidly, she was losing this war. "Wait, seriously, there is no need for us to live together, we can have the sex three times and move on. You're making it sound like we would be like married or something. What are you-"

He rolled off the bed to his feet. Smiling when he saw her gaze go instantly to his erection he smirked at her fists hitching the sheet up higher. He said, "I will have Onani bring your breakfast."

Blue eyes gawked from his shaft to his face. "Kultur, you can't keep me locked in your bedroom."

A gleam of lust flamed bright in his eyes burning a hole through the sheet to her, "Yes, I can."

Watching him stroll towards the bathroom she scowled. "Kultur, I have obligations. I promised Lori I would babysit their newborn. She wants to spend some time alone with Cortland."

He kept padding towards the bathroom in his bare feet. "So, the baby can come here."

"Kultur!" she said loudly with adamant insistence. He stopped and turned. Her eyes went from the top of his tousled dark hair over the muscles bunched in his powerful chest down to- she jerked her gaze back up to his face catching his smirk.

"I need to heal. Please don't harm the ill people because you…"

He crossed his arms. His erection had not diminished in the least. "Because I what?" It was pointless for him to hide his grin as her eyes drifted back down his body.

"Be- because of your lust. It's selfish."

That brought a quick scowl wiping out his grin. He glared so hard at her she had to drop her eyes. "All right." Giving in, his sigh was a piqued grunt. "You can leave my chambers, you can go to your workshop, but you have to promise you will not leave the castle. I trust you are a woman of your word." But he watched her carefully; she was sneaky in getting around his agreements.

Her face lit up so cheerfully he felt a pang in his heart, and his shaft jolted. It hurt that she was so happy to get away from him, but she was so lovely in her joy it also aroused him. Taking a step towards her he frowned when she held the sheet up like it was a solid barrier between them.

She said quickly, "I promise, Kultur, I will not leave the castle today." Such honesty and happiness in the broad smile she gave him made him suspicious.

"Uh," he hated the thought of her leaving his room. "Okay then. You can do your stuff, but just remember, the next golden moon is in a little over a week."

Her smile was so blank he felt another stab of suspicion. Maybe he should make her promise to come to him willingly for the second marking, his eyes narrowed, no, not yet. He didn't want her to lie to him, and he didn't want to argue more.

"All right. I have to be in the field all day today and probably most of the night. Can I perhaps have a kiss before you leave?" Brows high in hopefulness, dropped quickly at her expression and shaking head.

"No, Kultur. I know how you operate. First it's just one kiss, then it's 'just let me touch you a little,' the next thing I know you're pounding inside of me-" she broke off at the blatant graphic eroticism that struck his handsome face at her words.

He started towards her. She held up a hand to ward him off, "No, stop. I mean it. You swore if I said stop you would."

His head cocked, brow crinkled in chagrin at her denying him even a kiss.

"You need to unlock the door," Sislla ordered as she found the pajama top, pulled it on and shuffled off the bed. Finding the bottoms he'd left on the floor, she picked them up and sat back down on the edge of the mattress, slipped them on then rolled the legs up.

He stood with his hands at his sides considering what would happen if he broke his word to her and jumped her. Then he reluctantly went and unlocked the door but he wasn't going to open it for her, he didn't want her to leave. When she didn't move, he sighed and stepped several feet aside, away from the door.

Warily, she walked to the door, opened it and slipped outside scurrying down the hall.

Kultur stared at the door contemplating his next move.

Chapter Twenty-Seven

Two days later, Sislla's smoothed the sweaty hair off the little girl's head with her hand. The tot was sitting on the examination bed in Sislla's workshop.

Handing the child a sweet and a smile, Sislla said to the girl's mother, "She will be as bright as a star in no time, Mrs. Claright."

Mrs. Claright shook Sislla's hand, thanking her profusely as she helped the child down.

A shadow fell over Sislla, she recognized the shiny polished boots and white pants. "Yes, Ryan?" She smiled up at the guard.

A smile shone briefly over his stiff young face. "Begging your pardon, Miss Sislla, but it's been over three hours and you know the Atraam's orders. I've already sent the rest of the people away. You have to stop working now."

Surprised at how fast the time flew by, she glanced towards the door and saw the line of people was indeed gone. "Oh, okay." Knowing if she disobeyed Kultur's rule of her working no more than three hours a day it would risk Ryan's neck, she went ahead and started putting things away.

Then, a couple of the castle maids gathered in a cluster in the doorway. Ryan frowned at them and made a sweeping motion, "Ladies, Miss Sislla is done for the day, you may return tomorrow."

"Oh but we didn't come for healing." A girl in her twenties tucked her curly red hair behind her ears and said boldly, "We are

227

here for a lesson. Miss Sislla had promised she would do some more lessons. Here we are."

Sislla grinned with pleasure.

Seeing her immediately giving in, Ryan's frown deepened, he stepped forward. "Miss Sislla, with all due respect, I don't think the Atraam would be happy about that. He said no working longer than three-"

"Poo, Ryan, teaching a lesson in healing isn't work. He won't mind. Let's go to the big table out in the grand chamber, ladies," Sislla gestured with them to follow her. "I can lay out the herbs and leaves and you can look at them as I discuss their abilities, clotting blood, relieving pain, etc."

Short of physically restraining Sislla, and Ryan knew that anyone, including him, touching her would set the Atraam into a terrible rage unless it was a life threatening reason, he had no choice but to follow her.

Before she started, one of the young women took Sislla aside and keeping her eye on Ryan so he couldn't hear, whispered urgently in her ear. Sislla patted the woman on the back and whispered something soothing back to her. The woman tearfully took a seat with the others.

Sislla had been speaking for around thirty minutes when Ryan was finally able to flag someone down.

He motioned to another guard to come to him. "Jaspar," he said in a low voice so no one else could hear him, "go find the Atraam, I think he's still in the field, and tell him no worries but that the Miss is well past her three hours."

Thank goodness it was Jaspar who was there, he had shared guard duty with Ryan over Sislla and he understood quite clearly the Atraam's orders. The only one who seemed not to was Miss Sislla.

Jaspar nodded his acquiescence and strode out the door.

Ryan went and stood discreetly nearby but not right next to Sislla, sweat trickled down his temples. He could only pray that he'd done the right thing. The Atraam had said do not leave her under any circumstances, if something was odd, have someone fetch him. Ryan could only hold his breath and wait. He glanced at Sislla as she spoke animatedly at the women, his eyes drifted to her dress.

His cheeks reddened, the Atraam was going to be really pissed when he sees the dress she was swearing. It had a fairly low square cut bodice and her cleavage could be easily seen. However, her attire was clearly not part of his guard duties. He took a deep breath and held it.

Then as if Ryan's stomach wasn't clenched enough, worse came along. The Atraam's brother, Gabriel, spotted Sislla and ambled over to her.

The ladies taking the lesson were busy attempting a task Sislla had given them.

Gabriel greeted Sislla, "Hey little foreigner," he grinned at the nickname his brother had given her. "How's it going?"

She gave him a big smile. Gabriel was a terribly good looking man in a way that would be pretty if he was a female.

His wavy light hair sparkled, long lashes framed his light eyes twinkling with mischief, he had gorgeous kissable lips, as attractive but not as chiseled as Kultur's. Kultur was the only one of the three brothers who had a dimple.

Gabriel was big and heartily built as Kultur. Sislla had heard the gossip that Gabriel was quite the ladies' man. Charming with a casual but powerful sex appeal, he came across much more approachable than Kultur with his ready warm smile and saucy wink.

Kultur's hard, implacable face and cold empty stare, and the aggressive violence that sat rigidly in his shoulders kept everyone at a safe distance from him. Except for the more randy women looking for a dangerous liaison.

Lexi sauntered by and seeing Gabriel and Sislla immediately changed direction and went right to them. Greeting them with a cheerful smile and a perky voice, she chirped, "Hey, guys, what's going on?"

As Lexi joined them, Gabriel shifted next to Sislla and dropped a friendly arm around her. As the three conversed he occasionally gave her a little squeeze. He caught Ryan's petrified eye, the young guard was trying to signal Gabriel to let go of her without speaking out loud.

Gabriel just gave him a sassy wink. He was the only one facing the side door that led directly out to the field. Seeing the door open, his grin broadened as Kultur strode into the room.

Kultur's piercing gaze went right to Sislla, then to Gabriel's arm around her then to Gabriel.

Gabriel gave his brother a big shit-eating grin and hugged Sislla against his side. The hug pushed her breasts together and up in the low cut bodice, Gabriel dipped his eyes to peer down the front of her dress.

The fierce look on Kultur's face only made him grin harder. When Gabriel stroked Sislla's back, yanking at some curls, Kultur looked about to detonate.

Gabriel knew he'd gone far enough. He slipped his arm from Sislla's shoulders and drifted away. Sislla and Lexi were in deep conversation, they didn't even notice he'd left.

His hands in his pockets, Gabriel strolled over to where Kultur was standing. He looked calm with a hip leaned against the wall and his arms crossed, but Gabriel knew his brother.

Kultur's face was even more briery and hard-edged than normal, his smoldering eyes barely visible under lowered lids radiated volatile wrath. Gabriel watched him crank his neck like a grizzly on the attack.

Gabriel said cheerfully, "All right, calm down, little brother. I was just being friendly."

With hardly any movement at all, Kultur slammed his fist into his brother's side knocking the wind out of him.

Still smirking, but his eyes watered, Gabriel wrapped his arms around his torso and tried to keep from gagging from the strike. Breathless he complained, "*Kriité*, K, it was just a small hug."

"Aye, and that was a small punch. Touch her again and we will see how bigger the punch gets."

Rubbing his side, Gabriel's grin was weak but he still taunted his brother. "Chill, K, you haven't gotten to that third marking yet have you? Or even the second one?" Kultur's family was well aware that he had kept Sislla with him all night a couple of days ago on the golden moon.

Even past the necessary marking, they also knew Kultur was way too sexually robust and attracted to Sislla to spend the long night and late morning with her without being physically involved.

"Just shut up, Gabe, and keep your hands off her," Kultur warned quietly but with a chilled tone and eyes so slit they were almost closed.

Gabriel laughed. "No, seriously, brother, you haven't completed the markings, that means she is still fair game, still available for me to- *oof*-" he doubled over from the punch to the ribs Kultur gave him that was so fast even someone looking directly at the brothers wouldn't have seen it.

"She is off the list of available women. Don't fucking make me take you outside and prove it to you."

Gabriel laughed crookedly through the pain. "Okay, okay, I got it. I should give you a shot outside though, you'd still beat me but I'd make it tough for you. Anyway, you've never experienced territorial jealousy before, K, and tis sure taking you for a ride."

Kultur tucked his hands in his pockets; he hadn't taken his eyes off Sislla even when hitting his brother.

Beside him, Gabriel swore, "Holy shit, would you look at that?"

Kultur's eyes zoomed like a penlight at the women across the room.

One of the girls was standing in front of Sislla and had her hand on Sislla's chest. The girl then drew her finger around the inside of Sislla's low cut bodice. She ran her finger all around the inside of the collar from end to end.

"Holy fuck, brother, that is fucking hot!" Gabriel declared, stepping to the side; Kultur's punch missed him by a hair.

Gabriel couldn't help provoking him, "Seriously K, it doesn't turn you on seeing another babe with her hands all over your woman's tits? *Shi-it*, I'd take them both to bed so fast, watch them kiss while they undressed, grope them while they fondle each other- *aggh-"*

This time Kultur's fist connected with Gabriel's side. Gabriel squawked hoarsely at Kultur's back, "I think you broke my rib, K, don't you care?" He laughed watching the steam pouring off his brother as he stalked across the room trying to look calm and nonchalant.

When he saw Lexi's face lighten to ash at the sight of him, Kultur knew he looked fearsome; his casual stride wasn't fooling anyone.

"Uh, Sislla, you uh," Lexi stammered trying to get Sislla's attention.

Ryan was a frozen board, his eyes were stuck open wide, he didn't blink. The girl still had her hand inside Sislla's dress.

"What is going on?" Kultur demanded, his eyes on the girl's hand.

The girl whipped her hand out. "Oh, sir, Atraam," her face turned beet red then blanched white at the fury on his face. "We, I, I can sew and Miss Sislla was saying how she had to wear borrowed clothes from Lexi like this dress, I was uh, measuring her, uh, bosom, so…"

Kultur's gaze clamped onto Sislla's breasts half exposed in the low cleavage before rising to her face.

Sislla was angry, no doubt about it. Angry that he was causing a scene, well, she'd see later what anger really was. In fact, already the roses in Sislla's cheeks were paling like everyone else's at the thunderous look on his face.

Wisely, seeing the way he glared at her chest, she was suddenly afraid to be alone with him. She sidled nearer to Lexi.

Didn't matter, Kultur's eyes sharpened to cruel black ice. He looked every bit the harrowing warlord that reined with a heavy hand over the Chamaine-Gris, everyone present quailed.

232

His voice as cold and hard as his icy eyes, he said, "Put your gear up, Sislla, and come with me."

Twining her fingers together, Sislla brought them up to her chest as if to hide her exposed rounded flesh. "Uh, but, Kultur, I need to-"

He seemed to grow bigger, like an incensed goliath, his eyes spat black hell, but he said coolly, calmly, "Put your shit up."

Knowing Kultur was quite capable of throwing her over his shoulder in humiliation and marching off with her, or harming one of the others because of her obstinacy, her eyes flashed to Ryan who was standing so fraught with fear he looked like a tuning fork.

Without another word, as Sislla bustled around putting things in jars, the other women, including Lexi, slunk silently away.

When everything was put away in containers, Sislla went to gather them up in her arms to take them back to the workshop.

"Give them to Kirman Shaws."

"But he doesn't know where to-" seeing Kultur's impassive face, rolling her eyes, Sislla sighed and turned as Ryan held his arms out. As quick as he could, Ryan gathered up the containers and fled down the hall leaving Sislla and Kultur alone.

"Okay, I guess I'm read- oh!"

Kultur grabbed her forearm and roughly swung her around to face him. Taken by surprise, her eyes flew wide, her lips parted.

Kultur's black eyes like a shark's, dangerously emotionless, viewed her like she was a bloody baby seal. Holding her arm, he pulled her up on her toes and close to his chest.

"You know," the timber of his voice seethed so dangerously quiet and low a real shark would have fled from him. "If Shaws rolled his eyes at me he would be chasing his head across floor." Holding her arm he pulled her in close, said with chilling quiet, "And I am not being amusing."

Her lips flapped like she was trying to push words out, but the tighter he squeezed her arm, and the narrower his eyes slit, the less she could think of to say. "But- but-"

"You need to not talk right now." Moving his death grip to her upper arm, Kultur tramped across the marble floor, his heavy boots echoing with each hard footfall and up the stairs.

As they rounded the corner a guard hurrying around the sharp corner didn't see them in time and his tray caught Sislla in the head.

She reeled backwards and would have fallen if Kultur hadn't held her.

Pulling her close, he wound his long fingers around the back of her head lifting it to see if she was injured. An angry red mark was already swelling on her forehead.

Releasing her, Kultur's body swelled huge with fury, he stalked to the guard and slammed his fist into the side of his head sending the man flying. With a raging snarl he went after the guard.

The guard fell on his ass, scrambling to his hands and feet he tried to scurry away like a crab from Kultur's wrath, but with a thunderous roar deep in his chest, Kultur grabbed for the man's collar to haul him up, and drew back his huge fist to rocket a lethal punch to his head.

Screaming, "Kultur, no!" Sislla ran and threw herself between the men. Kultur was already swinging- he just missed Sislla and only nicked the guard in his effort to miss her.

"*Goddammit Sislla!*" Kultur bellowed. "Get out of the way, he is dead for hurting you."

"No!" Sislla leaped up on Kultur and facing him wrapped her legs around his waist. She threw her arms around his neck and clung to him, making it impossible for him to strike out without hurting her. "It was an accident, Kultur, an accident!"

"Sislla, get the fuck off-" he pried at her arms but she pulled herself up high enough to mash her bosom against his face. A slight hesitation, then his hands dropped to splay across her back and hold her harder against him.

She whispered against his hair, "Kultur, I beg, please send him away unharmed. I can't forgive you; I *won't* forgive you if you hurt him because of me. Please."

One hand slid up to the back of her neck, the other went under her butt to support her. He nuzzled her chest, for a few seconds rubbing first his cheek and then his mouth against her soft mounds. Instantly plunged in a white haze of desire for her, he had to fight out of it remembering the guard was watching them.

Dipping his nose in her hair, Kultur sniffed her unique scent. Through the thick curly locks he snarled at the guard, "You live, go to the dungeon, tell Horace 20 lashes."

He turned his face back from the guard and rubbed the side of his face and his jaw over her breasts. In the back of his mind he thought he needed to get them out of there before he latched onto a nipple and sucked it right through her dress in front of anyone coming down the hall.

But, her voice as serious and quiet as a heart attack, Sislla whispered in his ear, "No punishment, Kultur, I will harm myself if you harm him."

His blood ran cold, his head lowered, he believed her. The guard was struggling to his feet, his mouth bleeding, a look of stark panic smacked on his face.

Kultur forced himself to lean back from Sislla. He cupped the back of her head, his arm still under her butt, with a sharp nod of his head, he muttered to the guard, "Go to your quarters. Stay out of my sight." He watched the guard scramble to his feet and run off down the stairs.

So soft, her voice floated around his head, "Thank you, Kultur."

"Yeah." He turned back to her, brushed her hair off her face, then lowered his mouth and vehemently seized her lips. Their lips glued, Kultur carried her down the hall to his room.

At the door, when he fumbled for his keys, Sislla murmured against his mouth, "No, I need to go to my room, and…change my…" his tongue skating through and around and deep in her mouth did not stop at her words, but he did pivot and trot down the hall to her room.

All the way down the hall he dominated her mouth, barely letting her catch her breath. He kept his hand around the back of her head holding her against his lips. At her door, he opened it, carried her inside still straddling him and kicked the door closed behind them.

Without removing his mouth from hers, he kissed her all the way to her bed then swung around and fell on his back on the mattress bringing her down with him, on top of him.

He pulled her up his chest, her breasts almost spilled out the top of her dress. Both his hands wrapped around her head keeping their kiss going until she turned her head away to catch her breath and his mouth dropped to her neck.

Paying no attention to her struggles now to get off him, he sucked her flesh, pulling it, biting it, raising marks she would be angry about later.

He slid his hand into the top of her dress and palmed her breasts, filling his fingers with her suppleness he groaned. Kneading her too hard, she cried out and struggled harder to get away from him. When he wouldn't release her, she tried to hit him.

"Kultur, stop, let me go!"

Kissing and licking her neck like she was a feast made for him, he mumbled absently, "You can hit me all you want but you can't hurt me." He shoved his hand up her skirt, pulled his other hand from her top and pushed both palms down inside the back of her undergarment fiercely clutching her bottom.

"Baby," squeezing her and pulling her hard against his erection, he exhaled his hot breath misting her skin. "You are so fine. I've missed you so fucking much. You haunt my damned dreams."

But she squirmed and kicked, pushing at him. "No, stop Kultur."

Keeping one hand in her underwear, clinching her round bottom, he reached between their torsos and unbuckled his belt, tore impatiently at the buttons on his breeches.

He rolled her over on her back and moved on top of her. He pulled out his rigid throbbing erection, wrapped his fist around it and slid between her legs, shoving at her underwear, pushing them

236

down as far as he could reach. In a second he was going to tear them off in his urgency.

Sislla thrashed beneath him, hitting him and shoving him, but he was a moving brick wall, he could not be stopped.

Stroking his iron hard shaft, Kultur put his fingers on her sex and brought his erection to her opening- then Sislla screamed in his ear.

His head popped up in a lust thick cloud, he tried to focus on her face. He hadn't even noticed her struggles. Her hands were flattened against his chest trying to push him away.

Squinting confused at her, he asked, "What is it- what's the matter, *koritsi?*"

She hit one of his rock hard pecs with her fist. Sounding out of breath like she'd run a mile she huffed, "You said you would stop if I said no. I am saying no."

His dark brows disappeared up in his hairline with disbelief. "Are you kidding, *koritsi?* We are so hot, so ready," he rubbed his solid thrumming organ over her core and smiled. "See, baby," he murmured seeking to suck her lips, "you are wet. I feel your silk in my hand, on my shaft. You want me too."

"No." Her tone flat, her mouth set stern.

He just blinked at her for a minute. She was clearly serious. He rolled slowly off her to sit up, his brain in a sexual muddle, he fought to fix his pants. Then he pulled her underwear up and tugged her skirt back down.

She sat up and moved to the edge of the bed. Then she slid off and pushed herself up on shaky legs.

His eyes burned down her as if he would leave a charred mark every place he looked.

Sislla smoothed her skirt and cleared her throat. "I would like you to please leave." She was staring at the floor, but she raised her eyes warily to him.

His face had become a blank sheet of angled stone. He got to his feet, fixed his trousers and straightened his shirt, and then walked to the door.

His hand on the knob, his head lowered, he looked up at her through a tousled flop of black hair. "I've had a seamstress make you some outfits. You do not need to let that woman from downstairs feel you up again to determine your size."

Her cheeks blushed with embarrassment and anger. "She did not-"

His face darkened with possessive ire. "Yeah she did. She was groping the hell out of you. If I hadn't been there she would have had her hands all over your tits and gotten your bodice pulled down and would probably be sucking your nipples-" his eyes dropped to her cleavage staring at her nipples still hard from his rough caresses poking through the dress.

"Kultur! Stop that, that did not happen." She slapped her hands on her hips. "That wasn't going to happen, you are being vulgar and crude."

"No, that dress is vulgar and crude. After having his hands all over you too trying to cop a feel, my brother had you two women naked in his mind in his room with you-" he shook his head and scrubbed his hand down his eyes and over his mouth.

Taking a deep breath, he spoke over her sputtering anger, "Whatever. I've told you before, you don't wear shit like that unless you are on my arm." He shook his head, groused, "Even then, no. Your treasures are for my eyes only."

He stomped over to her, ignoring her flinch. "If I see you in crap like that again, believe me," his eyes glowed black as wrathful sin, he bent his head to get right in her face, "you will fucking regret it."

Sislla was furiously taken aback, she refused to cower. With her haughty chin in the air she sniffed, "Just because you are a crass pig you do not have to curse at me or speak to me like that, or assume everyone wants to maul me like you do. I don't know why you think you have the right to tell me what I can and cannot wear. I am an adult, I can choose what I want." She snapped her arms across her chest and stared him down.

The side of his mouth turned up in an unpleasant half smile. "Oh yeah?" His brow arched. "You think so? Go ahead and wear that shit again and we will find out."

It was crystal clear he could do what he pleased to her, which just infuriated her. "Why do you care, Kultur, what I wear? I am limited in attire, you know that, what difference does it make if a little skin shows? Besides, apparently you're the only one who notices. You're being kind of…prudish."

"Am I?" Taking her by surprise, he slid his hand under her jaw and pulled her closer to him and turned her face up to his. He saw the flash of fright strike her eyes before she firmed her lips and faced him boldly.

"When you were prancing through the field that day with my sister picking weeds wearing the tightest pair of pants I've ever seen, and a half a top exposing skin, every one of my men stopped their workout to gawk at you."

"Really, Kultur, I was new to the castle, they were merely curious. Lexi said you've never commented on her when she wears the clothes she loaned me." The harder Sislla tried to tug from his grasp the tighter he held her, and the closer he brought her to him.

There was hardly an inch between them. The carnal tension in Kultur poured of in sweltering waves. Worried that he would go after her sexually again, she put her hands on his abdomen to keep him back.

Little did she know that her hands on him incited his desire just as much as if their bodies were touching. Kultur lowered his face so his mouth was only a few inches from hers; he did nothing to stop the smolder in his dark eyes. Although his lust for her burned clear and vibrant, anger simmered under the surface.

"I care, *tiris koritsi,* because you are *tiris*- you are mine. Those men in the field weren't looking at you with curiosity; they were looking at you with lust. It seems I can't keep you protected every second. When you go waltzing around dressed like that, you're inflaming their desire, and some of those men are little more than wild animals and would not stop from taking you if they have the opportunity. Your other comment about my sister, she doesn't look the same in those clothes as you do. And I reiterate, she is not mine, but you are."

Sislla's lips parted. Different thoughts rippled across her face transforming her expression from confusion to denial, to anger. Her lids batted rapidly as she considered his words. He let go of her chin and she backed up a step.

"Kultur, I'm sure your men are gentlemen and would never think to accost a woman, like you have." She pointed an accusing finger at him with a frown. Her lips twisted wryly, "I do not prance or waltz, you make me sound like a flaky floozy."

"They are vicious warriors, Sislla," he scoffed, "not nice soft gentlemen."

She started to turn away and then her head snapped back to him with a look of ludicrous disbelief and perplexity on her face, "What did you say before? What do you mean I am yours? Why would you say something like that? I am certainly not *yours*. I do not belong to anyone, I don't care if you are king warlord of this land. You can't own people for heaven's sake."

A self-satisfied smile tugged at his mouth. He crossed his arms and looked down at her without lowering his head. "Sislla, make no mistake, you are mine. I have claimed you with my marking. It is not completed but that doesn't matter. I have informed you that you are my mate; you need to get it into your head. As your mate, I have the right to tell you what you can and cannot wear."

She couldn't be more flabbergasted, her mouth fell open but no words came out. Then she gathered up her thoughts and sputtered, "You- you- we are not mates. You marking me doesn't mean we are linked. Even if we were, I am an individual, you do not have the right to tell me what to do."

The smile deepened, pulling in his dimple. "Let's put it this way, sweetheart, as my mate, you would not want to do something that greatly displeased me. So out of your respect for me, your mate, you would not wear shit like those tight pants and those dresses my sister has given you." He watched her face redden, lips pursed hard together like she was going to explode.

"Kultur, get this through your Neanderthal brain. We are not mates. Even if you manage to get all three markings done with me, it does not mean we are a- a couple, that is preposterous. Why would we be?"

He was now almost down right grinning. "Ah, *tiris koritsi,* note that I am saying '*my* little foreigner.' First of all, there is no *if*, it will be when I, we that is, have completed the Epita, along with the Epita comes mating. At least it does with me. When the marking is complete, you will be mine for life. You already are. Get used to it."

Slapping her hands against her sides again in frustration she just glared at him.

Kultur glared back at her, but still the grin toyed in the corner of his mouth. Then, remembering his earlier anger about the woman feeling her up, firming his possessive lips, he said coldly, "No one, not man or woman, touches you, Sislla, but me."

He caught her chin again and gave her a hard, frosty kiss. Releasing her quickly and stepping back, he said, "My seamstress brought a dress here earlier for you, it's in your closet. Put your hair up," because he loved to pull out those pins and run his fingers through her tumbling ringlets.

"I will be gone for two days. When I return I will to take you to dinner, wear the dress."

Before she could swallow, he opened the door, stepped out, and was gone. Sislla stood for a moment. Kultur was like a tornado whipping around her, enveloping her with pure sexual dynamo. When he left, all the air in the room went with him.

Letting a long breath flow out, when he was on top of her a few minutes ago she had thought she wouldn't be able to make him stop. At the very least she thought he might expect her to give in to him as a sort of gratitude for not killing, she shuddered, that poor guard.

She was actually shocked that as far as he'd gone, Kultur had been almost inside her and hard as a steel rod, that he did stop as she asked him to. Just as he said he would. She said no, he stopped.

Wondering how angry he really was, his fury had been still quite visible simmering under the surface, what was next in store for her?

Chapter Twenty-Eight

Two days passed in a wink. Sislla nervously headed to the bathroom to take a shower to get ready for dinner. Her stomach clenched. His vile, degrading mother would be there.

Sislla could not figure out what Kultur wanted with her. He said he was saving her life by marking her, by why didn't he just let another man do it?

Why would he think they would be mates, and why on earth would he *want* to be mated with her, a foreigner? He didn't even know who she was.

Ruminating further on his words he'd spoken about her in his bed, why did he say he wanted her to sleep in his bed when he said he never did that with women?

Now, he insists on dragging her off to dinner with his entire family, and warriors and their wives, and that horrible mean woman, she took a breath and rolled her eyes, his mother.

Sislla just could not figure out what Kultur wanted from her. Maybe knowing how much his mother hated her, he just wanted to torture his mother with her presence.

Maybe he thinks if he pretends that he will keep Sislla as a permanent mate it will incense his mother. That must be it. He's mad at his mother for some reason and he certainly can't punish her, so he's going to infuriate her by shoving Sislla down her throat just to bug her.

"Well," she sighed, "we'll see what tonight brings. I guess I should just prepare to take hers as well as other's sniping shots. I'll just hold my head up high and do the best I can, keep my thoughts and feelings to myself."

Passing the closet, she hesitated, curious to see the dress Kultur had made for her. She continued to the bathroom, she'd see the dress when she was done.

He knew he could unlock her door and barge right in, but he unlocked it then politely knocked and waited.

When she opened the door everything inside of him melted. His feet stuck to the floor, he couldn't move. His gaze showered down her like a molten volcano.

"Baby, you look…" at a loss for words, how do you describe something so heavenly perfect? He stepped inside and closed the door behind him.

Sislla had put her hair up like he had asked, commanded. The ringlets flowed in a bright cloud around her head.

"Hold still one second, baby." He trickled his fingertips over the mark he made on her neck still present from two days ago when they'd made love. She had tried to cover it with makeup but it was still faintly visible.

A sly smile curved his lip, he pulled out a pin and combed a ringlet down with his fingers letting it fall and spiral down along her neck hiding the mark. No one but he, and Sislla, would know it was there. It aroused him to think about it and what they had been doing when he'd given it to her.

Murmuring, *"Koritsi,"* he reached out his hand and took hers, gently turning her around so he could see all of her.

The dress was golden diaphanous shimmer, so light and delicate it clung like gold snowflakes to her breathtaking feminine curves. Elegant and strapless, it clung snugly to her bust without being indecently low or tight, and all down her figure to widen slightly over the tips of the golden shoes.

"The dress, *koritsi,* is as exquisitely ethereal as you." Eyes like searing black velvet stroked her with admiration. Kultur slid his hand around the back of her neck to pull her in for a kiss, but then knowing he wouldn't stop at a kiss, he reluctantly let her go and stood back from her.

Sislla's cheeks were pink with discomfort. Her shy eyes lowered to look at the floor then rolled up to him. "I, uh, I'm...I mean I don't think I'm used to wearing something like this." She glanced over her shoulder at the mirror. "You don't think it's too...risqué?"

The rare dimple showed in his cheek with his foxy smile. He allowed himself a quick stroke down her lower ribs to slide his palm over her tiny waist. "You don't look cheap or slutty, honey, you look drop dead stunning."

Kultur put his hands on her shoulders and turned her to fully face the mirror, then stood behind her like he had the first time they made love. He refused to think of it as the day he raped her. It was the day he saved her life, the day he claimed her as his.

"Look at yourself, you're just too beautiful for words." He lowered his head and kissed her bare shoulder.

She smiled weakly at him in the reflection. "I thought you didn't want me to wear clothes like this?"

His big hands ran down her slender arms, his lips moved to her nape. His lips on her skin, he said, "I would not want you to wear it if you weren't with me. But you are with me tonight, I can enjoy looking at you and not caring so much if other men do too, because, as I said, you're with me."

Sislla looked so naïve and guileless with perplexity clear on her face. Sons above, with her at his side he would never want for anything more.

She moved from Kultur and turned to face him. Her gaze swept him from his shiny black waves neatly combed on his head, to the dimple that still lurked in his freshly shaven cheek, to his carved lips, so full yet manly. Taking another step from him to view his attire, she smiled.

"Kultur," she folded her hands in front of her, "you look so handsome."

He was wearing a black tunic and stiffly creased black trousers that even with a belt they still hung slightly low on his lean hips. His button down shirt was black as well, a stringed tie in red and black draped around his neck, and he had some sort of ancestral pins on the breast of his tunic. He'd changed his thick, steel-toed boots for slick, polished dress boots.

Now he grinned shyly. "Oh yeah? You think so?" His hands wiggled at his side looking for sincerity in her big blue eyes.

"Yes. It's strange," she put a finger to her chin studying him, "you still look ever the fierce warlord, but slightly tamed, and yes, very gorgeous."

His lips curved up in happiness. "Thank you, *koritsi*." Wow, a compliment from his little ice princess. Maybe there was hope for them yet. At least she didn't find his looks abhorrent.

Clearing his throat, he cupped her elbow. "We should get going." She moved to go with him to the door; he lightly brushed the ringlet on her neck, and smiled.

Walking down the hall, Kultur took her hand and pulled her close to his side. His eyes kept glancing down. The dress had a heck of a slit in it and every other step she gave a flash of slender shapely leg.

He could feel the heat roil up his neck, his groin tightened. They hadn't even gotten there yet and already he wanted to whisk her back to his room. He let out a deep breath, down boy, let her get to dinner before jumping her bones.

They were eating as they had a few times before in the fancy dining room. The huge octagonal room with the rich, pale peach wallpaper with the hint of sparkle in it and trimmed in white.

The huge crystal chandelier twinkled over the very long, crowded table. The servants as before were lined up near a door on the opposite side of the room. The cut crystal glassware sparkled with the chandelier.

Except it was different this time. This time as Kultur brought her to the doorway, he stopped, still holding her hand.

All conversation in the room ceased. The only sound was the scraping back of chairs as everyone at the table, including Kultur's siblings and his mother bowed their heads.

"Rise," Kultur said, his face stone, he squeezed Sislla's hand.

Everyone rose to their feet. Then bowing again, they spoke in unison a string of foreign words Sislla didn't understand, "Menwa Minste a Minstess, egairram ynomerec esre vinu. Taratan-un-kas Atra Sislla, avithé a' Kultur Kultiran, Atraam a' Chamaine-Gris.

Releasing her hand, Kultur slipped his hand on Sislla's lower back then moved it her waist and pulled her close to his side.

"Kultur," she whispered.

He lowered his head so he could hear her. "What is going on? What did they say?"

Her breath teased the hair on the back of his neck. His hand moved slightly up the side of her waist, he had to stop himself from raising it higher. His palm warmed from touching her.

Smiling, his eyes on the people with their heads bowed, he said very quietly to her, "They said something to the effect of, 'Welcome Master and Mistress, our fealty to you with hope of peace. Blessings to Atra Sislla, avithé of Kultur Kultiran, Atraam of the Chamaine-Gris."

She did as he had expected, blinked in total confusion, at the people, at him. "Come, *koritsi,* we will sit." He nudged her but she didn't move.

"Kultur…"

"Yes, baby?" His smile softened his deep voice.

"You, uh, said, they uh, said, Atra Sislla, *avithé- wife-"* her voice twisted in a strident whisper. "I don't understand, what is going on?" She remained unmoving when he nudged her again.

"Exactly as they said. I told you when I first marked you that we are mated. The third marking will make you fully, officially my wife. My queen. At this moment, we are technically married, *tiris avithé* – my wife. Now, we need to sit or do you wish for them to stand with their heads bowed all night? Come," he gave her a gentle push but with enough strength to force her to move.

Sislla's face was as white as a sheet. "Kultur," she whispered frantically, "you can't do that, you can't make me be married to you, you can't-"

"Hush, sweetheart, you can kick about it later. For now, you are their queen, act like one. Hold your head up. Keep your hostility to me for when we are alone." His hand moved up to the middle of her back as he ushered her down the long room to the head of the table.

His words had the effect he'd hoped for. She straightened her spine, held her head high, and moved with elegance and grace to the head of the table. Sislla's head was up but her eyes were lowered, she peered around the room from under the curl of her lashes.

Gabriel the goof winked audaciously at her, making her smile just a little, and Lexi kept her head down a little but gave her a huge smile.

Then she caught Darathia's venomous hate-filled glare at her.

When Kultur turned in his mother's direction she smoothed the vile loathing from her gaunt face.

Kultur pulled out Sislla's chair and helped her to sit, then he took his own. As soon as he sat everyone at the table took their seats. Kultur led the table in saying words of thanks for the food on the table, then he nodded to the head servant to begin serving.

During dinner, Darathia kept Kultur's attention by discussing household maintenance and relatives. The oblong table allowed Kultur to sit close to Sislla. He even pulled her chair closer every so often until their chairs were touching, he leaned his knee against her leg.

While enjoying his grilled fish and parsley potatoes, he chatted with his mother and laid his arm across the back of Sislla's chair.

When he brushed the sensitive skin of her nape with his thumb, she stifled a shiver then sat forward so he wasn't touching her.

Smiling politely at his mother, Kultur set his hand on Sislla's shoulder and pulled her back slowly, discreetly, so no one else would notice.

Taking no notice of her frown, he put his hand around the back of her neck and then moved it under the ringlet he had loosened. Using his thumb again, he brushed her skin, lightly thumbing the mark he'd given her. Her sudden rigidity indicated she was aware of what he was doing.

Still conversing with his mother, Kultur eyed the mark under half lowered lids so no one would see what he was looking at and continued stroking it with his thumb. In his mind it was like he was stroking his erection. He played their past love making in his head as he stared at the mark.

Remembering that day in bed, his huge dusky hand clutching her creamy round bottom holding her, bracing her while she stood in her lustrous nude glory. Her passion-filled eyes rolling back in her head then draping back limp. Her neck arched, her beautiful breasts thrust out in delirium as his mouth sucked and bit and licked her sex. His thick fingers plunging in and out of her soft pale sweetness, her hips bucking at his mouth and fingers-

"Kultur, how did the hunting go yesterday?" The man on the other side of Sislla broke into Kultur's memory. Frowning, he blinked, he hadn't realized his mother had stopped her monologue. Then a small sly smile pulled the corner of his mouth, he knew the man meant animal hunting but Kultur was thinking of Sislla hunting.

Highly aroused from his daydream, his fingers tightened. Feeling his hand clench her neck, his thumb pressed hard over the mark, Sislla pulled away.

Kultur leaned over and kissed her neck, enjoying the delicious shiver that rippled down her body that clearly pissed her off. His eyes dropped to her nipples that had hardened in that quick second. She shifted to turn her chest away from him.

Kultur gave his attention to the man. He brushed the ringlet back to cover the mark on her neck then slowly lowered his hand, moving it under the table, to her thigh.

He discussed hunting with the man, at the same time he slid his hand through the slit in Sislla's dress, for exactly the reason he'd told the seamstress to make it, and exactly where he wanted it placed.

Under her dress, he pushed the hand on her thigh between her legs. He heard her gasp and felt her tighten her legs against his invasion. Stiff as a board, Sislla kept her eyes straight, petrified someone would know what he was doing.

He prodded her thighs apart and kept pushing his hand right up against her core. He smiled again at the tremble she couldn't suppress. She turned her head to his profile, he could feel her scowling at him.

He leaned over and whispered in her ear, "Smile, *koritsi,* everyone has their eyes on you, the new Atra of the Chamaine-Gris, Queen of Aenlic Castle."

"Kultur," she whispered fiercely at him under her breath, "get your hand off my-"

His grin lascivious, he whispered back, "Off your what, honey?" The grin steeped evilly. "You say it and I'll move it."

Her undergarment was sheer. He could easily feel her mound, how warm and soft it was. Using two fingers, he pushed at her labia, separating the lips and brushed one fingertip up her slit.

"Uhh-" Sislla choked. Grabbing her water, she quickly and awkwardly gulped it.

"Are you all right, my dear?" Darathia asked with a faint sneer. *Good heavens, the girl was a gauche peasant. No class, no manners, just a lowborn harlot.*

As she gulped the water, Sislla couldn't look Darathia in the eye because Kultur had pushed one side of her silk underwear aside and was touching her bare skin.

He watched her blushing up a storm trying to discreetly wriggle away from his fingers; he had to bite his lip to keep from grinning at her struggles. Meanwhile, he stroked her clitoris, his hand was saturated with her wet silk. He bit his lip harder, thank the sons she wasn't immune to his dandling her.

"Dessert Atra?" A maid held a plate of pastries in front of Sislla.

Kultur thought she was going to faint with piercing arousal and sheer embarrassment.

His chuckle in her ear, she shook her head with a muffled "No thank you."

Sons above, he wished he could make her come, but he knew he couldn't go that far.

The maid offered the dessert to him next. He politely shook his head with a brief smile.

As she moved on down the room, Kultur laid his other unoccupied arm on the table in front of Sislla and set his hand on her hand curling his fingers around hers. She turned her face towards his; the look she gave him could peel paint.

He knew he was going to get lambasted later, but for now, he was almost out of his mind with salacious desire. His shaft was hard as a metal beam aching and swelling against his pants. He stroked and tickled her sex under the tablecloth, under everyone's noses, well, maybe not everyone.

Lexi and Gabriel were staring at them with bright eyes and funny grins.

Kultur figured his face was undoubtedly dark with passion, lust probably glowed in his eyes, and Sislla was red as a beet and looked so uncomfortable, anyone paying really close attention would know something was up.

Ignoring his siblings, Kultur nestled his nose in Sislla's hair, nipped her ear. As he pushed the tip of his finger into her, he whispered, "So, baby, you were going to tell me to get my hand off your, or actually now, it would be get my finger out of your-come on say it," he nipped her ear again.

Out of the corner of his eye he could see his mother glaring at them. He could care less. Dipping his finger in and out of Sislla's slick channel, he murmured, "Tell me *koritsi*, tell me what to take my hand off and I will." He grinned against her hair knowing she was too prim and ladylike to-

Sislla put her mouth right on his ear and said, "My pussy."

He about came in his pants. He froze, his finger inside her stopped moving, he looked at her with stunned surprise, and even hotter lust. His eyes dropped to her petal lips.

To hear the crude slang coming from her soft, puritanical lips was *so fucking hot*- and judging by the fresh crimson tide flooding her face it took a lot out of her to say it.

Hell, he's going to have to encourage her to talk dirty while they… his mouth quirked. He was going to have to get her to have the sex first.

He carefully withdrew his finger, and moved his hand from under her skirt. Pushing the slit together he lifted his hand to the table.

Lifting her hand up, he held it with both of his and brought it to his mouth. He kissed her knuckles, wanting to lick his fingers and taste her. His mother's snort carried across the table.

His lips on her knuckles, his eyes staring deep into Sislla's, Kultur whispered, "Let's go back to my chambers." Then he sighed heavily, that wasn't going to happen. She was so mad her plush lips had disappeared into a hard thin line. He kissed her hand again then set it on the table.

"Ah well," he sighed, he'd known she would be pissed. No sex for him tonight. He couldn't contain his grin, *but hell it was worth it.*

Dinner was over and people were getting up and leaving.

Kultur had to sit for a few minutes; there was no disguising the huge bulge in his pants.

Sislla hopped up and before Kultur could grab her, she dashed around the table to Lexi. She grabbed Lexi's arm and hauled her out of the dining room while Gabriel sauntered over to where Kultur sat scowling as Sislla blended into the crowd and disappeared out the door.

Gabriel dropped in the chair next to him with a devilish grin. "I don't know what you were doing, little brother, but judging by the looks on both of your faces, I can guess. I'd like to guess. Tell me, were you-"

"Shut the fuck up, Gabe." Kultur signaled a butler. When the man came over, Kultur said, "Bring me a drink, make it a double."

As the butler nodded and turned, Kultur said, "Better bring me two doubles."

"But, I'm thinking something went amiss, K," Gabriel snickered, "because she fled the room looking furious and mortified and left you sitting here with a," his eyes flicked down to Kultur's pants, "big 'ol boner."

Kultur flinched as his brother laughed in his ear.

Chapter Twenty-Nine

"Sislla," Lexi giggled as she was being pulled down the hall, "what is going on? Are you running from my brother?"

"Hush, just come with me." Sislla hurried, hoping to get to her chamber before Kultur left the dining room.

Hand in hand, the two girls rushed down the hall in their floor length gowns, Sislla's shimmering golden in the lantern light and Lexi's blue satin shining as the light caught the smooth material when it swooshed around her legs.

Sislla snatched open the door to her room and hustled Lexi inside, then slammed the door shut and leaned her back against it panting.

Lexi grinned at her friend watching her trying to catch her breath.

Sislla' face bone serious, she asked, "Tell me, Lexi, this business about the marking thing, three times to mark me to save my life. I- I know we discussed it before, but I just can't see why Kultur insists, why he cares whether I live or die. I think Kultur just wants to use it as a way to either annoy your mother, or to control me for some crazy ulterior motive."

Crossing her arms, Lexi leaned against the dresser and studied her friend. "Sis, seriously, why would he make this up? If he just wanted you, for sex only, he would just take you; force you when he wanted to, on any days and not just on days of unmarking."

254

She raised a sinister brow. "Or, he could have just thrown you in the dungeon, or killed you, or tossed you to one of the other factions, given you to one of his warriors, or put you on a boat and sent you home. Plus, believe me, he does not care a fig whether Mother is annoyed or not."

Sislla pondered her words, but shook her head. "I just don't understand it all…why mark me at all?"

Rolling her eyes, Lexi snorted rudely. "Duh, because he wants to save your life, and because he wants you. He wants to keep you, and not in prison, but in his bed, and by his side."

Sislla looked at her as if she was insane. Then shook her head again, the loose ringlet swept across the front of her. "No, he can hardly abide me, he's always yelling at me and bossing me around, no," shaking her head at the ridiculous implausibility of it. "No, I seriously think he has some ulterior motive, he wants to use me for something…" her eyes stared blankly contemplating what it could be.

A harsh guffaw blustered from Lexi's wide mouth. "Yeah, he wants to use you all right, he wants to use your body you dope."

She laughed naughtily at Sislla's indignant denying expression. "Really, Sis, I've never seen my brother be so gentle with anyone before, ever. Maybe me, sometimes, but with you he's different. He's so damned besotted he can't keep his eyes, or hands, off you."

Lexi flopped down on Sislla's bed laughing, uncaring that her blue silk dress was folded and mangled under her. She put her palms flat on the bed behind her to hold her up.

Shaking out her long dark waves, she said, "Now, tell me what is going on, Sis? I know Kultur was up to something at dinner. He looked like a tomcat slurping up rich cream, and you looked alternately fit to be tied, and hot and bothered. Tell me the dirt, girl."

Sislla trod over and sat down on the vanity chair with a huff. "Your darned brother, stop it Lex," she admonished at the smirking grin the girl was giving her. "Anyway, he was, uh, taking liberties," her face blossomed with pink.

"Oh, you are so lucky, girl."

"What? What on earth, how could you say that? He was- was molesting me under the, uh, table, that- that's wrong!"

Shaking her head with a leering grin, Lexi disagreed, "No, that's hot. I never knew my brother had it in him. I mean, he's the big tough, cold-blooded warlord, he seldom shows emotion and has a vicious soul and a heart of ice."

Smiling, her head shook side-to-side. "But for him to have his hands all over you, in public, basically anyway, in front of Mother for the sons' sake, damn Sis," she shook her head again. "You have changed him. The look on his face was absolutely dreamy. Mother, and Araina down at the far end of the table knew he was up to something and they were outraged but impotent, pun intended, to do anything about it. It was hilarious!"

Seeing Lexi shake her head again then her eyes gleaming laughter at her, Sislla frowned at her, asked her in irritation, "What?"

Chuckling, Lexi said slyly, "Honey, he wasn't fooling around with you under the table for just giggles, he's keeping you primed so you are ready whenever he makes his move again." She laughed out loud at Sislla's appalled look. "Come on, really, Sislla, you are married, betrothed,"

"No we are not." Adamant, confused, and mad, Sislla shoved her hair off her shoulders in a snit.

Lexi's brunette eyebrows shot up. "But he said," her brows lowered, brown eyes tapered at her friend. "You've made love, during the golden moon, right?"

Sislla nodded, blushing. "Yes, so, once, then...I mean, he," she looked away, "never mind."

"Did he rattle off a bunch of words you couldn't understand at a...let's say a crucial point?"

"I...I think so, maybe." Her face was so red; Sislla thought she was going to die of mortification.

"Let's see, let me say them and see if they sound familiar, okay?"

Lips pursed, unsure, Sislla was starting to feel really worried, "Uh, all right."

"Okay, did he say, '*Tiris devoleb, Iegdelp oteb sruoj rererof, ewera won eno?*'"

Sislla nodded slowly. "Yes, that sounds kind of like it. What does it mean?"

Lexi smiled broadly answering, "My beloved, I pledge to be yours forever, we are now one."

Sislla's mouth dropped in disbelief. "I don't understand, what does, I mean, why did he say that? We are not in- in love or anything like that, why-"

"Sislla, if during a golden moon, a man says that during lovemaking, when you are about to you, know, climax," she laughed at Sislla's embarrassed red face. "It means just as it sounds, that you are pledged to each other, forever. Basically, he married you guys while you were doing the nasty. Everything else after will just be a formality." She grinned from ear-to-ear then jumped up, ran over and hugged Sislla.

"You are my sister-in-law, Sis. I am so happy, you will be a wonderful influence on my brother." She clutched Sislla's arms and held her out to look at her, her expression turned a shade serious.

"Because of our father's brutality, plus having the protection and wealth of the village on his shoulders, and then the bitch he was engaged to, her betrayal and ambush, causing Father's death, well, Kultur has always been so dark and cold and brooding. He is too quick with his fists, and his punishments are extremely severe. But no one can question him, that is our law."

"You," Lexi kissed Sislla on the cheek, "are kind and caring, sweet and gentle, you're just what he needs to balance him. It's already wide spread how you have talked him down several times from either killing someone or ordering a harsh punishment."

She smiled wickedly. "Plus, you stand up to him. You and he both think he bosses you around but," she laughed, "it's really the other way around. He rules with an iron fist, but you rule, actually lead, him, with those soft, beguiling, big ol' blue eyes. One bat from them and he's dead meat!" She laughed and laughed, wiped an eye.

A bit more seriously, Lexi said, "Sislla, Kultur is a good, brave man who would never harm a woman or child, or an innocent person. He deserves something good for once in his hard life."

"Uh, hello, earth to Lexi." A blushing frown coloring her pretty face, discomfited but with a twinge of anger, Sislla said, "Your good courageous brother who would never hurt a woman or child- raped me." She watched Lexi's expression.

Her denial flared, but Lexi said, "Sis, he had to mark you to save your life. You refused; he did what he considered the lesser evil. Force you or leave you to the rabid hands of the Iminims."

"But he didn't leave me the choice to maybe wait and see if one of the local men-"

Lexi snorted. "Ha. Don't even pretend you would have chosen one of them over my brother. You may be beyond furious with him, but I can tell the way you look at him, that you-"

"I do not have feelings for Kultur. Don't even go there, Lex. He is a crude, sexist, overbearing, pushy, forceful brute who sexually assaulted me. For good or bad, whatever the reasons, nonetheless, he forced me. He had no right. If I wanted to die that was my choice."

"Ah, but Sis, you can see he cares way too much for you to have let you die." She shrugged. "Could you look at a weak animal choosing to starve itself to death because it's sick and stand there and let it? No, you could not. But, it is the animal's choice to die if it wants to, yet you would never allow that."

"Oh, Lexi, that's so different. I am not an animal; I am a human being with free will. He continues to take that from me. He doesn't treat me as an equal. He has, according to you, married me without asking me, or even telling me he did it!

"Even now, he decides how much I can work, and forces me to eat. I am forbidden to leave the castle, he tells me what I can and cannot wear, he molests me when I am asleep and unaware, or when I'm helpless to stop him like tonight at dinner." Her cheeks grew brighter.

"I understand your feelings, Sis. But this is how things are here in Aniniva. He is the Atraam warlord and he has the right to do what he thinks is best for his people. He is used to giving orders and no one even thinks of disobeying him. He limits your work because you don't, you work your fingers to the bone. And you get busy and forget to eat, you would be ill right now if he let you have your way." She held a hand up at Sislla's shaking head.

Lexi continued, "He won't let you leave the castle because he's afraid number one for your safety, and number two he is afraid you will leave him, and number three, technically, you are a prisoner. As an alien, until he knows who you are and where you're from," shrug, "he is protecting the people from you."

"Oh but, Lexi, I would never hurt anyone!"

"I know, Sis, but it's still a fact. So, let me continue, he dictates what you wear because he is a jealous son-of-a-bitch. I never thought I would see the day."

Her grin lewd, Lexi continued, "And, really, Sis, he molests you because he is enamored of you, you make his blood boil. Seriously, it could be worse. He could look like that Trogga creep that captured you, ugly and stocky, and stupid. Instead," her eyebrows wriggled up and down in a leer, "you have to admit, my brother is one huge, muscle-bound, damned good looking bastard, right?"

"Lexi! Your language! My goodness, you are as bad as Kultur."

"Anyway," Lexi got to her feet, stretched her arms over her head and yawned. "I gotta get going to bed. In the morning Van is taking me to a wizardly old woman who tends her garden differently and he says she grows superb, exceptionally succulent vegetables and she said she would show him and me what she does.

"If it's worthwhile, I'll bring the information to Kultur and after he studies it, maybe tests it, he might have everyone implement it. So," she gave Sislla a hug, "love you, sister-in-law, so happy you're part of the family now."

As Sislla opened her mouth to deny she was married to, or going to marry Kultur, Lexi spun from her with a pleased smile and left Sislla standing there in consternation.

Chapter Thirty

Sislla did not see Kultur over the next few days. She was kept busy healing the line of people that showed up at the door every day. Either Ryan or Jaspar was with her every second. They both had learned their lesson in letting her out of their sight, even for a minute.

They had been told, and they both meekly told Sislla that if she tried to leave the castle, or stayed overtime at her work, they were to physically restrain her. Not hurt her, they'd forfeit their lives if they injured her, but they were to restrain her gently until Kultur could be located.

And, Sislla sighed, the big brute would embarrass her by tossing her over his shoulder and taking her to her room and locking her in. Once was enough, she capitulated without further arguments. Kultur had a tin ear when it came to her health or safety, his word was law.

She'd heard the woman who had shoved her that day had been placed on a sort of house arrest. She's been exiled to a hut on the outskirts of Chamaine-Gris where she was allowed no contact by her family or friends. There were no aqueducts or hydraulic ram pumps, she had to haul her own water from a well. She was lucky Kultur allowed her the heating stones for cooking and warmth.

Sislla had begged Kultur to end the woman's punishment but he told her she had a penance to pay for her violence, especially

261

to a guest of his castle. The woman would have to complete 12 months of her sentence.

Sislla was putting her jars and medical supplies away as Jaspar walked the last patient through the marble grand chamber and saw them out, when she heard a soft knock at the back door of her workshop.

Removing an apron she had tied over her blouse and slacks she went right to the door and opened it. It never entered her mind to see who it was first.

A young woman, actually a teenager was standing there looking very frightened and very desperate.

"Dear, please come in, how can I help you?" Sislla swung the door wide and gestured for the girl to go into the workshop.

But the girl shook her head furiously. "No, no, please, I can't," her head swiveled back and forth as if expecting someone to jump her any second.

"Okay, calm down. What do you need?" Sislla asked her kindly.

Pushing back long, windblown dark hair, while looking anxiously all around with wide anxious eyes she said, "I was told I could trust you. That you wouldn't tell…it's my- my boyfriend. He and his little brother fell, down a ravine. They are both injured, severely injured. Please-" at the sound of Jaspar returning the girl ducked around the outside wall.

Sislla whispered, "Stay here, I will be back." She ran to her cupboards and filled a sack with supplies and slung it over her shoulder. When Jaspar came in, she gave him a big smile and said, "I need to use the facility before I clean up here. I'll be right back."

"Uh," Jaspar had been tricked by her before. He followed her. "I will wait outside the door, Mistress." He planted his body, dressed in the red jacket and white pants of the Kirmen Guard, against the wall as Sislla slipped into the bathroom.

Twenty-five-year old Jaspar had very short dark hair, dark brows and eyes; he was several inches shorter than the gangly Ryan and a few pounds heavier. Where Ryan had a hint of red in his hair and a long face, Jaspar's face was squarer with a shorter blockier nose, Ryan had freckles and Jaspar had a few pock marks from his teenaged years.

Jaspar waited and waited, and waited some more. When she didn't come out, he nervously knocked lightly and said, "Mistress, are you all right? Shall I get a woman to uh, assist you?" He waited. No sound, nothing.

He knocked again, then louder. "Oh sons above no, she wouldn't," he gingerly opened the door and poked his head in. The room, just as he suspected, was empty. The curtain fluttered gently at the open window. "*Shit!*"

He dashed through the grand chamber shouting out for Ryan and ran out the door to around the side where the bathroom window led to. He was searching for any sign of Sislla when Ryan came jogging up.

Ryan didn't need to ask, he already knew. He told Jaspar, "Someone came to the backdoor again. I saw what looked like one set of small footprints in the dirt coming to the back of the workshop, then a different set under the bathroom window."

He pointed, "I see some fresh footprints going that way, let's go." The two men ran off quickly following the footprints.

*****

Glad she had her hiking boots on that Kultur had obtained for her, Sislla stayed beside the teen girl hurrying down the lane. After Sislla asked the girl her name, and she said simply, "Tamma," they walked quickly without speaking.

They covered several miles before the girl stopped. She pushed through some thick shrubbery leading Sislla to a clearing.

In the clearing were some big rocks and fallen trees, the clearing butted up to a steep jagged hill. Two people, another teen, a male, and a younger boy around the age of six were sitting on the ground, leaning against the rocks.

Tamma scurried over and dropped down beside the teenage boy with a sob, "Matthew, I brought help."

After a moment's hesitation to take in the scene, Sislla hurried over to the young people. She crouched down in front of them and was shocked to see both boys were covered in blood.

The little boy was cradled in the older boy's arms. With haste, she set her bag on the ground and pulled out her supplies.

"Here," she said to Tamma, "take these leaves and put them everywhere there is bleeding."

Tamma did as she was told. Sislla looked to the little boy first. He was crying and trembling, appeared to be fighting to stay conscious.

"Hi honey, my name is Sislla and I've come to help you. What's your name?" She smiled warmly as she took out more leaves and pressed them neatly over the leaves Tamma placed down haphazardly.

His frightened voice tiny and shaking, he said, "Marky."

"Okay, Marky, I'm going to fix you and your brother right up, lickety-split." She took out more supplies.

Marky grinned weakly, showing a few missing teeth. He said, "Lick-split? That's funny."

Sislla worked rapidly, not stopping for past an hour until she felt the boys were set as best she could get them.

Kneeling, she leaned back on her heels and wiped her head. "I think you guys will be just fine. You need to rest. Don't move for a few hours and then you should carefully get yourselves home."

She turned to Tamma in question, "Why didn't you get their mother or father? Why did you come all the way to me?"

Her head lowered, Tamma clutched her fingers tightly in front of her. "Because, I am Ulmas, and my boyfriend, Matthew," she nodded with a loving smile to the teen boy who was drowsing, "and his brother are…" her lips pursed, she glanced around to see if anyone else had come across them. Very quietly, she murmured, "They are Tenthekens."

Putting her supplies back into her bag, Sislla said, "So? They should be home safe with their parents. Especially Marky." She smiled at the little boy, sleeping cradled in his brother's arms with the blood cleaned off, covered with bandages and with his thumb in his mouth.

"Tamma, if I hadn't been able to get here, Marky would have…" she didn't want to say it, but Tamma knew anyway. She'd seen the extent of little Marky's injuries. He would have died out there in the woods.

Tamma had laid her hand on Matthew's leg and looked lovingly yet bleakly at him. "I couldn't go to the Tenthekens, they would likely kill me, and I couldn't take them to my family, as Ulmas, *they* would have undoubtedly killed them. It's the way it is." She rubbed at tears filling her eyes.

"If either of our families, or our Atraams, found out Matthew and I, well," she sadly wiped at the tears and shrugged in defeat. "At the very least we would never be allowed to see each other again. We would be severely punished, if allowed to live at all."

"Oh, Tamma." Sislla threw an arm around Tamma and hugged her. "I'm so sorry, I wish I could-" a clanging bell drowned out her words. She looked up, "What is that?" The bell was deafening.

Tamma moved to sit beside Matthew. "There's a fire. It's the fire-bell calling for people to come and help. It's your people, your land, the Chamaine-Gris."

Sislla threw the last few items into her bag and jumped to her feet. "Get them home, safe, Tamma, and you be careful too."

Snuggling up to Matthew, Tamma asked, "Where are you going?"

Quickly making her way through the bushes, Sislla said, "There might be injuries, I need to go help." She fought through the shrubs to the trail and saw the smoke spiraling up the sky. She dashed towards it.

Traveling over the dirt path with tall, dense shrubbery bordering the trail, Sislla kept her eye on the grey funnel of smoke.

She was nearing the edge of village when she reached the scene. Several two-story houses were raging with fiery orange flames, plumes of black smoke roared out broken windows and around and up the buildings.

265

Sislla broke into the chaos of people running and yelling and crying in all directions, the sky had darkened to dim sooty blackness as ash billowed sucking the oxygen out of the air.

Seeing someone dragging a person away from the building and laying them on the ground, Sislla ran over and dropped beside them.

A man, his face black and slimed with soot was shaking the other man who was unconscious lying on his back. "Jo, Jo, come on, talk to me," the man was almost sobbing as he shook his friend.

Kneeling and digging in her bag, Sislla said calm and soothing, "Please, I can help, let me." She gently prodded the man aside so she could attend to his friend.

She helped the man then moved onto the next person, then the next. At one point she looked up, scrubbing at her itchy eyes she saw Kultur coming out of one of the burning buildings with an elderly woman in his arms.

He rushed over and laid her on the grass. There was a stream of blood flooding the woman's chest.

Behind her, Sislla heard some girls giggling. Kultur had removed his shirt to press it on the woman to staunch her blood flow. The girls were swooning over Kultur's bare chest.

"Oh would you look at our Atraam, he looks dyno in clothes, but look at him now, ooo," the one girl fanned herself while the other one laughed.

Although layered with soot and grimy ash, his sweating broad shoulders and chest were tremendous in their breadth and wealth of powerful muscles. Those muscles flexed and rippled with his every move. His biceps bulged, gleaming with perspiration as he pressed his shirt on the elderly woman.

Finished with the person she was working on, Sislla got to her feet and hurried over to Kultur and knelt beside the prone woman.

"Kultur," she said softly commanding, with a hand on his soot covered arm, "let me."

Bent over the woman, Kultur looked up in shock at Sislla. "What the- what the hell are you doing here?" He flipped his stunned eyes from her to the surrounding area and back to her. Fury darkened his face already dark with dirt.

He bellowed louder than the roar of the fire, "Where the fuck is Ryan? Jaspar? Sislla, what the-"

"Hush now, Kultur, you're not helping. You're only scaring this poor woman." She took out the supplies she needed and set them on the ground beside the woman.

Hearing frantic pounding footsteps racing up to them, Sislla's lips pulled in. Ryan and Jaspar had tracked her and were rapidly approaching.

She didn't dare peer up and see the looks passing between the three men, the ferocious deadly ire Kultur would assuredly be blazing at the guards, and the panicked terror of the guards fostered at him.

Next to Sislla, Kultur growled fiercely, "Sislla, what in the sons' name are you fucking doing here?"

"Someone said they needed all hands to help. Hand me that jar," her hands filled with leaves, Sislla said calmly, pointing to a glass jar she'd set out.

Glaring his wrath at her, he nonetheless picked up the jar and handed it to her. "All hands does not mean you, Sislla, and you fucking know that. Why-"

"Please, Kultur, you don't need to curse." Not looking up at him, she murmured soothing words as she patted leaves on the old lady who was crying.

Impatiently pushing his big hands away from the woman, Sislla said, "You are not helping this situation, Kultur. I'm sure you would be of better assistance elsewhere." Dismissing him, she didn't see the shocked glower of anger he bored into the side of her head.

When she ignored him, he climbed to his feet. "With her," he barked at Ryan. "You come with me," he snarled at Jaspar and stalked off to help a man who was trying to drag a heavy man out of the blaze.

Kultur checked on Sislla after an hour.

He crouched beside her. "Hey," he said quietly, "how are you doing? You okay?" He pushed her dirty ringlets off her shoulder letting them bounce down her back.

She raised a hand and used the back of it to wipe her forehead. "Yes, of course I am all right. It's the poor victims that are-"

"Damn Sislla, what happened to your arm?" Kultur snatched up her arm holding it out to examine it. "What's this?" A hideous burn marred her forearm near her wrist.

She tried to pull her hand away. "It's nothing, Kultur, it's just a little burn. I am fine. You don't need to-"

He grabbed up her bag and pulled out some of her jars. "Which are the pain leaves, Sislla? And the others, you tell me what you need."

When he didn't move, his hand holding her bag in front of her, she sighed and told him what to take out. He helped her apply the ointments she'd developed and other things and then wrapped gauze around the burn then pinned it in place.

"Okay, now you will go right back to the castle. The guards will take you. Get up." He stood and held a hand down to her.

Putting the supplies back in her bag, as she reached to another injured person someone helped sit down next to her, Sislla said calmly, "Do not bully me, Kultur. I will not leave people in need."

His hands on his hips, Kultur's infuriated glare didn't put a dent in her. "I can carry you-" he broke off. People were staring and listening.

He would look insane, heartless and a tyrant if he picked her up and dragged her off, but shit, she was hurt too, she needed to rest. He bent to reach for her but she was already laying out leaves on the person next to her.

Torn between letting her stay, injured, or causing more of a rift between them by carrying her off, he scratched his chest, leaving white trails in the black soot. *Ah shit*, he glared at Ryan, his message clear, for the guard to stay with her, and he stalked off.

A couple of hours later the fires were under control and the last injured person had been tended to.

Kultur told Jaspar who had been working steadily and faithfully by his side pulling people from the burning buildings, to tell Ryan to get another guard and take Sislla back to the castle.

Standing regally and still glaringly powerful even in filthy, torn clothes, skin black with soot and sweat, Kultur raked his fingers through his grubby hair and watched Jaspar go to Ryan and Sislla.

The two guards were too afraid to look at him as they helped Sislla get wearily to her feet, knowing she was there due to their dereliction of duty. Again.

Kultur's eyes quelled at seeing her so tired and as covered with ash and dirt as him. He wanted to go to her and carry her back to the castle, but, he glanced around, there was still so much left to do. Jaspar returned to stand at order beside him.

Sislla looked at him with a tired smile and gave a little wave then turned and walked away with her healing bag over her shoulder and the guards on either side of her.

Chapter Thirty-One

Finally satisfied he had done all he could, Kultur walked back with Jaspar and a crowd of other men that had come from the castle to help with the fire.

When they entered the castle, everyone went in different directions to get cleaned up and rest.

Jaspar, his skin pale with nerves under the grime, croaked full of anxiety and smoke, "Uh, sir, Atraam, sir, uh, should I wait in the dungeon, or uh, what do you, where do you want me to go?"

His smile lopsided, the dimple denting his cheek showed under the dirt, Kultur sighed, "I know, Kirman, she tricked you, again. I know you tried your best. She's just, wily, and determined to help and can't stop herself. And she's too smart for her own damned good. At least you and Shaws took the time and effort to track her, and find her."

He set his hand on the guard's back. Jaspar held his breath, but Kultur just patted him twice and said, "Just go to your family. See that they are all right."

When Jaspar stood immobile, his eyes wide with uncertainty, Kultur gave a short chuckle, "Go, it's okay."

Leaving Jaspar standing awestruck, the Atraam not only wasn't going to punish him for his terrible transgression, but, he had actually touched him! Holy shit! Watching Kultur stride away, Jaspar finally jolted himself out of his shock and ran off to tell his family of the Atraam's uncommon kindness.

270

Kultur shaved then took a long, hot shower. The hot water eased his sore muscles, he felt ten times better clean and shaved. While he dressed he stared at his bed. He pictured Sislla, all curvy alabaster nude, stretched out like a sinuous cat with her arms out to him, beckoning for him to come to her and cover her dainty feminine body with his huge manliness.

He finished buttoning his shirt and stuffed it in his trousers that were already tightening from his thoughts of Sislla. He was buckling his belt as he left his chambers to go look for her.

Treading down the hall, he tugged a comb out of his back pocket and ran it through his drying hair, palming the waves trying to flatten them.

When he reached her room, he knocked on her door. He didn't think she was there because Ryan wasn't stationed outside. He glanced quickly inside confirming his thought.

He checked Lexi's room, the kitchen, the dining rooms, the large one for their formal dinners and the smaller more intimate one they ate at when they were alone or in smaller groups. He nodded at a few family members that were enjoying a late dinner.

He poked his head in the tiny chapel way in the back of the castle they used when the weather was too nasty to go to the village church, the grand chamber, the several libraries and salons scattered throughout the structure, and her workshop but found nothing and no one said they had seen her.

They'd been fortunate that through several shipwrecks besides garnering new clothing ideas and vocabularies they were able to obtain books, as well as some of the locals had become authors. Berries, honey, vinegar and many other items grown on the island constituted the ink and the mills supplied the papyrus.

Scratching the side of his head in consternation, Kultur ruffled the neatly combed waves. Out loud he muttered, "Where the hell could she be? She has to be exhausted, her burnt arm must be aching…" scrubbing his hands down his face he refused to believe that she dared igniting his wrath by leaving the castle again.

He decided he would go walk the upper halls, if they were inside the building, Ryan would be out in the hall guarding her.

Striding to the stairs, he jogged up them two at a time then traveled the second floor where most of his family members had their suites. Nothing.

Up to the third level he trod down the carpeted hall, his booted footsteps becoming louder and clumpier as his anger started to simmer. Where could she- ah, there was Ryan. Standing outside Cortland McGovern's chambers.

Kultur's brows drew down in a frown wondering what she was doing there and not resting in her own chamber. Or his.

He strode up to Ryan who had been standing calmly, that alone told Kultur nothing was wrong, so his anger, and fear fell away.

Of course when Ryan spotted him, he stood at rigid attention with his eyes straight forward. He, like Jaspar expected punishment for letting Sislla escape the castle again. Even though Ryan hadn't been on watch, he still felt guilty as she was his charge, under his specific care.

"Kirman Shaws, what is going on?"

"Sir, Mistress, uh, Atra Sislla is inside, sir."

Kultur resisted rolling his eyes. "I figure that, Kirman, you're here. Why is she in the McGoverns' suites?"

"Oh," a bit of color oozed back into his pallid face. His eyes still straight ahead, Ryan answered, "The baby, their infant, wouldn't stop crying. Cortland and Lori became concerned. They had been up all last night with her. Miss Lexi, uh, your sister…"

Kultur's brow crimped with mild sarcasm. His hands clasped behind his back, his legs braced apart, Kultur nodded with a half-smile. "I know who she is, Kirman, continue."

His cheeks reddening, Ryan gulped and said, "Of course, sir. Um, Miss Lexi was trying to help the McGoverns. She decided it would be best to see if Mistress Sislla could help. Sir."

"I see." Unsure if he should knock, or just go right in, Kultur hesitated.

Reading his mind, Ryan offered, "I would just go in, sir. I haven't heard the baby for a while and a knock might wake her."

Kultur nodded at the Kirman with a smirk. "Thank you, Kirman." He put his hand on the knob and turned it quietly then stepped silently into the room, Ryan pulled the door closed behind him.

The comfortable room was lowly lit. Cream walls, tan carpet and powder blue furniture filled the large chamber. There was no sign of the McGoverns, but over in a corner in a big cushioned rocking chair was Sislla. Even from across the room Kultur could see she was asleep.

The lantern lamps glowed soft golden light making the room peaceful and cozy. Kultur trod quietly over the carpet until he reached her.

Sislla was curled up in the cushions, her head resting against the side of the rocking chair and the sleeping baby cradled in her arms.

He stood without moving, just watching her. The low lights flickering along her hair softly spiraling around her shoulders, the rise and fall of her bosom the baby was curled so peacefully against.

She came up silently behind him, but a skilled warrior, Kultur turned as she approached. Wrapped in a bathrobe, a tired Lori McGovern yawned behind a hand and greeted him quietly.

Stepping beside him, she smiled at the sight of Sislla asleep with the baby in her arms. "Finally," she whispered. "Lilybeth cried all last night and today. Sislla managed to do whatever it was to comfort her."

"Aye, she's good at that," Kultur agreed, nodding lightly. Then he leaned over and very carefully extricated the baby from Sislla's arms and handed her to her mother.

Lori cuddled Lilybeth against her shoulder and gently rocked her. "What shall we do with- oh," Lori watched Kultur deftly slide his hands under Sislla, and careful of her injured arm, lifted her up in his arms without waking her.

"Can you get the door?" he said quietly, walking across the room. He didn't notice Lori's lashes flicker and her brow curve up at the fact that he asked instead of ordering her like he normally would. Holding the sleeping baby, she moved to the door and opened it.

Without a word, Kultur carried Sislla, her head on his shoulder out the door and down the hall. Lori smiled sleepily after them as she closed the door.

He started for her room, then decided to take her to his. He waited while Ryan opened his door for them then said to him in a low voice, "Goodnight, Kirman. You may take your leave."

Ryan breathing a deep sigh of relief, quickly disappeared down the stairs before the Atraam remembered he was mad.

Kultur kept Sislla locked in his chambers for three days. He stayed in Gabriel's room at night. He ordered that the door to his chambers stay guarded, and had Onani bring Sislla food.

He didn't bother asking the maid if Sislla was angry, he knew she would be livid at being imprisoned. Well, he was mad too. She defied him again and she would suffer consequences. The Ulmas capturing her taught her nothing about her personal safety.

She must have heard the fire bells and slipped from Jaspar's guard to go help. That she ran through the meadows totally alone made Kultur's normally stoic heart race.

His first thought was to put her over his knee, but, unless she wanted to play at spanking for sexual fun, which he wasn't adverse to, he couldn't hurt her or demean her that way. So, she stayed in his room no doubt going stir crazy and watching out the window as the people were turned away from healing.

The third day late in the evening, he went to his chambers, unlocked the door and strode in. She was standing at the window as he had expected.

She twirled around at his entrance. His gaze moved from her furious eyes shooting blue sparks of anger and resentment at him, down to her cleavage. The dress was fairly low cut. Onani must have brought it to her from Lexi.

She ran to him, red blotches bright in her cheeks, shouted, "How dare you! How dare you lock me up like this, Kultur!" She stopped in front of him and slammed her hands on her hips.

"Ah," a crooked smile tugged up one side of his mouth. "A few days locked inside has done nothing to tamp down that little temper of yours."

"Oh!" Her eyes widened then narrowed to slates at him. "How dare you-"

He reached out suddenly sticking his hand in her hair at the back of her head, wrapped it around his fist and pulled her close to him.

Gripping her hair, he pulled it back forcing her head to bend back and drew her in until her breasts were pressed against his chest.

"I dare, Mistress Sislla, because I am the lord of this realm, this castle, the Chamaine-Gris, and of you, *tiris avithé, my wife. Everyone* obeys me for the good and the safety of the Chamaine-Gris."

His eyes rolled down to her breasts molding out of the dress. "I see again you defy me by wearing one of those slutty dresses." His blazing gaze devoured her rounded breasts.

She put her fists against his chest and tried to push away from him. "Stop this, Kultur, let go of me. I can wear whatever I want, you can't stop me."

He drew her closer, her breasts mashed against him so hard they almost pushed completely out of the top of the dress. "Ah, but I can, Mistress, as we have discussed before. However, in this case," his eyes never left her bosom, "as it is I alone who is enjoying this banquet, I am fine with you wearing that dress that you are almost falling out of. I wouldn't mind that happening either."

Ignoring her struggles and her fury, he bent his dark head and put his lips on her neck and sucked gently.

"Kultur, please, don't mark me, it's juvenile," Sislla complained, still pushing at him, but she tilted her head so her neck was more exposed.

Releasing her hair, his hands spread across her back. "Sislla," he purred against her skin, "it's been a week since I've bedded you. I miss you, I need you, I need release with you..."

She tilted her head over further, her eyes closed; he licked behind her ear and bit at her jaw.

Her breathy stammer hushed but angry, "Then- then, go find someone to- to release yourself with. Go to the village, you said they line the streets naked with their legs...opened..." he nibbled at her bottom lip as she spoke, "uh...ready...for you..." he drew her upper lip into his mouth and sucked on it.

"Uh huh, Mistress, you want me to do this to another woman?" His mouth closed over hers in a ravishing, penetrating kiss, when he released her lips she was panting for air.

"Or this," his tongue slicked her ear, then he sucked her neck. "Or, do you want me to do this to another woman, one of those lined up in the street..." he moved his mouth to her breasts and lapped at her soft flesh. His tongue darted in and out of her cleavage.

She tried to, but she couldn't hold back her moans.

He grasped a handful of her hair again pulling her head back, his eyes swept from her face down to her breasts that were straining against the dress from him arching her spine, they looked in even more danger of spilling out of the bodice.

Bending to her, he nuzzled her breasts with his face, then put his hand under one squeezing it, forcing it out of the dress.

"You want me to do this to another woman?" He cupped her supple mound and suckled it, then licked her nipple drawing it into his mouth. Biting it gently, he kneaded her breast roughly.

Releasing her hair, he dipped his hand inside her bodice lifting out her other breast, gripping them both in his big hands, strong fingers digging into her plump flesh, he said, "This Sislla? You want me to do this with another woman?" The sleeves of the dress slid down her arms making her bare almost to the waist.

Tiny wispy moans escaped her, she whispered huskily, "Where have you been sleeping, Kultur?"

"*Arghh*...Sislla, just," he shoved his face into her bosom, kissing her soft rounded skin, then biting the silky flesh hard, not hard enough to break through.

"Kultur..." Her voice hushed in strident ache, "Please."

He lifted his head and looked into her half-mast eyes. "Yes? Kultur what? Kultur please stop?"

Her lids fell heavy over her passion clouded blue orbs. Lips swelling from his aggressive kisses parted, she licked them.

He put his thumb on her bottom lip and whispered, "Or, Kultur please do more?"

"Kultur..." her eyes closed. Her hands settled on his hips, she didn't struggle to break free.

"Tell me baby, tell me you want me." He lowered his mouth on hers kissing her roughly again, still kneading her bare breasts. His thumbs rubbing over her nipples he said against her mouth, "Tell me, Sislla, tell me you want me."

Pushing against him, leaning her head back she forced her lids weighted with desire halfway open. Her gaze lowered to watch his hands on her, palming and molding her bare fullness.

She raised her eyes to his. Seeing white flames of heat burning in his dark eyes, she licked her lips, stammered weakly, her tongue thick, "Is it, is it a golden moon?"

His palms under her breasts, just holding them, his gaze seared right through her. "No," he said husky, wary, shaking his head. Black hair whisked over one eye. "Tis not." He tightened his grip on her flesh, his voice rough, he asked, "Does it matter?"

She covered her face with her hands, then shoved from him. Staggering out of his grasp, she jerked her bodice up to cover herself, then her sleeves. She crossed her arms tightly over her chest and lowered her head.

He propped his hands stiffly on his hips, dropped his head and shook it with a coarse laugh. "I see. I guess I'll go back to where I've been spending my nights."

He stalked to the door, snatched it open, stepped out, and slammed it behind him.

Chapter Thirty-Two

Storming down the hall with a raging hard-on, Kultur raked his fingers, digging them like nails through his hair, using the pain to distract from some of the lust that overwhelmed him like a blinding sandstorm. He went to his brother's room bursting in on him without knocking.

"Shit, man!" Gabriel startled at his abrupt entrance almost dropped his bottle of ale. His eyes narrowed in shock. The look of a thundercloud crowding his brother's face, sharpening the already harsh angles, his mouth a grim intractable dagger was enough to give Satan the chills.

The worst was, in the center of the white heat that still flamed in his dark eyes, was raw gnawing need. His brother actually looked…for the first time, hurt.

Kultur threw himself into a chair growling and grunting like a wounded bear.

"*Kratiis*, K, what the hell bit you on the ass?" Gabriel stood in front of him with a mocking grin.

"Shut the fuck up, Gabe and get me a fucking drink." Kultur slammed his back against the chair, drew one leg up and set his ankle on his knee and dropped his hands on the chair arms. His head flopped over the back of the chair. Facing the ceiling, he closed his eyes.

"Ahh," Gabe grinned big, "what's the little lady done now?" He squinted one eye at his brother. Noticing his high color, his

278

gaze dropped to Kultur's groin, seeing the still hard bulge straining at his pants, he chortled. "Shut you down again, huh? Gads, K."

Gripping the edges of the chair arms, Kultur sat up erect and roared, "Goddammit Gabe, get me a fucking drink and shut the hell up!"

Chuckling his way into his kitchen, Gabe came back with a couple of glasses and a bottle of alcohol. Four families were in charge of different stills and several others worked the vineyards. Alcohol was plentiful in the kingdom.

Gabe set the glasses down on the table in front of Kultur's chair, poured them both healthy drinks then put the bottle down.

He picked up the malt he had been drinking when Kultur so rudely barged into his rooms, drained the bottle, dropped it in a can near the couch and picked up one of the glasses of liquor.

Holding it up in the air, he chuckled a toast, "*Givili*, brother," and took a big gulp before plunking the glass down on the table.

Kultur leaned forward, shoved back his cinder black hair that fell over his eyes, grabbed the other glass, skipped the cheer and downed it, all of it, then slammed the glass on the table. He wiped his mouth with his sleeve and threw himself against the back of the chair, scowling darkly at nothing.

Gabriel's eyes went from Kultur's empty glass to his brother's sullen face and grinned. He picked the bottle up and refilled Kultur's glass. "I've never seen you like this, K, she's got you bad."

Kultur grabbed up the glass, drained it again and set it down more gently than before. The corner of his mouth ticked back dryly. "Aye. More." He pushed his glass at Gabriel.

"So," Gabriel said pouring half the amount he had the first two times, "what's the problem? You're a good looking guy in a rugged scary kind of a way, why is she shutting you down?"

The liquor warming its way down Kultur's insides, he sighed, calming down. When he'd thrown himself into the chair his pants had risen. Yanking at the knees to tug them back down, he turned a lopsided half-smile at his brother.

"Truth be told, Gabe, I don't think it's exactly because of me. Although she resists with all her might, her body reacts to my...touch. But, she denies us both pleasure." He dropped his head and shook it, then picked up his glass and only took a sip this time.

"So...you make her hot, you turn her on yet she says no. It's not like she's a virgin and," he caught Kultur's face crease then smooth back out. "Ooh-kaay, so, even if she had been a, you know, she isn't now. So what's the big deal, why does she say no to you?"

The leather squeaked slightly as Kultur sat back making himself comfortable in the chair.

Gabriel's room was all masculine comfort. Somewhat like his, with oversized black leather couches and chairs, heavy dark-wooded tables.

Like all the suites, it had a separate kitchen, two bathrooms, one regular scale and the other like Kultur's with a huge tub with whirling warm water, as well as several other rooms. They were sitting in the front area, a large living room.

His forearm lay along the chair arm, his hand draped over the end holding his glass with his thumb and a couple fingers, drifting it back and forth, Kultur watched the liquid slosh gently.

He said, "Actually, I do understand her resistance. It's the marking. She refuses to be marked, and I...ah...literally forced her for the first marking." A hint of red filled his face.

"Whoa, what?" Gabriel sat forward, his elbows on his knees." What the hell? That doesn't sound like you K. You don't force women; you don't *need* to force them. They throw themselves at you. You need to explain yourself, brother. Why doesn't she want to be marked? Doesn't she understand the vicious savagery of the Iminims?"

Kultur took a deep breath, let it out slowly. "I've explained until I'm blue in the face. She has some compelling, irresistible urge, which she can't explain, to go home. Even though she doesn't know where her home is, she thinks she'll be led to it somehow. She knows if she is marked she can never return to her people, whoever they are. She says she still has to try." His mouth turned up, "As I knew she would. I told you she would, she wants to hop in a boat and take her chances."

"Huh." Shaking his head at the crazy woman his brother had grown so attached to, Gabriel sat back in his chair. Shooting Kultur a disbelieving tense frown, his smooth forehead wrinkled, "Fuck- *alone*?" One look at Kultur's dark expression gave him the answer.

"But, you've already done the first marking with the oath, she is legally your *avithé*. Technically, you're married. It would be treason for her to leave you." His eyes narrowed at his brother, "You haven't told her who she is yet, and why she was sent here, have you?"

Kultur took a big swig of his drink. "No, and I'm not going to. I will at some point, but not now. She is already compelled to return home, it would only impel her to try harder to escape, especially if she knew she'd been sent to assassinate me."

Gabriel looked at him with interest, "She's tried to escape?"

He shook his head, "No, not yet. She's been too busy with her healing work. But I know it's on her mind all the time. I think she's been training some women to take over for her when she's…gone," he took another sip.

"I can't imagine what it would be like forcing myself on an unwilling woman." Gabriel mused, his lips pulled in and he shook his head. Cradling his drink between his hands on his lap, he said with commiseration, "So, you forced her to do the first marking to save her life. I can understand that."

"Aye, but she doesn't. She keeps throwing that I raped her in my face, and that I took her free will from her, her choice to live or die, or even to…" he scowled at his drink, "have the right to choose other men," he shuddered at the thought.

"The thing is, I am already so damned hot for her, her body and, just her, I like being with her. I would want her regardless of the need to mark her. But I never would have forced her if I hadn't had to. If she didn't want me I would have just bit it and stayed away from her. But the marking, you know I would not, could not, have given her to another man."

With an aggrieved sigh he grumbled, "The thing is, now that I have uh, tasted her so to speak, I cannot deny my need for her. She's like the very air I need to breathe." Kultur sighed again, then scowled. "All this doesn't matter, she is my wife, that's all there is to it. She will stay with me."

"Did you hurt her? I mean, when you, I mean you're a big rough guy and she's like this little dainty thing. Maybe she's afraid you'll hurt her again."

"Ha," Kultur snorted. Then grimaced. "Aye, she was hurt a bit, she was a virgin, and yeah, I'm big, but," he sighed with a reminiscent smile. "Believe me, after I warmed her up, brother," he wiped his mouth, "she was into it as much as me. It was dynamite, it was insanely-" he looked down at his glass shaking his head.

"Yeah." Gabriel pretended to plug his ears. "Okay, too much information. Anyway, you said her body reacts to you, you can turn her on. So," Gabriel crossed his legs and balanced his glass on his thigh, "have you had other...you know, encounters since the first marking?"

Kultur expelled a loud breath. "Yes." His mouth turned up in the same wry, reminiscent smile. "Oh, aye. They were just as," he peered at his brother with a leer, "un-fucking-believable. Better than anything I've ever- hell, ruined me for other women. Anyway," he took a hard swallow of his drink.

Gabriel's brows met in points, confused. "So, then what's the problem? If it's that good between you, why won't she do it even when it's not on the golden moon?"

Kultur's big shoulders shrugged. "I think she's afraid she will...like it too much, care for me too much, maybe get pregnant, and that will keep her from leaving. Plus, I think she's afraid I'll make love with her and not let her know it's a golden moon, sneak in the markings and then she will be stuck."

He looked at the glass in his hand and swore, "I can't let her die, Gabe." He said more vehemently, "I won't. If I have to uh, force her again to save her, even if she hates me forever, I'll do it." He threw back his drink, swallowed hard. "And," he took a breath, said severely, "she will live with me whether she wants to or not. She will accept it, eventually."

The two brothers sat in quiet contemplation for some time. They had a couple more drinks. Then Kultur slammed his glass down and stood up.

Gabriel eyed him warily, watching him walk purposefully to the door. "What's going on, K?"

Opening the door, Kultur smiled grimly. "I'm going to go make her react to me until she craves me like I crave her, until she wants to stay."

Gabriel's shouted cheer of, "You go, my brother!" followed him out the door. Kultur moved with quick confident long strides to his room.

When he reached his chambers, he smoothed his slightly damp palms over his tousled hair, straightened his shirt, took a deep breath, unlocked the door and went in slowly, not sure what to expect.

The lights were low, it was very quiet, Kultur could see a small lump in his bed. A smile softened his stern features. She was asleep, great. That had worked to his advantage last time.

He practically rubbed his hands together as he neared the bed. He couldn't wait to see what she was wearing. Her in his sleep top turned him on more than the sexiest lingerie could.

He kicked out of his boots and pulled off his socks, quickly unbuttoned his shirt and shrugged it off letting it fall to the floor. Unbuckled his belt, undid his trousers, shoved them down and stepped out of them.

Very, very slowly he slid onto the bed and lifted the covers. "Oh aye," he exclaimed under his breath. She was wearing his upper sleeping garment and a swath of underwear. Making as little movement as possible, he slipped under the covers.

She was lying on her side facing away from him. He carefully removed her undergarment then spooned up next to her back and slid his leg between her legs, separating them.

With his leg under her top leg, he lifted it slightly, took his shaft in his hand, it had never completely softened from earlier with all that talk about sex with her to Gabriel, and put it between her legs and against her womanhood. Reaching around in front of her, he unbuttoned the buttons on the top and carefully pulled it off her.

She stirred slightly but didn't wake. He pushed the covers down so he could view her naked body. He just let his eyes eat her up for a few minutes. He would never tire of seeing her nude. His wife.

"Sons above, Sislla," he whispered hoarsely. Both on their sides, her back to his front, he took a hold of both her wrists and gently pulled her hands up above her head, causing her back to arch slightly.

Sislla stirred, murmured a brief cadence of breaths and inaudible words. Her spine curved and he curled her legs back with his, whispered against her cheek, "You are flawless, *tiris plavas avithé,* my beautiful wife, are you waking? Feel my touch on that delicate satin skin of yours." He smiled when she murmured again, still inaudible.

Gripping her wrists with his hand, holding her immobile, he stroked his other hand from her nape then around to her throat, down over her breasts, palming each one, she shivered drowsily against his body.

He drew his hand lower, brushing over her belly then down to her core. When he touched her there she jerked so suddenly he almost lost his grip on her wrists. He stroked softly over her mound, her moan rolled out like a rough mew.

Circling her bud with his fingers, he caressed her slit, in seconds his hand was wet. He wondered what she was dreaming because she groaned and squirmed against his hand, like she was on the threshold between being asleep and awake.

Kultur gently pushed a finger inside her, she quivered violently and her body folded forward in half. Still holding her wrists he pulled her back, arching her spine again. He could feel her waking. She wriggled and sighed, then as he moved his finger deeper inside her she froze.

Her voice tremulous she whispered, "Kultur?"

His chuckle a low rumble against her ear, he said, "You were expecting someone else, baby, in *my* bed?"

As she woke more, she realized the position he had her in. She was buck-naked, he held her arms above her head, and was holding her legs curled back with his, forcing her spine to lightly curve back.

She tugged at her limbs but he held her. "Kultur, what are you doing?"

He chuckled again. "You know what I'm doing. And you know you want it too. It's not a golden moon so you are safe from marking."

Nuzzling his nose against her hair, sniffing, he murmured, "You smell like you, sweet, fresh, I can't get enough. I made Onani bring me the sleepwear you wore the other night and kept them in bed with me while I slept. They had your scent on them."

"Uh," her mutter was a shivery sigh. "I thought you were with another woman the past few nights."

Was there a trace of jealousy in her voice? Sons above he hoped so! "Don't be ridiculous, *koritsi*, there is no other woman for me. You are my wife."

Using his knee that was between her legs, he nudged them further apart, she was completely vulnerable. Her back arched, her legs parted, he still gripped her wrists over her head and slightly pulled back, she couldn't move at all to cover herself.

His heavy shaft pressing against her opening from behind, he skimmed his hand up her luxurious skin to fondle each breast, kneading and manipulating her globes in his fingers, pinching, twisting and pulling her nipples.

Surprised she didn't protest, or struggle to get out of his grasp, not too hard anyway, he kissed her neck. Gliding his hand down her body he fisted his achingly hard phallus and shifted it firmer to her core making sure she was completely aware of it. He rubbed it against her nether lips, smearing her silk all over his foreskin.

A deep shuddering breath ruffled out of her throat, but she said not a word. Holding his shaft at her opening it pulsed against her tender flesh.

Kissing and sucking along her neck, his breath warming her cheek, his voice raspy deep, he murmured heavily, "I have to have you, *koritsi,* I really can't stop myself." Reaching around in front of her, he caressed her clit until her hips were moving with his fingers. Her breaths sounded like scraping hums, and his hand was soaked with her honey.

"Okay, baby, it's now," he waited a few beats. She said nothing, no protest, no fighting to get out of his clutch. He pushed her legs further apart and fisted his shaft again positioning it at her core and sank into her.

"*Ahh*…Sislla, you are so fine," he groaned, pushing deeper, "you feel so fuck- uh, damned good."

Still she said nothing but she didn't tell him to stop.

Kultur laid his face against the side of her head so she could feel his breath, and he could hear her own breathing quicken. His thrusts were gentle at first, shallow, because of their position he wanted to make sure she was comfortable before he built them up.

Soon he was plunging but going very slow, teasingly slow, and deeper each time. As her sheathe eased apart for him, he wrapped his fingers around her hip to hold her and he thrust in harder and harder, pushing deeper.

Huffing harshly, his exhalations blowing her hair, sensation surged, firing his loins. He suddenly thrust so hard she gasped, he felt her vagina clench him. Backing off, he said gruffly, "Am I hurting you, Sislla?"

Her head slightly shook to the side, she let out a hushed, "No." Then, lacerated breath gushing through her parted lips, she said, "More, Kultur."

So surprised, he halted briefly, then smiled against her hair. Holding her arms more tightly over her head to stretch her body harder in a semi-circle, he grabbed her breast, squeezing it roughly, further detonating his scalding desire. At her cry, he released her and moved his hand down to press her core. He held his fingers over her nether lips feeling his phallus sliding in and out of her through his fingers.

"God, Sislla…" he huffed. "I can't hold off," He flattened his palm over her pelvis holding her tightly against him, then slammed again and again into her. The veins on his neck rigid and pounding with the strain of holding back, his teeth clenched, he was breathing so hard her hair was flying all over her face.

"I want you, Kultur," it was a breathless, low, needful keen.

At her words, blood rushed to his heart expanding it with such loving feeling for her it hurt. "I want you, Sislla," he murmured tightly, struggling to keep from climaxing before she did.

His palm lowered pressing her mound. His shaft still moving between his fingers, he shifted it marginally, slanting it to rub her slightly at a different angle. Rolling his fingers over her clit he suddenly pinched it sharply, it was enough to set her off.

He felt her spine bend hard, she pushed back against him with a ragged breathy cry, her head dropped back against his. He sucked her neck as her body stiffened to a rigid peak. Then trembling violently, with a release of a grainy exhalation and jolting spasms, she fell boneless against him her, body jerking while he still pounded into her.

His drubbing, grinding thrusts reached their zenith, bellowing her name in her ear, "Sislla!" he came hard and fierce, and his seed raced up his shaft and burst out.

Kultur's body convulsed as he emptied into her, his phallus jerking with each contraction. He paused, groaned, another few thrusts, and he surged to a shuddering halt, his splayed strong hand still on her pelvis clasping her against him.

Kultur knew he was breathing deep and fast like a wild animal in her ear, his heart in his chest beating against her back as his body struggled to calm. He released her wrists to pull her against him with both arms wrapping around her body holding her tightly. They didn't speak, they fell asleep that way, with him still in her.

Chapter Thirty-Three

When he woke in the morning she was gone. Kultur felt it even before his eyes opened. His arms were empty, his chest was cold.

He stretched out on the sheet reaching for her but, damn, she was gone. He knew it was useless to look around the suite, but just in case she was lounging naked surrounded with bubbles in his big swirling tub, he couldn't help giving it a cursory check.

A quick look, aye, his chambers were empty. She's probably sulking, getting all stiff with shame and guilt like before. He'd be damned if she was going to wallow in regret again for something that was natural and beautiful between them. When he saw her he would make it sea glass clear she was staying in his bed, every night.

He took off first for her room although he doubted she was there. He went in anyway. His sleep top was lying on her bed. He picked it up and held it to his face inhaling her scent. Setting it back down on the bed, he glanced around. His mouth quirked ruefully.

On the vanity was a plate with a half a piece of toast spread with creamy butter and nut butter with a few nibbles out of it, and a half a glass of juice. Shaking his head, her idea of breakfast.

Traipsing over to the window, he peered out, looked down. "Of course." A line of people trailed from the side door to her workshop. "Working her damned tiny fingers to the bone." The girl could not stand to see someone in pain.

On his way to his office, his mother slacked up to him in her low heels, skirt swinging like a pendulum around her ankles.

"Kultur, a word if I may?"

He fought down the rolled eyes and the frown, pushed a pleasant impassive sort of a smile on his face and waited for her. "Yes, Mother? How are you today?" he inquired politely, his mind on other things.

The grey hair was pinned in a bun on her head, hard dark eyes peeled at him in frustration. "Darling, please, we must talk about *her*."

Feeling his limbs turn to steel and his lungs suck in a deep breath, Kultur didn't hide his scowl. "Mother, no, tis done. I do not want to discuss Sislla. She is *tiris avithé*, my wife." He turned to go but she grabbed his arm. He looked down at the wrinkled, vein trailed hand clinging to him.

"You can give me a moment, son," she declared haughtily and with a slightly faux injured air.

He saw through her put upon distressed affect, but with an irritated sigh he allowed her to take him down the hall to one of the many salons.

She walked into the chamber in front of him. He followed her swishing skirt wishing he had gone straight to the field instead of doing paperwork first.

Darathia moved imperially to a sofa and sat down gracefully.

A tray was set in the center of the oblong table in front of the sofa. She had obviously planned on bringing him there; it was not by chance she ran into him. She must have been hovering in the grand chamber waiting for him to pass by this morning.

"Please sit, darling," she gestured in a waved arc of her hand for him to sit in the big chair diagonal to the sofa.

Ignoring his impatient huff as he sat in the chair, she graciously poured steaming herbal liquid into two porcelain cups and handed one to him.

Motioning to a bowl of sweet rocks and slices of square fruit to add to his drink if he desired, she sat back against the sofa with practiced dignity and took a careful sip of her hot drink.

Swallowing his impatient sigh, Kultur declined the sweet and the fruit; he leaned back in his chair and just held the cup without drinking. He wasn't going to initiate the conversation, she brought him there, he waited for her to speak.

Darathia reflected on her annoyed son. So huge and hard muscled, even dressed in neat pants and a button down shirt, his wild black hair tamed, he looked incongruent with the soft almost feminine chair he sat upon.

The room was pale yellow and pink walls, the sofa and chairs covered with pastel yellow and pink flowers. The children that didn't work at their family farms or in the fields, when not in school did embroidery when the weather dissuaded them from going outside. Some worked at the mills or glassworks after school.

The floor was thick buttermilk carpet. A fireplace in pastel stone took up part of one wall, a few bookcases and tables filled the rest of the room. His vibrant masculine energy was at odds with the soft room.

"Darling, this woman," she waited until he cleared the scowl and turned his fathomless onyx eyes to her. He was her favorite although he had always been her more difficult child to speak with, be close to. His father had beat obeisance, strength, and his duty to fight to protect his realm into him almost from birth.

The elder Atraam had had no conscience, no compassion, for anyone, least of all his own son. He had been cruelly cold and brutal to Kultur molding him into what he thought a warlord Atraam should be.

He had left his callous mark on Kultur, making him inscrutable, ruthless, and almost as merciless brutal and remorseless as his father. That's why this Sislla thing nettled her so much. Why did he care so much whether this foreign intruder lived or died?

Watching her from lowered lids, Kultur took a sip of his drink, said, "What is it, Mother? What else can you say about it?"

Her aggravated exhale carried to him. "Kultur, why is it necessary for you to mark her? There are thousands of available men in Chamaine-Gris more than willing to bed the whore."

Kultur clutched his cup so hard it was in danger of shattering. "Mother, I've warned you, I will not have you talk about Sislla that way."

The boiling anger under his calm tone made Darathia back off. "All right, all right, fine. Anyway, as I was saying, there are a number of men who would be happy to have sex with her, mark her, even keep her. Why-"

He slammed the cup down on the table next to him. His eyes glittered hard and ominously black. "I warn you, stop. Now. Not another word about her and other men. She is *my wife*."

Darathia sat up a little straighter, her spine like a fireplace poker. "Calm down, Kultur, for the sons' above sake, you sound so possessive. It's just, well, it is not necessary for you to throw yourself away on her. You haven't completed the marking, there is still time to turn her over to another-"

"*Goddammit*!" Kultur ground out leaping to his feet. "Enough! Sislla will not be with another man, ever. She is my *avithé*, and that is not going to change. I will not allow any interference from you or anyone else!"

Darathia got to her feet too, albeit not as energetically as her son and kept trying, "She is nothing, Kultur, a foreign peasant, a shore prostitute. She is not good enough for you, the Atraam of the Chamaine-Gris. Now, Araina-"

"Stop it, Mother." He didn't bellow it, he said it so quietly it sounded so much more dangerous than if he'd shouted.

Not stupid, Darathia of all people knew her son's famous temper and not to prod it. "All right, son, calm down. Now, please, if you would be so kind to sit back down like a gentleman, I have something to show you." She waited. He stood glowering at her. "Kultur, please sit."

Grumbling, "I never said I was a gentleman," *just ask Sislla*, he dropped back into the chair and shoved his back impatiently against the back of the chair.

Darathia smiled. "Thank you dear," she cooed, "now sit still, I'll be right back." She tripped over to him, bent and lightly kissed his cheek then left the room.

Waiting for her, Kultur leaned over and set his elbows on his knees, twined his fingers and cupped his chin in his hands. He could feel the heat of aggravation at his mother's continually maligning Sislla prickling his skin.

Sislla's bright blue eyes and sweet pretty smile floated in front of his mind, he smiled. How could anyone say anything bad about her? She-

Hands started at the nape of his neck and stroked down his back then rolled around to wrap around him under his neck.

He froze, could he only hope it was Sislla? A gleeful grin spread across his face as he grasped the wrists clutched together in front of him, swung her around and onto his lap.

She had already crushed her lips on his before he realized she was too heavy, bigger boned, and a strong floral perfume assailed his nose, not Sislla's gentle fresh scent.

His eyes flew open at the same time as the gasp at the door.

Araina was on his lap, in his arms, her arms twined around his neck and her lips pressing against his.

"Araina, what the fuck," grabbing her arms he pushed her back and just hated to look over at the door, but he did.

Sislla, her face drained of all color, stood with those beautiful eyes wide with hurt and betrayal, her mouth open in shock, she turned and fled.

"Oh fuck- Sislla! Come back here!" Kultur tried to push Araina off his lap but she kept her hands wrapped tight around his neck and clung to him. He barked, "Get the fuck off me, Araina!"

"Come, Kultur, you know you want this," she ground her butt into his crotch, then squirmed around to straddle him. She clutched him with both arms and legs.

"*Grrr...*" With an animal's fierce growl, Kultur stood up with Araina clinging to him, marched to the couch, jerked her hands off his neck and shoved her on the couch. Her legs flew up inelegantly as she fell sprawling on the cushions.

Insulted, Araina shrieked, "Kultur! Hey!"

He ran to the door and out of the room. Out in the hall he quickly scanned the area, but it was clear Sislla was gone and there was no trace of which direction she had gone in.

Dragging a hand through his hair, he cursed, "Fuck!" Thinking she probably went to her workshop, he headed in that direction.

"Kultur!" Lucas stormed into the grand chamber stopping him.

Snapping, "Not now," Kultur made to stalk past his brother, but Lucas held a hand to his chest.

"There's trouble in the field. A group of the warriors have separated and are fighting each other. Gabriel and I tried to stop them, but they need your iron fist to lay down the law."

Struck with ambivalence, Kultur paused with his eyes towards the hall leading to the workshop. His exhale grated out coarse and pissed. His duty was to keep the people safe.

Without a word he clumped across the marble floor and stalked out the door with Lucas behind him.

******

Her hand over her mouth, Sislla ran as fast as she could. As she reached the grand chamber, she panicked and ran out of the castle and kept going as far as she could for as long as she could.

After a few miles, she slowed and the tears fell. She slid to the ground heaving with sobs, her back knocked hard on the rock she leaned against.

Ryan stood awkwardly. He had been behind her all morning as was his job. He had been standing there at the salon seeing the same scene she experienced, he couldn't believe his eyes. The Atraam had clearly expressed his feelings for Mistress Sislla.

It was a gross shock seeing that demeaning bitch Araina in the Master's lap with their lips locked. If he hadn't been there when the Atraam's mother had told Sislla the Master commanded for her to come to the salon he would be believing what Sislla was right now.

It was obvious, at least to him that Darathia had set them all up. Ryan's heart broke seeing the sweet Mistress so devastatingly distraught, crying so hard she couldn't catch her breath.

But, he bit back the smile that threatened. She had fought and resisted the Master at every step, yet it was as transparent as those guileless blue eyes of hers that she cared for him. Yee-ha.

Her face in her hands, Sislla wept with hitching breaths and heart rending sobs. Ryan dropped down on his haunches in front of her. "Miss Sislla," he cleared his throat noisily, "uh, Mistress Atra."

Sobbing into her knees, Sislla said fiercely, "Don't call me that, I am obviously not *that*."

His voice soft, Ryan persevered, "Miss Sislla, don't let that woman do that to you, don't let her trickery win. It was a set-up, Mistress, it was done deliberately. I was there; I saw Madam Kultiran's face. You are too...pure...sweet, to see the malevolence in her eyes as she lied to you telling you the Master wanted to see you."

The tears still flowed; she gulped and hiccupped her breaths.

It was no doubt not his place to speak to her about this, but, damned if the poor Mistress' heart wasn't just bleeding out onto the ground.

"Miss Sislla, listen to me. I have known the Atraam and his family all my life. The Atraam, may be, uh, a cold ruthless man, but he is an honorable one. He would not hurt you like that, in that way, mean like that.

"Araina has flapped around him like an annoying buzzing fly ever since that whole engagement disaster thing of his, and he has shut her down at every step. His mouth curls with displeasure every time she paws all over him. If he had wanted her, begging your pardon, Miss, he would have had her long ago."

Sislla's sobs lessened, she wiped at her eyes with her skirt.

Ryan got close to her, but not close enough the Atraam would rip off his head if he came by.

"Miss Sislla, he cares so much for you, it's plain and bold in his face the way he looks at you, the way he treats you. I have never seen him so gentle and patient with anyone, even Miss Lexi, and Miss," he grinned and sighed, "if anyone has tried his patience, it's you."

She peered up at him through a blur of tears. Pushing her hair out of her face, a small smile wavered.

A bit of red tinged his neck. "Uh, I don't want to get too, ah, personal, but, you are the only woman he has ever, ahem, had in his bed. Uh, or bath."

Staring blankly at him, she sighed. "But maybe he finally gave into her wiles, decided I was too," her lashes lowered, embarrassed, "small...for him."

Ryan blew out a long breath. "Trust me, Miss, the Madam and that bitc- uh, Araina set you both up. Don't let them win. Don't hurt him because they hurt you." Saying his piece, Ryan fell silent.

Sislla gulped down her tears and her pain. Actually, she was shocked at her own behavior. What on earth had come over her, fleeing and breaking down in hysteria.

So what if Kultur had that- that- woman on his lap, and was...kissing her...Sislla touched her own lips remembering when he'd had his mouth and hands all over her, asking her if she wanted him to do that with another woman, and...begging her to make love with him.

Even then her heart had twitched painfully every time he had said, 'do you want me to do this with another woman?' all while caressing her breasts and kissing her until she was trembling to sink to the floor with him ready to-

"Mistress?"

"I...I'm uh, okay, Ryan."

He stood up and held his hand down to her. She accepted it and he helped her to her feet. His red brow furrowed, he asked with apprehension, "So…um…is everything all right, now?"

She started walking with her head down still wiping her eyes. "I don't know, Ryan, I don't know."

His hands tightly twined behind his back, tall and narrow as a pole, Ryan walked beside her, a half a step behind as the Atraam had instructed him so he would protect her from all sides, see any danger coming at her from any direction.

Chapter Thirty-Four

Sislla worked healing for hours putting the dreadful morning behind her.

Ryan was just about to tell her it was time to quit, when Kultur's big frame filled the doorway. His eyes on Sislla, all the patients still there quietly shuffled out of the room, along with her two assistants. He glanced briefly at Ryan with a signal for him to leave.

Earlier, when Jaspar had relieved him for a beak, Ryan had sought Kultur out and told him how he gone after her, and how he'd found her crying her heart out. The Kirman slid out of the room with a pursed smile that Kultur didn't miss.

Not looking at Kultur, Sislla put her herbs and leaves into jars and stacked them neatly in the cupboards, tucked her implements into drawers, hung up clean towels. He remained just inside the door watching her.

She was washing her hands in the sink when Kultur came up to stand right behind her. She could feel his virile heat enveloping her senses. Shutting off the water, not turning around, she took a cloth off a hook and dried her hands.

She could feel him untying her apron at her back, and slowly pulling it around and off her body. It felt like he was stripping off her protective armor. She felt his hands set on her waist, he left them for a second letting his warmth soak through her blouse.

Then, he spread his fingers wrapping them around her waist, rolling his palms around the front of her stomach he pulled her back against chest and wound his arms around her holding her tight.

Sislla didn't melt into him, but she didn't push away either. She felt his breath on her ear, the side of his face rough with unshaven whiskers on her tender skin.

He tucked her hair back and his lips touched her neck, he kissed her like the soft flutter of a butterfly wing. When she shuddered in his arms, he turned her around, his hands stroking down her arms to hold her waist again.

Eyes downcast, her arms hung at her side. His presence so close, his strength and energy reverberating like an aura against her body, his masculine scent wafted through her senses; she could feel his heat in her pores.

Kultur lifted her hands and set them on his shoulders; he tucked two fingers under her chin and tilted her face up to his. Her eyes moved to his chin.

"Sislla, look at me," his voice deeper than ever, quiet, firm.

Her lids lifted, the baby blues raised slowly to look at him, and she was taken aback.

Uncertainty glowed at her from the remote depths of his ebony orbs. He slid a hand to cradle her jaw and the side of her face and bent to kiss her, she turned her head. She felt his fingers tightened on her skin. He released her face and dropped his hands lightly to hold her shoulders.

"Sislla, you have to know what you saw wasn't…"

"What it looked like? I somehow hear the cliché of that," she said looking back down at his chest.

His heavy sigh stirred her hair. He squeezed her shoulders. "Baby, it was a total set up, I swear to the sons above. My mother lured me into the salon then left saying she had something for me. The next thing I know, I feel these hands stroke down my back, I'm thinking," he sounded almost bashful. "That it was you. When the hands rolled around the front of me, I, well, I grabbed her. I mean I thought it was you, and pulled her around to my lap. As soon as I realized it wasn't you, she's much bigger, definitely not as soft as you," seeing her frown he hurried on.

"Anyway, at the same moment I realized it wasn't you she slapped her lips on me and you were in the doorway." He gripped her shoulders. "*Tiris koritsi,* believe me, I didn't know, I-"

"Why did she take you to the salon? What did your mother want?"

"Huh?" His brow wrinkled. "She- she, *ah,*" he forked his fingers through his hair. "She wanted to talk me out of marking, marrying you."

Sislla stepped back from him making his hand fall away from her. "We are not yet married."

His eyes rolling with annoyed impatience he ran his hand through his hair again. "Aye, we must complete the ceremony. We have to make love again twice more on the golden moons, to complete the circle. I have told you this."

He reached out and took her hand. "We will be irrevocably married after that. As far as I am concerned now, we already are. I said the oath words as we climaxed, it is binding. You are, you will be my wife, my Atra, my queen."

The look of fear streaked across her face. She tried to yank her hand from his grasp, crying in a frantic whisper, "But why? Why are we to be married? Why didn't you just- just screw me and leave me be?"

His lips firmed. "I am not explaining this whole thing again."

Still fighting the issue she said, "You didn't ask me, why didn't you ask me if I wanted to be married to you, if I would agree to it?"

His smile wry, he replied, "Because you would have refused."

She was quiet, contemplating this, he was right. "You still should have told me before you did the deed, I had the right to know."

He squeezed her hand. "You were already fighting me about the whole marking thing. Telling you we would also be legally married at its completion, would have made you angrier, more frightened, resistant, panicked." He shook his head. "It was already bad enough. Telling you in advance that at the conclusion of the markings you would be irrevocably bound to me would have only made things worse."

She didn't respond, just stared blankly at his chest.

Holding her hand, he pulled her in close and put both hands to cup her face. "It's all done, Sislla. You, my mother, everyone needs to stop disputing it. I will not retreat, we will complete the circle, the Epita, and we will be fully man and wife. Now, all I care about is whether you're okay with that crap my mother pulled with Araina. You will believe what I tell you."

Her smile faint, Sislla snorted, "Just like you to tell me what to believe, not *ask* me if I believe you."

He drew her face up, his lips almost on hers. "Because I do not lie, Sislla. You must see that by now. If I say there is nothing between Araina and me, that I just about pissed my pants in horror when I realized she was on my lap crushing my *equipment* as you call it, and her big hard lips on mine, *ergh*," he shivered in repulsion.

When Sislla broke out in laughter, Kultur took advantage and lowered his mouth on hers capturing her sweet softness. Her mouth already open, his tongue pushed in like it belonged there chasing her tongue to mate with it.

When she didn't resist, and her hands stroked up his chest to cling to his shoulders, he deepened the kiss, crushing their mouths together until they were both faint and breathless with heady passion.

He finally pulled back. Sislla knew her eyes radiated the same hot glow that emanated from his depthless moons. He brushed back a spiral blonde lock, thumbed her cheek lightly, and kissed her pouted lips gently.

"I have to go out, in the field, *koritsi,* I'll be gone a couple of days. I really need, really Sislla, you have to promise me, I can't do the best job I need to do if I have to worry about you here."

A lick of black hair hung over his eye, Sislla smoothed it back. Warm lust struck his loins at her touch, she so seldom touched him.

"Please Sislla, don't keep putting Ryan and Jaspar's heads on the block by allowing yourself to get lured out of the castle. Promise me unless it's on fire, do not leave the castle. If someone is in dire need of your services, you tell Ryan. He will keep whatever it is in confidence so no one, including anyone from another faction will feel in danger. If they can't come to you, you tell Ryan and he will have guards retrieve them, again, no questions asked. Okay? Promise me, baby." He brushed his lips over hers.

Nodding, she wound her arms around his neck and pulled his mouth harder to hers. "I promise, Kultur."

At her response, his hands tightened. She drew back, "You have to go."

His eyes blurred, hazy with the delightful surprise of her wanting to kiss him, he held her, pulling her back for more. "I can go later," he mumbled at her lips trying to cover her mouth and shove his tongue back into her velvet sweetness.

She pushed away from him with a laugh. "Go on, then. I will be fine. I promise."

****

Kultur and his brothers were gone longer than expected. One of their warriors had been captured by the Tenthekens. It would mean certain death for the man, after excruciating torture.

It was the warrior's fault; he had been digging up and stealing metal. He should have gone in a protective group but he was greedy and impatient. Kultur would have left him to his own consequences, but he was Lucas' wife's brother.

Kultur and his men, invisible in dark clothes, their faces marked with coal, slipped stealthily through the woods. They were like unheard, unseen army ants moving as if their feet never touched the ground. Clay had seen Leo taken, saw where he was imprisoned before returning for help.

Clay led them in the cover of night to the Tentheken village. Most lights were extinguished as people slept. Warriors strolled the perimeter and the village, but Kultur and his men easily got passed them unseen.

Clay led them to an open hole near the soldiers' barracks. A guard sat cross-legged against a brick wall nodding off. Gabriel crept up behind him and snapped his neck without a scuffle or sound.

Lucas knelt at the hole and whispered, "Leo!"

Leo was lying like he was broken on the dirt floor of the hole. He wasn't moving. The hole was around fifteen feet deep.

Kultur tied a rope to a tree then looped it around his arm and sat on the edge of the hole, then jumped in.

Kneeling beside Leo, Kultur could see the man was in bad shape. His face was crushed to a pulp, his arms and legs hung at odd angles. Kultur put his face on his chest, Leo was just barely breathing. He looked up at Lucas at the top of the hole, his face grim.

Lucas pulled his lips in. The guy had to live or Lucas' wife, Cindra, would be inconsolable.

The village was dark, but a few lanterns strung around in trees and on poles streaked wide mild bands of illumination. Kultur could not see well inside the hole, but it didn't matter.

He wrapped the rope around Leo's chest and under his arms then looked back up at Lucas with a wave. Pulling together, the men pulled Leo up and out of the hole.

Lucas cringed when he saw how viciously Leo had been beaten. It was going to be a bitch to try to keep Cindra from seeing him like that. He untied the rope and slung it back into the hole.

The men held the rope while Kultur climbed up it. He and Gabriel lifted Leo onto Lucas' back.

In a dark pack the League started back through the woods.

Just as they entered the first line of trees a man came charging out with a sword drawn.

Kultur dodged the slice of the swinging sword, punched the man in the gut, as he folded over Kultur hit him so hard in the neck he broke it. The man dropped to the ground without another sound.

They met no other resistance on the way back.

When they reached the castle, they trooped in the back and took Leo straight to Sislla's workshop. As the men got Leo down off Lucas' back and onto the gurney, Kultur rushed to retrieve Sislla. His heart was beating like a drum. They'd been gone several days and he couldn't wait to see her.

Taking the stairs two at a time, he jogged to her room. Jaspar was sitting with his back against Sislla's door. He leaped to his feet at the sight of Kultur.

Well, Kultur thought, that's a good start. She was inside the castle, inside her room where she belonged. Well, he'd prefer she was in his chambers but at least she was here. Jaspar stepped aside,

Kultur knocked to give her a warning before he walked in and scared the daylights out of her.

The only light was what shone through her open window. He frowned, the window was probably way too high for someone to get into, but he didn't feel it was safe for her to have it open. He trod quietly across the carpet to her bed. She looked so small curled up under the blanket.

"Baby," he whispered, trying not to startle her. He sat carefully on the side of the bed and lightly touched her arm.

"*Koritsi,*" he said a little louder. Leaning over, he brushed her hair aside and whispered in her ear, "Wake up, little wife," he kissed her gently.

She stirred, her arms unwound. He set his hand on her arm, "Sislla, tis Kultur, wake up, you're needed, to heal."

Like smoke, his words seemed to seep into her brain and stir her more until she became aware that he was there. "Kultur," she sat up groggily, "what…"

"Hi there," he said softly and kissed her forehead.

"You're back…" she murmured redundantly yawning.

He smiled. "Aye. Honey, we need your help. Leo has been…hurt…pretty badly."

"Oh!" The sleepiness fled her foggy eyes, she moved to get out of bed, but she ran into Kultur wall.

He threaded his arms around her and pulled her against him, then plundered her mouth with frenzied abandon. *Ahh*, her body all snuggled in a nightgown pressed warm against his chest, her unique fresh scent made him hard in a flash. He started to push her to lie back on the bed and join her.

"Kultur, you said Leo," Sislla uttered breathless.

Steeling himself, he cursed, "*Shit*- we have to go," and moved away so she could get up.

She hurried to the bathroom to change.

Two hours later Sislla was putting her paraphernalia away and the men were picking Leo up to take him to his room to recover. Behind them, Cindra was wringing her hands for her brother. Lucas had a supportive arm around her, pressing her tight under his shoulder, whispering consoling words in her ear.

Kultur had hovered, helping when he could, staying out of the way when he couldn't. He waited until Sislla had her materials put up before going to her.

He was going to take her back to bed, his bed. As he reached a hand out- Gabriel came up to him.

"Sorry, brother," he said wearily, it's been a long few days. "But there's word there are Tenthekens sneaking through the forests on their way here to seek revenge for the two men we-" he broke off at Kultur's frown and his glance at Sislla. "Uh, anyway, we need to gather up a troop and go..." he glanced at Sislla, "uh, find them."

Kultur saw Ryan looming in the area, he called him over. "Take care of her." He bent down to Sislla and ordered, "You don't leave the castle." He kissed her quickly and was gone.

Chapter Thirty-Five

It had been a long day. Sislla was closing up the workshop when the last patient that was leaving came back inside. "Miss," the man said meekly, slightly bent over as if in pain.

She turned with a tired smile. "Yes, what can I do for you? I thought you were feeling better." She put her hand on his back and leaned in slightly to hear him.

They were near the back door; one of her assistants was taking trash out to be burnt in the fire tomorrow. The sick man staggered towards the rear of the room and groaned as if in great pain, he bent over further holding his stomach.

Wrapping her arm around the man's waist, Sislla called out, "Jaspar, quick, grab the gurney, it's out front where they were cleaning it!" The guard ran right out of the room to follow her orders.

"Now, you'll be okay," Sislla said to the man she was holding- when he staggered out of her arms and stumbled out the back door.

"Oh! No! Come back! You're ill, come back!" Sislla ran out after the man. She burst out the door into the pitch black.

She wasn't supposed to have been working so late, but several very sick people had come by and she kept moving even though Jaspar hovered over her saying she had to stop and threatened that any second he was going to have to bodily haul her out of the workshop. She kept telling him, "Just one more minute, Jaspar, I'm almost done," and kept working.

"Sir!" Sislla called out, hurrying around the rear perimeter looking for the ill man. Movement off in the bushes caught her eye. She ran over, gasping, "Sir, please let me help you, where are you-"

A hand reached out of the dark shrubbery, grabbed her hair and dragged her into the bushes.

Her first scream was piercing; her second was muffled by his hand. The man gave her a punch to knock her out, everything went black as he threw her over his shoulder then ran down a path into the night.

Sislla's face was banging against something, blood suffused her face. Then she realized she was upside down and her face was hitting a man's back as he ran with her draped over his shoulder. She started kicking and screaming and beating on his back with her fists.

"Fine girl," he snarled, yanking her forward letting her land hard on her feet, so hard she toppled backwards and fell on the ground.

He stood over her, unbuckling his belt and grinning like a deviant freak. "Gads," he drooled lustily as he crept closer to her, "you are so pretty, honey, I just had to have you."

On her butt, her palms scratched from the stones in the dirt, Sislla said kindly but her quivering voice was strained with fear, "Sir, you're ill, let me help you," she tried to sound calm but her face shone the fright.

He stepped closer. Almost standing over her, he yanked at his trousers pulling the buttons apart. Her fear seemed to accelerate his desire. Grinning down at her, he rubbed his crotch then opened his pants.

She tried to scuttle away from him; he dropped quickly between her legs and grabbed the waist of her pants hauling her back.

Sislla screamed, he slapped her and pushed her hard on her back. Her head hit a rock stunning her. Leaning over her, he grabbed her blouse with both fists and rent it, buttons flew in all directions.

His hands pried at her pants. Dizzy from the bang on the head, Sislla kicked at him, hit him, but he laughed at her and ripped the top of her pants apart.

The man fought to tug her pants down, she screamed, he clapped his hand over her mouth and yanked her pants down over her hips. He wasn't as big as Kultur but he was still twice her size, she fought like crazy but he was grabbing a hold of her pants and was about to jerk them the rest of the way down with one move- when he was suddenly gone.

Gasping frantically, trying to get a grip on the torrent of terror that shook her whole body, Sislla struggled to sit up and look through streams of tears in the dark to see what happened.

Suddenly a big body crouched down beside her, she screamed. He said quickly, "Sislla, honey, it's me, Gabriel, it's all right, you're safe now."

She saw him through a blur of tears, but then whipped her head around to the dreadful screams in front of her. A dark brute hulk was beating the man who was going to rape her. He was beating him into the ground.

"No!" Sislla tried to crawl on her hands and knees to stop Kultur from murdering the man, but Gabriel wrapped an arm around her shoulders holding her back. He said quietly, "Hush, honey, it's out of our hands."

Fighting Gabriel to let her go, Sislla screamed, "No! Kultur no! Don't kill him!" She screamed and screamed until her throat was raw, but Kultur kept hitting him, punching him over and over, until it was clear the man was dead.

Only then did Kultur sit back on his heels panting. His chest heaving, he dragged his bloody hands across his forehead. Black hair hanging over his wild murderous eyes dripped buckets of sweat.

Sislla had screamed so hard, and fought Gabriel she couldn't catch her breath. Kultur stood up and looked over at them.

"You-" Sislla rasped at him, "you killed him, how- could you?" the sobs clogged her throat. Gabriel pulled her into the corner of his shoulder.

His shoulders bunched and still heaving with rage, Kultur stomped over to her, bent over and put his hand one knee. He pointed a finger dripping with the man's blood at her. "You, this is your fault, Sislla. I told you never to leave the castle without my permission, this is why. His death is on you."

Lifting his shirt, he wiped the sweat and the dead man's blood out of his eyes. His eyes flicked down the front of her, at the torn shirt, her breasts heaving over very pretty lace bindings. "Fix her." He commanded his brother, then stomped off down the trail back to the castle knowing Gabriel would take care of her.

Sislla sat bewildered, disoriented, sobbing, and coughing from her hoarse throat while Gabriel pulled her torn shirt together keeping his eyes off her chest. He helped her up, fixed her pants, then half carried half walked her back to the castle.

Ryan and Onani were waiting for them. Gabriel gratefully passed her off to their hands.

When Sislla rose the next morning, she found her door locked from the outside. She hurried over to the window. There was not a line of people waiting for healing. He'd had them turned away.

"Damn him!" A rare curse burst hoarsely. "How dare he punish me like I'm a child!" She paced furiously, not stopping until the door opened.

It was Kultur. He came in and stood calmly, but his eyes were dark with anger.

Striding over to him, her hands on her hips, she accused him in an infuriated rasp, "You locked me in, you sent the people away, you *killed* a man!"

He crossed his arms over his massive chest. He hadn't shaved; his jaw was covered with black stubble, his cheeks and mouth concrete with aggression. Violence, and unrepentant bloodbath still filled his dark eyes.

His voice even, he said with cold dispassion, "He was dead, Sislla, the second he took what was mine. He was dead the second he touched you, he was dead the second he tried to rape you, he was dead," he suddenly reached out and gently touched the bruise under her eye with his fingertips, "the second he hurt you."

Her ivory face teeming with compassion, she cried, "Kultur, it's wrong, terribly wrong to kill, no matter what the reason."

His smile held no mirth. "You think it was okay he grabbed you, took you out of your home, beat you and was going to viciously rape you?" One black brow quirked up.

She glared steadily at him, her insinuation clear.

"Oh no, Sislla, don't fucking go there. Do not compare that sick fuck with me." Dark red seethed up his neck, covering his mouth hard with anger and grit teeth, up to darken his eyes further making them completely unreadable.

"Huh. You tell me what's different. Rape is rape." Seeing the rage turning his face to unrelenting rock, she spoke quickly, "You can't punish me like I'm a child. The man was sick, he staggered out the door, what did you expect me to do?"

"You went out the goddamned door with a strange man in the middle of the night." He sneered his sarcastic fury at her, "How stupid is that?"

"But, you are punishing the innocent sick people too!"

His voice was cold and emotionless as he said, "There will be no healing for three days." He turned and strode from the room. The door closed, and locked behind him.

Sislla was so mad she could spit nails. She ran to the window and waited. In a few moments she saw him leave the castle. It was clear he was filled with rage the way he stalked down the lane to the field, his shoulders blocks of unyielding granite, fists clenched.

He did not acknowledge anyone who waved or called to him, others shrunk back from the hard face and the black eyes that were like shadowed voids.

True to his word, Onani did not leave her door unlocked until three days had passed.

When Onani stood aside of the open door with her compassion and embarrassment flaming in her lowered head, Sislla tramped past her fuming, and went straight to her workshop.

It was a strain to push aside what had happened. A man had taken her and tried to violently rape her. Kultur had killed him with his bare hands, and without hesitation, even though she begged for his life.

Then he punished her like she was a child as well as the people who were denied healing. She was so mad she could scream, if her throat wasn't still hoarse. Still, she had to admit she'd been so terrified when that man attacked her she had been mindless with fear.

The worse thing was, as mad as she was at him, she kind of missed his large presence, his energy. The deep voice, the way he looked at her with desire, white flames smoldering in his obsidian eyes.

Sislla shook her head to clear the image. She had other more important things to think about. She smiled at her assistant who brought in her first patient.

******

Kultur worked himself past exhaustion, trying to push out the picture of returning to the castle late at night and Jaspar yelling that she'd been taken as he ran past Kultur out the door to look for her.

They had heard her screams; his blood had stopped dead at the sound. He and Gabriel, Ryan and a couple others took off in pursuit but they hadn't a clue what direction they'd gone in.

When they couldn't find her, he was beside himself with fear and anguish, then he heard her scream again and pinpointed where she was.

He'll never forget bursting through the bushes to see that animal ripping her clothes off and slapping her unconscious. He looked down at his clenched fists still showing the cuts on his knuckles. Aye, like he told her, the man was already dead before Kultur threw the first punch. He felt not a shred of guilt or remorse.

Except for the way Sislla had looked at him, so disappointed, repulsed by his lethal violence, she was physically sick with the killing. It twisted his stomach. Bah, like he'd told her, it was her fault. He didn't care what the reason, she had still left the goddamned building.

The prick would have had to kill her after assaulting her, knowing Kultur would murder him if he discovered who had taken her. Plus if the man had the balls to take her, his, the Atraam's wife right out of the castle, then no woman would be safe as long as the fucker lived.

He'd worked like a dog so he could sleep at night and not feel the torment of not having her lush little body to hold, not hearing her lovely voice in his ear, not laughing with her, not watching how she treated everyone with such sweet kindness.

His mood was so foul and black even Gabriel steered clear of him and didn't dare mock or tease him.

He paced his room like a caged wolf, running his hands again and again through his hair until he finally barked, "Enough!" Making up his mind, he stalked to the bathroom to clean up, shave for the first time in days, and go find her.

He tried her room first, then her workshop, although he figured, or at least he hoped, she wouldn't be there. If so, she would have disobeyed him again by working well past the three hours he allowed her.

Checking every room to no avail, he started steaming again, then his stomach lurched with a twinge at the thought that she might have left the castle, again. Maybe this time she would make good on her threat to leave, to go to the sea, to- no, he wouldn't let his thoughts go there.

Jaspar happened to pass by. Kultur stopped him. "Have you seen, the uh, Mistress, or Kirman Shaws?"

Jaspar clicked his heels together and stood at attention. "Yes, sir, Atraam. They, I mean she, uh, that is, Mistress Sislla, said she was bored of looking at the castle, not being able to see past the stone walls."

When the Kirman didn't continue, Kultur tried to hold back his impatient anger but the fright striking Jaspar's face indicated he had been unsuccessful. He gave up. "Damn it, Kirman, spit it the fuck out. Where is she?"

His Adam's apple bounced. "Oh, sorry sir, I misunderstood." He gulped and said quickly at Kultur's increasing anger, "Sir, she is in that study, you know, the one with that sort of closed lean-to leading to it. On the south side, that old-"

Kultur spun and marched away without a word.

Jaspar stood afraid to move, he was on the edge of either tossing his cookies or shitting his pants. When the Atraam was not angry he was the best of the best, but, he wiped his perspiring head, but when he was mad- he was terrifyingly deadly.

As soon as Jaspar saw the black hair and broad shoulders disappear down a hall, he let out his held breath, and hurried away in the opposite direction.

Kultur knew where she'd gone. He wasn't happy. Technically it was attached to the castle by a sporadic awning-like cover, but the walkway was still more outside than in.

It was an old outbuilding some of the men used as a make-shift office. Occasionally it was used as a place to have a discreet romantic tryst. That thought stung him, making him move more quickly.

His boots crunched on the pebbled walk leading to the building, passing under bits of cloth strung from a few poles as half-assed coverage. He snorted, leave it to Sislla to consider a few cloths clinging to poles to be considered 'inside the castle.'

A sigh of relief emptied his lungs when he saw Kirman Shaws standing guard outside the closed door to the small, one-room building. Although he didn't move, Kultur could tell Shaws saw him by the way his spine stiffened and he stopped blinking.

Kultur stalked past him, wordlessly opened the door, stepped inside and closed it behind him. He stood for a moment letting his eyes adjust to the dim light. Sheets hung over the windows to block peeping eyes.

Inside, there was an old weathered desk with dusty papers scattered on it, and glasses left from cocktails. A few chairs with faded cushions and stuffing poking out, and several plain wooden chairs and tables, old and scratched up, along with some books piled by a wall filled the room.

Across the scraped plank floor under a window was an oversized wide couch. She was curled up asleep on the worn cushions.

He stood for a moment observing her, trying to decide whether he was mad or not that she had kind of left the castle. But then, her bright hair spiraled over half her face and down her back, the meager light from the window brought out the soft roses in her round cheeks.

His feet moved forward of their own volition until he was standing next to the couch, his mouth, a crooked line of a scant smile seeing her pouty lips closed in a perfect bow.

Somehow, he found himself leaning over her, his hand tenderly pushing her hair off her face. She looked so young, so vulnerable. When healing, she seemed so composed and mature, it was hard to remember she was likely still quite young in years.

Chapter Thirty-Six

Crouching beside the couch, Kultur drew his big fingers across her cheek, so beautiful. Moving to his knees, he leaned over until their lips touched, his kiss like the stroke of a feather. Getting a sweet taste of her urged him to pursue a stronger kiss.

She made a tiny sound. Deep asleep, her mouth responded faintly to the press of his lips pushing hers open and his tongue foraging for hers.

Setting a hand on her shoulder, he pushed her lightly to roll her on her back to kiss her more easily, more fully. Her slender arms fell beside her head as if in gentle surrender. Then he looked down at the rest of her, his brows knit in a frown.

She was wearing something his sister had given her to sleep in. A tiny, thin cotton shirt that was so tight it was obvious she had no undergarments on under it, and it was cropped to just under her bosom.

Kultur's eyes were drawn like magnets to her full breasts molding tight like plump pillows against the cotton. His whisper silky sexy, "Wake up, Sislla."

Her lashes wafted at his deep voice but her eyes didn't open. Unable to stop himself, his hand went to one of her breasts. Brushing his fingertips over her nipple until it puckered, he lightly plucked it.

Watching the little bud grow hard, poking through the thin shirt, he could feel his own body growing hard. He covered her breasts with both hands, kneading the heavy globes until a ripple of a moan slipped from her.

"That's it, baby, wake up, be with me," he called quietly, moving his palms to the bare skin between the shirt and her pair of skimpy pants, like sweatpants hanging low on her slender hips.

His hands soaked up the warmth of her soft skin. His long fingers curled around her waist and her ribs, then he pushed them up under the shirt to clutch her bare breasts feeling their velvety softness. "*Oh sons*," he groaned.

Expecting her to wake up and either give him hell for touching her again while she slept, or hopefully, open her arms inviting him to join her on the sofa, he kept massaging her suppleness.

Her eyes didn't open, but her body was imperceptibly undulating against his palms. When she didn't push him away, although he thought she was might still be asleep, deep asleep as he could see her eyes rolling back and forth under her lids in REM, he pushed the shirt up until her breasts were fully exposed.

His shaft already hard as a rock, he fondled both plump globes, then put his face down and snuggled each one, kissing them. Murmuring in her cleavage, "Sweet *koritsi,* open those pretty eyes," a low growl urged, "can't you feel my touch, baby?"

Cupping her breasts with more vigor, he sucked on her nipples then bit and tugged at them with his teeth. He couldn't believe she didn't wake up. Becoming highly aroused, he was no longer being all that gentle.

She writhed faintly in her sleep, her hands still palm up on the bed next to her head, her legs curled to the side. Kultur leaned back and took her legs, pushing them down until they were stretched out straight, and then spread them slightly apart.

Sitting back on his heels, he just drank her in. Her face peaceful, her arms up, her breasts bare and her legs laid out straight in thin lightweight sweatpants.

"Damn, Sislla, you are so insanely beautiful, you know I can't resist touching you." He bent and kissed her. "Come on baby, wake up."

A tiny sound whispered in her throat, yet her eyes didn't open, they still moved behind her closed lids. Staring at her face,

Kultur stroked his hands down her ribs, over her stomach to her core, now her moan was louder, clearer, deeper. Her legs pulled together and up, curling back to the side. Her throaty moans stronger, she sounded like she was into his amorous petting.

Thinking she was waking finally, Kultur pushed her legs back down, then grasped her pants and pushed them down to her ankles. He palmed her sex over the wisp of underwear. With a raspy moan, her hips suddenly thrust up and into his hand.

"Ah, that's it, *koritsi,* be with me." His erection throbbing against his breeches, Kultur pushed her silky undergarment down then removed it and her pants, and separated her legs.

His gaze roaming from her reposed face, over her bare breasts, down to her apex, he caressed her core, watching her hips writhe ever so faintly on the couch cushion. Bending over her, he brought his lips to her sex and kissed the tender skin.

When her hips moved, he spread her legs further apart. He rubbed the sides of her folds with his thumbs, her ragged whimpers urging him on. Licking up her slit he gently bit her nub, her breath came in little hitches, her hips tried to twist side-to-side but he held them, and licked and kissed, touching and suckling her sex.

He sat back on his heels, his fingers stroking her, and watched every twitch and rasping moan she emoted. When she licked her lips, her head rolled, and her lips parted with a hush of breath, his erection pounded like a bolt of lightning.

Her eyes were still closed, his brows rose, *could she actually still be asleep*? His hand on her sex caressing her, he saw her nipples were hard as pebbles and a soft flush spread across her chest.

He nudged a finger inside her, bent and licked her clitoris. Her hands opened, splayed against the couch then closed and her back arched very slightly, yet her face was still in complete repose.

So turned on watching her shiver and writhe, asleep or not, his hand went to his erection, Kultur stroked it over his pants while still fingering and sucking her nub, rubbing circles around it, and in between moved his finger in and out of her.

Glancing at her face he whispered, "Your body, *koritsi,* was made to make love, with me, only with me." He put his lips back on her sex, stroked and licked her more aggressively.

When he sucked her entire mons into his mouth and lathed his tongue over her bud, her moan, almost a wail milled louder in her chest and her hips thrashed against his mouth.

Suddenly, her spine arched hard, her head dropped back, she sat straight up with her hands braced behind her back on the cushion, and with a guttural cry her eyes fluttered then flew open. He had brought her to the edge, her eyes glowed with heated passion. Until she came into full awareness.

"Oh my gosh, Kultur, what are you-" her eyes shocked to see his mouth on her sex.

Holding her thighs apart with one hand he lifted his head to look at her but he didn't stop stroking her swollen nether lips, his finger still moving inside of her trying to keep her on the edge.

With an aching sob, her spine curved backwards then she braced back on one arm, pushed her hair out of her face, her face flushed with rippling sensation, and mortification, she cried in a dry rasp, "*Stop, Kultur,*" her chest rose and fell rapidly with shallow fast breaths.

His face impassive, raging erection beating at his belly, Kultur narrowed his glittering eyes at her. Still holding her legs apart, his finger stopped moving but he didn't remove it from her wet sheath. He pinched her nub, holding it hard for a second, then released it with a caress. She cried out loud in pain and pleasure, her head dropped back and the rosy flush visibly spread up her body.

He said quietly, "Do you really want me to stop, Sislla? Tell me and I will." His hand still on her sex, his thumb lightly brushing her wet silk over her clit knowing he was keeping her on the precipice about to fall over the cliff into orgasm, he watched the skin above her bared breasts blush darker.

Gleaming misted eyes stared at him with transfixed passion, her tongue licked a circle around her lips and her chest heaved with heavy breaths. She took a deep shuddering breath, still drowsy she frowned at him, and then tried to push his hand away from her.

But he clenched her thigh to keep her from moving away from him or closing her legs.

Knowing he had her on the brink, he said, "Don't say stop, tell me yes, baby, please, tell me you want me, right now. Inside you." His hard face was completely blank of emotion as he watched her. It had worked before, he'd gotten her so high and hot she couldn't say no.

Her head dropped forward, she stared at her shirt pushed up exposing her naked breasts swollen and throbbing full with painful desire, her gaze fell to her nude lower part, her bare legs spread wide.

Kultur restrained her legs so she couldn't close them, his hand hadn't moved from her sex or his finger from inside her, just his thumb moved rhythmically over her clit. Her hips were unconsciously moving with his thumb's strumming.

"Kultur, you- you stripped me while I was asleep! You- you are touching me again when I can't, when I don't know, that is so wrong-"

"Yeah," he muttered, his eyes glowing like hot coals rummaged from her confused, passionately tormented eyes, to her breasts twisting as if trying to find his big hands to cover them, her hard nipples dying to jab at his palms. He knows her body wants him; he just has to convince her mind.

Sislla looked at his mouth, her face reddening with mortified awareness, she looked down to where his mouth had been when she had woken, and how incredible it had felt. She turned deeper red seeing his hand curled around her mound, his finger still in her. Her gaze drifted to his engorged erection straining against his pants.

When she didn't move, just stared blindly at his hand on her core, he brushed his thumb more firmly over her, tantalizing her delicate sensitized flesh, her cheeks bloomed brighter pink.

He did it harder and her breathing turned heavy again, gusty breaths hitched through her parted lips. Adding a finger, he slowly thrust them inside her deeper, curving and swirling, hitting her sweet spot.

Her hips twitched and bucked at his fingers, her head fell back with a drowning groan.

Shifting up, keeping his fingers working her, he grasped her head tilting it forward so he could devour her mouth while his fingers continued ravishing her sex.

Watching her lids slide down over her clouded eyes, feeling her response to his kiss, Kultur knew she was weakening.

Against her mouth he whispered, "What do you say, Sislla? Do you want me to stop, or do you…want…me inside you?" He thumbed her nub swollen and glistening with her silk, with circles and tugs; she bucked at his hand with a rib-wrenching moan straight into his mouth.

Her brain spinning in a lusted haze, she cried, "*Yes*." Breathy and angry, she declared, "Damn you, Kultur. Yes I want you."

Undeterred at her cursing him, he shoved his boots and socks off, yanked his belt open and ripped at the buttons on his pants. He shoved them down and kicked them off before she could change her mind. Not taking the time to remove his shirt he climbed between her open legs.

"Kultur…" With his hands and mouth no longer on her, her mind struggled to break through the ardent buzzing haze he'd brought her to. Starting to regain her senses she pushed to sit up.

His hand on her chest, he gently nudged her back down and put his hand back on her sex. Gingerly dominating her, he slipped the tips of his fingers inside her to get them slick then rubbed her clit with her silk, then he painted some on his hard aching shaft.

Feeling her withdrawing from him, he moved his hand back to her sex and pressed and twisted, churning and tugging his fingers in and out until he felt her chest panting against his. Soon her breathing grew wild and her hips were jerking, she was on the brink again.

Moving quickly, he slid up between her legs and pressed the head of his erection against her opening. Her hands suddenly came up to flatten against his chest to push him away. He lowered his weight on her, forcing her hands to move to the side, then thrust into her.

Her breath escaped in a rush, then it scraped back in with her cry at his sudden penetration, she cried out, "*Kultur!*"

He was only halfway inside her. "I'm sorry, baby. I'll stop and let you adjust." Feeling her vagina clutching him in tight pulses, he cradled a hand around the back of her head and kissed her lips, along her face then down her jaw. His other hand stroked up to fondle her breast.

The heat of her skin bored into his palm, his fingers wrapped around the vital swollen globe. Kissing, suckling and kneading her womanly flesh, when he felt her relax, her body accepting his intrusion, he started pushing in slowly until he was fully encased in her warm silken sheath.

Her legs lost their resistant stiffness, her hands slid up his huge biceps. Grasping his big arms, she felt every flexing muscle, every sinew. She rolled her palms over his powerful chest, stroking every steel bulge and every contoured dip. Her fingers fisted in the shirt he still wore, then she undid the buttons one-by-one.

Kultur could feel himself on the edge of coming just from her hands caressing him, and she was actually, for once, undressing him. He'd died and gone to heaven.

She pushed the sides of his shirt away and touched his bare chest, sifting her small elegant fingers through his silky chest hair.

With a groan, he lowered himself so he could feel her naked skin on his. "*Sislla,*" his groan rolled out in gruff rumble, "you feel amazing."

Her voice breathy and quiet she murmured, "You as well, Kultur." Sighing euphorically near his ear when he rubbed his hard chest against her soft curves, her palms stroked over his thick shoulders.

He pumped into her with a careful, gentle rhythm, then grasped her thighs and brought her legs up to wrap around his hips where he could get deeper with every more quickening thrust. Her body jolted with each plunge, her breasts bobbled.

His thrusts went deep but slow, and he withdrew very slowly, drawing them both to sizzling need. Her body curved serpentine against him, sliding her belly then her breasts up against his torso, her hips humped to meet his.

Suddenly he went wild, thrusting hard, deep, her grating cries- hoarsely calling out his name- urged him faster until he felt her reach her zenith. Her chest heaved, her knees gripped him, Sislla dug her nails into his shoulders and scraped them down his back,

When he felt her sheath squeeze around him then release with a loud keening sob, he followed with his own growling climax, pounding into her until everything in him surged into her.

He collapsed on her, keeping his forearms on the couch so he wouldn't crush her. Panting to catch his breath, he put his lips on her neck and sucked like a baby as the stars swirled in his head.

Her heart beat furiously against his, their pounding hearts mating. They lay still, twined together.

When both bodies finally calmed, Kultur tried to kiss her, but she turned her head, she was furious. Squirming to get out from under him she scowled, accusing, "You did it again, you took advantage of me sleeping, and with no protection, I can get pregnant!"

His voice heavy and gravelly with spent lust and deep with irritation, he scowled back at her. "I can't believe you are even pulling that card again. You wanted it, you said you did and your body responded immediately to my caresses."

"I thought I was dreaming, *again*. I can't believe after last time you would do this *again*."

His head dropped, his hair long enough to flop over, brushed her face. "Sislla, at first I knew you were asleep. I talked to you, I tried to wake you. When you responded I thought you had woken. It wasn't until you sat up that I realized you had still been out."

He shoved the hair back and looked down at her. "Really Sislla, how can you give me this anger and indignation the way *you* were all over *me*- I didn't force your hands to stroke me, I didn't force your body to slide all over mine, I didn't force your hips to buck-"

"Stop it!" Sislla yelled, her face scarlet, she turned away from the fury and hot desire that still blazed in his eyes. She squirmed out from under him and sat up, yanked the tiny shirt down over her breasts.

As she started to move off the couch, his eyes were drawn to the way her full breasts mushed against the tight, cropped shirt, jiggling with her angry movements. Before he knew it he reached out, pulled her with her back against his chest and covered her breasts with his hands.

He growled darkly, "You are my betrothed. If you would accept our betrothal and sleep with me in my bed you would not turn from my caresses, even if you didn't give prior permission for me to touch you. It would be expected, natural. You would awaken just like you did now, but you would cuddle into my embrace and accept and even want my touch." He tugged the shirt off over her head so he could feel her without barriers.

"Kultur, stop," she squirmed, pushing at his hands. "We are not normally betrothed, you can't just take me without my consent," she groaned when he cupped her sex then speared his fingers back inside her.

Probing her tender softness, he thumbed her pulsing bud, his other hand still massaging her breast. Her fighting lessened, against her will her spine arched back against his powerful chest with a deep growling moan.

He cinched his hands around her waist, turned her then lifted her to straddle him.

"Kultur!" Her mouth opened in a squeal, he covered it with his own. Slanting his lips for a tighter fit he invaded her mouth, her lips, her tongue. A hand under her bottom, he stroked the other up her stomach, to her breasts, squeezing each one then moved his hand to cradle her head while he continued his raid on her mouth.

A smile lit the back of his mind, her hands were winding around his neck, she threaded her fingers into his hair, the harder he kissed her, the harder she wrenched at his locks.

He slid both hands under her to hold her and stood up with her straddling his waist. He moved a few steps and braced her against a wall. Releasing his hair, Sislla dragged her fingers down the sides of his chest to his waist.

"Oh God, Sislla," he groaned into her mouth. She pressed her palms against his rigid abdomen, feeling his taut muscles, her fingers spread, she dug her nails into his flesh. It heated him like the sun was burning in his loins.

"Sislla," panting with desire, all the blood rushed to his erection. Breathing so hard his words jerked out in short grunts, "I'm telling you right now, I am going to take you again. Now. You have one second to say no."

She raised her hands to spread her fingers across the sides of his head while she crushed her mouth over his. That so turned him on he thought he would prong her right through to his hands covering her bottom.

He pulled back, lifted one hand to grab her chin for her to look at him.

Her eyes were so heavy-lidded and glazed she could barely focus on him. He kissed her then said, "You say right now, Sislla that you want this, and you will not say one word of recrimination, regret, or anger afterwards, you get me?"

She nodded and opened her mouth to kiss him again, but he held back. "Say it *koritsi, tiris avithé*, little foreigner, my wife, say it out loud. And no going back." He still had his shirt on, she clutched at the material crushing it in her fists.

Her lips curved in such a beautiful beguiling smile, it made Kultur's head spin. "Yes, Kultur, I won't take it back, I want you to take me. *Please-*"

As her last word was uttered, he impaled her, shoving inside before she could utter another. Although they just got done less than ten minutes ago, he was already hard as a rock. He entered her so hard he knocked the breath out of her. He heard her suck in a gasp, but her arms went around him. She held him against her as he drove into her, banging into her so hard and fast they both came to orgasm in minutes.

Holding her, he turned around and leaned against the wall until he caught his breath. Then he lifted her and set her on her feet.

Walking on wobbly legs, Sislla stumbled to the couch and snatched her clothes up off the floor. Stepping into the skimpy pants, she slumped on the couch. Not looking at him, she shrugged on the tiny shirt then finger-combed her hair.

Leaning back against the wall, Kultur panted, watching her. His eyes tapering at the mutinous set of her chin. He crossed his arms.

"You better not even be thinking it, don't you dare even say you didn't want it. Because there has never been another woman in my arms hotter than you, Sislla. There never will be, there will only ever be you." He trod over to her. "Sislla, look at me."

Her head turned from him, she kept combing her hair with her fingers, unaware the tiny shirt she wore rode up when she raised her hands exposing the lower curves of her breasts.

Kultur's eyes went right to the ivory mounds peeking out from under the shirt. She tugged it back down but that only made it tighter on her, molding her pillows of breasts like they were put on exhibition.

He sat down next to her. She still didn't look at him. "Sislla, remember what I said about those slutty dresses you wore?"

She didn't respond but he saw her forehead crease.

He reached down for his breeches, stood up and pulled them on, buttoned the fly and buckled his belt. He didn't button his shirt; he sat back down and leaned back against the couch cushion.

"I warned you that if you wore shit like that without me with you, there would be repercussions." She still said nothing but he saw her swallow hard, her skin paled slightly.

He stretched his arm across the back of the couch, she visibly shrunk from him. With a frown he said, "It's not fair to Ryan and Jaspar who are randy young men to have to be guarding you every minute and you tempt them wearing practically nothing."

Her mouth twisted and her brows knit. "That's ridiculous, Kultur, not all men run around insanely randy and lose control around women like you do." She could feel him tightening next to her, his muscles flexed and bunched.

But his voice was calm. "Really? That's why that man grabbed you and hauled you off to fuck you, right?"

He suddenly grasped her jaw and turned her to face him. He saw the flicker of fear in the same eyes that only moments ago were aglow with desire, kissing him passionately and crying out his name in a raging climax.

"You're the only woman I lose control over. You are my wife, you will act like a respectable woman and not flaunt yourself half-naked at every man in town." His angry eyes pierced into hers, he released her jaw.

Red flooded her face, angry red. Furious, she tugged the shirt down that had crept back up to just barely cover her bosom. She sniffed, "Maybe I want another man to-"

He grabbed her face pinching so hard tears come to her eyes. "Fuck that, there will never be another man for you, Sislla. If I ever found out you were fucking another man," he dragged in a deep breath, his eyes slit ferociously frigid. "I will kill him. Don't doubt me."

She blinked back the tears, her voice quivering, "You don't need to talk to me like that, use that language. I should have the right to choose the man I-"

He shook her jaw; eyes narrowed fiercely. "You had your choice the day my mother brought those men for you to…choose as a husband. You declined all of them. Recall that you had gone into the kitchen to hide." He let go of her face.

Rubbing her jaw, she complained, "You hardly gave me the opportunity to even think about it. I wasn't ready then. Maybe now, I still should have the right to-"

"I said no!" he roared standing up. Leaning over he glared hard into her eyes. "You and I will be married. It is too late for you to decide you want someone else." He grasped her chin again and threatened, "If I ever hear you are with another man, mark my words, Sislla, I repeat, I will kill him. End of discussion."

She stood up too. "If I want to see another man I will!" Her plump chest jutting out at him in anger, bouncing in the tight shirt drew his attention.

Warning her, "You push me too far, Sislla," he shoved his hands up the shirt and gripped her breasts.

She squirmed, trying to push him away but to no avail.

His fingers groping, squeezing, he said, "This is what that shit does to me, it will have the same reaction on any other red-blooded male. If I ever see you wearing this shirt or anything else like it again in public, I will take you down right then and there and fuck the shit out of you like every other man seeing you would be wanting to do."

"Kultur, that's not-"

"I would rip it off you right now and burn the damned thing, but," with a rare smirk he said in a lewd drawl, "if I have to look at your nudity again we will never leave this room."

"Kultur," complaint in her angry voice, she squirmed, "you're being abusive, your language, let go of me!"

"Honey, I told you, rules on this island are different than in other places. I'm just showing you what happens when you dress like that."

Still holding her breasts, he said, "But I do plan on seeing you wearing it again." His gaze at her pure lascivious lust, drawing his hands out, he pulled the shirt down. "In our bedroom. It makes me crazy hot."

"Kultur, my goodness, you are like a schizophrenic. Sweet and kind to me one minute, then horrible, abusive, domineering, sexually assaulting me the next."

The big blue eyes stared at him in bewilderment and sadness. "I won't stand for it. I will leave by the end of the week. I have some women partially trained, at least enough to take over-"

Grabbing her arms, he dug his fingers into her flesh and snarled, "I told you before, Sislla, don't ever think I'm kind or soft. I am a warrior, a soldier, those things don't have a place in my heart."

He shook his head at the pained desolation clouding her eyes. Dropping his hands, he ran his fingers roughly through his hair.

Seeing her distress, his tone gentled slightly. "It's just, I find I am insane when I'm around you and you've put your life in danger, or you wear stuff like that," his glare aimed at her nipples poking through the thin material. "And prance around in public. I am not used to being gentle with women, Sislla. I'm not used to caring about what my women wear. I'm used to just taking what I want when I want, and moving on, this relationship business is all new to me."

Crossing her arms over her chest, she cocked her head at him. "You could try, Kultur, you don't have to be the tough, ruthless warlord every minute. I've seen you be kind and tender to little Bardon."

Kultur realized his brutality was pushing her away from him just as much as her wanting to leave to see whatever family she might have. He sighed, "I will work on not being such a lascivious, crude bully. But I can't promise anything."

He raked both hands through his hair but he couldn't dispel the effect her body had on him. "I admit, I go a little nuts, I shouldn't manhandle you, I know. You bedevil me, *koritsi*."

Even as he said the words, he caught up her wrists, pulled her to him, her breasts crushed against his chest. His voice and expression had gone all hard again, "You are not leaving Aniniva. Ever."

Releasing her suddenly, he stalked to the door.

As he reached it, he turned back to her, his eyes stroked down her figure. Then he pulled his shirt off and tossed it to her. "Put that on. Kirman Shaws will walk you back."

Throwing the door open, he smiled and said with a slight mock, "By the way, tonight, *tiris koritsi,* is the golden moon. Isn't it funny that you said yes to me tonight of your own free will, for our second marking, and I didn't have to force you? Only one more marking to go, and you will be fully *tiris avithé,* my wife. "

Stepping outside, he closed the door to her stunned expression.

Chapter Thirty-Seven

everal days later, Kultur was in his office plowing through paperwork when a soft knock at the door interrupted him.

The door was open so he didn't get up or look up, just said a terse, "Come in." He heard movement but no one said anything. Assuming it was one of his brothers, he rapped impatiently, "What is it?"

"Kultur."

That got his attention. His head shot up. Sislla was standing in the doorway with Ryan behind her. Kultur immediately got to his feet and came around the desk to stand in front of it but not too close to her until he knew what she wanted.

His neck burned, he tugged at his collar not used to feeling awkward, or even, heaven forbid, shy. His gaze went unbidden from her crystal blue eyes to her tentative, slightly parted lips, down the while blouse with lacy collar and real pearl buttons from clams and oysters they dug out of the sand, and the dark blue denims they wove from their cotton fields.

He nodded to Ryan, but his eyes were on Sislla. "Wait outside, Kirman, and close the door," he caught the slight rise of Sislla's brow and muttered, "please."

Ignoring the faintly astonished look on Ryan's face as he left the room, the angles of Kultur's hard face softened to some extent. "Come in, have a seat." He gestured to the leather sofa.

She didn't move, "I only need a moment of your time, Kultur."

His hands linked behind his back, Kultur lowered his head but looked up at her through his dark lashes, he gave her a crooked lopsided smile, said, "Please."

Her lips curved up sweetly, "Okay." She went to the couch and primly sat down on the edge with her hands folded in her lap. She stiffened slightly when he came and sat next to her keeping several inches between them.

Biting back a sigh and a frown at her reaction to his proximity to her, Kultur asked, "How are you doing, Sislla?" He leaned back against the cushion and folded his hands loosely in his lap.

He had seen very little of her the past few days due to his working in the field and her busy with her healing work.

Meanwhile, he had been speaking to friends of his that were married, embarrassingly seeking relationship advice on how to win over a reluctant female. They all advised patience, perseverance and moving more slowly.

Too bad they were running out of time. The next golden moon was approaching and he was damned if he'd force her again, especially when he knew how splendidly she responded to his ministrations when he could get her mind shut off.

Unfortunately, that was only when she was asleep and when he went that route she accused him of being sneaky and taking advantage of her. And, he sighed, she was still bent on hitting the high seas- alone- to return to her home, wherever that might be. For some childish reason she thought she would be like a homing pigeon and just automatically find her way back.

Well, he did not want to force her again, but he damned well would if he had to. The thought of his beautiful betrothed succumbing to the perils of the ocean, or the Iminims getting their torturous hands on her.

Shivers if fear roiled up his spine at the knowledge that she would beg them to kill her while enduring the horror they would rain on her helpless body.

Her eyes dropped, then she raised them, licked her lips, and gave a tiny cough. "I, uh, everything is fine."

A slim grimness tightened his lips. The dark eyes studied her, no doubt he thought, she could see his ever present smoldering desire for her, and a shade of sadness in his eyes. "Sislla," he cleared his throat. "I thought, I had hoped after the other day we had come to, you know, an understanding."

His linked fingers tightened. "I expected you to sleep in my chambers the past few nights, but when I looked for you, Onani said you were staying with my sister. I'm, uh, assuming that was to avoid me." He could have gone after her, hauled her to his bed, but it would only make her angry and more resistant.

She didn't need to say anything; he could see the truth in her face. "Why?" He turned towards her and took one of her hands pulling it from the other and held it. "You know we're good together, you know I care deeply for you, and I'm pretty sure you have feelings for me."

She sighed, tugged at her hand but he wouldn't release it. Her tongue wetting her lips again, she said, "I've told you from the beginning I will not complete the markings. I need to leave." Her eyes lowered to their clasped hands.

Frowning impatiently at her, he exhaled heavily. "Sislla, it will happen, stop fighting it."

His other hand skimmed around her jaw, he held her gently asking, "Why can't you stay here? Would you if I was a different man, if I released you to another man?" He drew her close to his face. "Because I would. It would kill me, but to save your life I would. Is that what you want?"

She stared at his chin, not meeting his eyes. "No. I would still leave. Kultur," now she looked at him, "regardless of my having to leave, whatever, I could not stay with a man that does not respect me. Respect my wishes. If I say no, I would expect my…whatever you are, to do as I ask. I understand this is a different land with different rules and women don't have the same rights as men, but," she took a breath, "I am me and I won't be with a man who assaults me and speaks to me with ugly language."

Releasing her chin, he looked at her for a long time, dark eyes studying bright blues. "Sislla, last time we were together in that outside study, I told you I would do my best to treat you as you ask. You haven't given me the opportunity to do so."

She lowered her gaze to their hands. "It doesn't matter. I've told you, I cannot stay here and that is it."

They sat in silence for a few moments then Kultur asked, "So why are you here, what do you want of me?"

Slowly she pulled her hand from his. "I am out of herbs and leaves, and other natural items I need."

His lips thinned, he nodded. "So, write out a list and I will send men to go retrieve them."

Shaking her head, she said, "No, I need to do it. They don't bring me the right things. And some herbs and plants I need to look at to determine their readiness to be plucked, and other considerations. I need to do it myself."

"I will take you."

Her sad eyes rolled up to his. "No, I'd rather have Ryan go with me. Please."

He started to shake his head, "No, Sislla, I don't want you out there," seeing her adamant expression he sighed and closed his mouth. "Fine. But I want two more guards with you. Tell Kirman Shaws to get them."

"Thank you, Kultur."

His eyes narrowed at her. "Are you using this as a way to run?" He took her hand again. "Tell me honestly, Sislla."

Her big blues stared back at him guileless and honest. "No, Kultur. Not yet. I need the herbs for the people I'm training so they can carry on after I go."

Like a knife to his heart, Kultur felt the physical pain. His teeth grit so hard he thought he'd break them. "Stop it, Sislla," he hissed, "I'm telling you, you are not leaving this island to go die out on the fucking sea. I won't allow it. If that's disrespecting you, then, sorry." He stood up and went to the door and opened it.

She hesitated, then got up and went out the door. He stood watching her and Ryan trod away from him down the hall.

He started to turn to go back to his desk when he heard Lucas call to him. Pushing his hair back with frustration of not knowing how to deal with that stubborn, foolish woman, he scrubbed his fingers down his face and waited for Lucas.

His brother came into his office. The grave set to his mouth did not bode good news. "Kultur, something's going on out in the far north field. People have been spotted running through the woods. We need to check it out."

Kultur's brows went up in alarm. "I just gave Sislla permission to go collect herbs in the field, I need to stop her!"

"It's too late, I already saw her and three Kirman going out the back."

Seeing the rare look of anxiousness on his brother's face, Lucas said, "She'll be fine, she was heading to the south, opposite to where the strangers were. Let's go, we don't have time to sit around knitting a rope to tie her to you." He chuckled at Kultur's dark glare at him.

The brothers left to retrieve weapons and a team to search out the intruders.

Chapter Thirty-Eight

It was a beautiful balmy day with blue skies and a light breeze that tickled Sislla's hair. She smiled at the steady patience of the three Kirmen guarding her. They stayed near but not in her way as she studied and picked the things she needed.

When one basket was full, one of the guards took it from her and handed her an empty one. It was so lovely and peaceful, but Sislla's heart hung heavy.

She wanted to stay. She didn't know why she had to return to her homeland, wherever that was, she just had an overwhelming compulsion to go. She should have left long ago, but she hadn't. The healing, she needed to help the people, that's why she stayed.

A small smile lifted the corners of her lips, there will always be sick people and she could have started teaching sooner.

No, the reason she hadn't left yet, she had to be honest with herself, was Kultur. As much as she detested his violence to others, his disregard of her requests to not touch her without her permission, and his filthy language, she sighed.

Other than that first initial love making, he had never physically hurt her, he had done everything in his power to protect her, he was trying to save her life even though she fought against him.

As much as she struggled to fight it, she wanted to be with him. She wanted to sleep with him, eat with him, have his children. She loved the feel of his big arms holding her close, the

335

hard and softness of his kisses, his rough hands on her body, his masculine scent of shaving oil and his own virile heat, she shook her head with regret. It wasn't to be.

The last thing she wanted to do was to leave him. But an ever present pressure in the back of her head told her she had to go. She couldn't fight it. Every time Kultur looked at her with sadness and bewilderment in those black enigmatic eyes, her heart clutched. She needed to-

A horde of men on horseback suddenly surged from the dense forest. She dropped her basket and screamed.

Hooves pounded over the grassy field, clods of dirt and weeds flew as they raced straight at her.

She started run, the two extra guards ran too, away from her. Ryan put himself between her and the villains, his sword raised, but there were too many, they rode in a wicked quick circle around them.

One of the men said in a coarse loud voice to Sislla, "Tell him to put the sword down or we will run him through and take you anyway. You come now, he lives."

"No!" Ryan kept himself an inch from her and circled as they did swinging his sword in a continuous arc. "Stay behind me, Mistress," his breath gushed out in fear and valor.

The men on horseback moved in closer and closer. Sweat poured in Ryan's eyes almost blinding him, behind him Sislla was breathing so hard she almost squeaked.

Suddenly, Sislla pushed Ryan as hard as she could, and ran at one of the horsemen.

Ryan stumbled off balance falling forward. He scrambled to his feet swinging his sword, he yelled, "No! Mistress, stay with me!" The man on horseback reached down and grabbed Sislla around the waist and hauled her up in front of him.

She screamed, "Run Ryan, run!"

As the man's horse reared back with its front hooves scraping at the air, Ryan rushed him; a man behind him stuck his sword in Ryan's back.

Sislla screamed, "No!"

Ryan stood looking at her stunned, then he blinked and crumpled to the ground.

The men charged into the woods with Sislla captive.

****

"Ahh, there is nothing here, a wild goose chase." One of the Kirmen grumbled.

Lucas nodded, agreeing with him. "Aye, a false tale to get us out here for no reason."

Kultur looked at him, his forehead furrowed. "What reason could there be to draw us out? There's been no ambush, it has to be, the castle..." His heart screamed, "*Sislla!*"

No sooner had the words left his lips and he kicked his horse, slapped the reins and took off like the wind back to the castle.

They thundered into the front of the castle. Everyone dismounted and bolted into the grand chamber.

Kultur ordered his men to go in every direction and seek out who was there, and not there, and see if they could ferret out the reason why they were tricked, and who was the culprit.

Figuring she should have been back long ago, he ran to the workshop, then Sislla's room, his chambers, every room she could be in, but he came up empty. The vein at his temple beat like a frightening jackhammer. He struggled to stay calm, but his insides shook like leaves in a storm.

Two of his men came in bringing a Kirman. Kultur recognized him as one of the guards that had gone with Sislla. He was disheveled and scared, and had a guilty as sin red flush on his face.

"Atraam, sir," one of the warriors holding him said, "this guard has something to tell you," he pushed the man in front of Kultur. The man fell to his knees in a quivering puddle.

"I- I beg you sire, Atraam, it wasn't my fault, I didn't-"

Kultur whipped out his own sword and put it to the man's neck. "Speak, tell me right now."

"Uh- uh- uh," he stammered, his hands folded as if in prayer. "She uh, the Mistress, she had an assignation planned with a man. She- she ran off and just uh, left us, we didn't know what to do, uh, sire…"

His face as black as night, guttural words scraped out through clenched teeth. Kultur pushed the sword slightly into the man's neck. "You speak the truth? Tell me, you will die anyway for leaving her."

Tears poured down the terrified guard's face. "No, please sire, I speak the truth. She was picking weeds then- then we saw her run off and join a man in the woods. They hugged, and uh, kissed. Then they disappeared into the forest before we could stop them." His swollen eyes stared down at the floor.

Kultur glared at him, watching the man cower at his feet, then he slid his sword in its sheath at his waist. "Get out," he ordered not looking at the man.

"I told you she was a whore." Darathia came up to him.

His face a granite mask, eyes inscrutable, Kultur said nothing.

She sniped at him, "At least she is gone before you could finish the ceremony. You're free, my son." She set a hand strung with blue veins on his arm.

He stood frozen, a marble statue. He couldn't believe it. Not his sweet Sislla. She might have run to the sea, but she wouldn't have left him for another man. He put his hands over his temples and shook his head.

"It's all right, my darling. She's gone. Forget about her, you have a village teeming with beautiful young women to choose from."

"Shut up," he barked, "*shut- up!*" His eyes barely black slits he looked around. Even Gabriel and Lucas regarded him with misery. They believed it.

Kultur shoved his palms over his stinging eyes. What can he do? He has to do something, but what? Go run the heathen through as he had sworn to her he would?

338

The other guard that had been with Sislla trailed in behind the other Kirman like he was trying to blend in with them. But he was panting, clearly out of breath. When he saw Kultur, his eyes popped, his mouth dropped, he turned to leave.

"Back here!" Kultur bellowed.

The man, shaking in his boots trod very, very slowly to Kultur. He bowed, "Atraam."

Kultur's voice seethed low as a lion's growl, "What the fuck happened, Kirman? No song and dance, out with it."

The man looked like he was wetting his pants, his hands clutched so tight in front of him his fingers had no color. He was short and stout with light thin brown hair and piggish eyes.

"I don't know, sire." Seeing Kultur raise his hand, he spoke quickly, "I- I, men, men on horseback came out of the forests with swords raised. I-" his eyes darted at Kultur then to Kultur's brothers then he stared at the floor with mind boggling fright. His hair hung limp damp with sweat. The words inched out, "I ran."

Kultur's arm whipped out, his hand clenched around the man's thick neck. He grated fiercely, "What do you mean you ran? What the hell happened? Answer me or I snap your neck now." His fingers squeezed like metal stakes pounded into the ground.

The Kirman's piggy eyes widened. His flabby cheeks turned red, he spoke around his flaccid tongue hanging out of his terrified mouth, "When I saw the men, me and Dither the other guard, we both just- ran away. Kirman Shaws threw himself in front of her, I think, I don't know, I just- ran-" he closed his eyes tightly waiting for the end of his life.

Kultur's arm rigid, his fingers digging into the man's flesh, the man choked and gagged. He had disobeyed a direct order to protect Sislla, he had run like a coward, and he didn't have the balls to come and tell Kultur so he could do something to save her.

Two men, two different stories. Who to believe? Maybe this one said there were numerous horsemen so he wouldn't look so bad for running. Dithers had said she was meeting a man even though he knew that information could cost him his life. Besides him also running like a coward.

Louise Furley

Kultur stared down at the man wanting so terribly badly to crush his neck, but, Sislla's voice calling for mercy sifted through his head.

He scowled, no, he shook his head. Why should he care what Sislla thought about murdering someone who failed their job and left her- a defenseless woman, a coward soldier, warrior, leaving a woman to her fate...before he knew it, the man went limp in his hand and sunk to the floor then fell over on his back, his lifeless eyes staring up at nothing.

Without giving him another look, Kultur started for the door.

He halted when several of his warriors rushed in the door carrying a body. Kultur could see they carried Ryan. "What happened?" he asked the men.

"Sir, we were scouring the south field for the intruders when we found him. He was lying in the grass, he's been run through with a sword." At Kultur's questioning glance the man shook his head. "No sign of her, sir."

"All right." Kultur looked at Ryan, and let out a breath. "He is still alive. Take him to the workshop, and get the women Mistress Sislla has been teaching to see to him."

"Atraam," Ryan's weak voice ebbed out. White as a sheet, he tried to open his eyes.

Kultur laid a hand on his shoulder. "It's all right, Kirman, the women will help you."

He turned to go but Ryan said weakly with pained gasps, "She tried to save me...the Tenthekens..." he gasped for air, "took her," he passed out.

Kultur ordered, "Take him to the workshop, quickly," and he strode to the door.

His mother ran after him shouting, "Kultur! Where are you going?" Darathia grabbed at his sleeve to hold him back. He roughly shook her off and kept going.

"Kultur!" she shrieked. "She left you for another man, you've been cuckold, betrayed- let her go!"

Out the door, Gabriel and Lucas hurried to catch up with him. "K, what are you doing?"

Heading for the stables, Kultur said, "It doesn't matter what she's done. I love her. I won't leave her for the Tenthekens to tear her to pieces."

Not long and Kultur was leading his men to charge through the forest heading to where the Tenthekens' strongholds were. He left a few warriors to guard the castle and the village.

Halfway there, Danel appeared out of the thick woods to join them. No one knew he was there until he appeared, but no one said a word, they kept going.

It seemed to take an eternity to Kultur to get through the forest to the other side. They still had miles to go before reaching the Tenthekens. If he didn't make it in time, she would be raped and tortured for days then cut up in little pieces.

His gut twisted, his fists rolled into tight clenches, he would destroy them all. The entire clan. No one would live. The Chamaine-Gris outnumbered and out-powered both the Tenthekens and the Ulmas together. He spurred his horse faster.

This time he carried no flag of peace. Townsfolk screamed and ran as his men thundered into the village. Kultur led them straight to the Atraam's castle.

They slowed as they reached the perimeter. A stage for plays and festivals was erected near the castle. It was surrounded by thousands of villagers and warriors. As they neared the crowd, he could see the stage clearly. Kultur's blood froze.

Sislla was on the stage, her hands bound behind her. Two burly warriors on either side of her held her arms. Atraam Fraznee Colypssue stood near her, grinning from ear to ear. He steadily watched Kultur's approach.

Kultur and a unit of men reached the stage, the rest of his League stayed in layers around the castle and the grounds. His eyes went straight to Sislla and his heart felt punched.

She was terrified; no doubt about it, but the big blue eyes radiated her love to him. He could see it, he could feel it. He rode straight up to the stand, the people separated like waves in the ocean as he passed through.

Addressing the tall, muscled man holding center stage, Kultur said, "Colypssue, you have taken my woman. The entire clan of Tenthekens will die today. You will be wiped off the face of the earth." He didn't look at the horror on Sislla's face; he stared straight at the Atraam.

Atraam Colypssue chuckled. He drew long thick fingers through his thick, wavy light hair. He was a handsome man in a beefy kind of a way. He was muscled and broad like Kultur but he had a lot of extra weight on him.

"No, I don't think you will. If you kill any one of us, she dies. Terribly, and you know how, my olde enemy."

Not a person in the crowd spoke a word. It was too tenuous of a situation. Every warrior had his hand on his sword ready and willing to use it.

"What is it that you want, Colypssue? You set a deliberate distraction and came right for her. Why?" Kultur's eyes flicked from Sislla to the Atraam.

Colypssue chuckled again. "I wanted to hurt you, Kultur Kultiran. This seemed the best way to do it. I had spies in your meadows. As soon as she was out of the castle, we took her." His face hardened, eyes narrowed, he took a step towards Kultur yet stayed on the stage, he sneered down at him.

"You had the fucking balls to come to *my* town and take *my* captured prisoner and kill *my* men. No one does that to me and gets away with it, not even the supreme Atraam Kultiran. You know, Atraam, tit for tat. You killed my men, I take your woman as revenge."

Kultur stood motionless, his eyes on the Atraam. He was referring to his Lucas' wife's brother they had rescued.

"Your hands are tied, Kultiran. Either you see her die today if you attack us, or, you can come and get the pieces, later. If there are any. I may keep the woman alive for a while to play with her. She's a unique beauty, eh?" He turned and smiled evilly at Sislla.

She stuck her chin up in the air refusing to look at him or be cowed by him.

"Yeah, honey, you'll lose that arrogant look the first time I take you. We Tenthekens are not known for our gentleness. So," he grinned at Kultur, "what's it to be? I suggest you turn around on your steed and get the fuck off my land," he ended cold and harsh, spit flew out with his words.

Calm as sand, Kultur said, "I will trade for her."

Colypssue's brows shot up, then lowered with interest. "Oh yeah? What could possibly be worth a trade of Atraam Kultiran's woman?"

"Me."

A bursting wind of gasps and sudden utterances spread through the shocked crowd.

Sislla was aghast, her mouth dropped in horror. She shook her head at Kultur. Her captors growled, gripping her arms tighter to still her.

Colypssue's eyes narrowed at Kultur, then he smiled. He said, "You are fucking pulling my leg, Kultiran. No one, no matter how courageous and valiant a warrior would submit themselves willingly to our torture."

"You free her, now, I will take her place."

"No! Kultur, no!" Sislla cried out.

Kultur didn't look at her, his eyes were on Colypssue.

Atraam Colypssue studied Kultur to judge the seriousness of his offer. "Is this some kind of trick?"

Kultur crossed his arms over his chest. "No. No trick. Me for her. My word."

"Whoa, well now," Colypssue pawed his chin in thought.

Behind him Sislla struggled at the men holding her, she cried, "No, Kultur, he will kill you, no!"

Colypssue grinned with glee at her. "Actually, honey, not until we have sliced off an inch of him at a time. We start with the feet, and we cauterized as we go to keep him alive as long as possible to enjoy every agonizing second of it."

Twisting and jerking at the men and her binds, tears filling her eyes, Sislla looked hard at Kultur. "No, please don't do this. Just let me go, Kultur, leave me, I am nobody. You need to stay alive to lead your people." She could tell by the way his dark eyes flared then emptied he'd made up his mind.

Colypssue said to Sislla, "We would do the same to you, sweetheart, if we kept you. Of course," his grin merciless and cruel, "that would be after we used your body up." He turned to face Kultur. "Well, Atraam?"

"Release her. When she is with my brothers and clear of your perimeter, I will go with you. My word." Kultur took his eyes off Sislla to stare impassively at Colypssue.

Colypssue studied him for a moment then swiveled around and said to his men, "Release her."

The two men holding Sislla untied her and brought her to Colypssue. The big man cupped her chin and smiled with ruthless regret. "I'm not happy to do this, my beauty. I was looking forward to doing all sorts of interesting things with you," his gaze slithered down her and back up, his tongue snaked greedily around his lips.

"But, it's better to control an entire country than have one woman. With him out of the way," he gestured to Kultur, "I can take over the entire island. No one else is strong enough to lead, to fight as necessary to defeat me."

He nodded to the two men that held her. They handed her down to Kultur who instantly wrapped his arms around her and held her tight.

He whispered in her ear, "It has to be this way, Sislla. Be brave for me." He smiled at her, wiping her tears with his fingertips. "I love you, *tiris koritsi, tiris avithé*." He kissed her before she could say anything, then stepped back so quickly she would have fallen but Gabriel caught her and swung her up on his horse.

As soon as she was on the horse, Gabriel, Lucas, all the men turned and headed out of the village.

Sislla turned around crying, "No, Kultur, *don't*, your life is more important than mine- *please!*" She saw him standing alone, his hands at his sides, waiting, watching them leave. She tried to throw herself off the horse but Gabriel held her to his chest with a steel arm. "Let me go, Gabriel, I can't let them kill him, please," she hit at the arm that held her.

Gabriel whispered in her ear, "Hush, little foreigner, be brave for him. Don't let him see your pain." He held her so she couldn't turn around and look again at Kultur.

The troop of men rode like the wind back to the village. When they finally slowed, Sislla said to Gabriel, "Are you not going back for him?"

Gabriel smiled at her ruefully, "He said you were smart. Aye, we will go back and tear them all limb from limb. They won't kill him until tomorrow at their eve moon festival."

"But you might not be able to save him, right?" she whispered in horror. She saw the pained look on his face, Gabriel loved his brother. This had been the hardest thing in the world for him to do.

Gabriel said, "This was Kultur's command, his wishes, that we do nothing until you are in the safety of the castle." They kept moving as the sky darkened.

"Gabriel."

"Aye."

She was afraid to ask, "Ryan? He- I saw him stabbed with a sword, is he-"

"I don't know. Our men found him and brought him back. Kultur ordered the women you trained to work on him."

He cocked his head before saying, "Sislla, I have to ask, one the guards that was with you told Kultur, uh, that you had gone to run off with another man and that's why you didn't return." He coughed then cleared his throat.

She stiffened against his chest. "What? Who? No!" She twisted in the seat trying to look at him. "Never! The Tenthekens came roaring out of the woods. The two guards instantly turned tail and ran. Ryan, he- he tried to defend me. But they said if I didn't come peacefully they would kill him. But he refused to let me go. So...so I pushed him out of the way and let the man take me."

She shook her head and said bitterly, "Ryan is probably dead because of me. He still tried to defend me."

His voice gentle, Gabriel told her, "They would have killed him anyway. They lied to you. But, he still has a chance, so buck up."

They were halfway through the village when Sislla sat up straight. "Stop the horse, Gabriel, right now."

He kept going. "Why?"

"I have an idea, Gabriel." Her voice firm and determined, she insisted, "Stop the horse, I have to speak to the villagers. Please, I beg you."

When he brought his stallion to a halt, the other men gathered around them. Hundreds of hooves stomped the hard packed earth. Snorts from the horses mingled with the warriors' questioning rumbles.

"What's going on?" Lucas asked, holding his horse's reins to keep him still.

"I don't know," Gabriel said, "she asked me to stop. Said she has an idea." He said to Sislla, "Tell us."

After she explained what her plan was, the men thought she was insane, it would never happen. Gabriel and Lucas argued about it.

Lucas disputed, "No. Kultur said take her to the castle before we go back for him. That was all he wanted even to his own death."

Shaking his head, his light brown hair swinging over his ocher eyes, Gabriel argued, "He is our brother. If there's one slim chance to save him, I'm doing it. You come or not, but I'm doing what she says." He turned his horse into a lane that led up to a house Sislla was familiar with.

The men waited while she went in alone.

Gabriel and Lucas argued the entire time she was inside, that this wasn't Kultur's orders, that they should not have let her go in alone, on and on.

Chapter Thirty-Nine

Twenty minutes passed before Sislla exited the house. As she left it, the occupants all ran out behind her and rushed through the village to enter other homes.

Gabriel shook his head. He didn't even want to ask her how she knew who lived in the house. A wry smile touched his mouth; apparently she had gotten out and about a lot more than Kultur had been aware of. He gazed in admiration at her.

She still wore the lacy white blouse, albeit it had tears and stains from her abduction, the dark blue pants snug on her shapely hips and legs. The bright hair spiraled around her slender shoulders and down her back. Fierce determination radiated from the crystal blue eyes. His lip curved up, Aye, if they survive, she will make Kultur a worthy queen.

Sislla hurried to Kultur's brothers and the men waiting for her. She huffed, "Let's go."

Gabriel pulled her up on his horse to sit in front of him and they headed out of the village, away from Castle Aenlic.

The night was cool, leaves rustled from the light breeze. No one spoke, only the horses' hooves' plock- plock on the stone and dirt path made a sound in the dark.

When they reached the Ulmas' village, Gabriel held the blue flag while Sislla did as she had before at the Chamaine-Gris village, ran out on foot into neighborhood.

The men positioned their weapons at the ready, and Gabriel held his breath wondering if he'd let the girl race to her death. They were in one of their enemy's camp, while Kultur was being held prisoner in the other one.

The night offered little illumination but for the silver moon and stars winking amongst twilight clouds. It was as quiet as hundreds of warriors awaiting anxiously and warily on horseback could be.

This time, Sislla let out a low whistle before she slipped up the path and disappeared into another house she seemed familiar with. Gabriel's heart beat like a frenetic drum while she was inside.

Lucas moved his horse to wait beside Gabriel. "How on earth did she know what house to go to? The Ulmas are our damned enemies, yet they freely opened the door and welcomed her in like they knew her."

He turned to glower at his brother. "We are sitting ducks, Gabe, they could come around and massacre us while we sit here like pussies waiting for the girl to do, what??

Gabriel shrugged one huge shoulder. "I don't know. But," he squinted in the low light of outside lanterns at the house Sislla was in, "somehow, I trust her. Let's just wait and see, and fucking pray."

"Yeah, pray. You better pray that if Kultur survives and finds out about this, he will not extinguish both of us for letting her do this." His short smile slid askance at his brother, he saw Gabriel wore the same hopeful, nervous, grim smile.

Soon, same as before, Sislla hurried out, and the occupants of the house came out and spread to other homes.

Getting her back up on his horse, Gabriel, with some trepidation, make that a shitfreight of trepidation, shook his reins and headed even further away from their castle.

When they reached the next destination, hairs sprung up the back of Gabriel's neck. He felt his brother's dark gaze on him. They were back in Tenthekens territory.

"Stop the horse, Gabriel," Sislla's soft voice ordered him. He did as she asked. "Help me down, please."

He balked. He was a huge, heavily muscled powerful warrior and he was scared shitless, no way would he set this dainty female down on the Tenthekens' land.

She turned those brilliant blue eyes at him and said firmly, "Now, Gabriel. Time is of the essence."

Letting out a belabored apprehensive, then resigned sigh, he put his hands under her arms and lowered her to the ground.

As soon as he let her go, like before, she let out a low whistle, then moved quickly over the dirt path to a house. The door opened without hesitation and she disappeared inside.

Same as before, after twenty minutes or so, Sislla emerged, as did the occupants. She returned to Gabriel, the people spread throughout the village entering houses and calling out to one another.

Gabriel swung her back up on the horse. "What now, little queen?" Already it felt like he was dreaming.

Beyond belief, they'd entered both factions they warred with, tortured and killed with, and this slender young woman marched right through their strongholds and into their houses without a blink of an eye. And they let her in. And they didn't kill her.

"We need to wait, two hours I think, and we will be ready." She nestled back trusting against Gabriel's chest.

He had one arm around her to support her, but he was damned uncomfortable with her soft curvy body pressed against him. He understood she was tired. She'd been taken and held captive, and they've been constantly on the move all night while she ran around the villages.

She acted all innocent and calm, yet Gabriel knew if his brother saw her leaning against him with his arm around her Kultur would be pounding him into the ground. *Women, geesh, how does a man ever know what to do?* He studiously ignored the knowing smirk Lucas sidled over at him.

They waited just past the second hour when they heard them. Voices murmuring, hundreds of footsteps on the hard packed dirt.

The trees and bushes and grass crunched and crinkled and rustled with the flow of people passing over and through them.

A man emerged from the dark, spotted Sislla and cautiously went to her.

"Mistress Sislla, we are ready."

She smiled sweetly down at the man.

Gabriel recognized the enormous scar-ridden hulk as one of the most bloodthirsty brutal warriors on the island.

"Thank you, Christian. We will lead." She nodded at the warrior; he glanced warily up at Gabriel.

The two warriors eyed each other with suspicion, and uncertainty. They slid a glance at Sislla, then back to each other. With a hint of a shrug, Christian slipped back down the path into the darkness.

Sislla said calmly, "Let's go, Gabriel."

He hesitated, glanced at Lucas who just stared at him. They had decided what they were going to do; they would not pull back now. Lucas gave him an imperceptible nod to go.

Taking a deep breath, Gabriel let it out slowly as he lightly kicked his horse to move. The league started trotting along the path.

As they reached the beginning of the grassy perimeter surrounding Atraam Colypssue's castle, the dark night clouds were breaking up as dawn pushed yellow fingers through the blue violet twilight.

Unlike Kultur's airy, modern, pleasant estate, Colypssue's was hunks of craggy rock and black iron, dark and bleak, an ominous monstrosity. A thick vapor of doom hung like a gloomy cloud around the forbidding structure.

The castle sat on top of a low hill like a misshapen black toad with square warts and pointed turrets.

Sislla shivered as she heard faint, keening sounds roll over the hill on the wind, sounding to her like groans of a million agonized souls crying from the dank jutting walls covered with dark slimy moss.

At the pace they maintained, it took almost an hour for all of them to cross the tawny green grass.

When they finally neared the castle, they could see soldiers pacing the stage and a few villagers drifting around in a semi-circle in front of it.

Kultur's friend Danel rode up and spoke quietly with Lucas, then he left to find a strategic place to observe.

Colypssue strode back and forth barking orders; warriors traipsed up and down the steps of the stage.

A soldier brought a table to the middle of the stage. Another carried a bucket of hot tar; another had a box of swords, knives, machetes and a sharp bladed saw. Yet another brought the means for heating the tar.

Her hand flew over her heart, Sislla choked back a sob.

In the center of the stage, his arms bound behind his back, Kultur was on his knees, his head bowed.

From where they were they could see he had been brutally beaten. His clothes were torn and smattered in blood, sweat and blood dripped from his bowed head. The early morning sun streamed down gleaming on his hair making it shimmer like black oil.

Colypssue paused in front of Kultur. He crouched beside him with a nasty grin and grabbed a hunk of his hair. He jerked Kultur's head up. Kultur's eyes were closed, swollen and purple from the beatings.

 Colypssue said something to Kultur.

Even from a distance, Kultur's responding words through hoarse, bleeding lips were clear, "Fuck you."

Dark red infused Colypssue's face. The ferocious punch he shot at Kultur snapped his head back. He let go of his hair and Kultur's head hung down. His whisk of black mane swung dripping sweat over his eyes, fresh blood spattered the stage.

Sislla slapped a hand over her mouth to stifle her shriek.

Gabriel tightened his arm around her. "Brave little foreigner, you must be cool and bold."

She nodded, too distraught to speak.

They were almost to the stage when Colypssue saw them. He was standing beside Kultur pulling on black leather gloves to keep Kultur's blood off his hands. His face crinkled in a demonic grin.

"Ah, Kultiran's woman has returned." An ugly sneer with welcoming sarcasm he said, "So, you came to watch your man die? That doubles my pleasure, honey. Come on up here and I will give you a front row seat."

Colypssue was aware the Chamaine-Gris League was in the vicinity, approaching his castle. He had warriors all over the land reporting to him constantly what and who was about.

He knew Kultur's warriors were there, and he been had prepared to order his men to cut them off and slaughter them, but he had been completely taken off guard, shocked at seeing Sislla riding up like royalty to the castle on a horse. Something was up.

At Colypssue's words, Kultur lifted his head. Blood streamed down his face splattering on the wood stage under him. His swollen eyes widened in stunned disbelief seeing Sislla there. His gaze painfully flicked from her to Gabriel behind her, dismayed bewilderment narrowed the enigmatic eyes.

Blinking the blood and sweat out of his eyes, he looked to Lucas, obviously totally dumbfounded that they were there, with Sislla.

"Lucas, Gabriel, what the fuck-" Kultur glanced at Sislla. Her face was hard and red as she struggled to hold back her tears. He shook his head to toss his hair out of his eyes, blood and sweat sprayed; he blinked back the blood to look at his brothers.

His voice rasping from the pain of his wounds, Kultur gasped, "Goddammit, Lucas, my orders were to get her the fuck out of here and safe at the castle. "What in the sons' name do you think you're doing?"

Beside him, Colypssue chuckled. "I think your brothers thought to trade her back for you. I mean, they've probably fucked her enough and thought I would accept her in place of you."

Grinning like a crocodile, he snickered obscenely, "Too bad. I would never let you go, ever, for anything. You are my key to owning the entire island. I will be king, no, Supreme Emperor over all that exists here. Everyone will be my slave, all riches of the land will be mine. However, since they were so gracious to serve the lovely lady back to me, I'll take her."

His fat tongue slurped around his lips, his greedy eyes on Sislla. "I have unfinished business with the little bitch. When I'm tired of her, and my men are tired of her, we will see how long she lasts while I peel every layer of skin off her, inch by inch." He said to one of his warriors, "Get her and bring her to me."

Kultur coughed, spit out blood, his voice abraded with rage and impotence to fight, "No, fuck you Colypssue, we had a fucking deal. Let her go."

He peered up through sweat soaked hair at Sislla, and commanded, "Get out of here, get the fuck out of here, goddammit Sislla." His hoarse voice barked weakly, his every breath was a wheeze breathing through broken ribs and ruptured lungs.

The warrior who Colypssue commanded to get Sislla did not move. Colypssue turned to him, his eyes beading in anger he demanded, "What the hell is the matter with you, Kirman, get the fucking woman and bring her to me, now!"

Gabriel moved his horse right up to the stage. With majestic calmness, Sislla said to Colypssue, "No, Atraam. That is not going to happen. Look around," her arm out, she drew her hand across the land behind her.

Surprised at her total lack of fear of him, Colypssue took his lustful murderous eyes off of Sislla and glanced around as she indicated. His eyes widened into astounded spheres.

His gaze travelled stupefied at the not hundreds, but thousands, hundreds of thousands, of people gathered on the lawn and into the woods.

Not a blade of grass could be seen there were so many people there. They all stood stock still, men, women, and children, not speaking, all eyes on the stage.

Turning back to Sislla, his eyes levered open and closed like a now boggled crocodile. "What- what- what is the meaning of this? What is going on? Why are all these people-" he realized his warrior still had not obeyed his order, instead, the warrior was staring coolly at him. Other warriors gathered slowly around the Atraam.

Leaning back on his heels, Kultur labored to hold his head up and see what Colypssue was blathering on about. But his eyes couldn't move past Sislla, so courageous, and beautiful, sitting regally in front of him. Peripherally he saw the grounds teeming with people like swarming ants.

Her smile soft and sweet, and kind as always, Sislla said amicably, "What this is, Atraam Colypssue, is pretty much most of the people on the island, Aniniva. You see, all along, for years upon years, people from all three factions, the Chamaine-Gris, the Ulmas, and the Tenthekens, have been mixing, secretly intermingling."

She turned with a motioning gesture for someone to come forward.

Out of the crowd came Tamma, her boyfriend Matthew, and his little brother Marky. With them was another crowd of people, family members of the teenagers.

Sislla said, "These two young teenagers fell in love. Tamma is Ulmas, and Matthew and Marky are Tenthekens."

Still vastly puzzled, Colypssue eyed Tamma with a deadly stare. He said aghast, "You have been with my sons?" He turned to the Matthew, "And you with a filthy Ulmas?"

"Yes," Sislla answered calmly for the teens. "The boys were injured almost upon death. Tamma risked her life to get to me, a Chamaine-Gris," she shot a glance at Kultur who was watching her with a mixture of fear and stunned pride. "To help them. Both of their families, and I'm assuming you too, Atraam, were so happy they were all okay they didn't care about the mixing."

She turned to the crowd again and called out, "Noni?"

The young woman whom Kultur had brought into the castle came forward with her baby.

Sislla explained, "Noni sought help too. When I helped her baby survive his devastating illness, all I asked in return was that she try to work with her people for peace with all the factions."

Back to the crowd, she motioned.

A big man pushed through.

Both Kultur and Colypssue looked out with shock.

Atraam Rosh Boshor stepped forward.

Sislla leaned over her horse while Gabriel kept a grip on her belt, and Boshor have her a kiss on the cheek.

The crowd gasped.

"Atraam Boshor's baby sister fell into a pond. Joe Dougle," Sislla pointed at a young man nearby, he nodded and blushed. "Joe jumped in and saved her. She is Ulmas, Joe is Tenthekens."

Sislla stretched her arms in an arc around the grounds. "Everyone has been intermingling, secretly helping one another for generations. Only their fear of their leaders' wrath has kept them from being friends out in the open."

Colypssue's mouth flapped opened and closed before he said, "So- so what do you want? What the hell is all this?"

"What we want, Atraam Colypssue," Sislla said mildly, "is to live peacefully with each other. All three factions, without capturing and torturing and killing one another."

"But- but our products, we have to steal for ourselves and punish others who are caught." Colypssue's chest puffed up proudly, he stated, "We Tenthekens have the metals-"

Smiling, Sislla nodded but cut him off, "Yes, and the Ulmas have the papyrus to build special unsinkable boats so we can catch fish to eat, and their land has the most abundant and biggest variety of fruits and vegetables.

"And the Chamaine-Gris have the only land where the turesenes that make heat can be found, and the pine for their wood and roots to make the tar to put around the boats so they are sturdier in storms."

Sighing with impatience, Colypssue snapped with condescending irritation, "I know, we all know, honey, what's your point?" There was a rumble in the crowd but he couldn't tell whether it was for her or against her.

"Yes," Sislla said patiently, "we all have something each other needs. We," she arced her arms around the grounds again, "we have all decided we would prefer to trade, barter with each other instead of stealing and killing for it. The Ulmas are the finest carpenters, the Tenthekens the best ironworkers, and the Chamaine-Gris work miracles with glass and now the most skilled healers."

She smiled with pride, "And, the Chamaine-Gris have the particular fertile soil to grow the necessary herbs for healing."

Now, she waited. She glanced at Kultur, his expression on his bruised and cut face was unreadable.

They had discussed this before, the bartering instead of fighting. But Kultur had told her that long ago they tried a truce, but the Tenthekens would never stick with it. Colypssue would get greedy and screw with the other factions and still capture and kill, so eventually they'd all give in and the wars would start over.

Getting annoyed with her holding court on his land, Colypssue said with heavy sarcasm, "Yeah, honey, tried it, it didn't work."

Her hands folded neatly in her lap, Sislla said, "But at that time, the people hadn't realized how immensely intermingled they already were. Now, with clandestine lengthy and copious meetings and discussions, all of the people want to work together.

"They have agreed they are strong in unity and would stay strong, no matter how," her eyes bold and accusing on the gluttonous Colypssue, "*anyone* tries to grasp more than his or her fair share, or continues to kill and maim."

His brows high on his forehead, fury tugging at his mouth, Colypssue glowered at the delicate young woman sitting so brashly there telling *him* how to run *his* land. About to pull out his sword and slice off her head he said, "Listen, honey…"

"No, Fraznee," a man who closely resembled Colypssue walked across the stage.

Colypssue blanched. "Edward," he whispered. Swallowing several awkward times, he cleared his throat and pasted on a smile. "Uh, you have recovered…" Colypssue's smile did not reach his eyes.

His older brother, Edward, even taller than the towering Colypssue looked down at his brother and said, "Aye. Because I was so sick, Marta heard about this healer and took a courageous chance to bring her to me," he nodded warmly at Sislla. Her return smile was pure friendly and caring.

"After she studied my daily food intake, she advised me to stop drinking my morning juice." His eyes tapered harshly at Colypssue and watched his brother's eyes drop guiltily and his skin drain ashen with fright.

"She said she thought it might be...detrimental to my health. I remembered it was you who had insisted years ago that I drink it to stay healthy. Then," his eyes saddened, "I grew weak and sick, too sick to be Atraam, and therefore you," he stared hard at his brother, "took over. We see how well that has worked."

Kultur's brows arched at Sislla who was trying to look innocent.

Apparently times when she was supposed to be sequestered in her chamber, safe at the castle, she had really been out and about healing and meeting with the people of the island. He didn't know whether to spank her for her dangerous disobedience to his orders, or hug the hell out of her for her kind- hearted bravery.

She smiled meekly at him. But he wasn't fooled. He could punish her all day long for not obeying him and placing herself in dire peril, and she would go right out and do it all over again. And, for the sons' sake, she had even made a friend of Rosh Boshor. How the hell had she managed to do all this without either Kultur himself or his guards catching her?

There had to be people in the castle who aided and abetted her. He would have to do some deep soulful searching to decide how to handle the insubordinates. He glanced around, then sighed with relief. His sister Lexi, who he was pretty sure had her hand in this wasn't present.

At least his brothers were smart enough not to bring her. He glared at Gabriel then Lucas, he couldn't believe they had brought Sislla back here. But the actual outcome? He shook his head.

Edward turned with a sorrowful sigh and nodded to several warriors standing at attention. Two stepped forward and took Colypssue's arms.

"What! Edward! What is this? Release me!" Colypssue cried, struggling against the warriors.

Edward nodded to two other soldiers. They went to Kultur, unbound him and helped him to his feet.

Facing Kultur who stood on shaky legs, Edward said, "I am so sorry, noble Atraam, that my flesh and blood has caused all this terrible dissention and bloodshed all these years. It passed down from my cruel heartless father to Fraznee."

Kultur murmured through split lips, "As did from my father to me."

Edward nodded with deep respect to Kultur. "Aye, and it will end with us. We," he gestured to Atraam Boshor, and then Kultur, "will all live in peace and friendship. We can meet to devise plans to make a harmonious knitting of all the factions together, when you have, uh, recovered, Atraam."

His face darkened, he bowed to Kultur. "I have great shame that a valiant and fearless king who has shown mercy to us when we have not reciprocated, has suffered so much at my brother's wicked hands. My sincerest apologies and regret, Atraam Kultur Kultiran. I was not completely well enough until today to do this. To even walk on my own. It is because of your mercy that the people felt safe enough to seek the aid of your woman."

Kultur stood up as straight as his wounds allowed. His voice gruff from his beatings, he said, "It's over."

His inhale wheezed, "We move forward from this day. We can work out a bartering system, maybe ways to get all our people connecting through schools, or religious events, festivals, or something of the sort."

He struggled to draw a full breath, wheezed it in and went on, "The people will join in our talks so everyone has a say in how we live."

Atraam Boshor grinned his agreement. The three Atraams shook hands.

It was difficult for Kultur to stand on his unsteady legs. Wiping the blood out of his eyes with his sleeves, he said, "I look forward to creating our great new world. When we all come together as a stronger unit, we may be able to finally defeat the Iminims when they come. But for now, I have something I need to do," he turned around slowly.

Lucas and Danel were standing in front of the stage with their arms up. They helped Kultur to the ground.

Gabriel handed Sislla down to Jaspar to help her off the horse.

Kultur moved to stand in before her. They stared at each in outrageous relief, each thought the other was going to be tortured and murdered. Kultur took a step towards her, and Sislla ran and threw herself at him, almost knocking him over in his weakened state.

His arms wrapped around her. Ignoring his blood and sweat and bruises and her rain of salty tears, they came together in an aching passionate kiss. Around them, the crowd roared with cheers and clapping.

Atraams Boshor and Edward stood side-by-side beaming down at them like happy uncles.

With the first meeting dates set, Gabriel and Lucas helped Kultur mount his horse. When Gabriel motioned for Sislla to come with him, Kultur shook his head.

"No. With me." He held a hand out to her. Sislla smiled broadly through her tears and went to him.

Gabriel shrugged and lifted her up to sit behind Kultur. "Ah, well, that lush little body all cuddled up to me," he sighed, "it was good while it lasted." He grinned at the black scowl Kultur sent him, and with irreverent jocularity hopped on his own horse.

"When I'm better, brother," Kultur warned with a crooked grin, "you will pay for that."

With a roaring laugh, Gabriel swung his horse around and charged through the crowd and to the woods with the rest of the League behind him.

Chapter Forty

When they reached the castle, Sislla had the men help Kultur to his chambers, against his grumbling complaints that he could take care of himself.

Gathering her supplies, Sislla checked on Ryan while Kultur's servants helped him bathe and dress in comfortable clothes.

Satisfied Ryan would be fine, when she knocked at Kultur's door to his chambers, a Kirman opened it and waved her in.

She looked over to where Kultur sat on his bed on top of the blankets, his head resting wearily against the headboard. His lids almost closed, his gaze glistened like a dark light searing across the room at her.

Seeing the heated gleam in Kultur's eyes, the Kirman bowed and closed the door behind him as he left.

Sislla moved gracefully to the bed and set her bag of supplies on it, then she sat on the edge of the bed. The sheets rustled, the mattress barely moved under her light weight.

His wet hair hung across his brows, she tenderly sifted her fingers through the locks pushing them back off his forehead. The room was mellow golden from the lanterns. In the candlelight, Kultur's eyes glittered like black diamonds over her face and down her body.

His expression as inscrutable as always, Sislla couldn't read it, or his mood. "How are you feeling, Kultur?" The question hushed out softly. He had been beaten so severely it tore her heart to see him so horribly injured.

He leaned his head back against the pillow and regarded her through his half-mast lids. He said something, but so weakly she couldn't hear him.

"What, what do you need, Kultur?" She leaned closer to him, set her hand on his arm.

He motioned her with a faint movement of his hand to come closer.

Her heart bleeding for the pain he must be in, Sislla leaned over further. So fast she didn't even see him move, he snared her wrist, pulled her to lie half over his chest, and put both his hands around her head.

"I need this, *tiris koritsi,*" his lips enclosed hers in unbearable hunger. His thumbs caressing her jaw, her cheeks, slanting his head to seal them he carried her along in a breathtaking scorching kiss.

In only a moment Sislla was dizzy with desire, her hands splayed on his chest. When he lowered his hands to her hips and moved her more on top of him, she felt his erection throbbing first against her belly then her sex as he pulled her further up his body.

She pushed and rolled off the bed at the same time to break their link. She wasn't quite quick enough because he caught her wrist.

His voice as low and steady as ever, the timber deep and sexy he murmured, "Where are you going, *koritsi?"*

"Kultur," she gently chided him, "you have severe injuries. I will not be a party to making things worse."

His cut lip curled up in a leer, the dark eyes smoldered. He laid his big hand on his bulging erection and palmed it, a clear invitation. "Honey, not all of me is injured. A little love making with you will be good for me, it will help me heal faster, now come here," he tugged her wrist.

She resisted, gently pulling her hand from his grasp. "Kultur, I know what a...vigorous lover you are, and I know you won't settle for less. So, if you want my *willing* cooperation, and I promise it will be willing," she leaned over and slowly drew her hand down his shaft, then moved out of his reach, "you will wait until you are better."

"*Sons above, Sislla*," he groaned and grew harder, "how can you do that to me and walk away?"

"All right, Kultur," her stern doctor voice came out with detached authority, "unbutton your shirt and show me all of your wounds. The sooner I can put my leaves on them the quicker they will heal."

At the leering gleam in his eyes as he tore open his buttons she added with a squinted eye, "You will behave, and you will keep your hands to yourself, if you want my *full* cooperation for when you are well."

"Ah, sons above, Sislla, you just flog me and flog me with your commands and," his gaze darkened as it passed down her body, he smiled, "that luscious body that you forever withhold from me."

He sighed and put his hands behind his head, the biceps bulged, muscles flexed under the dark silky hair on his massive chest. "Go on, do what you need to do. I will dream of our next…date, while I feel your hot little hands on me."

*****

The next day, Sislla went to check on her patient. He had given her a key, so she knocked lightly in case he was sleeping and then went in. Surprised to see his bed empty, and made up, she heard rustling from another room.

Following the noise to a small office, she poked her head in. Kultur was dressed and sitting at his desk.

"Hey, should you be out of bed?" She trod inside worried that he was up and about after his horrendous injuries.

He swiveled his chair around to face her. The dimple in his cheek from the big smile drew attention from the bruises and cuts that were already rapidly healing. "Good morning, *koritsi*," he said, standing up with his hand held out to her, "come in."

Her eyes wide at the sight of his wounds healing so quickly, Sislla moved closer to him.

Instead of taking his hand, she gingerly touched the healing cut on his lip. "Kultur, the new leaves I gathered must be young and more potent, it's amazing how quickly you are recovering."

"Aye, it is." He opened his mouth and sucked her fingers inside.

At her startled yelp, he smiled and held her wrist while he sucked on her fingers. She tugged them out of his mouth and scolded him. "Behave, Kultur," she bit her lip trying to hide her smile at the tingle his mouth elicited.

He pretended to frown, scolding, "*Tiris koritsi,* you never allow me even the tiniest of liberties." He took her hand and brought her to a small divan. "Sit down, Sislla, I have something to tell you."

She looked at him warily; his playful tone had turned serious. She sat and pulled her legs up curling them next to her and rested her arm on the back of the couch.

Kultur sat down next to her leaving a bit of space between them. They both wore denim pants made in the mills on the east side of Aniniva, and both wore white tops. His a long-sleeved buttoned and hers a blouse with an embroidered collar.

She asked him with worry tightening the corners of her eyes, "You look so serious, is it bad news? Is someone sick?"

Kultur patted her knee reassuring, answered, "No, no *koritsi,* this is about...you." He watched her brows rise with confusion.

"Me? I don't understand."

He cleared his throat, uneasy as to how she would take his information. He fiddled with his sleeves, pulling the cuffs down over his wrists. "I know who you are, Sislla, and where you came from and why you are here." He saw her lips part, eyes exhibiting disbelief.

"I...I don't understand, how can you know when I don't?"

He reached to take her hand. Twining their fingers, he set their hands on the cushion between them and looked her steadily in the eye. "I know your name really is Sislla, Sislla Andersson. You are from the Ghesecular Providence."

Sislla stared at Kultur from his dark eyes to his lips to see if there was any chance he was joking. But, his eyes were unwavering and his mouth set. "How, but how do you know this?"

Letting out a heavy breath, still holding her hand, Kultur leaned back against the cushion and said, "We captured a man, his name was Apris Tinnian." He peered at her to see if the name meant anything to her. Her expression of bewilderment didn't change.

Kultur went on, "He told us who you were and where you were from. He said that many years ago, your grandfather, Haarold Andersson, was a very wealthy man and he," Kultur unobtrusively watched her, she showed no reaction at the name, "managed to float ashore here by accident.

"He spent a bit of time undetected, seeing what the land had to offer and who the leaders were before he managed to repair his boat and return to his home. Years later, after he lost most of his wealth, he decided to return here and take over Aniniva."

Absorbing what he was saying, Sislla's blue orbs intently watched Kultur as he spoke, but she wasn't any less confused.

"Um, okay, so what does that have to do with me getting here?" Then her mouth puckered. "What do you mean he wanted to take over Aniniva?"

Kultur scraped a few fingertips over his forehead in angst. He wanted so badly to not have to tell her this.

"Aye. His plan was to have me killed, and with me out of the way he thought the Chamaine-Gris would just crumble, fall apart, become weakened. Then the Ulmas and the Tenthekens would take us out and then fight each other until all the factions were weakened. Then Andersson could sail in with troops, take down whoever was left, and claim ownership of the land. Of course it's ludicrous to think taking out one man could handicap an entire faction."

"Well!" Sislla set a hand on her thigh, aghast at what he was telling her. "That's the most ridiculous thing I've ever heard!" She turned slightly to face him more. "Still, what does any of this have to do with me?"

For the first time since they sat down Kultur looked away from her. His eyes fell to their clasped hands. He took a deep breath and raised his gaze back to her pure, innocent face. "I'm sorry Sislla, but you were sent to assassinate…me."

"What?" Her mouth dropped. Disbelief and puzzlement chopped her words, "There is no way… I mean…are you telling me I was…I am…a killer?" Her skin paled, the roses fled from her round cheeks.

Kultur squeezed her hand then lifted it and kissed her knuckles. "No, you are not a murderer. That is the whole point. You were sent, actually forced to come here, to find a way to get inside the castle to get to me, but you refused to do the deed. The man with you, Apris Tinnian, said when you refused that if you returned home you would be put to death for failing to complete your mission, to kill me." Kultur squeezed her hand again.

"He, Apris, uh, was furious with you refusing to do the mission so he- beat you, then threw you off a cliff thinking you would die. But," he kissed her fingers one by one, "thank the sons above, you survived, and, coincidentally, made it to the castle anyway."

He waited silently while she struggled to comprehend what he was telling her.

Confounded with this information, her face scrunched with the stress of trying to make sense of it. She rubbed one eye, then the other, looked at him watching her with such concern, she smiled, then the smile disappeared.

"I…I still don't remember any of this, none, not even my name, or my- my grandfather. Nothing sounds familiar." Her distressed brow wrinkled in doubt. "My grandfather would have me- killed me for failing to murder you?"

He nodded somberly. "Yes."

She was quiet, contemplating, then asked, "What happened to the man, the one who came with me? Was he my…husband?"

Kultur winced at both of her questions. He answered the easier one first. "No. Apris Tinnian was nothing to you. No husband, no relation, he was only tasked with getting you here."

Squeezing her hand in hopes she would not go nuts, he said, "Mr. Tinnian, was, uh, disposed of."

Her eyes skewed sideways at him. "Disposed?" Her brows lowered, she said slowly, "Do you mean, tell me Kultur, you did not...kill him?" Her voice rose strident, but hushed.

He lowered his head, then looked up at her through a lock of hair hanging over his brow and replied, "He is dead. I did not personally do the deed, but I condoned it. Sislla-" he held his palm up to stop her words.

"His coming here with a scheme to kill me was violation enough, he would have returned to your country and told what you failed to do. That at some time in the future, when you returned home or when they came here, would result in your punishment for failure, death. And, if I let him loose in Chamaine-Gris, he could find you, and still kill you."

"Kultur..."

"Attempted murder on Aniniva is a death penalty offense. He tried to kill you, Sislla, you know me by now that I would not let him live after that." He didn't tell her the fact that the man admitted to beating her and trying to rape her, both would have been sufficient in Kultur's mind to take him out.

His mouth firmed, dark eyes hardened, he still held her hand though she tried to pull it from his grasp. The tears that welled in her eyes twisted his heart. He sat silently, waiting for the next shoe to drop. Then it did.

Her tone cool, she asked, "How long have you known all this, Kultur?"

"Awhile."

"How long, exactly, Kultur?"

His gaze lowered to their hands. "The day the Ulmas took you to Rosh Boshor."

Her gasp struck his stomach, turning it, he had known she would not take this well. When she pulled her hand from his he let it go.

"You- you- you knew who I was all this time and you- you did not tell me? How could you? You had no right," her voice shook with her anger. Her fists clenched as she slid to the edge of the couch.

"Sislla, please," he was starting to get used to saying that damned word, please. "I knew if I had told you, you would have hated me for disposing of that man, and for the deed you were sent to commit, and you would have gone straight to the first boat you could get your hands on and try to return to your home."

She started to get up, the white of her face darkened with her anger. "That is right. It would have been the honorable thing to-"

Snapping, "Fuck honor, Sislla," he got to his feet. "I will not have you die."

Her steps to the door hard with fury, she rebuked sarcastically, "Sure, honor is fine when it's yours in question. As a weak female mine means nothing."

He went after her grabbing her arm. "I didn't mean that, I just," he ran his fingers like a rake through his hair in frustration.

She jerked her hand from his. "No, again you took away my rights as a human being. You withheld my information from me, you didn't let me make my own decisions, you treated me like a child. I won't stand for it, Kultur, I won't!" She turned to the door.

"Sislla, you're right. I told you I'm trying to do better, treat you as an equal. I didn't have to tell you this at all, you would have no way of ever finding this out. I told you because I understand you would want to know, need to know, and as you said, it is your right to know. It's just," he dragged both hands through his hair,

"When it comes to you and leaving Aniniva, leaving me, and your imminent death trying to return home, I just," he waited for her to look at him but she didn't. "I'm sorry, Sislla, there are no more secrets. Can we-"

"No. We can't do anything." She stormed from the room.

He stood there staring at the empty doorway. "Shit, that went as badly as expected." Closing the door, he pondered what his next step with Sislla would be. It was time, he thought, to start romancing her.

He gazed out the window, but the golden moon would be nearing, he wasn't sure precisely when, and, he sighed, if he didn't get her warmed up again to him by then, what the hell was he to do? If he forced her again she might never forgive him.

But he would do it if he had to.

Chapter Forty-One

The next day was chilly. Kultur had gone into the village to meet with representatives of all three factions. He had been pleased at the outcome of their first meeting. They had all offered ways to get the factions involved with each other and would meet again in a few days to organize and solidify the first steps.

He wore a pullover sweater made from the wool of the sheep that salted the lush island over his shirt and heavier breeches. Early autumn was cooling the air.

Returning to the castle late, well after dinnertime, he went to Sislla's room. He was disappointed to see there was no guard outside her door meaning she probably wasn't inside. He opened the door anyway, did a quick check to confirm she wasn't there.

Treading down the carpeted hall, he considered where to look next. Lexi's room? He decided to go to his chambers first and put away the paperwork he'd brought from the meeting.

Trying to think about where else she could be, damn, he needed to tie a damned bell around her neck, he went inside his chambers and straight to his desk.

At the lateness of the hour, only a waning dulcet light shone into his windows. Setting the papers down on his desk, he went to turn on a lantern. Feeling a prickling along the back of his neck, he hesitated with his hand on a knife stashed at his back, one of the many he had tucked away under his clothes.

"Kultur."

Wow, he'd never heard Sislla sound so sultry before. Her voice wafted around and through him, his knees felt weak. Turning around slowly, he saw her standing in the archway between the office and the hall.

She wore a soft yellow sweater with buttons and a skirt. The best thing was that she was smiling. His heart did flip flops. Guardedly, he asked as he moved towards her, "Not that I'm complaining, but why are you here, *koritsi*?"

Her head ducked shyly, the bright ringlets fell over her shoulders, she peered at him through her lashes. "I, um," she chewed her bottom lip, her cheeks blossomed prettily. "I promised you I would be…willing."

His brows jumped, could she be…serious? Kultur moved slowly closer to her. When he was directly in front of her she raised her head, her smile still shy, but he could read the heated passion glowing in her eyes, for him. It was what he'd dreamed of since he'd first laid eyes on her.

He reached out one hand and wrapped it around her nape. Pulling her gently to him, angling his head so he could encompass every bit of her velvety lips, he lowered his head to take her mouth.

Her lips spread open eagerly, her tongue meeting his with the same excitement that quivered in Kultur's body. The kiss deepened, he cradled her face with both big hands. Her delicate fingers strode up around his neck. By the time their bodies touched his erection was already straining against his pants.

His head and his penis throbbing with desire, Kultur pulled back and looked at her. Sislla's lips were wet and parted, eyes blurred with desire peered dazed and seductive from under her limp lids. "*Koritsi*," he whispered, "there is no doubt that I want you, always, are you ready, for me?"

Her smile so soft and pure, and loving made her cheeks round higher. "Yes, Kultur. I want to make love with you, now. Right now."

He hesitated, he wanted her to be very sure, he couldn't stand another rejection from her afterwards. But, she was in his room, of her own volition and she says she wants him, that's good enough for him. He grabbed up her hand and led her out of the room and down the hall to his bed chamber. Releasing her for only a moment to light a few lanterns he went right back to her.

Brushing wispy tendrils off her face, he slid his big hand around her neck as he lowered his lips to hers. The heady kiss went on until Kultur felt he would die if he didn't get inside her.

Breaking the kiss, their eyes connecting, he undid each tiny button on her sweater. When done, he parted the sides and pushed the sweater half off her shoulders and gazed at her bosom.

"You melt me, *koritsi,* with your beauty." He drew his palms over the swells of her breasts molding out of the lacey binding.

Sislla's spine arched slightly as she enjoyed his warm touch, she murmured, "Beauty withers, Kultur."

He smiled, bent and kissed her lips then her chin then the swell of each breast. "Ah, but yours never will, *koritsi,* because your beauty is from within. Even as your body ages, my beloved, the beauty of your soul will still radiate your sweetness, warmth, love for all mankind, you will forever be beautiful. I will learn compassion and mercy, and to tamp down my temper from you."

He pushed the sweater off letting it drop to the floor. Then, their eyes still linked, he undid her bindings letting them drop with the sweater.

His gaze moved from her eyes to her bare breasts and groaned, "So full and soft and perfectly round, baby." He cupped them, kissing each one, his grip tightened as his pants did. He lathed each nipple with his tongue before pulling them into his mouth to suckle on the hard little beads.

Her gruff moan made his lips a little rougher. He sucked the firm flesh of her breasts, tugged at her nipples with his fingers while licking them.

His mouth loving her breasts, he felt her small hands tugging at his belt. "*Ahh, koritsi,* my sweet wife," still cupping her breasts he looked down. She was pulling but couldn't get it undone.

Smiling, he said, "Here, baby, let me help." He unbuckled his belt, when he reached for the button on his pants she shooed his hands away. He let his hands fall to his sides.

Sislla stood on tip toe, kissed him, then reached for the bottom of his sweater and pulled it to his shoulders; he bent so she could push it up further, and helped her pull it off.

Letting the sweater fall to the floor, Sislla reached up and unbuttoned the top button on his shirt until she had them all undone. When she pushed the lapels over his shoulders he shrugged out of it, letting it drop.

Kultur stroked his hands around her head again drawing her up to kiss him. Her fingers twined around his neck, they brushed their nude upper torsos together.

"Sislla," he sighed happily, "I'll never tire of feeling your naked body against mine, never."

She leaned back dragging her fingers through the downy hair on his chest, then down to his pants. Cooing, "You are so solid, Kultur," her hands stroked over his abs, "so strong." One hand reached up to caress his face. She smiled and added, "So handsome," her head tipped up to receive his kiss.

Then she slipped down to her knees and undid his boots. He kicked them off, she removed his socks. It took a few seconds for her to tug the buttons on his pants loose, it was more of a struggle to push them down. He stepped out of them.

Still on her knees, he held his hand down to help her up, and said, "Come here, sweetheart, let me-" He broke off when her hand touched his erection over his briefs. "Uhh, sons above, Sislla," he swelled under her touch.

Tucking her fingers under the waistband, she drew his undergarment down. When his phallus heavy with arousal sprung out, she touched it gingerly, studiously, smiling at his groan.

Brushing one fingertip down the length of it, she watched it swell and harden even more. Then, she wrapped one hand around it like she'd seen him do. It jerked almost out of her fingers, she giggled. Very slowly, carefully, she skimmed her hand under it to his testicles and cupped them very gently.

"I'm gonna die here, baby," Kultur's moan growled low and gravelly.

Remembering his mouth on her, she tenuously put her lips to the crown of his shaft and lightly kissed it while strengthening her grip on his testicles. When she put her tongue on it and tentatively licked his iron hard manhood, his body clutched in spasms, he caught her head pulling her away.

On her knees in front of him, she looked up worried. "Did I hurt you? You don't like that?"

Gritting his teeth, he crushed her hair in his hands as he got control of his body. "Ahh, sons above no, baby, I like it, I like it beyond belief. But," he took a deep calming breath and smiled down at her. "I want to release inside you. We can do...other things...later. Come," he held his hand to her again.

This time she took it and he helped her to stand up. He turned her around and undid the button on her skirt and pushed it to the floor, leaving her in her scant undergarment.

He pulled her back against his chest and palmed her breasts. "I love holding you, Sislla," he crooned, dipping his head to kiss her neck. His lips pulsed on her throat, he asked, "Will you let me do it forever?" He slid her undergarment down her legs and off then drew her against his chest again.

Her head rolled back. His mouth on her neck, his hands caressing her breasts, her moan a deep susurration of delight strummed in her throat, she replied huskily, "Yes, yes, Kultur..." Her breath hitched at his hand that suddenly stroked her core.

Feeling her silk wetting his fingers, with a sensual growl raging in his chest, he lifted her in his arms, carried her to his big comfy bed and laid her down. He climbed on the bed and knelt beside her.

She looked up at him with glowing eyes. He set a hand on her leg. "Sislla," the desire for her a black heat in his dark eyes, his expression serious, he asked, "will you stay here, on Aniniva, with me?" He held his breath waiting for her answer.

She set her hand on his. Quietly, she told him, "Yes." She didn't hide the pain in her eyes as she said, "Kultur, when I saw you on that- that stage, bound, beaten, about to be..." she took a deep breath, sighed it out. "I knew at that moment I could never live without you."

Sislla watched his brows rise, his mouth curve slightly with hope. Her voice tender, she said, "Anything else, my home, family, duty, honor, nothing, nothing meant anything to me without you, nothing was as important to me, as you."

He threaded their fingers together. "Baby, are you sure?" He'd waited so long to hear these words he couldn't believe she was finally saying them.

Sislla sat up partway leaning back on her palms. "Yes, I've been fighting it. Even when I was afraid of you, my heart soared every time you were near. I didn't want to leave you, I just had...you know," she smiled at him.

"I had that unbearable urge to return to wherever my home was, it was irresistible. But, I realize now," her tender smile broadened, "my home is where you are. You so bravely, selflessly gave your life in lieu of mine. There is no greater sacrifice to show how much you care for me. How do you say husband?"

The world stilled around them. His heart clenched so hard he thought he would be unable to draw a breath. Through squeezed lungs he rasped, "*Sauvyaun*."

Steadied back on one palm, she reached up and held her other hand against the side of his face. "Kultur, my *sauvyaun*."

He felt the back of his eyes sting. Kultur could not believe he, the ferocious, heartless warlord king, Atraam of the Chamaine-Gris had tears blurring his eyes. His feelings were so strong for this petite woman, she held his soul, his life, in her dainty hand.

His hand cradled the back of her head, he leaned over and savored their kiss, finally they were united.

His lips on hers, he pressed her to lie back on the mattress. Her arms wound around him. He lowered his hand to between her legs, caressing, stroking, feeling her soft body quiver under his touch. When his hand grew wet, and her hips rose to his fingers greedily he moved over her, gently pushed her legs apart with his knees.

"Are you ready, my wife?" he whispered. His face inches from hers, their eyes collided and held.

Her fingers tracing the back of his neck, stroked into his hair. "I am, husband." Her gasp from his sudden thrust into her body melted into a moan as her sheath hugged around him.

He waited for her to adapt to his thick, hard shaft, savoring their union, before he started moving slowly all the way to the end of her, then dragging unhurriedly back.

He felt her fingers weave in his hair and as he picked up speed, the faster he plunged the harder she pulled on his locks. The steamy gurgles and erotic cries squeezing breathless from her incited him to surge harder into her with long, deep penetrating thrusts.

Kultur could take no more. Reaching between them, he swirled and pinched her nether lips and her head fell back, the beautiful eyes rolled and she gasped his name.

Driving into her saturated depths, their mutual earthy moans entwined, tying their hearts together. Her slender hips meeting his ravenous plunges, his gruff growls blending with her hitching moans, roiling waves of pleasure pulled at them as they spiraled into mindless oblivion together.

When he could thrust no more, he collapsed on her, his heart beating out of his chest heaving against hers. Rolling to the side, he stayed inside her, his hand over her heart. Together they enjoyed after tremors as their bodies settled into normal functions, pulses slowed.

They lay there content, their minds and bodies sated, for the moment.

Kultur rolled slightly to hold her jaw while he kissed her. *"Koritsi, tiris avithé, ki prana vealla harted mein sleten a biin."*

Their lips lightly touching, Sislla asked, "What did you say?"

He smiled against her mouth. "I said, little foreigner, my wife, I love you with all my heart and soul."

"Kultur, teach me to say that." She licked his upper lip.

The smile turned to a lustful grin. "You keep that up, *avithé,* and we will never get out of this bed."

"Hmm, fine with me. Teach me." She licked his lower lip.

He pulled at her lip with his teeth, biting it gently. His erection was already turning hard still inside of her. "Just say, *ki prana vealla, tiris sauvyaun.*"

Slipping the tip of her tongue into his mouth, Sislla asked, "What does that mean?"

His mouth closed over hers, he murmured, "I love you, my husband." His thumb caressing her cheek, he deepened his kiss and moved his hips slightly against her leg.

Pulling back a shade, she whispered, *"ki prana vealla,* Kultur *tiris sauvyaun."*

He groaned at her soft mouth, "Sislla, you just break my heart it's so full of love for you." He rolled on top of her, nudging her legs apart.

As his head lowered over hers again she saw the golden moon shining through the window, its amber light stroking Kultur's muscled body.

Chapter Forty-Two

Later, the steady knock at the door stirred them as they were indulging in more lovemaking.

Dragging his pants on, Kultur stomped to the door flinging it open. "This better be fucking important." His cross growl would have put the fear of death in most men. But Gabriel just grinned at him while trying to peek inside the room.

Kultur stood in the doorway blocking his view. "What the fuck, Gabe, we're busy."

Gabriel's light brown eyebrows arched. "Oh yeah? Sislla's here?" His eyes went to Kultur's tousled hair to his bare chest to his unbuttoned pants to the bulge in them to his bare feet.

Dawn was barely breaking. Gabriel's grin went ear-to-ear. "Good for you, K, you finally nabbed her. It was a golden moon last night."

"We know," Sislla's drowsy, sultry voice drifted from behind Kultur. She was wearing his shirt and was also barefoot.

Kultur turned with amazement. "You knew?" At her tender smile he bent to kiss her.

"Geez, K, I came here for a reason," Gabriel complained.

His arm around Sislla's shoulders, Kultur faced his brother. He asked impatiently, "What is it?"

"There are ships coming. We're pretty sure it's her people," he nodded at Sislla. "The Shenna-grans from the Ghesecular Providence. Old Viktor knows of them. Viktor was one of the few that has travelled to other lands and returned home here. He was on the shore with us when we went down to check them out."

A dark frown rutted Kultur's fac. He hugged Sislla closer to him. "Do they appear peaceful?"

Gabriel glanced from Sislla to his brother, a slight shake of his head. "No. We've already had reports of them murdering some of the people fishing on the sea. The sirens have been sounding; you can't hear them in here. Probably wouldn't have noticed them anyway," he said with a wink.

"I'll be right down." Kultur closed the door in Gabriel's face. Facing Sislla, he reached for her hip.

"Kultur, we need to go-"

"Aye, in a minute." He set his hand on her thigh and slid it up lifting the shirt she wore. She had nothing on under it.

"Kultur…"

"Look at that, baby…" he brushed his fingers over the side of her hip.

Her brows drew down. She looked to where his fingers were. "Oh!" Her hands went to cover her mouth. There was a tiny faint star on her hip. The Epita. "Oh Kultur…"

"Aye, you are one of us now." He crouched and kissed the star, then quickly swept the shirt back down or they would be right back on the bed. "We can play more with it later," he leered then leaned over and kissed her.

"But now I need to get dressed." He hurried off to change his clothes.

When he came out buckling his belt he saw Sislla standing there fully clothed in a long dress. His brows lanced down together. "What do you think you're doing?"

She started for the door. "I'm coming. Don't even think about forbidding me. This is my family, you will not keep me from them." She fled out the door with him staring after her with his mouth open.

"Ah fuck," he spat. His heart jumped, just as they got together would her family come and take her away with them? He shoved his boots on and ran after her.

******

Kultur and Sislla stood with most of the people from all three factions gathered along the shore and into the woods. Even though the siren sounded, all the people stayed.

A group of ships floated up close. Several men got off one and climbed into a smaller one. That boat paddled to shore.

When they reached land, the men in the boat climbed out, their boots making imprints in the hard damp sand. A male in his mid-sixties trod right up to Kultur who tightened his arm around Sislla.

The man said, "Ah, Atraam Kultur Kultiran, I recognize you, you look just like your father. A bloodletting soulless panther."

Tucking Sislla slightly behind him, Kultur said, "And you would be Haarold Andersson."

Nodding, "*Ya*," Andersson answered with a slight bow. He turned his attention to Sislla.

She regarded him with eyes indicating zero recollection, but she did not hide the anger in them.

He spoke coolly, "Granddaughter, you look well."

Kultur nudged her further behind him. "What is it you want here on our land, Andersson?" His face dark and cold, enigmatic eyes clearly exhibiting no hesitation in ruthlessly dispatching the foreigners. "Let me tell you, sir, you need to speak quickly and without extraneous words."

Andersson's gaze travelled the entire area that was teeming with Ulmas, Tenthekens and the Chamaine-Gris, all armed to the teeth. His attention returned to Kultur then Sislla.

"Granddaughter, don't you have a kiss for your grandfather?" He held out long arms, his hands open to her.

Kultur tightened his grip on Sislla, but she squirmed forward.

Her blue eyes sharp on the elder man, she said politely, also coolly, "Grandfather." She tried to step closer to him, but Kultur held her back.

Eying him speculatively, she said, "After I landed on this island, the man you sent to bring me here, Apris Tinnian, tried to kill me."

She watched Andersson's expression, only the flaring of his pupils belayed his understanding. She continued, "Obviously, he failed. However, *he* is dead."

Andersson's forehead furrowed, but nothing else on his face indicated any feeling.

"He brought me here to assassinate Atraam Kultiran. As you can see, I did not. Instead, I married him." She smiled up at Kultur. He didn't smile back, yet his love for her was clear in his deep eyes.

Sislla turned back to Andersson. "So, your plot failed. Behind and all around us are all three factions of the island. We have come together as one. We have a truce. We will fight you together if you choose to attack us."

Without moving his head, Andersson's eyes swept around the shore and back to Kultur.

As usual, Kultur's eyes were completely blank, which only made them more threatening, more terrifying.

Andersson said to Sislla with distaste, "You married this warlord barbarian? How dare you sully your family name with-"

Sislla snapped, "Be quiet, Grandfather."

Everyone within earshot looked with shock at the sweet young woman telling her own kin to shut up.

He looked stunned as well. "Sislla, how dare you speak to me in that way? You need to step aside. There will be a bloodbath today. These people," he motioned to the islanders with revulsion, "will not live to see tomorrow."

She tried to step forward again but Kultur's arm on her shoulder was like steel holding her back and to his side.

She responded to her grandfather, "I am not going to lower myself and tell you what I think of you, sending your own flesh and blood to murder, and to be murdered."

Taking a tremulous breath, she told him, "You are wrong." Her voice dropped to a whispered warning, "It is you who will die if you do not get back on your ships and sail the heck out of here. Now."

Kultur silently hugged her, showing his solidarity.

She was grateful he let her speak, and no one else interrupted her either. Gabriel and Lucas flanked them.

Andersson's face deepened to dark red, his brows slashed over furious eyes. He opened his mouth to say something, but he heard the rustling of the natives preparing their weapons. Blanching slightly, he tried again, "Granddaughter, your family, you must come with me. They miss you. They-"

Keeping her amnesia to herself, Sislla said, "Since they allowed you to send me here on this suicide mission, please give them my best when you get home. Tell them I am well, and," she looked up at Kultur and smiled again, this time he smiled at her. "That I am happy. Now," her voice hardened, "do not make these people have to kill you and yours. Leave. Do not come back."

She steadily stared at him, her eyes unwavering at his. She could see other than cruelty and greed; his eyes were empty, void of any compassion or love. They say Kultur was soulless, but, no, this was truly a heartless man.

Andersson stared for a long time at her. Then, without a word, he turned and sloshed back through the waves to his waiting boat.

His men followed him and they paddled back to their ship. In thirty minutes none of the ships were any longer visible.

Kultur turned and put his hands on Sislla's shoulders. "I love you, my precious wife."

She smiled. "I love you, my husband," and they kissed.

Oblivious to the people watching, Kultur asked, "How soon do you want to start our family?"

Her smile broadened, she leaned into him. "How soon do you want to?"

"Ah, my beloved," he pulled her closer and replied, "now sounds good to me."

Sislla laughed. "Right now?"

Chuckling, he said, "Well, we have to go through the wedding ceremony that is expected of the king and queen of Chamaine-Gris, but that will be next week, or as soon as my dear mother can arrange things. So, how about we leave this crowded shore and go start practicing for that family? Perhaps we may get a head start on that little prince or princess."

"Oh," Sislla beamed. "I hope for a tiny prince with his da's dark eyes and ebony locks."

"Hmm," Kultur grinned. "I am hoping for a beautiful princess with her mother's blonde curls and big blue eyes. But, for truth," he wrapped his hand around the back of her head drawing her face up to his. "I would be happy with whatever the sons above bestow upon us. As long as I have you, my darling, everything else is superfluous."

Their lips connected, eyes joined, and the loving couple melted into a tender kiss.

Behind them, the crowd roared, yelling, "Long live Atraam Kultur and Atra Sislla!" Their cheers echoed over the land.

The End

Dear Reader, thank you for purchasing Kultur's Keep! *I know you could have picked any number of books to read, but you picked this book and for that I am extremely grateful.*

I hope you enjoyed this novel, and if you did, **please leave a review** *where you purchased it, and look for other exciting titles in my name!*

About the Author

Louise Furley loves writing romance with a huge helping of suspense. She finds it exciting to study new lands and learn everything she can about the area and the natives that call it home.

Her idea of fun is researching ideas, studying enigmatic modes of science, archeology, and different ways to kill someone.
Her Significant Other finds the last to be particularly notable. He remains wary yet gives Louise his full support with her writing adventures.

Louise Furley

Sunny Florida is home where Louise is a graduate of St. Thomas University with a master's degree in Mental Health.

This degree is essential for exploring the deviant soul, and understanding the mind of a killer, while finding it exhilarating, frightening and sad all at the same time. With artistic license, Louise can be judge, jury, and sometimes executioner!

Louise is the author of numerous published novels. When not researching or writing, she is dreaming of unique plots, and discovering fresh ventures she hasn't yet experienced in the world.

Ride along with her as she travels new and thrilling journeys!

Please enjoy the first few chapters of my book, Cini and the Beast.

Chapter One

It was broad daylight yet danger already lay in wait.

A perfect blue sky domed the two carriages bouncing and lurching over the rocky, hard-packed dirt trail.

The trail had been wide open across a vast savanna, but now it funneled into an archway of trees that rapidly thickened into dense forest. So dense, the occupants of the coaches could not see more than a few feet into the leafy woods bordering the trail.

Without warning, a nightmare sprang up right in front of them.

Bandits!

"Ya-ho!" The team master yelled, alerting the other carriage while whipping the reins. The eight horses screeched out whinnies and took off at a hard gallop, spitting clods of dirt in all directions.

They didn't get far before the bandits cut off their flight, blocking them from the front, and more came up the rear, inescapably trapping them.

In the chaos of shouts and hooves stomping, dust kicked up in clouds shrouding everything.

Bellowing commands to the carriage drivers to cease moving, the bandits waved swords and rapiers in warning, a few held rare firearms.

The men on the carriages slowed the horses and raised their hands in surrender.

An enormous black stallion, nostrils flaring, marched forward through the pack of bandits, his bold fetlocks lifting and stomping in bullying high steps.

The man atop the horse allowed the steed his dramatic, treacherous dance in front of his confined audience.

His seat arrogant, smug face streaked with filth and sweat, the bandit crowed with squalid mirth, "Good day, my friends," he leaned forward with an arm resting lazily on the short saddle horn, reins dangling in his hand.

His greedy grin nasty, he informed them, "They call me Tetek, Terror of the Spider Thread Trails. You have by now determined we are here to take your trades, your money pouches, your valuables. You will all depart the carriages and stand aside peacefully while my men divest you of your treasures."

The mean face flattened in ugly threat. Eyes narrowed at the men, he warned them, "Any resistance, *at all*, will result in your instant and likely painful, death. Do I make myself under-"

Suddenly dropping from trees and rushing out from the thicket, warriors surrounded the bandits.

Instantly hurtling into battle, they leapt off their steeds with clamoring shouts of, "Take no prisoners!" Slashing swords and daggers, the warriors were quickly and easily beating hell out of the thieves.

In the noisy turmoil, Tetek leapt up onto a coach wielding a sabre. Pressing it against a driver's throat, he shrieked in fury, "I will cut off his head if every warrior doesn't back off! Now!"

Long black hair streaming as he ran, *Dominio* Lord Kazak Adarken vaulted onto his steed. Racing the few yards, he jumped up to his feet on the saddle and launched himself onto the carriage.

He landed with a hard thud and kept moving with the blinding speed of a wild ravaging animal.

"Back! Back!" the now panicked bandit screamed. "Get back or I kill him!" Recognition of the warlord approaching him with deadly speed, the Emperor's top *dominio,* struck Tetek's face like a frightened slap leaving it stark white.

Gripping the sabre in his sweat-loosened grasp, he tried to turn keeping the driver between him and Lord Kazak.

As swift as a north wind, Kazak had his hands on Tetek's own neck before the bandit could react.

Screeching his terror, Tetek moved the sabre from the driver to stab and slice maniacally at Kazak- but in a blink, Kazak tore him to pieces with his bare hands and teeth. Like a feral beast he savaged the man until the carcass dropped in the dirt beside the carriage.

Without hesitation, Kazak jumped from the carriage and ran to the next brigand and ripped him into gristle and bones before the man could take a breath to scream.

Warrior Bo'orchu 'Bo' Targutai captured a bandit, and beat him until he barely clung to consciousness. Bo clutched the thief's collar keeping him on his feet, the battered man's head hung.

Through blood flooding in his eyes, the robber watched the bearded Kazak tear into man after armed man without raising a weapon.

The robber cried, "Who the hell is that? Is he man or savage beast?"

Bo laughed, "Both. But to be honest, I'd say more beast than man." Bo held the beaten thief and they watched the warriors viciously slay the rest of the bandits, until none was left breathing.

The sniveling male Bo restrained, shook with terror. Spitting blood and teeth he cried, "What kind of **hideous** *monstru* is he?"

His chuckle demonic, Bo told him, "Lord Kazak Adarken was dropped in the Black Forest they believe at three years old. They think three because when they found him, he had very few words they could understand. Some of what he supposedly said was, 'I three,' and 'I *alb tirgis*.'"

"White tiger? What the fuck does that mean?" The thief snorted up blood and spat it out. It splatted on the dirt already mottled with blood and sprawled grotesque guts.

Bo shrugged, then explained, "The legend goes that they studied his nails and hair and other things and determined he'd been all alone in the forest for around a year making him around four if what he said about being three that he remembered was accurate.

"He spoke few words, he more growled, and stalked, and preyed like an animal. On his back is supposedly a tattoo of the Siberian symbol for king, and at his shoulder there are stripes of claws, and the impression of a paw.

"They claim the Siberian symbols are not tattoos, or, henna, but birthmarks. The paw," he shrugged, "no one can tell. Looks like it was literally imprinted, clawed into him by a..." his lip twitched at the man blanching at his words, "tiger."

The bandit's mouth dropped in disbelief. "So, you're saying that- that half man half creature was...raised by...white tigers?"

Nodding with a grin, Bo replied, "*Da*, Siberian Tigers. However, he was marked by the white one, not the yellow with stripes. They named him Kazak after the Romastik word for savage, and his surname of Adarken for the words dark killer.

"He is *dominio*, prime warlord of *Împărat Radoslav's* army, Emperor Boris Radisalvo's royal **league of drujinos, his elite warriors.** "

The bandit gasped. Panting and wheezing in pained breaths from punctured lungs, he about fainted when Kazak, wiping his sleeve across his mouth, over the thick black beard, stomped on a moaning man splayed on the ground, silencing him with death.

Kazak looked up at Bo and came to them.

Huge with cordons of hardened muscles strung across his powerful shoulders and over his thick chest, Kazak combed bloody fingers through black hair saturated with sweat and blood that hung over brilliant blue eyes.

Those merciless eyes studied the bandit Bo held, broken and bleeding, now on his knees sniveling and begging for his life.

The bandit threw himself at Kazak, frantic fingers dragging down the **chainmail and leather plates sewn in under the leather vest.**

Clinging to Kazak's breeches, he wailed, "Please, my Liege, I beg you for my life! I was carried along with these other fellows, I have nothing to do with-"

Whack- Kazak backhanded him, knocking the man backwards flat on his back and out cold. The warlord stood beside Bo, one of his lead warriors and his best friend, their eyes emotionless and placid on the unconscious, butchered man.

Bo said matter-of-factly, "He's the only one alive. I guess he's the one we let go free to warn the others about us."

Kazak grunted. Standing with boots akimbo, hands clasped behind his back, his face behind the thick beard and long hair a cold brutal mask.

Sighing, Bo crouched beside the bandit as the other occupants of the carriages milled about thanking the warriors for their help. He tacked a note to the unconscious man, it stated:

"Warning to all who travel the Ita Cale, the Spider Thread Trails. Thievery, kidnapping, accosting and murder will not be tolerated. Doing so will result in immediate death. There will be no second chances.

By Orders of Lord Kazak Adarken."

After every battle, the warriors left one bandit more dead than alive, to describe the horrific carnage, the bloody slaughter dealt by Lord Kazak Adarken and his warriors to any that dared disobey the Lord's written warning.

Chapter Two

*H*olding her long skirts up, Cini hurried down the hall praying to the good God she didn't run into anyone. Slipping into the shadowed stairwell, her swiftly pattering footsteps were muffled on the grey stone steps leading up to the towered roof.

As she stepped out to the pitch and stone floor, she chastised herself for not bringing a scarf to cover her bright hair. The corn-silk color was such a light yellow it bordered on white.

Her Aunt Marta always embarrassed her saying Cini had the flaxen curls of a toddler and could have easily blended into a field of early daffodils.

But Cini wanted to be likened to a woman, not a child. However, right now, she had to move carefully to stay in the shadows lest the sun reflect off her fair hair giving her away.

Sneaking to the side of a turret, Cini was careful to keep as much of her body hidden behind the gable while she peered over the edge. Parts of her blue flowery gown brushed the dusty stone wall as she stood on tiptoe.

Chills prickled up her spine at the sight of Prince Gavrill Andreyev's retinue. Fear and anger stiffened her back.

The nerve of the marauding cad. Traveling back to Russia, he had decided to take his soldiers trekking through Sweden to Chalon-sur-Sônn where Cini's family had emigrated from England to join her father's people.

Prince Andreyev had made it clear he was sending word to his home in Russia to send more troops of soldiers to come and seize Chalon-sur-Sônn, where he would pronounce himself king and lay claim to Cini.

Cini's uncle had died and her father Garund was crowned king. Not only was Cini breathtakingly desirable, marrying her would solidify Prince Andreyev's desire to be king, although capturing and taking over the entire region would ensure that alone.

Yet, being king was not all Prince Gavrill Andreyev aspired to, his plan was to lay siege upon his own emperor, Boris Radisalvo, and take his sovereign royalty for his own.

"Cini," a hushed whisper drew her from her anxious viewing of the horses and men that rambled around the compound.

Cini spun around to see her best friend peeking out from behind a waist-high stone wall.

"Melisandra Maciel!" Cini scolded with her hand at her throat, "You scared the feathers off a goose." Her warm grin negating her scolding, she took a few steps from the edge of the edifice towards her friend.

The girls were night and day. Cini's palest of blonde curls twirling in fat ringlets down her back were a striking contradiction to Melisandra's raven black hair that hung straight as a whisk to her bottom.

Cini was petite and much on the thin side yet blessed with amazing curves, whereas Meli was tall and all willowy grace. Under sky blue eyes, Meli's generous mouth was full and always with a ready, if timid, smile, Cini's lips were tiny yet lush.

"Shh!" Meli warned, staying behind the pillar of rock. "Don't let anyone hear you. You don't want to draw that horrid prince here."

Quietly, Cini moved closer to her.

Her expression worried, Meli spoke hushed, "Do you think he meant what he said about sending his soldiers to occupy our town for good? They've already taken over."

Concern darkened her golden skin, she tugged the sleeves of her tangerine gown over her wrists. "And his crazy idea to marry you. The nerve! One kingdom isn't enough for him he has to have ours too?"

Cini petted Meli's arm in comfort. A steep serious tone roping through her words, she whispered, "Oh I believe every word he says. His countenance is too mean, severe, his smile twists cruelly when he strikes out at his men and our people."

Blonde curls bounced as she nodded hard and repeated, "Oh yes, I believe everything he says." A brow cocked, she asked Meli, "Why are you not at your lessons?"

"I was sent to look for you. Cook said you haven't finished the baking for tomorrow's dinner for the prince. She says you have the hand of a magical faerie when it comes to the lightness in your baked specials." Meli laughed then turned stern with suspicion. "You are not still planning your ridiculous escape?"

Cini took a step from her friend, fingers clutching her long skirt to lift it slightly from under foot.

"Meli, the prince has the village imprisoned, surrounded by soldiers, everyone who has tried to leave to go for help has been murdered. I know I can get out without being caught. I must go, I must get to the emperor and beg his aid."

"No, Cini, you can't-"

"There you are my summer blossom, my naughty Princeza Činnosti," Prince Gavrill Andreyev stepped out onto the stone landing. He didn't see Meli ducking down the second his voice barraged into the space.

The fifty-year-old king moved towards Cini, his barrel chest pumped up, he shook his dark brown head with a scold, "My dear, I've had my men looking everywhere for you."

He strode to her; the back of his dark red coat draped to his knees, the front was partially closed with gold buttons. Gold embroidery decorated the coat, his knee-length boots laced up the front also gilded, covered most of his black slacks.

Cini moved back from him, leading him away from where Meli was hiding.

At first he scowled, then with condescension oiling his tongue, Andreyev said, "It is time for you to stop being obdurate my child, embrace your destiny to marry me and combine our kingdoms."

"But you don't want to blend our clans together, Prince Andreyev, you want to raze our village to the ground, kill the native populace and take over completely." She discreetly motioned for Meli to leave while she could.

"'Tis true." His hands clasped behind his broad back, he sauntered over to her. "Count yourself lucky you won't be a victim of my extermination. You will be safe as my wife."

He was physically fit and good-looking, but the mean bead in his brown eyes, and cruel curl of his heavy lips marred his classical features that were slightly thickened, squaring with middle age.

Hands slapped on her slender hips, small nose turned up in the air, Cini admonished him, "You are old enough to be my father, my grandfather," she could see Meli was creeping behind the prince and slipping down the staircase.

The prince huffed with irritation, "Stop whining. Many girls are married at your age and even much younger. I must return with my soldiers and make ready to gather more men to come and take this land over. In the meantime, I will leave a force to contain your people. Execution will be the only punishment for any who try to escape."

Cini tried again, begging, "Please, Prince Andreyev, you must reconsider your campaign!"

Coming closer to her, his smarmy smile unpleasant. Brooking no argument, eyes narrowed, he directed coldly, "We will be married. For now, I must have a little taste to hold me." He grabbed at her, she jerked to the side to avoid his grasp.

Off-balance, the prince staggered, tripped and toppled into the low wall.

Cini took her chance and bolted for the door. She rushed through it, slammed it shut and pulled down the plank that crossed over locking it.

The prince's roars were barely audible through the thick wood, and became less so as she streaked down the stairs.

Chapter Three

In the field, Kazak Adarken fenced and parried, then moved on to lance practice, and later to javelin throwing then onto hand-to-hand combat with his men.

In the cosseting warm day, knee-deep in grass, wheat fields wafting to the east, buffeted by pillars of glossy forest, the men, and a few women, sweated, grunted, groaned as they battled each other.

They worked hours upon hours of practice before Kazak allowed a break. Sweat pouring down his face, dragging his fingers through his long hair, he headed to a well.

Dipping a cloth in a bucket of water, he drew it over his wet face, scrubbing the thick dark beard, then rubbed it over the black mop that waved just past his shoulders.

Peeling off his chainmail and leather vest, he dipped the cloth in the bucket again, and wiped down his arms and bare chest, then pulled a dry shirt over his head. A shout drew his attention.

Two warriors on horseback clopped into the yard stirring the dirt into dust puffs.

"Liege," one laughed, "you should see. We were coming in from past the plum orchards when over the far hill we saw a…" His eyes darted back and forth with mirth and mischief, and a bit of wonder. "You won't believe, but we saw a *zână*- a-a bloody fairy-"

"Nay," the other warrior disagreed shaking his head, "it was an elfje, a *mica creatură*, a wee creature, Liege."

The first warrior argued, "Nay, could have been a *zburătoare-*"

"Nay, fool, it was not a damned flying bird-"

"*Basta*!" Kazak barked in a mixed guttural language. "Your bickering gives me a headache." He tossed the cloth on the mortared edge of the well.

Beside him, Bo said to the men, "Why do you care if there is a bird or a fairy or an elf, or whatever-the-fuck is out there?"

The first warrior responded, face aglow, "Because it was colorful, beautiful, a vibrant female on horseback, whisking over the hilltops with hair the color of the brightest sun waving behind her."

Frowning, Kazak said, "A stranger in the area our men did not detect?" Heading for his steed, voice of cold, rough iron, he barked, "And you let it go, and did *nu* ring the alarm?"

The second warrior watching his lord, more like an ireful bear stalking to the stable, he called out, his voice shaky with impending fear of future discipline, "There were others chasing after it, her, whatever it was. But," gulping nervously, "it suddenly disappeared, so we came to tell you about it-"

Kazak was already at the stables.

Soon he was racing as one with his stallion, **Falium**, across the farmland, and through the meadows filled with violet wildflowers then to the foothills.

Eyes as sharp as an eagle's, he scanned the hillside but saw nothing except villagers gathering berries, and a small crowd of men on foot and horseback meandering in and out of the thinly treed woods bordering part of the fields.

Kazak slowed his horse, gaze flicking from trees lavish with thick leaves to the softly rounded foothills. He saw nothing like the soldiers described. No elf, no fairy, no colorful bird on horseback.

13

He shook his head, crimson ire burned up the back of his neck at the foolish warriors. Wiping a hand across his thickly ridged brow, he cursed, "They will feel the lash of the whip, the bastards-"

Wait, one of the males traveling about on horseback in a group, a young boy, shot a nervous look at him under the bill of his cap, then quickly averted his gaze.

Too many battles burned under Kazak's weathered skin to not feel the tingle of suspicion trickle along his broad shoulders.

"Tck tck," his tongue clicked, spurring the horse to move. A slight knee to the side directed the horse in the direction of the boy. The stallion hardly took a few steps in that direction when the boy suddenly bolted from the loose group of men.

Kazak's heels jammed into the horse's belly and Falium took off like a flash of black lightening.

The boy had a good head start on Kazak, he was already over the first hill and bounding towards the cover of woods. But he was a piss-poor rider.

Falium streaked across the land as if he had wings.

The boy made it to the grove of trees.

Used to the pounding of Falium's hooves, Kazak finely-tuned his ears to the separate sound of the fleeing horse's galloping steps and easily followed the horse and rider.

Darting around trees, Kazak quickly caught sight of the boy.

He was clinging to his horse with a death grip, bouncing and jerking as the horse took off on its own, coming back out of the woods to run on the waves of flowing grass.

The reins snapping on his back, Falium turned sharply to follow the boy.

Within seconds, Kazak was riding alongside the boy. He caught a flash of huge, round, terrified orbs glowing green at him before the boy futilely tried to turn his steed away and rush back into the woods.

Falium's hooves pounded beside the boy. When their stirrups knocked together, the burst of terrified green surged as the boy struggled to maintain control of his mare.

Horseflesh battered against horseflesh, long tails stuck straight out with their speed, and Kazak reached out with long powerful arms and snatched the boy right off his horse, dropping him hard on the saddle in front of him.

The boy was so small and slender he fit between the butt of horn and Kazak's strong thighs.

Kazak's lips pursed at the scream the boy emitted, high and piercing as a girl's. Holding the young man against his hard chest, his broad hand clasping the panicked boy against him, he felt a weird softness.

Worse than weird, it caused his groin to suddenly burn. Even the most privileged of young men in their neck of the woods was taut and muscled with battle practice, but this boy was soft.

Pulling gently on the reins, Kazak slowed his horse. The shock of green glowing eyes and the delicateness of his captive confused him. He moved his arm around the lad to hold him tighter lest he attempt escape, and was astonished at the big lump he felt under his hard hand.

Before he could register it, the boy wrenched from his arms, and dropped hard to the ground.

He cried out, apparently injuring himself, but nonetheless was up and running, well, hobbling, towards the forest.

His bewilderment growing, Kazak slid off his steed and easily stalked after the lad.

The boy younger and smaller and obviously injured, Kazak quickly caught up with him.

When he grabbed his arm, the lad squealed and burst into a frenzy of punching, kicking, twisting, emitting a few English words said so frantically Kazak couldn't grasp them.

Grumbling a string of foul curses, Kazak had a mind to slam his fist into the lad's head, a good pop and as frail as he was, the kid would be out like a light, if he survived the blow.

Instead, he wrapped an arm around the boy's waist, hugged his back to his chest and lifted him up off his feet. He barely weighed a stone he was so light. Kazak could feel thin hands struggling to pull Kazak's arm off him.

"Calm the *føkk* down," Kazak commanded in his own language knowing it was unlikely the lad understood what he said.

The boy arched his back, tried to kick Kazak and attempted to slam his head into Kazak's.

But the lad was half Kazak's height and weight. Even if Kazak hadn't easily dodged and blocked his blows, the boy's attempts at strikes would have been like a fly swatting him.

"*Basta*," Kazak's deep voice a harsh rasp in the boy's ear, "enough." In thick mixed dialects he warned, "You fight me, I break you." Roping an arm around him and over his arms, Kazak gripped the boy's jaw and held it up, holding his chin hard in the air.

The lad kicked harder and screamed through his jaw clenched tight with Kazak's hand, "Let go of me!"

That weird feeling zinged up his spine, Kazak paused, then dropped to his knees laying the boy not gently on the ground on his back and straddled him.

The boy immediately tried to sit up and punched ineffectively at Kazak with gritted screams.

Kazak leaned over, staking the lad's wrists to the ground and glared at him. He ordered in heavily accented broken English, "Nay move."

His eyes drifted from the face blotched with dirt, so much it appeared to have been deliberately placed there, down the very slender neck, over the pulse pounding as the lad gulped hard and rapid, down to his waist-length jacket buttoned up tight.

Under the jacket, his chest rising and falling with his frantic breaths, looked funny, odd.

Kazak's gaze swept back up and was taken aback by the delicate bones of the boy's face. The high, round, childlike cheekbones, and he felt that peculiar tingle in his groin at the very small, perfect bow-shaped lush-as-hell lips.

Tearing his eyes away, he raised them to the lad's own terrified, crystalized sea-green orbs fringed in the longest lashes the warlord had ever seen, all the way to the curled ends that fluttered frantically over the frightened eyes.

With a grunt, Kazak sat up, gripped the lad's jacket with both hands and ripped it and the shirt beneath open. His pupils blazed at the linen breast-band that was wrapped so tight, full breasts mounded over the rim, Kazak wondered that he- she- could draw a breath.

He grabbed the stranger's hat, yanked it off and dropped it. Long, vivid yellow curls tumbled out. The boy-girl- squealed and thrashed anew.

Kazak could see why, and now understood those burning spikes to his manhood as he loomed over the obvious female who lay grunting, squealing, struggling to throw Kazak off her.

With every punch, and bucking writhe she made, the fair breasts bobbled even in the tight band, holding Kazak's attention.

Seeing the heat flaring in his ice-blue eyes, and the dark color spreading up his neck, under the layer of dirt her own cheeks flamed crimson. Kazak leaned over pinning her hands back to the ground over her head.

"Who you?" his guttural question ground out, aware he was barely intelligible to her.

He spoke many languages, but he hadn't been around a lot of English speaking people in his rough life and was well out of practice with that language.

At first, confusion laced through her fear. Then by the way her lashes lowered over those striking eyes, and the turn of her head, Kazak could see she grasped his question, and clearly had no intentions of answering him.

Kazak lowered his body over hers to partially cover her, holding her in place with his weight. Long, hard fingers gripped her jaw, holding it roughly, stiffly. His face already hard as chiseled granite didn't change, but his brilliant blue eyes darkened with impatient wrath.

"One time more," he muttered harshly, squeezing her tender flesh with the hard pads of his fingertips. Feeling her squirm beneath him, not a good move on her part as the friction heated his manhood, he demanded, "Name?"

If possible, the sea-green goblets grew wider with renewed fear at the harshness of his voice and the hard grip of his fingers.

Or maybe it was the other part of him that was growing bigger, longer, harder pressing against her thigh that made her struggle more frantically to push him off her.

He was like an ox, she couldn't budge him a hair. Except for the grunts from her struggles, the tiny, lush lips stayed firmly closed.

Kazak allowed himself a moment to lay his hard body on hers. She wasn't sturdy and strong like most of the women he dealt with.

He felt the fullness of her soft breasts frantically panting, pressing into the heaviness of his rock solid chest. The pure femininity of her flat belly, slender legs struggling, entwined in the musculature of his thighs.

Her girlish breathy gasps and whimpers as she fluttered desperately against him like the beautiful fairy they'd called her, the delicate scent of her soaked into his every pore.

The feel of her so heady, his body felt on fire, and heavy as lead, he couldn't, didn't want to move.

She paused in her struggles when he stuck a hand in a bunch of her curls. Feeling the silken tresses between his fingers, he crushed them in his fist and lifted them to his face and breathed in deeply.

Kazak was drowning in this girl. This exquisite, foreign fairy was encompassing all of his senses. The fire building inside of him threatened to quickly push him out of control. He was going blind and deaf with lust. He nudged a knee between her thighs and pushed them apart.

Falling into those frightened sea crystals, under lids heavy with arousal, he watched the flair of a new kind of terror strike her dirty face as his burgeoning manhood dug against her sex.

But, she was fighting so hard to get free she was harming herself.

Blinking back his lust, *"Bună-* ah, fine," Kazak grunted, rolling off her and to his feet. He jerked her up with him.

A cry of pain and her legs buckled.

Kazak struck his arm around her to steady her, and saw her face crease in pain as she favored her left leg.

"Serves right." He swung her up in his arms and trudged to his waiting horse, grumbling, *"Prost fată,* stupid girl jumps off moving horse, deserves hurt."

She continued to struggle as he carried her, but he ignored her as if she was just a pesky flea squirming in his big arms.

When he reached his steed, he threw her over his shoulder. With her squeal against his back, he mounted Falium then dropped her in front of him.

He wrapped a steel arm around her and over her arms roping them to her sides, this time she would not be jumping from the horse. His heels jabbed in, and Falium bolted for the compound.

Twisting side-to-side, "Let me go!" she screeched. "You have no right!" Her words were haughty and brave, but her back trembled against his chest.

Feeling him stiffen and his head bow, she peered a glance at him, he was staring down at her exposed breasts. "How dare you! Stop!" She jerked and tried to throw her body, which only made her full flesh bounce more.

If he kept her restrained as she was and her half-bared bosom joggling over his arm, Kazak would have her back off the horse, tossed flat on the ground and him impaled deep inside her.

Reluctantly, Kazak slowed the horse and moved his arm to her lower belly, freeing her hands.

She immediately buttoned the few buttons he hadn't torn off her blouse and the filthy jacket.

www.ingramcontent.com/pod-product-compliance
Lightning Source LLC
Chambersburg PA
CBHW050859250626
47155CB00001B/31